EYE OF THE FALCON

A Psychic Visions Novel
Book #12

Dale Mayer

Books in This Series:

EYE OF THE FALCON
Dale Mayer
Valley Publishing

Copyright © 2017

This is a work of fiction. Names, characters, places, brands, media, and incidents are either the product of the author's imagination or are used fictitiously. Any resemblance to actual events, locales, or persons, living or dead, is entirely coincidental.

ISBN-13: 978-1-773360-18-8
Print Edition

Back Cover

As a young girl, Issa bonded with her pet falcon and was the lookout for her father's smuggling operation in Ireland. After everything went south one night, and her father and brothers were killed, her mother brought her to America to start over.

Immigrating was hard, but eventually Issa grew up and pursued a career in environmental sciences and continued to follow her passion for falconry. But she doesn't find the same special bond with other falcons. Until one fateful day when her world tilts again ...

Eagle, a former military pilot, has retired to his small ranch outside Denver, Colorado, where he runs a rescue center for raptors in need. One falcon is acting irrationally. Eagle's only recourse is to euthanize him, but the falcon rips free. Although injured so badly he shouldn't be able to fly, the falcon disappears into the skies.

The next morning the falcon returns with a beautiful but seriously injured young woman in tow—carrying a message of death and destruction for all of them ...

Sign up to be notified of all Dale's releases here!

http://dalemayer.com/category/blog/

Your Free Book Awaits!

KILL OR BE KILLED

Part of an elite SEAL team, Mason takes on the dangerous jobs no one else wants to do – or can do. When he's on a mission, he's focused and dedicated. When he's not, he plays as hard as he fights.

Until he meets a woman he can't have but can't forget. Software developer, Tesla lost her brother in combat and has no intention of getting close to someone else in the military. Determined to save other US soldiers from a similar fate, she's created a program that could save lives. But other countries know about the program, and they won't stop until they get it – and get her.

Time is running out ... For her ... For him ... For them ...

DOWNLOAD a *__complimentary__* copy of MASON? Just tell me where to send it!

http://dalemayer.com/sealsmason/

CHAPTER 1

ISSA MCGUIRE'S HEART was sick as she took a last look around her mother's apartment, saying goodbye to the space she had once called home and that would soon be empty after Goodwill came to pick up the boxes. Walking out into the night, she could hardly believe her mother's life had been reduced to those few possessions she'd seen in her mother's final residence.

Among other belongings Issa had chosen to keep had been a leather keepsake box—about the same size as a large wooden cigar box—and a cardboard box full of papers. She'd taken a peek inside both but had found some of the information shocking. Surely the extensive criminal activities listed inside the topmost manila envelope in the banker's box had to be wrong. She knew her father had been a smuggler, but that had been a way of life. The other charges, ... well, those made no sense. Something, somewhere, must clarify all that had gone so wrong. She couldn't trust her own childhood memories and wasn't at all sure she could believe the papers found in her mother's belongings either. Some things just didn't add up.

Back in her vehicle, jammed full of her mother's possessions and memories, she hurriedly got into the driver's seat and slowly drove toward her small cabin.

And away from the remnants of that era of her life.

After years of the concrete city, she couldn't do it anymore. She had died a little every day she was forced to exist without the space and sky that was secondary to her soul. Such an elemental thing, but, to her, it was the main priority. She'd made it through school; she'd made it through her degrees. And now she was beholden to no one.

Except for the birds. They were part of her soul.

At the nondescript turnoff to her road, she slowed for the corner and bounced hard, wishing there had been more money so she could've filled the pothole and done a better cleanup of the driveway. Not too much though. She certainly didn't choose to pour down concrete or asphalt. Maybe a layer of gravel for the tires to grab in winter. All she wanted was a little more ease of living. But without it being too modern.

Her cabin illuminated in the headlights of her car, she could hear the birds already crying to her. Humbug, the huge snowy owl, who'd crawled inside her heart and made a place for himself, sat on a corner of the cabin's roof, staring at her.

Roash, the beautiful falcon she'd found in the field, sat on a fence post—he too was waiting for her. She knew the golden eagle would be around somewhere. And then there was Gillian, the tiny saw-whet owl who wouldn't be far away. Smaller than the others of her kind, a little more damaged than the other birds of any kind, the one who needed her just as much as she needed her birds.

Leaving the vehicle on for the headlights to shine on her front door, she quickly moved to the cabin and back to the car.

It might be summertime, but, once the sun went down, it didn't matter where you were in this area of Colorado, a chill settled in. Inside she lit the woodstove and put on the teakettle. She had electricity but used it sparingly, choosing instead to use kerosene lamps. She wasn't against some modern conveniences, but she didn't appreciate the related monthly bills that came her way. Until she had a regular paycheck, she had to find and save the pennies wherever she could.

So far she had yet to discover anything of her mother's worth selling, and she hadn't figured out where her mother's bank accounts were. She'd unloaded the big box of paperwork, hoping the information would be in there. Along with the answers she needed on her father's criminal activities. But she didn't want to look inside; she couldn't bear it. Not right now.

Not with the grief of losing not only her only living relative but her mother. They'd had a complicated relationship, but, when it came down to it, she'd been family. Issa wanted to keep the little bit of fantasy about her father for as long as possible. Not that she had much in the way of illusions. It was hard enough to face the reality of losing her mother. How could a woman in good health, and only sixty-two, have a heart attack and die, while Issa was at the university collecting the paperwork on her doctorate? To come home and to find her mother in her own apartment like that—on the kitchen floor, already cold from taking her last breath hours ago. Issa shook her head, tears never far from the surface, once again rising.

Nothing had been on the kitchen table or on her mother's bed that explained what her mother had been doing right before her death, and, after the chaos of the police and the morgue attendants, Issa hadn't been able to return to her mother's apartment and had crashed at home with tears of loss and grief. When she finally awoke midday the next day, it was to the cold harsh reality of being all alone at twenty-six. She was much too young to be the last one of her family still living. And to be facing the grim job forced upon her to contend with the reality of burying a loved one unexpectedly. It had taken days, almost a week, as she couldn't even consider starting the process for several days. The fifty-five-mile drive, one way, between her secluded cabin and her mother's apartment had only added to her exhaustion.

Her mother had hated that she lived so far away.

"Why can't you live nearby me?" she'd whined. "It's as if you want nothing to do with me."

"Mom, I just need to be out on the land. One with nature. I can't live like this. I can't live in these concrete boxes," Issa had said.

"They're called *apartments*. Everyone lives in them."

Issa had turned and said, "No, not everyone wants to. There are places with open spaces and real trees and dirt beneath your feet."

Her mother had shaken her head. "Dear God, why can't you ever leave that alone?"

"I can't. It's who I am."

"No," her mother had argued. "It's part of who you *were*. It has nothing to do with who you *are*. That was twenty years ago. Two decades have gone by. You should've adjusted. You should be somebody else by now."

Issa's teakettle started to whistle in her little cabin. Issa pulled out a teabag and a very large ceramic mug and poured hot water over the top of it. It was the way she always drank her tea. Strong and black. Her mother, Maier, liked hers with a little bit of milk and a little bit of sweetener.

Issa liked the comforts of home—but what *she* considered *home*. Her mother's place had never been home. Apartments made Issa feel closed in, like a prison. Maybe she'd only spent her first six years of life on the hills of Ireland, but those six years were ingrained into who she was. And every day that she was not outdoors felt like a prison sentence with no end.

"I can't live up there with you," her mother complained. "And I don't want to live away from you."

Issa had nodded. "I know that. So I'm the one who will come back and forth. I'll stay here sometimes, but my life will be there."

"How can that possibly be?" Her mother had walked away and sat down on the couch, looking so lost that Issa had felt guilty. "You have no job up there. And to do that drive back and forth …"

"It's not that bad, it's only an hour."

Her mother nodded as she always did. "Only an hour. It's an hour that you are away from me."

"It's an hour where I'm coming to you or going away from you, yes," Issa had said quietly. "But it's also an hour where I'm closer to the life I need to live."

Her mother had turned such sad eyes her way. "Why is it such a sacrifice to be away from there?"

"I can't explain it, Mom. It just is."

Holding the big ceramic mug in her hand, Issa stood in front of the fire, letting the waves of heat wash over her. And now, with her mother dead and gone, Issa didn't need to make the drive again. She didn't need to do anything in the city again as she had no job to go to either.

She'd completed her PhD, but, so far, unfortunately she had found only concrete city work available. But, when you were a biologist and had your doctorate in environmental

sciences, surely jobs in her field existed where she could live
out here like she needed to.

Her cell phone buzzed in her pocket. Yet one more sign
of the trappings of civilization. She pulled out her phone and
looked at the Caller ID on her screen. It was one of the
university professors, one of the men on her doctorate team,
sending condolences to her for her loss. She raised her gaze
and stared into the darkness beyond the windows. "How is it
they all know?"

She shook her head, not understanding. Her mother had
been big on social media. And on secrecy. Her mother had
made up a fake account and thought that was the best part.
She could do and say and be anyone she wanted to be and no
one knew.

Issa didn't know that was possible. She was big on computer technology and having all the research material at her
fingertips, but she would never want to be on those sites her
mother had thought were such fun. Issa had been amazed
when her mother showed her how many friends she had.
The ongoing question in Issa's mind was, *Were they actually
friends?*

The one time she'd asked, her mother hadn't cared, saying, "These are people I interact with, people who share
what's happening in their lives and are watching what
happens in my life. I don't feel so alone when I do this."

Issa had nodded. The last thing she wanted was people
prying into her world, into her life. She'd gone through
school making friends but keeping few. She wasn't wired to
be a social butterfly. She wanted no part of the global
fascination of other peoples' lives.

She lived in the open air, the silence of the forest. Still
waters and amazing forms of life dwelled within. But only a

few special people cared to look for those wonders. She hadn't tried hard to make friends. For that she knew the fault was hers. Her heart wasn't in it; neither was her soul. She'd come alive when she joined the local falconry club. That was something she could relate to. She'd become as attached to the birds there as she had to the members.

They had rallied around her, understanding on some elemental level she was one of them. She hadn't realized, growing up, such a group of people who did this was over here. She hadn't understood her life as a child was in some ways unique and yet, to others, deprived. It made her both heartbroken for not being so special and yet grateful for having others who understood. And, despite all the time she spent with these people, she hadn't yet found a hawk or falcon or another bird that could give her what she sought. And she'd spent decades searching. Two of them to be exact.

When she heard an unnatural sound outside, she froze. Making a fast decision, she blew out the kerosene light. But for some reason her instincts were on alert. And then she heard the rumble from her birds outside. Humbug screeched into the night, and she heard a gunshot. Her blood ran cold.

She raced out the back door, and two hard hands grabbed her. Not a word was said as she fought and screamed and tugged to get away until finally something was shoved over her head. It was long enough to drop down over the rest of her. She was knocked to the ground and trussed up like an animal. Finally she was picked up and tossed over someone's shoulder. Blind, hurting, and terrified, she continued to struggle until something hard slammed into her head. And she knew no more.

CHAPTER 2

Weeks Later

EAGLE SAUNDERS WALKED onto the long veranda and stared at the sky. He saw no sign of the falcon who'd taken off on him yesterday—the falcon still so badly injured it shouldn't have been able to fly. And that was after Eagle's attempts to heal the bird who had showed up a few days ago.

Out of habit he yelled, "Rikker? Come home, boy."

The sky was empty. The falcon long gone.

That didn't stop Eagle from searching the sky's vast blue depths. As always it drew him in, like a wounded soldier to the hope that something—someone—was out there. He was no stranger to hope. Lying in Afghanistan, waiting for rescue with his bullet-torn body, he'd stared upward for hours as his hope waned.

He'd woken up in the hospital weeks later, realizing sometime hopes and wishes did come true.

Now he gave homage to the sky on a regular basis, the blue depths giving him the courage way back when to stay alive until the shooting around him had died down and his team could come for him. He'd rebuilt his life outside of the Special Operations unit he'd been in. A life as far away and as unregimented as possible. He had over a hundred and twenty acres here. Part of it was an inheritance from his grandfather, and the other parcel was purchased as a barrier to keep the rest of the world at bay.

He'd seen enough of what humanity could do to one another. He couldn't stop them anymore, but at least now he didn't have to witness it. Here he worked to save those birds that had always rested at the edge of his heart. Something about the majesty of the raptors called to him. He hadn't planned on creating a refuge for them, but, no doubt, that was exactly what he'd done.

A biologist buddy, also former navy, had found an injured eagle and had brought it to Eagle as he'd been the closest help at the time. The concept had snowballed.

And that brought him around to wondering about Rikker and what had happened. Something impossible.

Rikker had a badly broken wing, broken leg, and a deep cut on his back. Eagle had found him when out riding several days ago. Instead of panicking when a human approached, the falcon had stayed still and let Eagle pick him up and bring him to the center for treatment. Due to the animal's more docile behavior, and, by now out of habit, Eagle had checked for leg bands, then with the local falconry clubs.

No one was missing a falcon. Or no one wanted to own up to it and possibly be handed a bill for the bird's care. Not that Eagle would have charged them, but he'd seen how people's behavior shifted once money was involved.

In fact, he hadn't expected the raptor to survive that first night. He'd stopped the bleeding, set the leg and the wing, and stitched up the cut, but the bird had been off his food and water and barely holding on to his perch. None of which were a good sign. Yesterday morning he'd been even worse. He'd given up the fight to live until he suddenly tried to rip apart Eagle's hands.

When Eagle had taken the falcon outside into the sunshine, thinking it might be a kindness to put down the bird, the raptor had exploded from his arms—as if the falcon had read Eagle's mind—and flung himself into the sky in a last attempt at freedom. Except, with his injuries, no way in hell should that falcon have been able to fly. And he was one of the largest Eagle had ever seen.

But Rikker had taken to the skies with a vengeance and disappeared.

With his rescued dogs, Gunner and Hatter, at his side, Eagle walked to the raptor cages. The two big dogs went a long way to keep a lot of the wildlife back at the interior fence line where they belonged.

Caring for the large birds brought in a multitude of other prey looking for an easy meal. Although Eagle's property was well fenced—both an outer and an inner fence line—the birds often hurt themselves as they panicked in their pens, trying to get away from the threat of predators.

As Eagle approached the birds, he realized something was wrong. He picked up speed and ran the last few yards. Instead of the normal rustling of feathers, calls, and chattering among the birds, there was silence. He approached slowly and quietly now, feeling hundreds of eyes turn his way. And yet not one bird made a sound.

Unnerved, he walked around the perimeter of the multiple pens, looking for the predator that had them all tense. He pulled his gun from his holster and approached the corner cautiously. Glancing to all sides, he could see nothing that would put the birds on full alert. Peering around the corner, he saw the same high grass and bushes leading to the tree line farther back. He kept walking. Predators of all kinds had one thing in common. They were sneaky as all hell.

His steps as soundless as his raptors, he automatically checked the fences, looking for holes. Foxes were notorious for getting inside both fences but still could not penetrate the raptor cages. And, if the foxes were smart, they'd stay clear. Coyotes often stayed just off to the side and taunted the birds, letting them know that, given any weakness, the coyotes would be there to tear apart the raptors' throats. But the wolves were even more intimidating. They would howl from a distance, knowing the birds were within reach, almost salivating at the luscious meals inside the cages.

But Eagle found none of those four-legged creatures.

And still behind Eagle was only silence. Every bird watched his progress. He kept glancing into the pens for any clue. Something was seriously off. A thick dark growl erupted from Gunner's throat. The huge sheepdog ambled forward, his ears up, his back raised. Hatter raced behind with a lesser sense of smell. More concerned with the joys of puppyhood, he pranced and jumped around Gunner, trying to figure out what this new game was all about.

Unfortunately Hatter was no puppy—he was just stunted in growth and seriously stupid.

Eagle walked past, dropping a soothing hand on the back of Gunner's neck. "What is it, boy?"

Gunner hunkered down as the hair on the back of his neck rose again. Eagle studied the long grass and the thick forest beyond. The air was still, heavy. Nothing moved. Not even the wind.

A negative space was up ahead where the ground cover appeared flattened. A trail of broken and trampled grass led to it, but, unless the animal left the same way, no path exited the hollow. With Gunner at his side, Hatter loping behind, Eagle slowly approached. Reaching the first fence line, he stood on the bottom rail and stretched up, hoping to see what was hiding.

Just then something erupted from the long grass.

He watched in amazement as Rikker soared high above, splitting the air with its piercing screech, only to circle back around again and again and slowly lower itself down. Eagle could see its broken wing, and yet the bird still flew straight. Eagle didn't understand—but he wanted to. He swung a leg over the top rail of the fence and jumped down on the other side.

He ordered the dogs to stay. Gunner broke into furious barking, as if warning Eagle not to go there. But the big heavy dog couldn't jump this fence easily. With his weapon ready, Eagle slowly parted the long grass. Just as he caught a glimpse of something white on the ground, the falcon rose once again, flapping its big wings in front of him.

"Easy, Rikker. Take it easy now. Let me see what's going on."

Unable to see around the irate bird, Eagle stepped forward, using his arms to brush back the raptor. His gaze dropped to the ground, and he froze, his mind struggling to compute the scene before him.

A nude woman—bloody, bruised, and scratched to hell—lay collapsed on the ground unconscious.

Or dead.

"Jesus Christ." He put away his weapon and dropped to her side. She was on her side, but Eagle could see she was young, with long dark-red hair half covering her face, skinny to the point of being gaunt. Her bare feet were bloody and torn. As if she'd run until she couldn't take one more step ...

Instinctively he searched for a pulse, only to have Rikker flap his dangerously large wings in Eagle's face and claw at his hands.

"Stop. I must help her. Just like I helped you."

With a wary eye on the bird, Eagle was determined to subdue the falcon if he wouldn't let Eagle check out the woman. He slowly outstretched his arm again. Rikker made a harsh cry but settled onto the woman's shoulder.

Not the best place, but it would do for the moment. Eagle found a pulse at her wrist. Slow and steady. He did a quick check for injuries. He ran experienced fingers down her spine, her extremities, looking for breaks. He couldn't find any broken bones, but her right ankle was swollen, and one shoulder badly cut, and any internal fractures would be hard to confirm without X-rays. He frowned, his mind racing to identify the wounds and their cause.

Keeping his face and eyes protected from the falcon, still uncertain of the reason for the bird's presence, Eagle searched the woman's back and chest again and found a small hole on the shoulder she lay on. He settled on his heels. He knew that wound.

She'd been shot by a small caliber handgun at close range. He gently rolled her forward and found no exit wound.

"Goddammit." He glared at Rikker. "What the hell is going on here?"

In a move that shocked Eagle into silence, Rikker slowly lowered his head and stroked the woman's cheek with his beak.

"Well, shit," he whispered. Eagle pulled off his shirt, throwing it across her form. Wishing he had a blanket with him, he glanced at the house and realized it'd be better to pick her up and take her back, but how badly wounded was she? He worried about internal injuries the most. Still, she couldn't stay here. That's when he noticed the bright red blood on the grass beside her head. As soon as he probed that side, she moaned. In a gentle voice he whispered, "Take it easy. You're safe now."

Just then she rolled to her back. Her eyes opened, and cloudy midnight-blue irises gazed at him. She seemed to focus, only to have her lashes slowly drop again. Her mouth worked, and he could sense the effort behind her need to speak.

"It's okay. You're safe."

Her eyes opened, this time with more clarity, and landed on Rikker. Instead of crying out or screaming in terror, she murmured, "*Mo chara*, you found me." She gently stroked the falcon. He crooned at her touch, and her eyes drifted closed again.

Aware of time passing, but also aware of something magical happening, Eagle studied her waxy features, his gaze catching sight of the fresh blood on her forehead.

He slipped his arms under her frail form and lifted her. As if Mother Nature herself was helping, the wind picked up, making the trees bow around him, the branches forming a protective curtain for him to carry her through, unseen by others. The air held an eeriness, like something otherworldly. The dust swirled up at his feet, taking away his footprints, even though it had rained just that morning. And then a rumble sounded, ... as if someone gave them cover to hide the noise Eagle now made.

Unnerved, but understanding an opportunity had presented itself, he cradled her against his chest and strode back to the dogs. He awkwardly made it over the fence and froze. Rikker stood on Gunner's back, both ahead of Eagle as if urging him to move faster, with neither complaining about the odd transportation system. Even Hatter was out in front, for once a serious look in his eye.

Eagle didn't have a clue what was going on, but, whatever it was, it had to do with the injured woman in his arms. He picked up speed, almost running to his house. As he came to the large falcon pens, the silence was suffocating. His heart slammed against his chest, and he could hardly breathe for the tension coiling inside.

As soon as he pounded up the steps to his house and bolted inside, the dogs barked and the raptors screeched, filling his world with a cacophony of sounds—like some invisible command had been released.

He stared down at the frail woman in his arms and asked in a low shocked voice, "Who are you? And what the hell just happened to my world?"

SHE WOKE UP in a dream. Fog surrounded her; pain filled her. Like being on a roller coaster of agony as she shifted and moved, yet she wasn't the one doing the shifting or the moving. Was she being carried?

Her body shifted again but in a gentle wavelike motion. Not choppy and jerky as she would have expected if carried. The sound in her ear was warm and reassuring—a heartbeat—a strong, vibrant, rhythmical pulse that drove through her consciousness and found a surprising response in her own chest. She was alive? Really? After all she'd been through?

She didn't think it was possible. She hadn't given up hope, but she certainly hadn't thought a rescue was possible. She remembered running through the bushes, through the trees, falling, picking herself up and carrying on again.

Although desperate to find help, when she crossed a road, she'd stopped, considered it briefly, and then realized she couldn't trust anyone. And she'd bolted across the road and over the fence to the woods on the other side.

The fence meant somebody owned the land. Somebody cared. She could only hope they weren't like those she'd left behind. Just the thought of anybody from that group following her had her picking up her feet and running again.

She'd yet to make a sound, but, in her mind, she could hear her screams. She couldn't stop crying out in pain at each step, but she wasn't sure her voice worked anymore. The last time she had screamed, it was as if her voice had been broken. To be forever a raw echo of her former voice, one she'd barely recognized. Something else she could lay at her captors' feet.

If anybody would ask, all she could say was they were male—one to three, maybe four; she didn't know anymore. They'd all taken turns one way or another. But there'd been one boss. He'd ordered everything that had been done to her. She'd started with clothes and ended up nude. And yet she hadn't been raped. Although grateful, she didn't understand. It was more about power and humiliation. *Stress.* The boss had used the word *stressors* over and over again when he spoke to the other men. She didn't understand. She'd retreated like an animal, curled into a ball, trying to get away from them. But failed every time. And they'd go at it again. Tiny razor blades, cigarettes. She kept screaming, and nobody would listen.

The boss kept asking her questions. She didn't understand what they wanted. At the end she didn't even understand the questions. The endless pain became too much. She'd retreated inside herself deliberately. It had taken her a while to figure out that acting one step away from death was the only way she would get the men to relax enough that she might escape.

And it had worked. But even now she didn't remember exactly what she'd done. Except she swore she'd heard voices in her head. Voices telling her to run. But it was all confused with the men's voices, fighting. Something about her guard cheating at poker.

One had stormed off, and the other had gone to the door, screaming at him. The words a blur but the heat unmistakable. And she knew he'd probably come at her as an outlet for his anger. Instead he'd gone outside, slamming the door, but he'd slammed it so hard that it had bounced open again. She'd gotten up off the pallet on the floor. And raced to the open door. She looked through a crack to see where they'd gone. And, sure enough, they both headed off in the same direction, the fight continuing even outside the cabin. She stepped out to find one man had stayed behind. He chased her back into her room, a baseball bat in his hand. But he'd been so looking forward to beating her that he tripped and fell, the bat falling from his grasp. She was on him in seconds. She didn't remember how many times she hit him, or how hard, but she'd thrown the bat to the ground afterward, climbed through the window, and kept going. She never looked back.

And now here she was, another meadow, another fence, somebody else's property. And that was the last thing she remembered.

Until now. The man shifted her in his arms, and a wave of pain rose up so sharp, so achingly clear, her stomach—already empty—strove to escape her mouth. She shuddered.

"Easy, take it easy. You'll be fine now. I won't let them

hurt you again."

She didn't know why, she didn't know how—and maybe it was just because of that strong heartbeat under her ear—but she believed him. She sank back, back into the unconscious world she'd been in, grateful that, maybe this time, somebody would help her.

CHAPTER 3

E AGLE WENT STRAIGHT to the spare bedroom, wishing
he had more hands available as he struggled to pull back
the blanket so he could lay the broken woman on the
mattress. She moaned softly as he pulled his arms free from
underneath her. He raced to the bathroom, grabbed towels,
and returned. With a warm wet washcloth, he quickly
dabbed her forehead, checking to see how severe her head
wound was. His military experience let him know she likely
had a concussion and would possibly need stitches.

He was loathe to call a doctor. And even more so to call
the sheriff. He did a complete second check over her body,
noting the ankle continued to swell, and the injury was
recent. The scratches he assumed were from running. Her
feet would need to be soaked to see the extent of that
damage. Her ribs were bruised, her arms lacerated, the soft
skin on her breasts reddened with angry burn marks. Grimly,
he realized she'd likely been held captive somewhere,
somehow. And for a long time.

Until she found an opportunity to escape. The shoulder
wound was the one that worried him the most. How long
had she been tortured? She could have any number of
internal injuries he couldn't see. There was an odd green
tinge to the right side of her back near her waistline. That
also worried him as did the multiple layers of bruising all

over.

The bullet had to come out of her shoulder.

He could handle the rest, but he didn't want to make a call on that one if he didn't have to. He didn't want her to suffer permanent shoulder injury if he could help it.

He gently covered her up, feeling the clammy coolness to her skin. As he pulled the blankets over her, a screech sounded beside him. He turned to find Rikker walking up and down the bed.

"I brought her inside. Now give me a chance to fix her up."

The falcon tilted his head and stared at Eagle. An intelligence both unnerving and bizarre stared at him.

"I don't know who and what you are, my friend. Just know I'm not here to hurt her."

An odd rumble sounded from the falcon's throat. It fascinated Eagle as he stepped back and pulled the phone from his pocket. He dialed a number he knew by heart. When a grumpy older man answered the phone, Eagle said, "I need you."

Gray snorted. "That's nice. Always nice to be wanted by someone."

"Come here now, as fast as you can. Bring your medical bag." Eagle hung up the phone and pocketed it. Gray would come. If nothing else, curiosity would force him.

Eagle returned to the bathroom, grabbed several more washcloths, and made a quick trip to the kitchen for warm water and a bowl, then headed back to the bedroom, and sat beside her. Once again, he pulled the covers down, hearing the woman protest as the chill settled in.

"I'm sorry. I'm trying to clean up the scratches as much as I can." With a washcloth, he gave her a thorough, and, as fast as possible, bed bath, paying attention to the scratches that needed further cleaning. He knew he was hurting her, but she never made a sound.

Then she was likely unconscious yet again. When he made his way to her feet, he knew a simple wash wouldn't do it. He should have shifted her the other way on the bed, hanging her knees over the edge to get her feet set in the water.

Deciding that would still be the best way to do it, he quickly realigned the bedding, slipped his arms underneath her, and shifted her position. He covered her body again, leaving her lower legs bare, feet dangling just above the floor. Then, with clean water in the larger basin, he lifted her feet and carefully put them in.

As soon as her feet came in contact, he realized she wasn't unconscious at all. She cried out in pain, her body jerking up only to murmur in joy as the heat soaked in. He needed her body temperature to warm up fast. He should have just placed her in a bathtub.

Still the bullet hole was the bigger issue as long as she was warming up. He glanced at his watch. "Come on, Gray. Where the hell are you?" With an antiseptic soap, Eagle gently smoothed some over the bottom of her feet and then let her feet rest in the warm water.

Just as he finished, he could hear the beat-up old Ford come down the driveway.

Gray. Thank God.

Rikker, at the woman's side, stared at Eagle, almost as if ready to give a screech should Eagle do something wrong. For some reason Eagle felt like he needed to explain to the bird what was happening. "Gray is coming to look after her. I can do a lot of field dressings but that bullet? We need to make sure it comes out. Can I get it out? Yes, but not as clean as I would like. She also needs a doctor to look for any other internal problems."

He took several steps to the doorway, turned back to look at the bird, and said, "I'll be back in a few minutes." And he raced out the front door and unlocked the gate. He locked it up behind him and walked back up to the house.

Gray was getting out of the cab of his white truck. He slammed it shut and glared at Eagle. "You could have given me an explanation."

"It would have taken too long," Eagle said calmly. He nodded inside. "You need to see this."

Gray's name matched the closely cut short head of whitish hair and beard. He shook his head. "It's not like you to be so mysterious."

"Did you tell anyone where you were coming?" Eagle asked belatedly. Shit, he should've warned Gray first. Eagle glanced around the area, his gaze searching the shadows. Had someone chased her? Tracked her here? If so he had to prepare. He had no intention of letting anyone at her again. Not once she'd finally escaped.

He motioned the old man inside.

Gray walked up the porch steps, almost being deliberately slow to aggravate Eagle.

Unfortunately Eagle didn't have any time or patience. "You didn't answer me," he snapped. "Did you tell anyone where you were going?"

Gray raised both hands in exasperation and walked into the house. "Who would I tell? I live alone, remember?"

"I wonder why," Eagle said.

"No sass, boy," Gray muttered. "You live alone too, remember?"

With the door locked behind them, Gray raised his eyebrows, and the two hairy lines shot toward his hairline. He stared at Eagle wordlessly.

"Follow me." Eagle led the way to the bedroom to see the woman exactly as he had left her. Like Rikker's magical disappearance, Eagle had been a little worried she'd disappear as well.

Gray stopped in the doorway and studied her. "Shit," he whispered. "Who is she, and what happened to her?"

"I don't know the answer to either question."

Gray was all business now. He dropped his bag on the floor beside the bed and rolled up his sleeves. "Explain," he barked.

Eagle shared the little bit he knew, leaving off much of the mystical stuff he still struggled with himself.

Gray shot him a hard look, carefully pulled back the covers, and sucked in his breath. Then he proceeded to check her over. With Eagle's help, they gently rolled her to her stomach. With her back exposed, Eagle took the opportunity to wash and clean the scratches that went up and down her frail body.

"I don't like that bullet hole or the bullet graze alongside her head," Gray announced. He tapped her good shoulder. "Not sure what kind of life she's lived, but that looks like a very old bullet hole too."

Eagle studied the small scar. "Not an easy life obviously. But these new injuries ... Why do you think I called you?"

"You should've called for an ambulance and the sheriff."

"Not happening." Eagle wouldn't budge on that issue, not until he knew who had done this to her.

Gray settled back on his heels. "Why do you have to be so damn stubborn? She isn't your problem."

At that, Eagle said nothing.

Gray raised both hands again, this time in frustration. "Fine, don't be sensible. Don't let the authorities know where she is. Don't let her family know she's safe."

"You get a point for that last one. But not the rest."

"That's the thing about family. Nobody gets to be her age without having parents, siblings, or somebody who cares about her." He picked up her ring finger. "No evidence of a wedding ring, so you might be off the hook of any husband. That doesn't mean she can't have a live-in partner of the last five years."

Eagle nodded. "It also doesn't mean that live-in partner isn't the same asshole who held her captive and beat her to the point she ran until her feet were skinned bare to escape him."

Gray let out a slow breath. Then gave a clipped nod. "Okay, point to you too." He turned to look down at her. "What is it you want me to do?"

"Help me get the bullet out, patch her up, and deal with the head wound. If you have any antibiotics to stop some of the infection waiting to take over, that would be good. Plus any painkillers in that bag of yours too. There's no flesh on her bones, and whatever trauma she's been through would've been more than just physical. She's a fighter," Eagle said quietly. "She got this far on her own. She needs every chance we can give her."

"And if the men who did this to her come after her?"

Eagle gave him a grim smile. "As soon as we get that bullet out, I can set up the security system outside." His gaze narrowed. "Then I'm loading up every weapon in the house, in case I get a chance to empty them into the asshole who did this to her."

Gray warned, "You can't take on every ill in the world, you know?"

"No, just those that come to my front door." Eagle turned and walked out.

"DID YOU FIND her?"

Dylan stared at his longtime boss and swallowed hard, then shook his head. "No. We tripped his security system," he said bluntly. "As we bolted, Jordan here fell back and took some kind of a spear in the belly."

The boss looked down at the man gasping for breath on the floor and nodded. "And yet you weren't injured?"

"It looks like he runs some kind of raptor center."

"Raptor?" the boss said, his voice low, sharp with interest. "Anything of importance?"

"I don't think so. Honestly it was dark, and I couldn't help but see a thousand eyes staring at us the whole time. It was damn spooky."

The boss nodded quietly, contemplating the sky over their heads.

"Boss, can we get some help for Jordan here?" Dylan asked, motioning to the man collapsed on the floor, still groaning. "I know he deserved the punishment for letting her escape, but surely he's suffered enough?"

The boss nodded. "Absolutely." And, right in front of them, he pulled out a handgun, pointed, and fired, placing a bullet between Jordan's eyes.

Dylan swallowed again and again. He stared down at the man he'd worked with the last few months. He hadn't known him well. He'd been a laborer the boss had picked up, but he'd been here the whole time they'd held Issa captive. Dylan had even wondered himself if it was safe to keep Jordan around when this was over and done with. He wasn't sure the man could keep his mouth shut.

Not to mention the boss had asked Issa a lot of questions. Dumb questions. Dylan had thought they were more stupid curiosity, but still the boss had the power to shock him. The boss got colder every day. With the boss's breath slowly calming down, Dylan turned to look at him. "Where do you want me to dump him?"

This wasn't the first time Dylan had disposed of a body. But this was the first time a man was gunned down beside him. Dylan didn't dare show any nervousness. There was a whole lot of mean in the boss—especially lately. And he appeared to no longer have any boundaries as to what he'd do or wouldn't do.

"Take him out to the ditch in the back. Bury him deep enough we don't have to worry about the animals. Make sure the job is done properly."

Dylan nodded. He glanced at the big man at his feet and sighed. "Maybe you could hire a smaller man next time." He bent down, grabbed Jordan by the hood, and dragged him out the front door. There wasn't much for flooring here thankfully. Just dirt, but he still left a blood trail.

A trail he knew he'd have to clean up fast. When he got to the front step, he walked around the building, turned on the tractor with the bucket on the front, hopped on it, and drove around to the front. Reversing the front-end loader so the bucket was down in front of the porch, he got off the seat, dragged the body into the bucket, and, with his chest heaving, straightened up again. Wiping his brow, he walked back around to the driver's seat, hopped up, and raised the bucket. Then he drove around the side of the cabin and parked. He knew better than to leave that blood trail visible for long. There were too many people around this place.

He went back in with the bucket of dirt that sat outside and spread it on top of the blood. Then grabbed several more bucketfuls. He gave it a couple minutes, then grabbed the heavy rake and smoothed over the area. It wasn't a perfect solution, but there wasn't any other way. Blood was blood.

The boss never said a word. He sat beside the fire, his laptop on his legs, and wrote notes. He was a hell of a smart man. Dylan had to admit he was worried that maybe the boss had bit off more than he could chew. His fascination with that damn girl and her birds had cost him a lot. Then he was haunted by so much more.

The two were actually old friends in many ways but not when push came to shove. ... Dylan spent his life looking after the boss. Not the other way around. The boss was very clear on that.

When the inside was cleaned up, Dylan hopped back onto the tractor and drove carefully along the trails.

There'd been a lot of rain lately, and the ground was soft. At the back of the property were a couple ditches. He was pretty sure he could find a place to put Jordan and not have anybody ask any questions. When he got to the spot he was thinking of, he hopped off and took a good look. They'd had a spring runoff, and some of the ditches had ended up very deep. He considered one that was well over six feet deep, almost a crevice.

He turned the front-end loader around to get into position, and, when he could, he dumped the body into the place he'd thought would do for a deep-enough grave. Then he maneuvered the bucket to pick up rocks from close by and slowly filled in the area. When he was done, he got off, grabbed some of the deadfall from around the area and dragged it over the top.

Then he backed up the tractor, and, with his boots, he made scuff marks so the area was clear of any tire tracks.

Inside, his mind was in turmoil. Had Jordan been shot because he had failed to guard the girl? Or because he'd been injured, and that made him a liability? It didn't matter what the answer was because Dylan got that much closer to being the next one forfeited. In fact, as he drove back, he worried he would get a bullet right away. The boss had kept him around to take care of Jordan's body, but now what? Just because they'd been together for years didn't give Dylan a free pass.

He walked back into the cabin and headed for the kitchen. There he washed up and started dinner. He did all kinds of jobs here. None of them mattered. He didn't have any other life. He had given his life to the big man eons ago. Dylan was too old to do anything different. He was a wiry monkey man, strong, but there wasn't a whole lot to him now. He'd aged and not well. He used to be as bombastic and fiery over issues as his boss was. The boss was much younger, but the years were becoming more noticeable as he aged too. The question now was, how long did Dylan have?

For a long time he thought loyalty was the answer to longevity. Now he had to wonder if a bullet was in his near future. He prepped the potatoes and tossed them into the pan to start frying. He could hear the boss on the phone.

Bits and pieces of the conversation came his way. None of it made a lot of sense. Dylan and the boss were both Irish, but it was as if his boss spoke a different language. That was okay. The less Dylan knew, the better.

It might stave off that bullet for a while.

CHAPTER 4

I SSA LISTENED TO the footsteps retreating from the bedroom. She had no idea who this man was. She'd only awoken to the pain—fingers poking and prodding.

It was hard to lie motionless as they continued to explore her wounds. Her feet felt funny—warm, yet cold; stinging, and yet healing. She couldn't figure out what they'd done to her feet. Everything hurt so damn much. Now if only she knew where she was, why she was here, and who these men were. The one thing she did know was that Roash stood guard beside her.

As if sensing she was awake, her falcon leaned forward and gently stroked his beak along her temple. Hot tears came to her eyes. She didn't know if anybody could possibly understand how bereft her life had been, how empty since she had lost her own falcon two decades ago. Roash had filled those footprints more than most, but their relationship still didn't have the same depth as what she'd had.

It seemed like she had spent all that time searching for another feathered friend, an animal that would give her the same connection. Something about this one made her hope and, at the same time, made her fear. This was the second time in her life everything had blown up.

The first time had cost lives. And everything she'd known—her father, her brothers, her homeland, and the house she'd spent every day in. The fields and the hills, the cliffs and crannies, she had climbed and crawled and laughed and played on them all. But the loss of her own falcon had hurt the most. It turned her into a mute for many months. Nobody understood. Specialists said it was the shock and trauma of losing so many family members. But, in fact, it was the trauma of having the voice in her head go silent. It had been ... special. The two of them together had been ... incredible. But she'd been a child, and nobody had believed her. They understood the falcon came when she called, that he had been trained, and, even though she was young, she had worked hard to develop the bond between them. Of course she had. Her father had always threatened to take the falcon away if the two didn't do their best for him.

Her dad had been an opportunistic man, gleefully dealing in activities that the government would've done a lot to stop. But it was the only way he knew. It was how he fed his family, how he'd been raised. And it was a life he took to naturally. He led a large group of trusted men just like him.

She'd had an odd relationship with her father. As long as she was of value, she was treated fairly. But, even though a mere child, dare she cross him ... As such, her memories were conflicting. Most of the time she was happy with foggy memories that allowed her to see him in a warmer light. But she was an adult now. She knew he had been a smuggler. But the other charges she'd seen on that criminal record sheet had shocked her. Made her question her childhood.

The covers were pulled off her body yet again. She knew she should be worried that whoever checked her over was someone she didn't know. And that her body was entirely exposed and just as injured. But she had heard nothing but compassion in either of the men's voices. Soon blankets were pulled up to her neck, and a welcomed warmth invaded her body.

She was so very cold. In her homeland, she was used to the cold, as they all were. You got up in the morning, and you could see your breath in the air, and she found a certain joy in the experience. Evidence of the freshness of the world around them. And she missed it.

She missed so much. Everything that had happened in her twenty-six years of life, she could label into parts: part one being before the nightmare, before she lost all but one family member.

Part two being the aftermath. That horrible stage of immigrating to America, forced to see doctors and specialists, looked upon as an oddity, attending school, which she had no interest in. A life without her father or her brothers. Or her beloved falcon. A life inside the concrete city with concrete boxes stacked on top of other concrete boxes and stuck beside more concrete boxes.

Life where there were no green hills, no waves crashing on the shores below. And worse yet, no breath hanging frozen on the air when she got up in the mornings. And no falcon ever at her side. The loss had been overpowering.

Part three was the adjustment. Growing up, going to schools, multiples of them, finding a life worth living, learning to understand what relationships were, her first boyfriend, her first kiss, her first affair, and then her first graduation and her second graduation, followed by a third. Those were the normal steps in life here. Although she'd been behind when she first arrived in the States and had been held back from school for a long time until she began to speak again and could pass her placement tests, she'd eventually made the most of her new reality.

Until part four. When her physically healthy mother, at only sixty-two, had a heart attack and died on the kitchen floor, while Issa had been working on her research at the university. She'd found her mother when she had arrived for dinner. And all that part one pain and shock and loss reopened, and she realized how little she'd dealt with that original pain.

Now an adult, she had been forced to go through the motions of organizing her mother's body for cremation and finding a place to lay her to rest. It had been tough to go back into her mother's apartment to clean up her personal belongings.

And just like Pandora's Box, she'd opened the box of paperwork and then been kidnapped—her world split anew and part five began.

Part five tore her world apart.

The footsteps returned. She couldn't stop the shudder rippling down her spine. She didn't know who this first man was, but she recognized caring when she felt it.

He'd brought her in from the cold, but, more than that, ... Roash trusted him.

For her, that said everything.

Until she heard a second voice. And the thick Irish accent.

"HOW IS SHE?" Eagle hovered as Gray cleansed and then stitched up the head injury.

"She needs a doctor," Gray snapped. "How do you expect her to be?" He twisted to stare at Eagle. "I get that you don't want to bring in the sheriff, that you want nothing to do with authority anymore, but what you can't have is this woman dying on you."

Eagle's voice was hard. "That's why I brought you in."

Gray shook his head. "That's not good enough. I don't have the proper facilities here to take out that bullet."

"You do it, or I do it," Eagle said firmly. "No law enforcement types."

Gray twisted on the side of the bed and glared at him. "Why? Why would you choose to put her life at risk by not calling for help?"

"Because she's running for her life. Somebody shot her. No way in hell am I letting anybody else know she's here."

He watched as Gray's face worked. In many ways Gray was like Eagle, somebody who didn't do well with the establishment. But Gray would call the sheriff or EMTs. Or a lawyer. Whoever was needed, he would reach out for help, whereas Eagle had *been* the help for a long time. Being in the military, he'd spent time all around the world, helping military coups, fighting against insurgents, saving people, rescuing kidnap victims. He'd been the one everyone called for when they needed help.

Besides, how could Gray understand the bizarre events that had occurred when Eagle found this woman? Eagle didn't understand them himself. But he knew, from that moment on, it was his job to protect her. In whatever shape or form was required. In his personal experience he'd seen the enemy in many different disguises. He often intuited when and where the attack would come from. And he was damn sure it was coming. And soon.

If he hadn't trusted Gray, Eagle wouldn't have called him. As he studied the older man, he wondered just how much he trusted him now. Because if he told anyone she was here, … then Gray had suddenly become the weakest link.

Eagle dropped his gaze and walked to the window and studied the yard around the house. The birds had returned to normal in their pens. They were one of the best security systems he could possibly have. Along with the two dogs.

He turned back to Gray. "Are you with me?"

Gray was already prodding the woman's shoulder. "I think the bullet went through the soft tissue and missed the bone."

Eagle walked over and sat down. "Stop."

Gray's fingers froze.

Eagle pointed. "On that side, a lump is under the skin."

Gray whistled. "Pass me the scalpel, will you?"

Eagle reached over to the towel that held the surgical instruments. He picked up the scalpel, passing it to him. He knew what came next. He grabbed one of the antibacterial cloths and quickly wiped the area. He watched and waited as Gray made a precision cut through the skin and went digging for the bullet so damn close to the surface that it had almost gone through by itself. When he grabbed the tweezers and pulled it out, Eagle held out his hand for it.

Eagle studied the bloody bullet. Then shook his head. "A .22. Somebody shot her with a .22 rifle."

"Good squirrel gun but it doesn't do so much for humans."

"She isn't much bigger than a squirrel."

Grimly Gray nodded. "How long do you think she was kept captive?"

"That's something I need to find out. Do you think she's naturally skinny, or is this malnutrition? As in, could this have developed through weeks to months of captivity?"

"It's malnutrition. It's prolonged stress. I'd say she's been a captive without food for at least a week, potentially with skimpy rations for a couple months, but she's naturally lean."

"Once again we've come up against the nicer side of humanity." Eagle's voice was sarcastic, even though he tried hard not to let it out.

But he'd seen too much of the world to hold much faith in people. He settled back and watched as Gray stitched the tiny wound closed and placed a bandage over it. When he was done, they shifted her position so her shoulder was up and her arm supported with a pillow under it to stop the shoulder blade from pulling on the wound.

"You better find some clothes for her. Her skin tone is turning gray, and she's seriously anemic. We need to give her some vitamin shots. But, if she's hypothermic, that's another thing altogether."

With the same thought, Eagle straightened and walked upstairs into his bedroom. He pulled out a pair of sweats and a T-shirt. When he came back, he said, "I'm pretty sure these will swim on her." With help from Gray, Eagle quickly dressed her, being careful of her shoulder and her many other bruises, scrapes, and cuts. As they pulled the sweatpants over her hips, Eagle said, "I'm worried about that green spot."

"You should be," Gray said. "That looks like a blow to her right kidney. Probably a direct punch to gain compliance."

A muscle worked in Eagle's jaw as he nodded. "And the rest?"

"I'm hoping they're all superficial. But I think this rib on the side is cracked. Without an X-ray, I don't know for sure." He turned and glanced at Eagle. "Do you know anybody who would give her an X-ray without asking too many questions?"

Eagle shook his head. "No, I don't."

"What about the vet you use for the birds?"

Eagle shrugged. "I don't know that anyone would let me bring in a human patient." He studied the frail woman. "How badly do you think she needs it?"

"It would be the first thing I'd have done if I was in a hospital. I don't like some of these bruises. I don't like the fact multiple colors are in the same spot."

Eagle pulled a big sock over her foot, tucking it under the loose sweatpants leg, almost smiling when it came to her knees. With the second one on, he tucked her under the bedcovers.

As he walked out of the spare bedroom with Gray, Eagle said, "I saw lots of that out on missions. Systematic torture. The same bruises day in and day out. And the sustained damage never quite heals."

"And they're all strategically placed of course."

"The one on her right kidney is for sure."

Gray nodded. "That's where I think she was somebody's punching bag for longer than a week. Given her condition, I suspect she's been missing for several weeks."

"Why? Why would somebody do that?"

Gray stopped to look at Eagle, shoving his hands into his pockets, his medicine bag packed up beside him. "You have to realize there is a good chance she's been sexually molested. There could be damage on the inside too."

Eagle leaned forward. "There was no bruising on her thighs or around the pubic area."

"I know. I saw that. And maybe that's a good thing. But people will rape as a punishment. As a power and dominance thing, not for the sexual pleasure of it. And they're also quite likely to use an object for the same purpose."

Inside his gut Eagle felt something tighten down. It was

pure anger. "There was no blood," he said slowly. In his mind, he searched back to when he'd first seen her. "There was no blood except from the fresh bullet wound and on her head. There was no dried blood anywhere else."

"That doesn't mean she didn't go through a creek, and it washed off." He nodded toward her. "However, I agree no bruising was there, and, given the colors on the rest of her body, I'll surmise she wasn't sexually assaulted."

"I'll keep an eye on her." Inside Eagle sighed with relief. It wasn't a guarantee of course, but he trusted Gray's skill. There wasn't much he hadn't seen in his life either.

"You do that. You might want to consider contacting Annie too." Gray picked up his bag. "I'd say it's been a fun time, but I'm not sure I'll sleep tonight, knowing she's here. Call me if her condition changes."

"I will." Eagle hesitated a moment. "Thanks for coming."

Gray lifted a hand. "Don't make me regret that I didn't drive her to the emergency room myself—or that I should've called the sheriff."

"If you do," Eagle said in all seriousness, "you just signed her death warrant."

Gray shot him a hard look. "And likely your own." He turned and walked out.

Eagle didn't give a damn if he took a bullet. But, as he considered all the birds that needed his care, it made him contemplate what backup plans he should implement, just in case something *did* happen to him. It was an issue as he was the sole caregiver to so many. Several young men in town gave him a hand when he'd built the new pens. They continued to come out on an irregular basis to help out around the place, so Eagle had no idea how long until their next visit.

Eagle hadn't worried about his death up until now. Realizing that a real threat was imminent, he needed to consider it. And fast.

STEFAN ROLLED OVER in bed. When he opened his eyes, he could see blue sky all around him. He glanced down at his mattress. But there wasn't one. Instead it was just a big fluffy cloud supporting him as he floated in the sky. Amazed and filled with wonder, he let himself drift, wondering who and what he owed for this experience. He traveled in the ethers a lot.

But he had yet to float on a cloud.

He smiled in joy, closed his eyes, and reached out with his arms, letting a burst of energy from his heart go free. When he opened his eyes again, the sky had darkened. Not with a cloud or a storm approaching but with night. And somehow the dark midnight sky was even sharper and clearer. He still floated on his crisp white downy bed, but the stars were so clear, it was as if he could touch them. He was amazed at the feeling.

He didn't quite understand what was going on, and he wanted to because, as soon as he could, he'd repeat this—at least he'd try to. He twisted his head to see land below him. But it was a long way down there.

As he searched, he couldn't identify his location. There were trees and meadows, forest and fences, plus the odd house dotted the landscape. But not any recognizable landmarks to tell him where he was. He sent out a cry in his mind, asking, "Who needs help?"

There was no answer. None. He frowned and then realized a tiny faint trail of energy surrounded him, as if somebody had floated in this spot in recent times. There was a familiarity to it. He didn't quite understand. He tried to track the energy, but it disappeared beneath him. As he rolled over to stare below, the world disappeared as clouds moved in.

He tried to brush away the clouds, but there was no moving them. He rolled off the cloud, pointed himself toward Earth and dove. Just as he thought he was about to break through the cloud cover, he sat up in bed.

His beloved Celina rolled over and placed her hand on his arm. "A nightmare?" she asked gently.

He scrubbed his face, pulling his hair back off his forehead. "I have no idea," he admitted. "But it was the same energy as before."

"The woman crying for help?"

He turned to look down at his wife and nodded. "I haven't heard or seen that energy in a few days. I was afraid she'd died."

Celina sat up, wrapped her arms around him, and just held him close. He knew how lucky he was to have her love him like she did. Well, he was more than lucky. He was truly blessed. He burrowed his face in the nape of her neck and crushed her close.

"Can you sleep again?"

A shudder rippled down his body. "I don't know," he whispered. "Maybe."

They lay back on the sheet, arms wrapped around each other, just giving comfort, both knowing that, at any moment, he could be pulled into another dream, another vision, or, the worst case, another nightmare.

And he could do very little about it.

CHAPTER 5

ISSA OPENED HER eyes, her body frozen, afraid to move for the pain she knew would shoot through her system. She studied the coverlet over her, the white pillowcase under her head, wondering how long she'd been here. She had no sense of time. No idea how long she'd been away from her own home, how long she'd been kidnapped. She didn't know if the men who'd done this had enough time to track her down or if they'd chosen to run. An insidious anger flowed through her. For what those men had done to her. What they said they'd done to her pets ...

She had so much hatred that she didn't know how to stop it from poisoning her soul. Those men had enough hatred for everyone in the world. And all because of her family apparently. Although the kidnappers hadn't explained, she didn't understand and couldn't even begin to sort out why they needed her. ... Yet the boss would use any method to get the answers he wanted. Answers she hadn't been able to give because she didn't have them.

At least she was alive.

She focused on that. She didn't know if she'd gone from bad to worse because pillowcases did not mean she was safe here. Somebody had treated the wounds on her feet. Although sore, even as she lay here, she knew they'd been cleansed. And the hands on her body had been gentle, caring, but that didn't stop the fear inside her.

So whoever this was, she'd thank him, but, at the same time, she needed to get the hell away. Potentially the sheriff would be after her too. In the deep recesses of the confusion of her brain, memories were mixed up. She was so afraid she might have killed one of her guards.

She'd been covered in blood when she'd crossed the stream, falling as her raw feet struggled to keep her footing. It had been a relief to realize, when she stepped out on the other side, that most of the blood was gone. And then Roash had found her. She'd seen his broken wing and done what she could to make it easier for him.

That he brought her here was a miracle. But, as someone who needed more than one miracle, she hoped more were available. Her bladder was full. She had no idea how long since she'd gone to the bathroom. Neither did she remember the last time she'd had water.

Her body was dehydrated and broken. But, using the same methodology she'd always used to connect to Roash, she'd used it to help herself. Hence, Roash still sported a broken wing as she'd taken enough of his spirited energy for her own use, but that had left him short. How sad was that? She felt bad about that, but she'd been in desperate need. At the crooning beside her ear, she turned her head slightly to see the big falcon standing guard on the headboard. She murmured, "Hey, big guy. How are you doing?"

Roash rumbled back at her. Not a cry but more a murmur of gentleness. She smiled and took that comfort back under again as she slept. This time deeper, easier, and more peaceful.

When she woke the next time, she still didn't feel better, but she needed to get up and empty her bladder. It refused to be silenced. She pulled off the covers first and stared down at the oversized T-shirt and massive sweatpants that she wore. Even her feet were covered. She should've been sweating in this getup. Instead it was a cozy nest she hated to leave. From where she lay on the bed, she could see a bathroom across the floor. And yet the distance appeared to be miles away.

She had to stand up. Slowly shifting to a sitting position, she only cried out once as her injured shoulder jerked. She had to sit straight because of her ribs, and so many other body parts screamed for attention, yet she couldn't do anything for them. But what she really needed was to get up onto her feet and make it to the bathroom. She took a deep breath and gathered her strength.

"Let me help you."

A huge man strode across the bedroom. She froze, her eyes dark as they watched him without an expression. She'd learned a long time ago to never let anybody know what was going on inside. But he didn't appear to care one way or the other.

She was scooped up, her breath coming out in a harsh gasp as her ribs were dislodged.

"I'm sorry," he murmured. "I'm sure all of you hurts. And I don't quite know how to stop that but with the passage of time."

She never said a word.

He stood in front of the toilet. "Do you want to risk standing on your feet?"

She contemplated the toilet and then said, "Yes."

Her voice was so faint he leaned closer.

He nodded and gently lowered her until she had a hand on the vanity beside the toilet and a hand on him. Then she slowly dropped her feet to the floor. She blew her breath out and put weight on them. Waves of pain rolled up through her stomach, slamming into her ribs and her throat.

She shuddered, and he quickly dropped her pants, plunked her butt on the toilet, and pushed her head to her knees. He grabbed a large bowl out of the bathtub and held it near her mouth. She fought to hold back the acid in her stomach. When she finally managed it, she sat back and groaned. "That was worse than I thought it would be."

He nodded. "We will have to do this for several days until your feet scab over."

She opened her eyes and stared at him. "I don't think I want to ask."

"Don't then," he said reasonably. "When you're better, we'll discuss some of these injuries. Right now I need you to go the bathroom and then call me, so I can pick you up and carry you back to bed." He stared down at her. "Got that?"

She nodded. She really wanted to protest that she could get there on her own, but she wasn't so sure she could.

As if reading her mind, he said, "Do not do anything on your own right now. Your feet are in bad shape, and so is the rest of your body."

The corner of her mouth turned down. "Got it."

He walked out of the bathroom but didn't shut the door. He was out of sight, but she had no idea where he was. And it didn't matter.

Her bladder released as if it finally knew it was safe to do so. When she was done, she managed to pull up her pants without standing. He walked back in, scooped her up, and softly sat her on the vanity. "Can you reach the water?"

He turned on the faucets, and she washed her hands. It was the first time she'd really seen her hands. Lots of scratches were over her fingers; her nails were bloody and filled with dirt. She shook her head. "You saved my life. Thank you."

"You're welcome. Now let's make sure we get you back to health again."

She lifted her gaze to him, seeing a hard-chiseled chin and a slight dimple in his cheek when his mouth twitched. "I didn't mean to be such trouble," she said in a voice barely above a whisper.

He shook his head. "None of that. You're in trouble. I can help."

She gave him a ghost of a smile. "I don't think anybody can help. And the longer you keep me here, the greater the chances are my kidnappers will come after me and kill both of us."

He studied her face, his gaze intense as he searched deep into hers. She wasn't lying. She was at the end of her rope. If she couldn't even walk to the bathroom, no way could she run.

Finally he gave her a clipped nod. "Let them. I don't die easy. And I'd be sure to take as many with me as I could."

"There could be one less," she whispered. "I think I killed one with a bat. But I don't know for sure. The memories are all mixed up."

His arms came around her. He picked her up and walked into the bedroom. As he sat her on the bed, he said, "Good. That's one less for me."

She lay back down, her face pale from the pain … everywhere.

He pulled the covers over her. "Now sleep. Your body needs to rest." He turned out the light she hadn't realized was on, and the room was instantly showered in darkness.

Then he turned and strode out, leaving her once again alone.

BACK IN THE kitchen, Eagle set out fixing a simple chicken soup. His grandmother had been a diehard believer that chicken soup would fix anything broken in the body. He figured it couldn't hurt. He didn't consider his chicken soup to be on par with his grandma's, but, over the years, he'd gotten darn good at it. He also figured he deserved a hell of a reward for not plying the injured woman with questions. A dozen or more were ready to spill out. At the very least he should've asked her name. She hadn't been terribly forthcoming. Stoic—that was a good word to describe her. Fearful, she had been ready to run. Although he wasn't sure she could. He figured the damage to her feet had been early, to stop her from that very thing.

When he'd cleaned them, Gray had said someone had taken a knife and sliced the bottom of her pads, not very deep, but just enough that, with every step, they would split and cause her excruciating pain. The torture had been extensive and continuous, so that she was either held for someone's sadistic pleasure or somebody wanted something from her very badly. That she'd been tortured for as long as she had been, he figured she hadn't given it to them. Now the real question was, did she have what they wanted, or had she been tortured for nothing because she didn't know anything? He'd seen that happen too. He'd also seen an insurgent leader who liked to torture for fun. For him it was stress relief. The screams of others made him feel better.

Darkness settled outside. With the soup simmering to his satisfaction, he turned his attention back to the weaponry he had laid out on the kitchen table. He took very good care of his arsenal. Right now each was getting a special bit of attention. As he cleaned and oiled them, he lined up the ammunition he might need. No way in hell would somebody get into this house and get at her without him being ready. There was still no guarantee he would fight off an attack, as that would depend on what they had for weapons and the sheer numbers of those coming. If it was one or two, no problem. But, if fifteen to twenty, his body was still organic, and it took bullets like anything else.

He'd heard what she'd said, that maybe she'd killed one man. There hadn't been any emotion in her tone when she'd said it. He hadn't known if that was deliberate or pure detachment so as not to feel the pain of having taken another's life—and possibly the loss of clear memory over the event. He'd done enough missions and seen enough action that the pain of killing someone in self-defense was something he could deal with.

In her case, he suspected trauma was responsible for her lack of emotion.

He glanced through the open doorway where she slept once again. He'd tucked her back into bed, and she hadn't moved. He didn't even think she had rolled over. He worried about her ribs though. Remembering what he'd planned to do earlier when he heard her getting up, he reached for his phone and called Annie. When the gruff old veterinarian and ex-military nurse answered, he asked, "Do you have a portable X-ray machine?"

"Yes," she answered testily. "But it's still not *that* portable."

"Portable enough to put into the back of the vehicle and come to my house to take an X-ray of something extremely damaged?"

"Maybe."

"I got an unopened bottle of Jack Daniel's sitting here for you."

"As much as I like my liquor," she said with a snap, "I still have bills to pay."

"The price?"

"What's the broken item?"

"A secret."

"Goddammit, what kind of trouble are you in now?" she asked in a huff.

"Maybe killing trouble."

He heard her suck in her breath. "You could call for help."

"I am," he said quietly and hung up the phone.

CHAPTER 6

W HEN ISSA OPENED her eyes again, the sharp agonizing pain was back. She moaned as she was gently straightened out, her shirt raised up to her neck, then cold hands poked and prodded her chilled skin. She cried out in pain.

"It's all right. Take it easy. We're checking your ribs. We need to make sure you haven't broken anything."

Issa gave a garbled laugh. If they only knew. Breaks upon breaks. Small ones, nasty ones, meant to extract information. Information she didn't have. When she was twisted ever-so-slightly the wrong way, she cried out again, a scream of pain echoing around the room. She shuddered.

"Damn. Wished that had made her black out," a gruff voice muttered.

Issa whimpered, wishing for the same. She opened her eyes to see a bright light overhead. Some weird machine was beside her. "What are you doing?" she asked fearfully.

"Taking X-rays," the gruff woman said, but compassion was in her voice at odds with the harshness of her raspy tone. "Stay still. We need to see the extent of the damage."

"It's bad."

"We'll see. Just let me get all the pictures I need."

In pain and too exhausted to do anything other than lie here, she let them do what they would. As soon as they were done with her shoulders, arms, hands and chest, her pants were removed, and her lower body was X-rayed. Finally she was redressed and tucked back under the blankets. She curled eagerly into the heat. She could feel the shakes starting all over again. "Roash?" she whispered, calling to him in her mind.

"I don't know what that is. Eagle, do you know what she's asking for?"

She made a tiny calling sound. She could hear Roash. There in the far reaches of her mind she could hear his response.

"Jesus Christ, those damn birds. Why did you let them in the house?" the woman asked.

"This one came with her," the man said.

Roash landed on the bed, his beak gently stroking Issa's cheek, an odd rumble once again coming up his throat. She rumbled back at him. Content, knowing at least he was safe with her, she let herself fall back asleep.

But her dreams weren't pleasant, and her sleep wasn't restful. She surfaced again and again, each time to see the room in shadows with nothing but the moonlight shining through the windows. It was the same room. She didn't know if that was a good thing or a bad thing. She didn't dare try to run. The memory of the last time was enough to make her stomach start heaving. But she could still hear the raspy voice, only farther away now.

"I have to get my laptop out of the truck," she said. "I should be able to transfer them to that. It's a new system. I'm still learning how to use it."

"And this is a good test subject."

"Hell, no, it's not."

Isolated in her room, Issa heard the front door close; then, in the distance, a vehicle door opening and closing.

Her mind catalogued the sounds. Footsteps as the woman returned.

"Give me a cup of coffee. This could take a bit."

"Will do."

"What the hell's that I'm smelling?"

"Chicken soup."

The woman snorted. "What? Your grandmother's recipe?"

His tone neutral, he said, "Absolutely."

"Well, she was a hell of a cook. So are you sharing?"

Even Issa had to smile at that—her movements difficult, awkward, as if rusty from lack of use. Maybe it was the mention of a grandmother that brought her own mother to mind. Whatever had happened to her apartment? She'd left it for Goodwill to come pick up the boxes. The manager knew what was happening. Had they shown up? How long ago had that been? And the ashes? She'd put them in her root cellar with the boxes. How pathetic was that. Her mother reduced to a spot in a root cellar, of all places.

A strong aroma wafted toward her. She lifted her head and sniffed. How long since she'd eaten? She had no answers. So much was a black hole. Yet so much else she couldn't forget. The beatings. The systematic torture. The questions. *Where is it? Tell us where you hid it all.* Repeatedly. It hadn't taken them long to expand their vocabulary to *What did you do with it? We want what is owed us.*

She frowned as that came into her mind. She lay here, wishing for a little bit of the warm broth. Roash flew off from her bed and headed to the kitchen.

"Goddamn that thing …" Eagle said. "Yet it never really leaves her side. He must have had a reason."

Roash cried out suddenly, his wild call filling the room.

"Maybe the bird's hungry," the woman said.

There was an odd silence. Issa smiled, only to gasp in silent wonder as her rescuer made the connection. And said, "Maybe he's telling us she's hungry."

The gruff voice snapped, "This is already past spooky. Let's not go straight into the bizarre."

The man laughed. "You have no idea how spooky and bizarre this is. Eerie even."

"Eagle, you call me out of the blue to bring my brand-new machine over to check out the woman's condition. A woman who's already so badly broken she should be in the hospital, and yet you refuse to take her there. You are taking in broken animals, but even you know when to call a vet. Yet, when this woman needs so much more, you don't give it to her."

"That's not true," he protested. "I help every animal that comes across my path. She's just another one."

"Then why shouldn't I call the sheriff?"

Issa strained to hear his answer. She didn't want the authorities involved, yet couldn't explain that instinctive response either. The men who kidnapped and tortured her should be stopped. They shouldn't be allowed to get away with what they'd done to her. Yet she didn't think they'd do this to another woman. She'd been their target for a long time. She just didn't understand why.

His voice was hard when he finally answered the gruff woman. "Will you?"

After a heavy sigh, the harsh voice said, "Hell no. Where's that damn soup?"

There was clang of dishes, and Issa could follow the sounds as the man served up a bowl followed by the *clunk* as he placed it on the table. Then she heard Roash's cry in the dark.

The woman gave a cackle. "I can't believe you have those two here. You should feed them. After all, you're feeding me."

"I planned on it."

Moments later she heard footsteps approach. She didn't know if she should pretend to be asleep or not. But, as the aroma drifted closer, she realized she was desperate to put something in her stomach other than acid and whatever blood might still be there.

A soft light was turned on at her side, and a bowl placed on the night table.

"I know you're awake. You don't need to be afraid."

"Thank you for treating my wounds." She shifted in the bed and turned to look up at him. "You've been very kind to me."

He shook his head. "I might've killed you, not knowing how bad your injuries are."

She glanced at the bowl. "I was hoping you would share."

"It's not in my nature to *not* share. Particularly with someone who's hurting."

She studied him and then her position. "I don't know if I can sit up," she confessed softly.

"I doubt you can, at least not easily," said the gruff woman from behind him. "Let Eagle help you."

Issa glanced out the doorway to see a large burly woman in a plaid overshirt, her grizzled hair gray and her face lined with wrinkles.

"I have some of the X-rays processing on my laptop now. What the hell happened to you?"

Issa let her gaze drift toward the gruff woman and saw

such a sense of wholeness about her. Issa was determined to do the right thing but by her own honor code, not necessarily by the one others followed.

"I was held captive, but I don't know for how long," she tried to explain to the two tall silent people staring at her. "I don't know by whom, and honestly I couldn't even tell you where."

The woman walked farther into the room. Issa could feel the compassion in her worldly eyes. She stopped beside the bed. "Well, lucky for you, you are here now." She motioned to the man at her side. "This is Eagle, and I'm Annie."

"My name is Issa." She frowned as she searched for her last name. Then shook her head only to stop as pain slammed into her. She winced, half closing her eyes in response. When she could speak again, she whispered, "I'm not sure what my last name is though."

"That's the head injury," Eagle said. "The memories will come back soon."

"Maybe I don't want them to," she said, careful to not move her head.

"What can you tell us about yourself?"

"I have a PhD in biology, a masters in environmental science. Falconry is a hobby. Roash and Humbug and a few others are my passion."

"Humbug?"

Talking was taking too much out of her, and Issa found it hard to keep her eyes open. "Humbug is my snowy owl. He lives with me at my cabin."

"And where is your cabin?"

Her gaze flew open as she studied him, her mouth trying to form the words. She frowned and looked at him. "I'm not sure. I can see the driveway in my mind ... and the road ...

and the cabin itself. But I ..." She fell silent.

He shook his head. "Not to worry. It'll come back."

Annie walked out of the room.

"Humbug needs help," Issa said quietly. "He can't feed himself well. How did you find my falcon?"

"He showed up one day. I run a raptor center for birds. His wing was broken, and I tried to help him. But he stopped eating and ripped off the splint. He would cry, and then he would go silent."

She nodded. "His crying was to find me. If he fell into a despondent state, it was the lack of communication with me."

Eagle nodded, slowly walking closer. "I had him in my arms. He just lay like he was ready to die. And I thought maybe it would be a kindness to put him down." He shook his head in wonder. "But he bolted from my arms as if he was just playing dead, and he flew into the sky. He shouldn't have been able to fly with that wing. He shouldn't have been able to do anything he did that day. He disappeared like an arrow in one direction. I looked for the rest the day. I came out several times later at night and in the morning calling for him. Later that day, when I found you, he was sitting on your shoulder."

"How did you find me?" she asked curiously. She studied the man Roash trusted. "Did he call you?"

He frowned. "I don't know what you mean by that. The other animals alerted me something was very wrong. My dogs led me toward you. And when I climbed over the fence and found you in the hollow, Rikker was sitting there."

She smiled. "Thank you for bringing me home. His name is Roash, by the way."

Just then Annie returned.

"I could do nothing else." He glanced over at Annie. "Can we move her to sit up?"

Annie nodded. "I suggest you tape the ribs first. Just two fractures, one on both sides. The collarbone is cracked, right arm is cracked, several toes cracked."

"Is that all?" Issa said, her voice full of pain. "I was pretty damn sure the men had broken more than that."

"I'm still waiting for a couple more pictures to process," Annie said quietly.

Eagle said, "I have an idea. At least for this time. Then, after you've eaten, I'll find the tape and bind those ribs."

"I don't know that I can eat very much," she whispered, adding, "but I would love to try. It smells delicious."

Roash stepped forward as Eagle disappeared and then returned with a travel mug and a metal straw. He poured the broth from the soup into the cup, put the straw and the lid in place, and then gently lifted her head to take a few sips. The heat filled her stomach, sending waves of warmth through her.

When she drank what was in the cup, she lay her head back down again. "I presume all the injuries are small enough they don't need to be reset or casted."

"Yes, you're correct," he said quietly. "And you're right, they were directed, very controlled."

She gave a tiny nod. "That makes sense."

"How does any of this make sense?" Eagle asked. "That somebody would deliberately do that to you is not normal."

"No, but I think for those men it was very normal." She closed her eyes, and now, with a warm tummy, she let herself fall back into the healing state of sleep.

"WOW," ANNIE SAID. "When you pick a mystery, you really pick a doozy."

He shook his head. "This is bizarre." He lifted the bowl and cup, checked to make sure Issa was covered, and ushered Annie out. "But at least she's eaten. It's not much, but it's a start."

"Her stomach is not likely to handle much more than this."

He nodded. "Agreed."

"I'll see what these last two X-rays bring up. I have tape here. The ribs are hairline fractures from very focused blows."

"And that green spot on her back to the right?"

"Her right kidney. I'm not a medical doctor, but I've not seen anything in the X-rays that shows it's bone related."

"*Great.* I thought maybe her liver or spleen."

"That she's even alive is amazing."

Annie turned to look at Roash, who was busy drinking some of the chicken soup broth. "He must be starving if he's drinking soup?" she said, pointing to the bird.

"I think its survival. For him and for her."

Eagle got up and grabbed a loaf of bread from the side and plucked a bunch of the seeds off the top. He put them down beside the bird and watched as he ate them. "He's a raptor. I need to get him something from the pens. The next batch of eggs don't come out of the incubator for two days."

"I never did understand how you could do that. You raise a couple hundred chicks from the eggs so the birds can eat them."

"Chicks are a natural food for raptors," he said absent-mindedly. "And I know the world would look at me in horror because I let one hundred chicks die every day, but they are much easier to look after than mice."

"Now don't get me wrong. I'm not against it. It's survival of the fittest. Mother Nature's food chain. In your case, those birds need sustenance as well as anybody."

"Besides I have to supplement it with roadkill I get from neighbors. And from the town. That deer I was given last week helped."

"You're lucky you could get the birds to eat that. Most need to catch their prey live. Too bad they won't work on the bones."

He shot her a look. "No, but the dogs will."

She laughed and nodded. "Isn't that the truth?" She pushed her bowl off to the side. "I could use a second bowl."

He got up and filled the bowl again for Annie, then got himself a bowlful. The entire time Roash continued to drink chicken broth and peck away at seeds. He needed food as much as Issa. Unfortunately Eagle didn't have much for him here. He'd have to go out and do the chores soon and check on the security system for the night. Especially tonight. He had an electric fence on part of the cages. He wanted to make sure they were all charged. He didn't have a clue what the night would bring, but he'd be ready no matter what.

"I checked the other X-rays. But I can't see anything else. There could be some stuff I don't know how to read as I deal in four-legged critters, but you got the gist of it."

"I really appreciate this."

"I'm sure you do. As far as breaking in the machine, you were right. This was a good one." With the second bowl of soup in front of her, she set about eating, dipping her bread into the broth. When she was done, she said, "Now that was good."

She picked up the bowl, walked over to the sink. She

turned and stared at Roash. "I'm a vet and spend my life helping animals, but I've never seen anything like this."

"I wish I knew more about the bond these two have," he admitted. "I've never seen anything like it either."

"Find out who she is, and then you'll find where she was, where her cabin is."

"I'll do that." He glanced out at the night. "I need to set up security and electrify the fence around all the raptors."

"Forget about around the raptors. You need to make sure you got something set up around her." And she nodded at the bedroom. "Call me in the night if you need to."

Eagle smiled gratefully at the woman with a heart of gold. "Thanks."

When she walked out, he stood at the front door and waited until she turned on her truck and took the battle-beaten old brown Ford out of his drive. She and Gray should get together. They had at one point, but they were both too damn stubborn to make it work. And yet they were two of a kind. And both damn good people.

As soon as he saw the headlights heading down the road, he turned around and walked to the gate and locked it. With the dogs at his heels, he did a quick walk around the property checking on the inner security system. He turned on the electric fence near the raptors. Annie was right. He should have something around the house. It never occurred to him that he'd be in a situation where that would be necessary in his own home. He thought he'd left all that behind when he was honorably discharged from the military. He'd hated having to watch his back day and night in the navy, but that's where he was all over again.

He returned to the kitchen, turned on the lights to finish cleaning the guns, laid one by every window on the main floor, took three more upstairs where his bedroom was, and stepped into his big room.

He didn't feel comfortable being a floor away from her. He grabbed his bedding and went down to the living room couch to make himself comfortable. No way to know what the night would bring. He just wanted to make sure he was ready.

STEFAN WALKED INTO his studio. He hadn't had the urge to paint in several days. The break had actually been kind of nice. He'd come off a difficult case—a serial killer in Maine, of all places. Stefan had connected with the killer through his painting. Stefan had shut down his art for a few days afterward, needing the break to heal.

The case had ended successfully, but it had left Stefan feeling worn and weary. As he walked through his studio, he opened up windows, pulling back the blinds to let in the sunshine. Something knocked at the back of his head, telling him to pick up a pen. He could ignore that a lot of times.

But sometimes there was no help for it. He was forced to comply. He picked up his sketchbook and then dropped it immediately.

No, apparently he wasn't supposed to sketch. He shrugged and walked to an easel, randomly chose a canvas, and put it up. One of the most difficult processes in his life had been to learn to trust his psychic process. To trust that what was coming through needed to come through.

If it meant destroying the canvas or making something completely not saleable, then that was okay too. As he reached for his paints, his hands stayed in the air, and he realized, no, this image had to be charcoal. Something he hadn't worked with in months.

At the sideboard he found a long piece of charcoal with a sharpened end and came back to the white canvas. He stood in front of it.

"Who are you, and what can I do to help?"

And then, in the process that had taken him years to perfect, he surrendered. Seconds later he watched as his hand lifted—his hand still attached to his arm, attached to his shoulder, and then to his body—but a hand following directions from some other soul.

He watched the black lines show up. And they made no sense, and he realized this was one of those times where either he wasn't meant to see what was coming or a message wasn't coming through clearly. He closed his eyes and sent out a message of hope and love to whatever desperate soul was screaming at him.

Mentally he kept getting a garbled sound of screeches and cries. Not the same as the woman he had contacted several days ago. But similar in an odd way. With his head bowed, he let his hand do what it needed to do.

When he finally stepped back, his arm dropping to his side, he took a deep breath and opened his eyes. And stared. He'd done this many times, and often the results were shocking. Sometimes they were brilliant. Sometimes they were horrifying. And sometimes they were just childish blotches that meant nothing.

But this, ... this was exquisite.

The door opened behind him, and Celina walked in. She stopped and gasped. "My goodness, that's beautiful." She raced to his side. She slipped her fingers into his hand, and the two stared at the beautiful snowy owl on the canvas. "Who is it?"

The name when it came out made no sense. But even as he tried to make it into another name it refused to comply.

"Humbug," Stefan said. "That's the only name I get. *Humbug.*"

"That's not a name," Celina argued. "That's more like an expression of disgust, like Scrooge saying, 'Bah humbug.'"

Stefan gave her a crooked grin and said, "This isn't about Scrooge. But what I can tell you is, this owl is called Humbug. And he belongs to somebody, and somebody belongs to *him.* And he's missing that person."

"They've been separated?" Celina whispered, her fingers stretching out as if to stroke the downy feathers on the canvas. "Wow, poor thing."

He wondered if the charcoal would smear, but he didn't need to worry. Her fingers actually never touched, just wafted across the air above the canvas. "Yes, they've been separated."

She turned to him with a smile and said, "I think I like this new direction of your talents."

He shook his head. "I don't know that there is anything new about it."

"You're connecting with animals. Animals in need. That will never be a wrong thing." She turned back to the painting. "How can we help Humbug?"

Stefan put down the charcoal, picked up a rag, and wiped his hand. "I have no idea."

CHAPTER 7

ISSA AWOKE WITH a start. Her heart slammed against her chest, and images flashed through her mind. Humbug on the roof of her cabin. Roash on the fence post. The sound of the men sneaking around the cabin. The panic, the fear. She lay frozen, her body trembling as she relived the moment she'd realized she was in danger. Staring straight ahead at the ceiling above her, she worried and wondered. What was going on? Were the men coming yet again? Was that why she woke from a nightmare?

In the back of her mind she heard a faint screech.

It was Humbug. Did Humbug have the same abilities to communicate as Roash? The trouble was, she hadn't known Roash could do that until this started. And even now she wasn't exactly sure just what was going on with him. But he understood her pain. That he brought somebody to her aid was amazing but fell short of the connection she'd had with the falcon soul buddy of her childhood.

Her mother had always mocked her, telling her that she was imagining things. That the falcon was just a well-trained bird, and the bond between them wasn't extraordinary. Issa knew her mother was wrong. But there'd been no point in arguing with her then.

The minute she brought up her falcon's name or the old country or the life they'd led, her mother would shut her down with a sharp voice, telling her that life was gone. They were all gone, and Issa was never to speak of it again. And, if she persisted, her mother would get up and walk out.

And Issa got the cold silent treatment. She remembered the pain and loneliness when her mother went silent, letting Issa know so clearly that her mother wanted no part of her. Growing up, that had been as hard as anything. So she went out of her way to avoid upsetting her mother. As an adult, she recognized the controlling tactic. One she hated. No one should ever withhold love and affection from a child. She didn't give a damn what the reason, it certainly should not be simply for asking questions about your history.

She wondered at the images and the memories that flowed through her mind. As much as she loved her mother, certain things her mother had done Issa hated. Once again her mind went to the box she never had a chance to go through. Both boxes.

She needed to know what was behind all this. She could only hope her captors hadn't found the boxes. She was sure they'd searched the cabin many times over. She'd only discovered the root cellar accidentally after she bought the property. It made sense as it was an old homestead originally. With the cabin modernized and upgraded for electricity and running water, the cellar might have been forgotten over the years.

The trapdoor blended into the rest of the woodwork. Even the latch itself was wood and lay flat, matching the grain. When she had moved in, she'd made one pass on the floor on her hands and knees with a scrub brush, clearing away the years of emptiness and disuse. When her brush had caught on the handle, she'd been delighted with her find.

Her eyes drifted closed again, only to be startled awake

as more memories slammed into her mind. Men in huge trucks. Her heart caught in her stomach. She didn't recognize the trucks, but they were driving in the city. She highly doubted they were anywhere close to here, as, from what she could see out the windows of Eagle's house, the countryside spread to all corners around her.

Tired and sore, she rolled over in bed, grimacing as her shoulder pulled. She tried to settle back into sleep. More images slammed into her mind. Disjointed, yet some completely in sequence, but in a different country. Sky scenes, urban scenes. As if the blow to the head had unlocked or shaken loose the filing system she had used to tuck everything away. Now it floated free through her mind, the chaos of mental folders tossed to the wind with bits and pieces going everywhere.

She tried to blank it out. Tried to go back to sleep. Just as her eyes closed, once again a beautiful white face popped into her mind. *Humbug.* Tears welled up. Her kidnappers had said they'd shot all the birds they could find on her property. She had no doubt they had. Those men were monsters, uncaring of life, big or small. They had a goal, a mentality that said they came first. And everybody else was roadkill, so get out of the way or join them.

According to them, she'd been in the way. And she still didn't understand how that worked. But if they'd hurt Humbug ... He was the gentlest big baby she'd ever met. But he needed care. He'd be lost without her. A bullet would've been the easiest death for him. Troubled, she fell into a deep sleep.

EAGLE SHIFTED ON the couch. He'd slept on it before but

not in a long time. It was hardly the top-of-the-line accommodations. His military days of sleeping on the hard ground were over. It certainly was not that he was old, but some injuries were just so much worse when springs pressed against them. He shifted again and then froze. What was that?

Eagle threw back the blankets silently, straightening up and padding across the floor. He checked out the windows first. There was nothing moving in the night. But something was wrong. He moved from window to window and slipped across to Issa's bed. There he froze. Her eyes were wide open; she stared straight ahead at the ceiling above her, unblinking ...

"Issa, are you okay?"

There was no response. Neither did she blink or shift at the sound of his voice. Unnerved, but knowing catatonic states could be caused by many issues, he approached quietly. Roash rose from the night table beside her.

He frowned. "What are you doing in here still?" He glanced at the window open barely enough for the falcon to squeeze through. That was reassuring. He didn't want to have to consider any more metaphysical events. Because he was just out of explanations for those. He was a straightforward man, believed what he could see, what he could touch. But he'd used his intuition enough times to save his life to know he couldn't discount that sixth sense either. *Proving* it was something completely different. And the weird events since finding Issa were something else again.

He studied her face and that huge gaze staring straight up. He swore he saw something move across her features. Not like a grimace of pain or wave of fear but a shadow, ... shaped like wings. He gave his head a shake. "Man, you need to get some rest."

But he couldn't tear his eyes away from what he was seeing. He leaned over her, feeling this buzzing sound in his ears. He stared down into her eyes. His head was slammed with images: blue sky, clouds, green forest below. He pulled back, his heart bouncing around in his chest. What the hell was going on? He walked around her bed to approach from the other side, and one of Roash's beautiful golden eyes glared up at him.

"I'm not trying to hurt her. I just need to know what the hell's going on."

That incredible gaze of Issa's turned slowly as if tracking his progress. But he didn't get a sense she knew he was here. No recognition shone in her eyes, no sense of awareness of her surroundings. Like a galaxy floated through the bright color of her irises. A blue that glowed with mystery—and shone with an odd sense of timelessness.

He leaned over her so he could stare straight down into her eyes, and immediately the tingling started. Wary, he forced himself to stay in place. And images caught and held him again. Blue sky, clouds, raindrops dripping off leaves. This time the view from inside the tree up against the trunk. Water droplets rolling down branches and twigs. And in the early morning, sun peeking through, differently this time and yet stunning.

The needles were sharp with clarity in the morning light. His jaw dropped, and he was afraid to break free, to move in any way to stop this. Yet he was sure he could reach out and touch them. His hand was already in the air ...

And just like that, it shut off. The images were gone. Issa lay as still as before, but now her eyes were closed. He let out his breath gently, trying not to wake her. Yet how could he not? He was desperate to know what had just happened.

What she had done?

He sank to the edge of the bed and stared. Who was this woman? This woman who could be anywhere from twenty to forty, who lay on his bed, her body so badly damaged, and yet her mind, her energy, so alive. So unique. And, yes, so special.

And maybe that was the part that bothered him the most. It wasn't like those images were on the movie screen or were still photos on the monitor. They'd been in front of him. Fully 3-D. As if coming from his own eyes. Shaken, he got up and slowly walked to the doorway. He kept his gaze on the woman who now appeared to be resting as easily as a child. Whatever had affected her earlier was seemingly gone.

Just as he was about to exit through the door and put on coffee, knowing sleep was long gone for him, she sat up, completely unaware of her injuries. Her head turned almost like a robot, and she stared at him. "I have to get Humbug."

His mind struggled. Humbug? Humbug? Then he remembered. An owl in her care named Humbug. He took several steps toward her, hearing Roash lift his broken wings protectively … over her. She held out her arm, her gaze locked on his. Roash shifted position to settle on her forearm. Eagle couldn't tear his gaze away. The bird settled right between her bruises. He would've said the bird's claws caused the bruising if he had not seen for himself how very carefully and gently the bird placed his feet to minimize her pain.

"Why do you need to get Humbug?" His voice was harsh, cold, and he admitted, but only to himself, maybe a little terrified.

"He's in trouble. They want to kill him to get back at

me for escaping."

He could see that. His heart went out to the owl. Because the men who would do something like they'd done to her would do so much worse to Humbug. And, if they thought they could use it to hurt her more, they would. They'd shown no conscience yet. This would only get worse.

"Do you know where he is?"

She blinked and stared at him with a frown. It was like she just came back to awareness. "What did I say?"

"You said we need to get Humbug. That they want to kill him."

Her gaze widened in shock. "I did?"

Slowly he nodded, but he only saw confusion on her face. "Do you know where Humbug is?"

She turned to him and shook her head. "No, but I wish I did." Tears came to her eyes. She collapsed back onto the bed, pulling the covers up. Roash walked up to her shoulder, crooning, and she started to cry.

DYLAN STARED AT the property. He couldn't believe it was possible for her to have made it this far. He liked the fighting spirit of the woman. Of all the things he'd done over the last fifty years of his adult life, this was the worst. They not only had kidnapped a woman and beat her, but she was family. What they'd done to her ... He shook his head. His mother would roll over in her grave, and his father would've given him a hiding, a good flogging. He didn't much like it himself.

But the boss had been adamant. Something about stressors. Something about her having knowledge. Something about her abilities. None of it made a whole lot of sense. But the one thing Dylan did understand after all these years was, he didn't argue with the boss. If Dylan didn't like what he had to do, he needed to keep his mouth shut and run as far and as fast as he could, in such a way that the boss could never track him.

So, when given a job, Dylan accepted it with a smile and nodded agreeably. Anything else, well, that wouldn't go over well. He wasn't much of a tracker, but nowhere did it say she had come this way. Except that little bit of blood he'd found on the fence post. And quite by accident.

He thought she'd be in a hospital by now. He'd called around, looking for her. He had checked with the clinics. But there was nothing, no sign of her. Then he'd called the morgue, but no females matched her description. He winced and stared down at his hands. He was sixty-five years old. He could hold his head up with pride until a few weeks ago. Now what was he was supposed to do? He had a high standard, his morals strict. He didn't have the same belief in law enforcement others did, and he didn't care if he broke the law, but he had his own moral code.

For the first time in his life, he'd broken his own code. And he struggled with that. He also knew he'd had little choice. It was either do this or take a bullet. The rules with the boss had always been the same. Easy to follow, clear to understand. Never any misunderstandings. Do as you were told or take the consequences.

Dylan hadn't had a problem taking the consequences for doing as he was told. But, as the body count mounted up over the last twenty-odd years, he often wondered if he'd done the right thing. Life had been easier in the old country. He understood that way of living. He loved the country and the people, even the lifestyle. America was faster, harder, …

crueler.

Dylan couldn't trust anyone, not the men beside him whom he'd been friends with, nor a stranger across the street. The friend beside you was just as likely to stab you in the back, and the stranger to give you a helping hand. It was bizarre and made for extremely uncomfortable day-to-day living. Back in the old country he'd known exactly who his friends were every moment of the day. And, if any one of them went rogue, the punishment was instant.

CHAPTER 8

WHEN ISSA WOKE the next time, her heart was heavy; her eyes burned from the acid of her tears, and the pain went so much deeper than muscle and bone. Humbug, who she had thought was dead, wasn't. Overjoyed to know her feathered friend had survived, it was horrible to now know Humbug was in mortal danger.

She closed her eyes and whispered, *"Humbug, please stay safe. Please, if anybody is out there who can help him, please do so. Humbug's an innocent victim. ... And he's very special. He needs me."*

"Who are you talking to?"

Her eyes flew open to find Eagle standing at her door. Something about his stance, his arms, his body language, was not quite stiff but a little more unyielding than she'd seen before. She understood. It wasn't that he was afraid; he was wary. Everything so far was a test of his beliefs.

And maybe he was right to do so. Maybe the rest of the world should keep their distance because she knew she'd go after these men if they went after Humbug.

She now knew beyond a doubt those men were evil. The world would be so much better off without them.

"I was praying, hoping somebody would find Humbug." She studied Eagle for a long moment. "You don't trust me."

He raised an eyebrow. "You don't trust me."

Her gaze widened. "I trust you more than I have ever trusted anyone."

At that, a surprised look came across his face, and he took a step inside, his arms still across his chest. "Why is that?"

She tilted her head toward the falcon. "Because Roash trusts you." And for the first time she saw a crooked smile cross Eagle's face. "You love birds," she said in a low voice as she studied him for any sign of the evil that had already touched her life. She knew that, even though he'd been good to her, evil sometimes took its time to show. "So you can't be that bad."

He nodded. "Not only do I love them but I save them. When you are healthy enough, I can take you out to meet the more than two hundred birds I keep here."

Her breath caught in her throat. Her gaze widened in shock. "Seriously?"

If there was ever a dream job for her, this would be it. To help more than just a couple would be beyond amazing. And then she remembered that evil came in many forms—especially walking on two legs. She shuddered. "How far away from the house are they?"

"Not very far at all. I have pens that go for several hundred feet."

"Pens?" Her heart sank. To be caged was not the ideal life for a bird.

He nodded. As if reading the look on her face, he said, "Most are injured. Most will never fly again. And, if they do, they can only lurch from side to side. They just become easy food for other predators."

She nodded. She understood Mother Nature was a hard taskmaster. Life was for the fittest. She wanted to reach out

checked his watch and realized it was too early to make a phone call. On a notepad, he wrote down the names and phone numbers. He still hadn't had any luck searching for the name she'd given him.

But there could be many ways to spell her name. Without a last name, it was damn near impossible to narrow down the search. He continued to delve into the mythological world until the sun rose. Then he got up and set the pot of soup to reheat for her and put on a pot of coffee for him.

As soon as both were ready, he went to the bedroom to see her lying there, staring at him. He let out his breath gently. "Well, you scared me once again last night."

She narrowed her gaze at him. "Why?"

"You screamed out of the blue. We'd just been talking. I turned to get some soup started, and you cried out in terror and passed out." He shook his head. "Are you sure there is nothing more you can tell me about who you are, where you're from, about your family?"

Her gaze widened. "My name is Issa."

He nodded. "You said that before. How do you spell that?"

"*I-S-S-A*," she whispered.

"I tried that version of the spelling but couldn't find anyone with that name."

"Why did you look?"

"To see if there were any missing person bulletins. Are you in a falcon club?"

She blinked and then smiled. "I belong to one, I believe." She turned her head slightly, her gaze staring off into the distance. "I have friends there."

"And you have a last name?"

"I must have, but I can't remember it."

He nodded agreeably. "You ready for a cup of coffee?"

Her gaze widened in delight. "Absolutely. Is there any chance of that soup?"

"I'm heating it up again." He turned and walked back into the kitchen. "I'll be back in a few minutes with both."

STEFAN PICKED UP the phone. "Tabitha, have you ever connected with an owl?"

"I've never tried to, and I don't recall any ever connecting with me," she said slowly. "Why?"

"I drew a picture of a bird, a big snowy owl called Humbug."

She gave a startled laugh. "I love the name."

"Humbug has been separated from someone he cares about."

"What? Oh, poor guy," she said. "Are you thinking a human partner?"

"I can't see any other reason for me to have picked up on Humbug's distress. Because, if I start connecting with every distressed animal, you know I'll never get any rest," he said with a note of humor in his voice. "Animals are injured and separated from family all over the world all the time. Almost as often as humans."

"So we have to assume he's important to somebody and that somebody is either important to you or you're important to them." Then she added with spirit, "Any idea who the owl is connected with?"

"No, I don't know. But, for several weeks now, I've had some very strange visions connected with Humbug, and I've heard a woman's cries of distress, but I haven't been able to find her." His voice was filled with great regret as he added,

"And I don't know why."

"Meaning you can hear her cry out, but you can't speak to her?"

"Yes. It seems to be that way. But often I can track someone's energy regardless. I'm not even seeing her energy. It's like I'm up in the sky floating, and I can hear her cries, but I can't find her."

"A disconnection?"

"Possibly. I don't really know what it is or how to explain it. Then the visions stopped, and I was afraid she'd died."

Tabitha gasped. "That would make sense, sadly enough, and it could also be why Humbug is distressed." Tabitha paused.

Stefan could see her smiling when she said the bird's name.

"He's looking but can't find her," Tabitha said.

"That's a lot of assumptions. I'm not even sure about my visions because they weren't normal. In the past I've always been able to track something down somewhere in one way or another."

"Sure, we're making assumptions. But we make those every day in this type of work." Her tone turned brisk as she asked, "Maybe I can track him down myself?"

He told her the little bit he knew. "Now almost nightly I wake up, and I'm floating on a bed of clouds. It's full of sunshine and blue sky. Within seconds it turns to a midnight sky."

"That certainly fits with an owl because they're night hunters. So are many other animals and birds. Let's hope we're sticking to birds," she said. "If we start into the whole animal kingdom, it'll get even more complicated."

Stefan glanced down at the feather in his hand. "I found a falcon feather a few days ago on my deck. I didn't understand what it meant." He corrected himself. "I still don't understand what it means. But, when I put it down, I feel compelled to pick it back up again."

"Interesting," she murmured, her voice low and deep. "Were you able to get any energy off the feather?"

"No, not much. But I can't seem to stop touching it."

"You sure it's not Humbug's feather?"

"If I'm assuming Humbug is an owl, then this is not Humbug's feather."

She chuckled. "You know? In Mother Nature we have attractions that don't always make sense. It's quite possible other birds are willing you to help Humbug."

Stefan rolled his eyes and walked over to the windows. "I'm looking at my railing and my deck, and there is no other sign of any other bird, so I doubt it." But the words were no sooner out of his mouth than a huge crow came and landed at the railing, right in front of him. Stefan let out a broken laugh. "Okay, I stand corrected. A crow just landed on my railing. But then they're always around."

"Keep watching," she said quietly. "You've put out the word, and now they're responding. See how quickly it happens. Does that tell you that you're on track?"

The sky turned dark as birds flocked toward his house. Celina walked to his side. She took her cell phone and started taking pictures, then said, "Tell Tabitha what we're seeing."

"Tabitha, you won't believe this, but there could be hundreds of birds outside my place now, some flying around in circles, and it's like the sky has gone dark. They're landing on the railing, on the patio, and on the rooftop. Several birds hit the window just now as if trying to get inside. It's like they've gone mad." He'd never seen anything like it.

"Not *mad*," Tabitha said quietly. "They're desperate. They need help, or somebody they know needs help. Somehow they've learned you can connect to them. And they won't leave you alone until they can save the person or animal they're trying to save."

"But I don't know anything about Humbug," he said in astonishment. "And certainly not about whoever it is he's missing."

"Guess what, Stefan?" Tabitha said, her voice gentle but firm. "You'll have to find out what's going on, who's in need, and how you can help."

CHAPTER 9

THE SOUP WAS just as delicious the second time as it was the first. "Thank you," Issa murmured as she handed the empty bowl back to him. "You're a very good cook."

"No, I'm not," he said cheerfully. "It's my grandmother's recipe."

She gave him a ghost of a smile, hating that just the act of eating a bowl of soup could exhaust her to the point she wanted to rest.

And she knew those sharp eyes of his missed nothing. He'd seen the weakness on her face yet again. But there was one thing she really hoped she could do, and that was wash up. "I don't suppose there is any chance of a bath?"

He stopped, frowned, glanced at her, toward the bathroom, and back again.

She shrugged. "I'm not exactly sure how extensive my injuries are, but it seems like a warm bath couldn't hurt," she said hopefully.

"I'd love to see you actually get to the bathtub on your own first," he said as he stood, tapping his foot on the floor, his hands on his hips as he contemplated it.

She winced at the reminder of how much she still depended on him to get to the bathroom. The bathtub was just another trip. And she'd need help to get in and out. "Never mind," she said hurriedly. "I don't want to cause any more extra work."

He snorted. "Running a bath is hardly extra work." He walked into the bathroom. "The only way to get in is if I carry you, lower you into the water and then scoop you back up again."

The last thing she wanted was to have this man carry her and treat her like a two-year-old, but her hair was dirty. And even worse, she knew her feet would be also, for, although they had been soaked with antiseptic, the bottoms, the tops, and her toes were grimy. He'd given her a sponge bath, so she certainly shouldn't be worried about her modesty at this point. But being unconscious and bathed by a stranger was a whole different story than being carried nude into a bathtub and tucked into bed afterward.

"If you're willing to give me a hand, I should be able to get into the bathtub on my own," she suggested.

He shook his head. "No, I can carry you to the toilet, but you're still not able to walk to the bathtub."

She nodded, resigned. "Maybe in a few days then."

He gave a muffled exclamation. "If it'll make you feel better, why the hell not?"

He walked into the bathroom, and she could hear the water starting. And she smiled. She'd do a lot to just get into that tub and soak. Whenever her troubles overcame her, she used to crawl into the hot water and soak. If she could have a natural hot spring on her land, she'd be in heaven. On the other hand, she'd probably stay there every waking moment.

She remembered reading about a certain species of baboon in China that lived at the hot springs. She thought that would be a great animal to reincarnate into.

"I'll get you another change of clothes. Be right back." He returned soon enough and left something for her to wear in the bathroom.

When her nose twitched, she realized he'd put something into the bathtub. She wasn't sure that was the best idea, given all her scratches, and she knew getting in would hurt like crap. Something she hadn't thought about when she'd asked. Not to mention the stitches on her head and shoulder.

He walked back toward her. "I put a bit of tea tree oil in the water. It's strong, not terribly nice smelling, but it has antiseptic properties, and all the scratches would benefit from a very good soak." He paused. "But I've got to warn you, it'll hurt like shit when you get in."

Her gaze went to the bathtub and back to him. "I was just thinking that."

He shrugged. "We can give you a bed bath?"

"No, that would hurt also. A real bath would be lovely. The stinging will go away soon enough." She pulled the blankets back and slowly sat up. She'd been making some headway with moving a little more each time. She rested her feet on the floor and studied them. "Do you think I can put weight on them?"

She was plucked off the bed, held in midair as Eagle said, "Drop your feet to the floor now."

She slowly stretched her legs out and realized he held her just above the floor. He lowered her until her feet touched the floor.

"Now, with just one foot, try to stand."

Her feet were swollen, puffy, and felt like there were great big cushions underneath, yet the minute she put her weight on one, she cried out.

"That answers that," he said, lifting her back up again.

"No wait." She closed her eyes. "I have to get used to it

at some point."

"Hell no, you don't. Another few days and we'll try again. A week, ten days at the most. You don't have to walk on them when they're bad." He walked over to the bathtub, sat her down on the edge, and said, "You might be able to manage this from here."

Sitting on the edge of the tub, she realized there was a bar on the far side. She glanced at him. "Actually I think I can."

He frowned, hesitating.

She waved him away with her hands. "Let me try. I promise I'll call if I get stuck."

"You have to call anyway when you want out," he warned. "We can't risk you falling."

She nodded. "Let me try first, please."

As if hearing the sincerity and the need for privacy in her voice, he nodded and walked away.

She slipped the big heavy socks off, hating to leave the warm cocoon. She didn't realize just how cold she was until she stripped off her clothes. Clothing which was obviously his because the shirt went down to her knees and the pants went up to her armpits.

When her bare bottom touched the edge of bathtub, she gasped. She kept her voice low, but, Lord, it was cold. She pulled her arms inside the T-shirt and carefully pulled it over her head. With all the clothing on the floor, she pivoted gently and slowly dipping her feet into the hot water. Tears filled her eyes. It felt wonderful and terrible at the same time. Every slice, every scratch, every bruise screamed as soon as it met the water. But a few moments later, after the initial pain, everything started to cry with relief.

"It's a start," she murmured.

It took another twenty minutes to fully seat herself in the hot water.

When she was stretched full out, she lowered her head to just below the stitches. She lay that way letting the heat soak into her bones. Even though she'd been warmly dressed and under covers, there was such a chill inside.

"Are you okay?" Eagle called out from the hallway.

"I'm better than okay," she answered. "I'm warm and feel great."

"Good, watch out for that head injury."

"It's the only part of me that's out of the water."

She heard him chuckle.

"The tea tree oil ... I don't know how good it is for my hair. It's probably not the best, but most of the scent is gone anyway. I don't know if you have any shampoo, but my hair is in rough shape."

"Soap and shampoo are on the side."

Twisting slightly she could see both. "Okay. I'm good. I don't plan on moving until the water turns cold."

"Good enough. I need to check on the raptors. If you think you'll be okay, I'll probably be outside for a good hour."

"Go," she called out. "Go look after those that need you more than I do."

"Will do."

She heard his boots walking across the floor. And then he was gone. She sank into the water and let her eyes drift closed.

Once again images of wastelands, clefts, oceans, and lakes flew across her mind. She could see the sides of the cliffs, snow dappling across the crags—akin to memories of a flight a long time ago. Yet the only flight she remembered taking that had gone over an ocean would've been when they had traveled to America from Ireland. She'd been so young that she didn't think she remembered anything of that trip.

The more she tried to remember, the more her head pounded. She didn't know if it was from her head injury or a mental block.

No doubt what she'd been through was horrific, and the details would hurt all that much more when she did recall them. For the moment, she was content to just lie here and rest.

Roash flew into the room and landed on the side of the bathtub. The ceramic was hard for him to grip, so he eventually flew up and landed on the back of the toilet and stared at her.

"It's okay, Roash. I'm fine."

Wanting to feel the warm water over her injury just for the peace it would bring her, she dropped her head ever-so-slightly lower, feeling the heat soak into the rough edges of the skin that had been torn. She didn't know if it was smart or not. It was stinging, but then any water would sting. Taking a chance, she pulled her head completely underwater, swallowing her cries.

After a moment, she came up for air, loving the feeling of her entire scalp soaking in the warm water. With low reserves and not wanting to ask Eagle if she didn't have to, she pulled herself into an upright position and started with the soap. It was only as she started to lather up and wash her body that she could see the tiny slices in her skin—the details of the damage to her body. With her face to toes scrubbed, she turned her attention to the shampoo.

That was a whole different process. She was forced to stretch out to rinse it, then back up for a second shampoo.

By rights her hair should be rinsed the second time under running water, but what she'd done was already awesome. She twisted the long reddish locks to a tight coil and tucked it on itself high on her head. She reached for the towel on the floor, dried her face, neck, shoulders, and hands. Then using the bar at the side of the bathtub, she pulled herself up to sit on the tub edge again.

Her whole body throbbed, but it was a good kind of throbbing. She was drained by the time she finished getting dressed again.

Perched on the bathtub, she studied the floor, wondering if she should try to walk to the bed on her own. Then considered an alternative. With a smile on her face, she slipped down until she sat on the floor and proceeded to scoot slowly to the bed. But the penalty for that was exhaustion. She stretched out on top of the blankets and closed her eyes. She was asleep in seconds.

EAGLE'S WORK HAD backed up. As efficiently as possible, he went to the cages—feeding, cleaning, checking on his charges. Some bandages had to be switched; one had been ripped off, and another splint had been pried apart. The things that some of the birds would do to avoid treatment. Even if for their own good. He patched and soothed from one end of the property to the other.

By the time he was done, he knew he'd burned through the time allotted for Issa's bath. He'd kept an ear out but hadn't heard her call. He and the dogs walked back inside; he washed his hands and headed for the spare bedroom. He stopped at the doorway in surprise.

She was fully dressed and stretched out on the bed atop

all the covers. There was a damp trail back to the bathroom. A soaking wet towel still lay on the floor. He picked it up, hung it over the shower railing, pulled the plug in the bathtub, not surprised to see the grayish-blackish water as it disappeared. He used the showerhead to give the bathtub a quick rinse and turned back to check on her.

As he got closer, he could see her hair was twisted into a knot. And, of course, she'd soaked her stitches. They looked pretty good. The skin was less angry, and she hadn't torn anything open. So, no harm done.

He shifted her lower half, pulling the blankets free, tucked her underneath, and covered her back up again. She murmured gently in her sleep but didn't wake up.

Back in the kitchen he put on another pot of coffee. Just as he was thinking about food for himself, his cell phone rang. He picked it up, but there was only static. "Hello?"

No answer. Frowning, he ended the call and placed the phone on the counter beside him. He had a thawed steak in his fridge. He popped it into a frying pan and added a couple eggs. When the time was right, he took it off. Just as he sat down to eat breakfast, his cell phone rang again. He glanced at it, but it didn't show a number. "Hello?"

Again static, nothing else. He tossed it down on the table. Obviously somebody was having trouble getting through to him. He shook his head. It was just one more of the many odd things going on right now. He dug into his steak, and his cell rang again. He picked it up. This time it displayed Gray's number. "What's up?"

"You could give me an update," Gray said testily. "I know you like to be alone, but the least you could do for an old man is let me know if she's alive or dead."

"She's alive. She's in bed and improving."

"That's it?"

"I know this sounds bizarre, but she really wanted a bath." He wasn't sure what made him add that part except, to him, it was a sign of progress.

"So, she's conscious? Who the hell is she? What the hell happened to her?" Gray exploded. "Jesus, man, you could've at least told me that she woke up."

Eagle pinched the bridge of his nose. "I'm sorry, Gray. I've been a little busy."

"I get that," Gray said quietly. "But a little common courtesy for somebody who is part of this would help."

"Sorry," Eagle repeated, knowing his friend was right. There'd been time to call, but he hadn't thought to.

"Whatever. If she is doing better, can I come by? If not today, maybe tomorrow? Do you need anything?"

"No, I'm fine and yes you can come by." Gray hung up, and Eagle studied his phone. *At least his phone worked this time.* But if Gray had been upset that Eagle hadn't updated him, he could just imagine how Annie felt, and she was even tougher with Eagle. He took another bite of steak, chewing while he dialed Annie's number.

"A progress report?"

He smiled. Annie, she didn't sound any different. "She's better. Still can't put any weight on her feet. She just had a bath."

"You put her in a bath?" she asked in surprise. "Isn't that a little fast?"

"She requested it. She was bloody, tired, and cold."

"That cold isn't good. Her body should be dealing with the chills by now."

"I don't know how to warm her up any more than I already am. She's eating hot soup. She's under the covers, and she's wearing my old sweats. She should be warm. The house is hot." He turned to glance at the woodstove, realizing he probably needed to bring in another armload of wood to keep it going for her. "I'm hot."

"You're not injured. And you're not lacking nutrition from the last however many days or weeks. Her body is fast burning through everything you can give her to eat."

"I'd give her more, but I don't think her stomach could handle it," he admitted. "She's had a bit of coffee and a bit more soup."

"That's good. I presume she's asleep after the bath. When she wakes up, try to get some protein in her. Even if it's just a couple scrambled eggs."

"Will do." He hung up and proceeded to finish the steak.

When the phone rang again, he didn't see a caller ID on the screen. He answered, "Hello?"

Static and yet not static. As if somebody really was trying to get through to him. "Hello, anyone there?"

There was a funny odd buzz, like a voice from a long way away trying to reach through the static. Eagle shook his head and shut down the phone. "Sorry. Don't know who or why you are trying to get a hold of me, but it's not working."

He checked his watch and realized it was past ten already. All the work he needed to get done today was done. He had phone calls he'd planned to make but hadn't gotten to. He grabbed his phone again, pulled up his notepad with the list of local falconry clubs. The first number, he got no answer; the second number, a man answered.

Eagle said, "I'm looking for a woman named Issa. I thought she was a member of the falconry club."

"She's a member, but we don't have any contact information for her. Even if we did, it's our policy not to hand out personal information," the voice said apologetically.

Eagle glanced at the notepad and realized he'd called a Tom Folgers. "Tom, is there anything you can tell me about her?"

"Why? Who is this?"

"I run the raptor center out of Colorado, and I have a couple falcons I was looking to have her help me with," he improvised. "I tried calling once before but couldn't reach anyone."

"Sometimes no one's here to answer the phones." Tom seemed to calm down then. "Issa comes in sometimes. But we haven't seen her for months now."

"I was trying to get a list of her credentials. Can you spell her last name?"

"The last name isn't so bad, but the first one is deadly." He chuckled and said, "Issa's last name is McGuire."

"She's not on your website."

"No, she's not a full member because she doesn't have her own falcon, so she's not on there. All the pictures there are members with their own falcons."

Eagle nodded. "That makes sense." He now realized all the pictures were of one human and one falcon.

"She went to the university here too. I know she just finished her doctorate, so you might find more information from them on her."

"Thank you very much." He hung up, not wanting to push the issue and ring any alarm bells for Tom. Eagle looked at her last name, typed it into the search bar, and came up with several articles. One was an obituary with another name. Marie McGuire.

Age sixty-two, deceased on August 26. That was five

weeks ago.

Pulling on his search skills, mostly learned in the military, he hunted down property records to see where Issa might've been living. Her mother's apartment came up. As well as a PO box for Issa but no physical address.

Interesting. Eagle remembered she had talked about a cabin, which could mean very rural, as in it didn't have anything other than a lot number.

With the PO box number, he phoned the post office and asked about her.

"Not sure I can tell you anything. She comes and goes. Haven't seen her in a while though."

"I'm trying to find her place."

"I talked to her a couple times. She lives up north of the city. Lots of wide open country up there, and that's the way she likes it, she said."

"Good enough, thanks." He realized the area was over an hour away. He could take a trip out this afternoon and a part of him felt like she should go with him. Only she wasn't in any shape to handle that. As he sipped his coffee, static, like he'd heard on the phone, slammed into his head. He grabbed his hair and yelled, "What the fuck?"

Instantly the static toned down to a dull, dry background noise. And a voice said, "Sorry."

Eagle hopped to his feet and spun in a circle. "Who just said that?"

But instead of a voice, a number kept flashing in his head. He grabbed his pen and wrote down a ten-digit number. He frowned. Was that a phone number? As soon as he had it on paper, the confusion in his head emptied. He grabbed his phone and dialed. When a man's voice came on the other end, Eagle asked, "Who the hell are you?"

A tired but humorous voice answered him. "I'm Stefan. I'm calling on behalf of Humbug."

And Eagle knew his world would never be the same.

CHAPTER 10

BRANCHES BANGED ON her window yet again. Issa listened to the scratching against the glass. Although the sound carried an odd note, she didn't sense any fear coming from Roash. Ever present, he stayed at her side—sometimes on the headboard, sometimes on the bed, other times on her shoulder. She wondered if he knew what her nightmares were and came to give her comfort. She wondered if he understood how much his presence helped. She hoped so. Just to know he'd survived those assholes filled her heart with light.

Now hopefully she could find Humbug. She knew many men were attached to their dogs. But if there was ever a cuddly stuffed animal—but in a live form—it was Humbug. She adored him. She'd had him for nine months. Nine months where he enriched her life every single day.

She stared dry-eyed at sunlight outside the window. The days were rolling into nights, rolling to days, and she had no idea of the passing time.

A sound at the door had her slowly rolling onto her back so she could see who leaned against the frame. Eagle held a cell phone in his hand. "Who is Stefan?"

She frowned and racked her brain. "No idea."

"He knows you."

She stared at Eagle for a long moment. "I don't know

anyone by that name."

"I know what your last name is now. McGuire. I know you belong to the falcon club, but you don't have your own falcon. And I know nobody has seen you there for a few months."

She gasped as images filled her mind. "Oh my," she said, and she broke out in a big smile. "McGuire *is* my name, and the man you spoke with is Tom."

Eagle nodded, took a few steps forward. "He seemed like a nice young man."

She smiled. "In many ways, yes. He has a very young-sounding voice. He's in his mid-forties." She watched a whisper of a smile cross Eagle's face. "I know. When I first heard him speak, I thought he was a teenager. So tell me about Stefan."

"I'm not sure what to say. There was a phone call, and I couldn't hear anyone for the static. It happened three times. On the third time it was like I could hear numbers through the phone or through my mind, or I'm just crazy." He waved the phone in his hand. "And that's all too possible. Nothing about this is straightforward or simple."

"What number?" she said, trying to bring them back on track. He was obviously perturbed over something, but she had no idea what.

"Thinking it was a phone number, I dialed it. And the man who answered was expecting my call. He said his name was Stefan. He was calling on behalf of," he paused, looked at her, and said, "are you ready for this?"

She frowned. "Just get on with it. He's calling on behalf of whom?"

He took another step forward, his gaze hard and inflexible, as if he could dredge through the recesses of her mind to get the answers himself. "He was calling on behalf of Humbug."

She gasped, and her face lit up. "That's wonderful!"

Eagle looked at her. "And how do you figure that it's wonderful?"

"He must've found him. Humbug has a name tag on his right foot."

"And how would he know to phone me?"

She blinked. And blinked again. She gave a slight shrug. "I don't know. Didn't you say you run a raptor center? Maybe he looked it up. Besides, that's not the point." She froze. "He does have Humbug, right?"

Eagle's voice dry, he responded, "Not quite."

IN FACT, HE wasn't sure it was safe to tell her at all. Because it was just a little too bizarre.

"What do you mean?" she snapped. "This really isn't something I care to joke about. Humbug is very close to my heart."

"Apparently he's *special* in many ways," Eagle said as he still tried to figure this out in his mind. "Stefan didn't have a ton of information."

"What information did he have that was so cryptic?"

"He said he had heard from Humbug, and Humbug was in distress and was looking for you." He leaned forward and glared at her. "You did say Humbug was an owl, right? Or is he your lover, some crotchety old man whose name would actually fit him?"

And damn if she didn't blink at him again. The slow blink of huge eyes in her face that reminded him of the damn birds outside. Especially the owls.

"What exactly did he say?" she asked slowly. "He said he *heard* from Humbug?"

"Yeah. I would put him down as being completely crazy, except for the owl's damn name." While he watched, she turned her head to stare outside.

"Fascinating."

"Oh, no, that's not quite the word I would use," he said. "Nothing since you arrived has been fascinating. *Daunting, perturbing, disruptive, unbelievable,* any number of other related terms I could use. *Fascinating* isn't one of them."

She waved a hand in his direction as if dismissing his concern. "That's because you're the kind of man who only believes what you can see in front of you. If you can touch a table, and it looks like a table, and it functions like a table, you'll lock into thinking it's a table. Whereas, if I see a table, touch a table, and use it as a table, it still has the functional ability of being something completely different. For example, if I throw matches on it, it becomes a source of heat. But if you always let it be a table, the table you might be forced to sleep on for a night, it will never be a bed. You see what you see and nothing more."

"And how is it that you would see Humbug?"

"He's a snowy owl, extra-large, with a bum wing. I found him injured in the fields. At the time I assumed he'd escaped from a predator. But he is also cranky. He likes things the way he likes them. He wants the food he wants. He likes his comforts the way he wants them. And, if you want him to go outside and do something for fun, he's very much back to being Humbug."

Eagle stared at her and, despite himself, started to laugh. He pulled a chair up close beside her bed and sat down. "So how the hell did Stefan hear Humbug? How does he know

Humbug is in trouble?"

She slowly glanced his way and then back to the window again.

And he knew instinctively she was hiding something. "Spit it out. Nothing but mystery has shrouded your visit from the beginning. I'd like to know some things for sure. How does Stefan know about Humbug?" Eagle demanded.

Her voice was so low he had to lean closer to hear her repeat it. "He might be able to hear Humbug."

Eagle stared at her. "So, a man might actually hear Humbug's cry-in-the-night type of thing?"

She winced. "I don't mean *hear* in that sense."

He groaned. "In what sense do you mean?"

"Maybe Stefan is psychic."

He knew he lived out in the middle of nowhere, and he knew he'd turned his back on humanity, but some things he couldn't turn his back on. And that was some of the stories he'd heard over the last decade. They weren't stories you read in the newspaper. But they were stories you heard through special friends in certain law enforcement departments. He bolted to his feet and raced to the kitchen, grabbed his laptop, and returned. He had the laptop, notepad, and Stefan's phone number as Eagle sat beside her. He typed in the name to search and up came dozens of articles. He checked the bottom row to see Google had matched fourteen pages of online data to Eagle's search criteria without even clicking again. "Shit."

"What did you find?" she asked.

He watched her pleating the blanket front, fear and worry spilling into her fingers. "He *is* a psychic. A very well-known one."

She frowned. "I don't know him."

"Is there any reason why you should? Are you psychic?" A look of horror crossed her face, and he chuckled. "I'll take that as a no." He dropped his gaze to the laptop and said, "He lives on the West Coast."

"Not exactly neighbors," she said drily.

"How far could Humbug fly?"

"Barely at all. From the kitchen table to the couch. From one fence post to another. And, if he was going in a straight line, you can guarantee he'd end up in a forty-five-degree angle on a downward slope," she said. "He's funny, cuddly, smart—sometimes," she qualified. "He's also very silly and very inept. He would not survive on his own for long."

"So, considering we don't know how long you were held against your will, and the only thing I have to go on is the falconry club time frame, are you sure no one would notice you were gone?"

"No, not after my mother died."

"She died on August 26, just over five weeks ago." So she'd been held for, at most, five weeks. No wonder she was in such rough shape. To survive that showed stamina, mental strength, and a fight to live. He loved that about her.

She paused, swallowed hard, and added, "If Humbug found a place to get food on a regular basis, and he was warm enough, he could survive. Of course he'd need water as well."

"How is it that you have anything to do with these birds?"

"They are my passion. I specialized in animals for my education. Animals and their environment," she said, fatigue in her voice. She shifted deeper into the blanket again. Her head relaxed.

Fascinated, he leaned forward. "Why birds? Why did

you specialize in birds?"

"I didn't have a choice," she whispered. "They chose me."

And damn if she didn't fall asleep again. He checked his clock; it was almost eight. If she slept through the night, she'd be a lot better tomorrow. She was healing rapidly. He was astonished at how the bruises were quickly running through the different colors. Even her head wound looked much better, the edges growing together, and, although they still slightly puckered, they were already starting to close. He didn't know how that was possible. It was too fast.

When his phone rang again, he stared down at it. That was way too many phone calls for him in one day. He answered it cautiously. "Hello. Who is this?"

"Stefan asked me to call."

Eagle pinched the bridge of his nose. "Why?"

The beautiful light voice chuckled. "My name is Tabitha Stoddard. Apparently you need me."

"For what?"

"I'm a sensitive. I pick up on animals' energy, particularly when they are in distress. I run Exotic Landscapes, a refuge for animals. And I have deep intuitive connections with a lot of animals. But I don't have a ton with birds. Stefan called to let me know Humbug is in trouble."

"The bird can't fly. I understand it's a snowy owl with an injured wing."

The woman's voice softened. "Oh, poor thing. The fact it hasn't been taken out by a larger predator is a good sign."

"Not unless we have a way to get to it. When you say you have a deep intuitive connection, what the hell does that mean?"

That same laugh filled the air. "It means different things

for different animals. I'm not trying to be cryptic. I'm not trying to be vague. Some people call me a psychic, but I'm very connected to the animal world. Stefan is connected to people."

"And, even if I pretended to believe you, Stefan is the one who connected to Humbug."

"True. But then Stefan is very different. He's connected to the ethers. He does a lot of work on the divide between this world and the next."

"Whoa. Okay, now that's getting just way too far to the left for me."

"I know," she said sympathetically. "You're much more the norm. Believe me. My gift has made my life difficult. Chances are you have never come up against someone like him or me. Regardless Stefan and I will continue to combine forces to locate or otherwise aid Humbug."

"I have a falcon here that appears to be very connected to a person."

"Oh, that would be interesting. It doesn't happen to have some unusual markings on its left foot, does it?"

He bolted to his feet and walked back into the bedroom. Roash looked at him and cawed gently. And, sure enough, his left foot, the lower part was scraped clean. "I don't know what you mean by unusual markings," he said, a question in his voice. He wasn't prepared to give her any more than that.

"Does it look like a band has been there, but it was removed, and the skin rubbed clean?"

"Yes, that's exactly what it looks like."

"Well, that's a good sign."

"How the hell can you say that? You just described a bird you've never seen sitting in my spare bedroom."

"The real question is, and it is very important that you

tell me the truth"—she took a deep breath and let it out slowly—"is there a beautiful woman with you as well who came with the bird?"

"Jesus." That was all he could say. Anything else was beyond him.

"You need to keep her safe. She's very special." With that, Tabitha rang off, leaving him staring at the dead phone in his hand.

"WE'RE HEADING BACK out again to scope the land."

"Wait." The boss handed him a sheet of paper. "The owner of the property is ex-navy. He earned himself several medals in combat."

Dylan's heart sank. "How long ago?" Please let this guy be in his nineties and ready to drop. But he knew it wouldn't be that easy. He'd seen a strong healthy male around the place. And that was the worst kind. Young men became protective when they found an injured female. And, if this one had skills, then this job just became that much harder.

"Make sure you take him out too."

Dylan swallowed. "Is that wise?"

"If you can get the girl without killing him, then fine. But you'll need to blow off his kneecaps to stop him from coming after us."

"True." Dylan grabbed his rucksack, nodded to the new guy, and headed to the truck.

"Blow off the guy's kneecaps?" the other guy asked. "Is he for real?"

"Not only is he for real, he'll do it to you too if he doesn't like your performance. So keep that in mind." Dylan didn't want to see the look of shock on the man's face. He'd seen it all before.

Sometimes the boss said things to the new guys to scare them.

Not this time though. Dylan had been given orders. Get the girl; cripple the owner for life. If that didn't do the job, then Dylan was to kill him.

Really all that meant was he was to kill him outright.

Dead men couldn't talk.

CHAPTER 11

W HEN SHE WOKE up next, she saw the early morning sun shining through the window. And heard a strange call. She sat up in bed slowly. Roash was at the window, pecking at the glass. "Do you need to go out?"

Roash turned, and she was pinned with a golden look. She studied the distance from the bed to the window and then decided she should try. Carefully she stood, surprised to find the pain tolerable. Her feet still felt swollen and puffy, like she was walking on cushions, and each step sent spikes of pain through her—but to a lesser degree than she'd felt so far. At the window, she opened it wide enough for Roash to fly out.

She stood there for a long moment, studying the acres of land, and, from where she stood, she could see the corner of a pen. And birds. An incredible number of them stretched out. Some lined the interior fence; some were in cages; some were sitting on top of the roof. She didn't quite understand what was going on out there, but she wanted to. She'd understood Eagle had pens but hadn't expected wild birds resting on every surface around the yard.

A door was at her side. She realized what she'd thought was a closet was a door out to a small deck. She opened it, winced at the cold air reaching her, wrapped her arms around her chest, and stepped out.

The chill in the air in no way took away from the beauty of her surroundings. For somebody who had spent her life getting back to nature, it amazed her that this man lived in what she'd easily call God's Country. Rolling hills, trees everywhere. She looked but saw no sign of other people. And yet birds were everywhere. She didn't understand, but one cried insistently. She studied the mass of birds, looking for the one calling. His cry wasn't a sign of pain, so she didn't understand his distress. It was like a warning.

As soon as that thought crossed her mind, she felt a shiver deep inside. She stepped back off the small deck, back into her room. She closed and locked the door. Walking to the window, she called for Roash to come in.

But there was no flood of wings. She stood with the window open ever-so-slightly and took a few steps to the bed. Just as she was about to sit down, she realized she should do a bathroom trip first. When she got back to the bed, she pulled off one of her socks and took a good long look at her feet. They felt sore, but she'd managed to walk. That was huge.

The bed needed straightening. Then, as she sat down once more, that same odd cry came again. Only this time it was muffled. Too curious to ignore, she got up and walked back out on the deck. And there stood Eagle. Talking to what appeared to be a blue heron. She studied it in amazement. Blue herons were hardly inland birds. They always clung to rivers, streams, wetlands. Normally a fish-eating bird, she wondered if Eagle had a lake or river around here with a constant source of food for the heron.

She watched as he placed a bucket in front of the heron, who immediately dipped down and pulled out a fish. He threw his head back and swallowed it whole. She watched as it slowly slid down his long neck. The bird stood at least four feet high. It was a darn impressive sight.

She smiled, absolutely loving the interaction. This place was special. How unusual was the man who cared for the birds. Most were predators, which required a special diet. Mice, hatched chicks, fish, and the odd chunk of meat would be needed, depending on the different species. She wanted to go out and talk to him. But, at the same time, she felt an odd, creepy feeling of being watched. She stepped back into the doorway. As she did so, Eagle spun, and his gaze pinned her in place. A look of surprise whispered across his features. Then he smiled. She gave him a shy small finger wave, stepped inside, and closed the door.

She was sure of one thing. Eagle was a good man.

She also knew someone—or something—was watching the property. And, although there had been something animalistic about this, she wouldn't have said it was threatening. Yet, a definite menace hung in the air.

Back in bed she found a bottle of cream on the night table. She studied the label. It was an antiseptic cream. She smoothed it all over the soles of her feet and would let them dry before putting her socks on again. She still didn't know where Eagle's property was located, but there'd been such a chill to the air outside that she figured the altitude of his property had to be higher than at her cabin. Had fall weather descended on them?

She'd lost track of time long ago. Five weeks since her mother's death? Definitely fall then. That was one hell of a long time that she basically didn't remember. As she did recall the torturous days and nights, she was damn lucky to have landed here. Even now thankfulness invaded her very soul.

She was barely under the blankets when she heard Eagle's footsteps at the front porch. She really wanted to see the rest of the house, but she was too tired and sore for more walking. And going outside was out of the question, especially now that the house was being watched.

He was at her doorway within minutes. "It was good to see you up," he said quietly. That gaze of his never missed anything. He studied her face, seeing the fatigue. He saw her feet partially out of the blanket, the evidence of the cream glistening on her soles. "How was it to walk?"

"Not as painful as I expected. Yet, I won't be running marathons anytime soon."

"You think you'll run one later? That would be worth seeing." He grinned. "Do you feel like having breakfast at the table?"

"I'd love to, but I just put some cream on my feet."

"Put the socks back on and walk carefully so you don't slip."

She nodded and sat up. "Did you see where Roash went?" she asked anxiously. "I let him out a little bit ago."

Eagle shook his head. "I wouldn't worry about him though. He seems to have a pretty good instinct for what's important."

"I gather it was feeding time at the zoo?"

"Actually, yes."

She chuckled. "Yeah, I can see that. That is the hard thing about keeping raptors. For them to live, another animal has to die."

He nodded. "I supplement with fish and any roadkill I can. But nothing takes away from the fact these birds need live food most of the time."

"I've known several big raptor rescue centers that incubate eggs. Doing a constant rotation of hundreds of incubating eggs at a time seems like the most economical answer."

"I do that too. And somehow it makes it slightly easier."

She nodded with understanding. "I know. Nice to keep mice. I found that very difficult though." While talking, she put on the socks, and, with a hand on the headboard, she stood. She shook her head. "What is it about actually standing on your own two feet that makes the world suddenly a whole much easier place to live in?"

"We're meant to be on our feet."

"So true." As he watched, she took several hesitant steps toward him. "Did you feel it out there?"

"Feel what?" His tone never changed; his gaze never left her progress.

"You know what."

He lifted his dark-chocolate-colored eyes to study her face. Then gave a quick nod. "Yes, I felt it."

"Did you see anyone?"

"No. But it's not the first time we've been watched."

"Did they follow me here, do you think?"

"I think they probably followed your tracks. The question is whether they saw you on the side deck this morning."

She froze. "I never thought of that."

"That little deck is partially hidden by one of the wind barriers. But depending on what angle they looked from, you might have told them you were here."

"Shit," she said softly.

"Yeah," he said drily.

When she reached him, he held out an arm. She held his forearm, not surprised by the steely strength of the muscles under her fingers. At the same time, she *was* surprised. The man was solid. She'd expected him to be strong but not this rock-hard steel.

With his assistance, she made her way down the short hallway into a very large open kitchen, dining, and living space. She stopped and smiled with pleasure. "This is beautiful."

"It's been a labor of love," he admitted. He helped her to a kitchen chair and pulled it out for her. "Sit down here, and see how that'll be. If you need a pillow, tell me."

She sat down on the hardwood chair, wiggled slightly, and said, "It might be just fine."

He had already returned from the couch with a couple cushions. He pulled another chair from under the table, plopped the cushions down, gently lifted her feet, and put them on top of the pillows. "When you walk on them like you've just done, it draws all the blood to the surface, and they'll swell because they've been injured. Let's keep them raised as much as possible."

"Thank you."

"Not a problem. But as far as being watched, any idea who it is?"

"I'm afraid it's the kidnappers."

He spun slowly to look at her. "You've never said anything about that. Have you remembered what happened?"

"Bits and pieces of it are coming back. Nothing clear, nothing I could seriously identify. I remember cleaning out my mother's place almost a week after her death, being emotional as she had just passed away, finding something that upset me in her belongings. So, when I got home, I wasn't as aware as I could have been. I unpacked the car and stored a bunch of it in the root cellar and might even have put on the teakettle, when I heard something outside. I raced for the back door and was grabbed. I fought, but they pulled a long hood over my head and body. I was picked up, thrown over somebody's shoulder, screaming the whole time, until somebody hit me in the head." She shrugged. "I don't remember much after that."

Instantly he was at her side. "Do you know which side you got hit on?"

"Yeah," she said drily. She pointed to the left side of her skull. "I do remember it bleeding quite a bit off and on. But it was the least of what they did to me."

He nodded. "I had a doctor come in to look at you."

"The woman?" she asked.

"No, an old Irishman was here first."

She stiffened slightly at the description. "Did he say anything?"

"Only that he'd seen stuff like this before and hoped never to see it again," Eagle said. He poured her a cup of coffee, brought it over to her, and set it on the table within her reach. "He said you were systematically tortured. The bruises were multiple colors, indicating you were hit repeatedly in the same spots. Just as you started to heal, you'd get slammed again."

Her throat closed with the memories, pain choking her even now. "They wanted something from me that I couldn't give."

"What was it?

"I don't really know," she admitted. "They just kept asking, *Where is it?*"

He stopped and turned, leaning against the counter, holding a big hefty ceramic cup full of coffee. "Tell me more."

"It's still kind of fuzzy. I know they were looking for information about what happened back in Ireland when I was a child."

"Ireland?"

She studied him carefully and nodded slowly. "I heard your friend's accent. I have to admit I stayed silent while he was here. I was scared of him." She gave a sigh. "I was afraid he was one of the kidnappers. They had accents too."

"That makes sense. I had wondered if you were conscious through any of that."

"I was briefly awake as I was being checked over. I forced myself to stay quiet because I didn't know who you were. And because of his accent," she admitted.

"I guess the accent was just a little too close to those you had already heard?"

"Yes."

"Tell me what they were looking for."

"I'm from Ireland originally." She gave him a lopsided grin. "My whole family was involved in smuggling. I used to be the lookout as a young child. My father and his men had coves up and down the shores that they used. They landed in various places, unloading their goods, keeping them hidden until they could be sorted and divided up. My mother was part of the lookout crew."

"What happened?"

"One day, when I was six years old, it all went to hell," she said in a matter-of-fact voice. "I never did get an explanation from my mother. She would never talk to me about that time in my life. When I tried to ask, not only would she hit me to silence me, as I grew up, she would turn cold and distant, as in she wouldn't talk to me for days. The minute I would bring up something about the old country, I would be punished with the silent treatment. I very quickly learned that the pain from withholding love was more effective than any physical punishment she could have inflicted." She shook her head. "So I really don't know what happened back then." She picked up her coffee cup, slowly turning it in her hands, swirling the hot liquid faster. "I just know I lost my father and my siblings to the disaster."

She raised her gaze. "I had three brothers. I was the youngest by twelve years. But I don't remember any of them."

"Did the kidnappers work with your father?"

"They didn't say that specifically. I thought, from their questioning, that they were looking for someone who had betrayed them. That betrayal caused the death of my brothers and father. There was also mention of money, as if they didn't get their share of the loot, but I don't know what that means," she said. "It was decades ago. They should have just moved on, like I did. But the one thing you need to know about the Irish is that they never forget. And these men, ... my family included, lived on the edge of the law. They were smugglers. They didn't believe the law applied to them. We all lived a secret life."

"A lot of people in the world are like that." He snorted. "But, if the kidnappers were cheated out of their share of a deal, it could be what they are looking for. But why now? Maybe they were looking for your mother, and, when they realized she was gone, they went after you."

"They kept asking for answers," she said, puzzled. "They wanted to know why I didn't know what was going on. They wanted to know why I hadn't seen it coming." She shook her head at his confused look. "I was six at the time. My mother was around somewhere, but I had no idea what was happening that night. I didn't even understand the logistics of what they were doing. I understood my parents and brothers were doing something illegal. But what *illegal* means to a child, well …" She raised her shoulders in a shrug. "How much of any event can a young child understand?"

"But your mother was a lookout too?"

"She was. But she always stayed inside the house." Issa didn't know how much to tell him. Why did any of this matter? But still he needed to know enough to get a clearer picture of these men and what they might have been after.

"Alone?"

She nodded. "Of course my mother would say she was with me all the time, and my father believed her. At the time, I thought that's what her being with me meant. I would stay outside. She would go inside and wait. I didn't realize until later that 'being with me' didn't mean the same thing to everybody."

"She went inside, and you were left outside? And this is how your family operated?"

"We'd do that every month," she said. "Until that one fated night when everything blew up, and I have no idea what happened." She shook her head. "I just know there was a huge fight down below. There were gunshots. There were multiple men involved, not just my brothers and father and those who worked with them. And, no, I don't know who they were or how many there were. You have to remember, I was only six."

"Your mother never said anything about it?"

Issa gave him a hard look. "I went through hell trying to get information from her. But she would never talk."

"And what upset you in your mother's belongings?"

She frowned. "Something in one of boxes I opened."

"What was in it?"

She shrugged. "Envelopes. Lots and lots of envelopes.

Along with that was a leather keepsake box from my mother. I didn't get a chance to look at any of it clearly." She stopped, then realized there was no point in keeping the information from him. It had all happened a long time ago. "I caught a quick glance of one of the documents about my father having a criminal record or criminal charges pending, but I didn't read it so don't know the details. At the time I didn't think I was up to dealing with the loss of my mother *and* my memory of who my father was."

"We need to look at those."

"That was the plan all along. Escape, find the boxes, get revenge."

"Revenge?" he asked carefully.

Her lips quirked. "At the time I thought the kidnappers had killed Roash and Humbug. The men took great delight in telling me how they'd tortured and killed all my birds." She sighed. "And, if I'm honest, it was the thought of getting revenge that kept me going. I wanted to make them pay for what they did."

"This might be a good time to tell you that I got a phone call last night from a woman saying she runs an animal reserve called Exotic Landscape."

Issa tilted her head and studied his face. "Interesting. Do you know her?"

"No. Her name is Tabitha. She said something about Stefan. She had been in contact with Humbug herself."

Issa stared at him. "That's the second person who's said they've spoken to Humbug. Is that possible?"

"You tell me. Stefan appeared to be almost resigned. So we have somebody who called himself a psychic, and someone who runs an animal shelter and called herself a sensitive, both talking to Humbug."

"What did they say about Humbug?"

"He's in trouble, and he needs you."

She straightened, wanted to race outside to find Humbug, but she'd barely make it to the doorway. "We have to go help him."

"That's a nice thought. Any idea where he is?"

She turned to stare at him. "No. But, if you could drive me home, we could get those boxes and look for him too." A frown whispered across her face. "That is, if anything is left of my cabin. It could be all burned to the ground. If so, it's all gone."

"Where do you live?"

"Denver," she said. "Just south of the city."

"That's a good start because I live outside Denver too, but to the north."

She frowned in confusion.

"You're at my home, which means somebody transported you to a place within traveling distance from here."

She stared at him. "I don't know how many days I was on the road. I just kept putting one foot in front of the other. I'm not really sure where I am now."

"I highly doubt you came from more than one day's walk away from here."

She mentally thought about the distance she'd walked and said, "I traveled for several nights. Just not very fast."

"Drink your coffee, and get some food down you, and, if you think you're up for the drive, and you know how to get to your place, we'll take a trip."

She brightened. "Can we go now?"

He shook his head. "Food first."

He brought out some homemade bread as black as the ace of spades and chock-full of seeds.

120

"That looks fantastic," she said in delight.

"Good because it's the only kind of bread I eat around here." He placed the butter in front her, big slabs, and gave her a knife.

With him at her side, she worked her way through the first slice of bread and halfway through the second one. She put it down and shook her head. "Sorry. My eyes are bigger than my stomach."

He looked at her for a long moment and nodded. "That's fine. I thought you might be overdoing it." He took the remainder of bread, broke it in pieces, and gave the rest to the two dogs lying quietly by the door.

She watched the pair enjoy the treat. Both were a decent size. One had more a sheepdog with a pinch of Rottweiler look to him, giving him a guard-dog air. The other one could have been a mix of dozens of breeds and appeared to be an overgrown pup. "I don't remember seeing the dogs."

"That's because I kept them away, afraid they would hurt you just by their sheer size. I haven't let them in your room. This is Gunner and Hatter."

She smiled. "Will you let them come see me now?"

"Yes."

At his command, both dogs approached her. The larger one laid his head in her lap and looked up at her with a sorrowful look that said he had wanted to come to her for days. The second dog nudged her hand, looking for his fair share of love too. She fell in love. She crooned to them gently as she said hi to both dogs. "Can they come with us?"

He shook his head. "They stay here with the birds."

She didn't say anything to that. "It would be great if I could go home."

"Let's just be clear about one thing," he said as he

grabbed his keys, shoving them in his pocket, and putting on a holster with a sidearm. "I will take you home to get the paperwork, but no way in hell are you staying there."

She frowned. "Are you saying I'm a prisoner?"

He shook his head, his gaze clear and direct. "You're here until this is over. You're not leaving my side. Got it?"

She studied him for a long moment and found there was none of the anger and terror rippling through her that she'd had from the other men. This man wanted to protect her. The others wanted to harm her. This man was honorable; the others were full of hate. Eagle stood casually, confident in his decision. He wasn't looking to terrorize her. Neither was he looking to comfort. But his statement was a fact. She could take it or leave it.

For the moment, she took it. She'd make up her mind about the rest later.

OUTSIDE THERE WAS a sense of urgency to the morning. The birds knew it. They'd never been wrong yet. He just didn't know in what form the trouble would arrive. Before it did, he wanted to get her the hell away from here. Preferably where he could get answers. And, if she had answers back at her place, then that was where they were going.

She looked like a tiny waif in his extra-large clothing. He grabbed an old afghan, brightly colored, as if someone had used yarn ends, indiscriminate of one color palate. With that spread out over the truck passenger seat, he came back and scooped her up, ignoring her protests that she could walk on her own, and stepped outside on the front porch. He set the alarm and carried her out to the truck. He buckled her in and closed the door, walking around to the driver's side. He drove to the gate, opened it, drove a bit farther, then closed and locked the gate behind them, leaving the dogs to guard his property.

He turned onto the highway. "You okay?"

"I'm fine, just surprised at how fast we ended up pulling out."

"We need answers. Too much shit is going on."

She nodded. "I'm not arguing. I'm just surprised. When I woke up this morning, I was thinking it was the day I needed to start living again."

"What you need is to be back in bed. Hopefully we can pack you some clothes and get you back home again."

She didn't say anything for a long moment. And he realized the term *home* was probably what she was stuck on.

"You need looking after until the kidnappers are caught and until you're back to a hundred percent."

"Thank you very much for looking after me," she said in a formal tone.

And it pissed him off. "I'd do it for anybody," he said in a brisk tone.

Silence was her only response.

He hit the highway and floored the gas pedal. He wanted to get back as soon as possible. Preferably without being followed. More than that, he didn't want anybody to see Issa beside him. He'd seen many cops, lawyers, and judges on the wrong side of the law so knew better than to trust anyone.

"Tell me about your mother," he said. "It doesn't sound like you had a great relationship with her."

"I don't know that it was bad, but it wasn't a loving one. With no other family members, it was just the two of us."

"When did you come to the States?"

"Soon after my father and brothers were killed."

"Interesting."

"Why?"

"It's a long way to run," he said quietly.

"Well, if we were running, she didn't show it. I didn't have much to do with her in the last few years. Sure, I saw her on weekends, but it seemed like we were almost strangers. She was always on social media. I couldn't stand to be in town, and she couldn't stand to be out of it."

"If she was on social media, then she might have been found earlier, if anyone was looking."

"I doubt it. She had Americanized her name when we came over here."

"You each dealt with pain in your own way."

She nodded. "Doesn't everyone? What about you? Do you have any family?"

He shook his head. "My mother passed on ten years ago."

"I'm sorry. What happened?"

He gave a bitter laugh. "I was in the military, in a Special Operations unit. She always worked with Doctors Without Borders and traveled the world—dragging me along with her when I was younger. She had the biggest, most compassionate heart. Her life was her team. She went into a small village in Afghanistan where they held her and the whole group as hostages. Of course the United States doesn't deal with terrorists and certainly doesn't deal with hostage demands like that. We went in with a small unit to rescue them. They found out we were coming, and they shot her right in front of me. I had a few moments with her before she died. She said she would've done it all over again if it meant saving my life." He shook his head, shaking off the memories that still brought tears to his eyes, plugging his throat with sorrow.

"It's one of the few times in my life that I let vengeance control my actions. When I walked off that mountain with my mother's body in my arms, the other hostages by my side, no adult male was left standing." His tone was harsh. "You see? You don't know me. I'm just an asshole soldier, and you happened into my life. The fact is, I was having a weak moment."

When she remained silent once more, he shot her a hard glance. If she showed one bit of pity for him, he would dump her on the side of the road. He couldn't stand that. What he had said had been very true, yet he couldn't leave somebody in trouble.

She shook her head. "You might like to show your prickly exterior, particularly when you talk about things that are very emotionally hard for you. *Whatever.* I know who you are on the inside."

Now it was his turn to be silent.

He drove steadily, not wanting to get into any more emotional conversations, still in shock he'd brought up his mother's death. That was so unlike him.

After another ten minutes, she said, "What about your father?"

"He walked out of my life when I was a toddler. He didn't want me then, and I don't want him now."

"You never felt the urge to look him up?"

"No. He made his decision. No way I'd let him in my life now. I lost my mother, and that asshole of a father is no worthy replacement."

"Hardly a replacement. How about another person in your life? You don't always have to be alone."

He looked at her. "Really? So how come you're so alone? Or is there someone I don't know about? A lover? A casual friend for the night? Or what about your mother? Did she remarry? Date anyone seriously?"

She shrugged. "Honestly, I don't know. About my mother or me." She played with her fingers. "I have no rings and no ring marks that I can see, and so far there aren't any memories of anybody. And my mom spent all the time I was there visiting her on social media, pointing out stupid posts and stuff. If it wasn't a meaningful conversation, I didn't want to waste my time on her either."

"Meaning, you wanted answers. She wouldn't give them to you."

"That probably sums it up. But I didn't know about the two boxes she had. She could have given them to me at any time in the last ten years. It's not like I'm a child anymore," she cried out passionately. "What a way to find out, now that she's gone."

"But it was the easiest way for her. She didn't want to deal with the guilt, the pain, or the fear of whatever is in those boxes."

"I understand that. But neither did she want to explain it. To tell me her side of it. And that is something very difficult for me to understand."

"Hopefully we'll get the answers soon. Do you remember where you live?" When there was no answer, he turned to look at her, his eyebrows raised in question.

She shook her head. "I'm sorry. I don't remember all of it," she said in a small voice. "The whole drive I kept hoping it would just magically come to me."

"Are there any routes you took all the time that you would know by routine?"

"The university to my mother's. University to home. My mother's to home."

"That's easy then," he announced. "I'll take you to the university, and we'll start from there."

She settled back with a bewildered smile. "I know it sounds silly, but how can anybody forget pieces of their life?"

"You were grazed by a bullet, shot in the shoulder, knocked unconscious, tortured, and terrorized for weeks. I'm sure you would like to forget lots of things as well. The mind is a funny thing. It's got the capacity to forget what's painful, and it's also got the capacity to shut down anything that will slow your healing. The head injury could also have caused a temporary memory loss."

"Oh." After that she sank into the blanket, pulling it around her shoulders.

"Are you cold? Do you want me to turn on the heat?"

She shook her head. "No, I'm fine."

But he could see from the tight way she clenched her fingers that she wasn't fine. He pulled onto the off-ramp and into the parking area of a busy franchise coffee shop. He entered the drive-through, ordered two cups of coffee and several muffins. Once he paid for and collected his order, he pulled back out onto the road. "One of those is for you."

"I'm not hungry."

"Not right now, but you might be later." He lifted the small pop-up lid on the coffee cup and took a sip. He liked his coffee dead black. This one was perfect. He put it into his cup holder and made his way through the town. He knew where the university was, but he hadn't been there for a long time. "I think we're about fifteen minutes out from the university."

She nodded but never said a word. As he glanced over at her again, he could see the blanket pulled tighter around her shoulders, up around her head. Was she hiding from anybody considering the truck or hiding from what was coming? He didn't know. "Where are we likely to find Humbug?"

"I have no idea," she said quietly. "I'm hoping he's close to home, but I'm afraid he's trying to find me or trying to follow me. He probably started in one direction and got himself thoroughly lost."

"Are you sure you never heard of Stefan or this Tabitha person before?"

She shook her head. "No," she exclaimed. "Not that I can remember." She turned to look at him. "What about you?"

"Not until they called me," he said cheerfully. "I'm not exactly sure what a sensitive is, in terms of animals either."

"It generally means they can see, feel, hear, and sense an animal, either in the present or their spirit form." She laughed at the surprise on his face. "I'm from Ireland, remember? So I'm more accustomed to some of that than you are over here."

"Well, as you pointed out, I only believed in what I saw, touched, and felt, but, since you arrived, I have to admit the boundaries have been pushed."

"And they'll get pushed a lot more most likely," she said quietly.

He pointed up ahead to the turnoff. "I'm heading out university way. Tell me when you start to recognize your surroundings."

"At that big intersection up there is a roundabout. Take a left."

Soon enough he was on the road heading back out again into the city when she said, "Stop. Turn right here."

He swore and quickly shifted lanes. "I know you are

probably struggling to remember, but a little more warning would help."

"My mother's place is just around the corner."

Following her instructions, he turned into a large apartment building. He glanced at it and then at her. "Do you want something here?"

She stared at the building. "I don't know. When I left, there were boxes Goodwill was supposed to pick up. I had everything else in my car. The place should be empty."

"You stay here. I'll go talk to the manager."

She nodded.

He hopped out, locked the truck, and walked over to the small office. The manager was in. Eagle mentioned Issa's mother and told the manager he was a friend. "I'm just checking to make sure all the boxes were picked up and the apartment is fine."

The manager nodded. "It's all good."

They shook hands, and the manager gave him the deposit owing on the apartment. Eagle signed Issa's name to the bottom of the receipt, handed it over, and returned to the truck. He searched his surroundings for anything that appeared suspicious, but he couldn't see anything. Back in the truck he gave Issa the envelope and said, "Here is the deposit on your mother's apartment. I assume she was renting it."

Issa stared at Eagle in surprise. "Yes, I forgot about that," she exclaimed. "I gather the things were picked up."

"Picked up and checked off. So there's absolutely no purpose in coming here again."

Issa sat back quietly. He glanced at her and realized how difficult it must be. "I know it's hard to see your mother's place up for rent so soon, but we can't stay here. Where would you have turned to get out of here?"

She pointed out the next few turns. He found himself back on a highway, heading to Issa's cabin. She leaned forward as the excitement grew on her face. "Up there, at that intersection, take a right." For the next ten minutes, he followed her instructions until she said, "Now we just stay on this road to my place."

"And how long again?"

"Thirty minutes."

He settled back for the ride, keeping an eye on the traffic. But the farther along they went, the less traffic they saw. When he realized he hadn't seen anybody for a good fifteen minutes, he said, "How long have you actually lived here?"

She shrugged. "Five years, I think. Slow down," she yelled suddenly.

He hit the brakes and saw a dirt road up ahead.

"This is it."

He stared at the dirt road that barely passed for a driveway and the heavily wooded area that cloaked where their destination was. He took a turn onto the road and slowed to a crawl.

She gave him an apologetic look. "I was planning to get it fixed."

He nodded. "A rough dirt road is not anything to be ashamed of."

They traveled along the half-mile driveway until he saw a small cabin.

"Oh, my God, there it is," she said. "For some reason, I was so afraid they would've burned it to the ground."

"Not likely. That would've caused a hell of a fire. And we're very short on rain this year." He pulled up in front and came around to her side. There he unbuckled her, lifted her in his arms, and carried her to the front step. He set her down and then stepped back.

"I don't see any of my birds," she said quietly, her gaze searching the treetops and the fence line. She hobbled to the front door that stood partially open. He knew the inside would be trashed. He kept protectively at her side as they entered. She tried to flick on a light, but there was no power. She might have been cut off if her bill hadn't been paid.

When he stepped inside, he saw a very plain, simple cabin with an old worn couch and chair on the left side and a Formica table from the eighties on metal legs on the right side. Everything was upside down and tossed to the floor. "Let me check to make sure no one is here."

The place had that cold, empty, deserted feeling. He made a quick search anyway. Better to be safe. When he came back, she stood in the middle of the living room, dismay on her face. "Why would they destroy everything?"

"Because they were looking for something. Or maybe just to hurt you."

She nodded. "Both, I believe."

With his help, she navigated through the debris on the floor. She made it to the bedroom and stopped. "There's not much in the way of usable clothing."

He'd seen that for himself. They had dumped the drawers, emptied the closet, and poured something like paint and paint thinner over them. He wasn't sure, but a whole collection of liquids had been thrown all around.

She stood in shock. He watched her shock turn to anger. And of that he approved. "Good. Get angry," he said quietly. "Because otherwise you'd stay a victim, and victims are completely helpless."

"I was a victim," she said, her tone so low he could barely hear. "And you're right. I was completely helpless. But I'm not now. They might've ruined a few clothes, and maybe nothing is salvageable, but this will not break me."

She turned to study the bathroom, a simple affair with a small shower, toilet, and a sink. The few toiletries were tossed on the floor. She wandered to the kitchen, straightened up a chair, and sat down. He opened the fridge and slammed it closed.

She glanced at him. "You hungry?"

"No." He shook his head. "I was wondering how long since you've been here. The food in there is bad."

"I have no power. I'm not sure how long it takes food to turn in a sealed fridge."

He shrugged. "Three to seven days."

"I'm pretty sure I was held for a lot longer than that."

"So, did they get the boxes?"

"That's why I'm sitting down. I'm scared to look." She pointed to the floor under his feet and said, "A root cellar is down there."

He glanced at her in surprise and back at his feet. He studied the floor layout, but it took him several minutes to see the wooden handle completely flattened into the floor, its grain matched up. He bent down, lifted the handle, slowly raising it. "Do you have a flashlight?"

She shook her head. "I did, but I don't know where it is now."

He pulled out his cell phone, turned on the flashlight, and shot the beam down there. "Doesn't look like they found this." He heard the small cry of relief in her voice. He slowly made his way down the ladder to see several boxes of canned goods, some camping gear, and a crematory urn. *Her mother?* With her guidance, he found the boxes they were looking for. He asked, "Do you want your mother's urn now?"

She shook her head. "No, we can leave that here for now."

When he climbed out, he replaced the lid, leaving the cellar hidden again, and carried the two boxes out to the truck, putting them behind the seats. Then he came back and said, "I'll take a quick look around outside, staying near the cabin, to look for Humbug. You stay here. Just give me five minutes, and then we'll leave."

He returned, shaking his head. She shook her head too. She stood and, with careful movements, walked to the front door. She still wore his big socks and oversize sweatpants.

He scooped her up, closed the front door, and carried her to the truck, noting her watchful scan of the area again. Once inside the cab, he reversed and headed back to the highway.

"Close to my place are a couple clothing stores," Eagle said. "I suggest we get you something to wear." Seeing her expression, he asked, "What's the matter?"

"My Suburban," she said quietly. "It's gone. I hadn't had a chance to unload everything. I was so concerned about getting the boxes to safety that I left my purse to get in the next load. Now it's gone too—along with all my identification." She stared at him in shock. "That means I can't prove who I am."

CHAPTER 12

S HE DIDN'T KNOW why that should bother her so much. But, without her ID, she couldn't get a driver's license, couldn't get her bank cards, or access any money she had in the bank. So many instances in everyday living required her identification.

"I don't suppose you remember any of your numbers?"

"Does anyone?" she asked in astonishment.

He chuckled and poured out a stream of digits.

When he stopped, she said, "What the hell was that?"

"My Social Security number, driver's license number, and my credit card numbers. With your numbers you could at least transfer money."

"I still need a card to go to the bank to get it out."

He shrugged. "Sure, but we could transfer the money into my account, and then you'd get some cash, while you wait for new cards to arrive."

"Oh." She shook her head. "It never occurred to me to memorize my numbers." Then she remembered losing her purse while in the field over a year ago. "My bank keeps a copy of my passport photo on my account in case something like this happens."

"I know it's probably not the time to ask, but are you sure your name is Issa McGuire? Any chance it might have been changed?"

"That's my name," she said firmly.

"And you know for sure you're from Ireland?"

She stared at his profile. "Meaning, my mother might've changed our name when we came to the States?" She frowned at his nod. "It's our name but she Americanized hers, but I don't know why."

"Depends on what happened that killed your father and brothers," he said. "If she thought you were still in danger, she might very well have."

"But my first name is very unusual," she murmured. Any other name felt and sounded foreign to her. "Wouldn't she have changed that too?"

"Unless you refused to answer to anything else."

Another memory popped into the confusion in her brain. "Actually, for a long time I didn't speak." She stared out at the world passing by. "After what happened to my father and brothers, I became mute for a long time. I know she was really frustrated with my slow return to normality. The specialists said to just let me be, that I'd recover after I had a chance to process the trauma."

"How long were you like that?"

"At least six months. But I really struggled that first year. Not only was I behind in school, coming from Ireland, but I was also dealing with the trauma of so much loss and change, and it took several more years before I really got started with my education. I spent a lot of years playing catch up. Once I got it—once I understood this was my life now, and there was no going back—then I adapted. I took off, raced to the head of my class, and stayed there."

"And why was that important to you?"

"Choices. I figured, if I was at the top of the class, I would have choices for my future. My mother didn't appear to have any. She worked in a local retail store, running the cash register at minimum wage."

"There was no money? She had no assets from Ireland?"

Issa shook her head. "Not that I know of. From my understanding, we arrived penniless, and there was never any spare money while I grew up. My mother was always penny-pinching to make things work. I got a job as soon as I was old enough, and it was the same kind of job she had. When I realized I could be working for minimum wage for the next forty years"—she shook her head—"I worked even harder at school."

He nodded. "I can relate to that."

When they hit Denver, he drove through the big city until they were on the side closest to his place. He pulled off at a restaurant. "Do you want to stop and have some lunch?"

"I can wait until we get home."

"You might be able to, but I can't."

He waited until she got out the truck, and, even though she still was dressed in his clothes and felt like a hobo, he took her in and seated her at the first empty table. Positive everybody must be wondering who the hell she was, she kept her head down.

When she finally peeked around the space, she realized nobody even looked at her. A waitress came to bring them coffee and menus. Never was Issa more aware of her lack of funds than she was right now. In a low voice she said, "You do remember I don't have access to my money?"

He stared at her, hardness coming into his eyes. His tone like flint, he said, "Did I ask you for any money? No. Lunch is on me, and make sure you order something substantial. Otherwise I'll order for you. And we will stay here to make sure you eat it."

She glared at him. "Are you always this bossy?"

"When people piss me off, yes."

And she realized she'd offended him. Muttering, she said, "I'm sorry." She settled in to study the menu. Her stomach was still touchy. She didn't dare fill it too much. They had a beef and barley soup. She put her mind to that. "I think I will have the bowl of soup. That might stay down."

He considered her for a long moment and nodded. "Too much of anything would likely upset your system." When he placed their order, he added French bread to her order.

She sat back, feeling the fatigue of the long drive in her bones. "How long until we're at your home again?"

"About thirty-five minutes. Do you think you can handle a clothing store for a couple pairs of pants and T-shirts, shoes and socks?"

She shivered and pulled her arms around her chest tighter. "I'm not sure about T-shirts. I'm still so cold. I need sweaters."

He frowned.

She leaned forward. "Is there a thrift store around? Obviously my body weight is very low. We could find some sweatpants and sweatshirts cheap until I can put some weight back on. And right now I don't care what I look like, as long as I'm warm."

He lifted his gaze in surprise.

She shrugged. "I know. My mother was a skinflint, and apparently I picked up a few of her habits."

He chuckled. "It's not necessarily a bad thing."

The food arrived. He'd ordered a burger and fries, and her soup bowl was an impressive size. When the French bread was delivered, she knew she couldn't eat both. She shook her head. "If I keep eating like this, I will build my weight back up with no problem."

"It'll take months." He kept his gaze locked on her. "What was your body weight before you went missing?"

She frowned and glanced down. "I've always been lean," she confessed.

"One hundred and twenty-five pounds?" he hazarded a guess, and she nodded.

"My mother had a scale. I think the last time I weighed myself, I was about a hundred and twenty-four pounds." She wondered at a man who could pin her weight so accurately. "What would you expect me to weigh now?"

He shook his head. "I'd be surprised if you weighed a hundred and eight."

It was hard to stare at her hands, the skin so thin that the veins showed through. "I got mononucleosis when I was in high school. I dropped down under the one hundred mark to around ninety-four pounds, but, even then, I wasn't in this condition."

"This condition isn't just loss of weight. It's malnourishment, stress, and injuries. What they did to you has accelerated the damage."

She picked up her spoon and took a sip of the soup. It was delicious. "Well, at least they won't have a chance to do it to me again."

"It's still a lot of damage and a lot of physical decline for just a couple or three weeks."

"They were very rough weeks." She took another sip of the soup, and suddenly she couldn't get enough. She was hungry, and the soup hit the spot. She stopped all efforts of maintaining her calm and literally inhaled it. She did try to dip the French bread into the broth, but the slice was thick and not a whole lot of the broth came away with it. By the time she hit the bottom of the bowl, she broke up the French bread, softening it, but she couldn't finish it.

She sat back. "Now that was good." She stared in amazement at the bowl. "I didn't think I'd be able to eat it all."

"That's because your body has been starved."

She nodded. "We should probably pick up some multivitamins or something to help me get back on top again."

He didn't say anything but worked his way through his fries and burger.

She sipped her coffee and asked, "How do I go about getting my ID?"

"Hopefully we'll find some documents, like your birth certificate, to make that job simpler."

She brightened. "Right. I forgot about the boxes."

By the time they went back out to the truck, she was in a pleasant state—feeling warm, cozy—and the fear had fallen back.

When he pulled into a large thrift store, she laughed. "See? This was a good idea."

"I don't know that it is," he admitted. "But I couldn't figure out what kind of clothing store would have clothes in your size. I was tempted to take you to a kid's store."

She shot him a look of outrage. "I'm sure we can find something here that works. And I'd feel much better if it didn't cost an arm and a leg. I do intend to pay back every penny you spend on me."

She ignored the fact he slammed the truck door hard at her words. She'd been raised to be independent, and she had no intention of taking advantage of the situation. But she needed to find something that would somewhat fit at this store.

With his help and a cart, she pulled out several pairs of sweatpants, a couple pairs of jeans, a few leggings, long-sleeve shirts, sweaters, and sweatshirts. When he looked through the winter jackets, she protested, seeing the tickets on some of these items were quite large.

He shot her a look and held one out to her. "Winter can land in Denver very quickly. No way you can wear my winter jackets."

She struggled, not wanting the coat, as it was still way too big. Two jackets later, she found one. She glanced around for shoes as she still wore his socks. Noticing her interest, he found a used pair of sneakers that had some life in them, a couple of slip-ons, and a pair of boots for her to try on.

By the time she was done, she had a whole new wardrobe. She winced at the full cart. "What do you think all this costs?"

"It's Tuesday. Everything is half price."

She stared at him in delight. "Really, they do that?"

He chuckled. "And even if they didn't, it wouldn't matter." He hesitated. "They might have socks that fit here too."

One of the women who worked there heard them. She walked them over to several baskets full of heavy socks and lighter socks. And mittens as well. He took several that looked to be in good shape and added them to the pile. There he slid her a sidelong look. "With your low body weight, you don't need a bra."

Surprised, she glanced down and realized that, of course, when her body was so skinny, her breasts had shrunk. She shook her head in disbelief. "I used to be a B cup."

"Well, now you're maybe a double A," he said with a

smile.

She shot him a look of outrage, but, chuckling, he turned and walked to a different counter.

He motioned to the bras on the rack ahead of them. "This is your department. I don't know anything about them."

She found several brand-new sports bras hanging on a rack. They were very small, but she checked the sizes and then glanced down at her chest. She realized they were only a size smaller than what she would normally wear. She chose two and added them. "These will do, at least for now."

"And panties?"

She winced. That was a great reminder she hadn't had any underwear on for days now. She groaned and walked back to the lingerie section. It wasn't the time to be squeamish. She should be grateful to have any. She found packages of unopened underwear set off to the side with tags on them, as if a store had just handed over all their old stock. The sizes were once again big. She chose a size she normally would have worn. One had six in the package. She held them up with a question in her eyes.

He nodded. "Absolutely. Can you get a second pack too?"

She looked, but there weren't any more in that size. At the cash register, with the sale, the entire purchase ended up being less than fifty dollars. She stared openmouthed as he paid cash and carried her three large bags with her purchases.

When she got to the truck, she said, "You think she made a mistake?"

"What kind of mistake?"

"There are three bags full of clothes here, and you only paid fifty dollars." She laughed. "I'm loving this."

He helped her into the front of the truck, placing the bags in the back with the boxes. "Next up is home. Go to sleep if you can."

She shook her head. "I don't think I'll be able to."

But she was wrong.

The excitement of getting clothes of her own again had helped to give her a sense of peace. And, as the wheels turned under her, and Eagle drove them steadily homeward, the calmness around her stroked her mind, and she fell asleep.

HE GLANCED OVER and smiled as she gave up the ghost. He'd loved seeing her in the secondhand store. Her reaction to the cost was priceless. He didn't know what her mom might've been like, but he himself had been raised traveling around the world. He and his mom often ended up getting secondhand clothing, if only to replace those destroyed by his rough play. He didn't see any reason not to shop that way. He couldn't have bought a decent jacket in a real store for the fifty dollars he'd spent for everything just now. And, as she regained her weight, these purchases would become too small.

While she'd shopped, he'd sent texts to a couple friends, giving them a few important details. He'd used a code word they'd often employed in the military, letting them know the level of danger he suspected they were in.

Chances were the kidnapping assholes had already checked his license plate and probably knew everything there was to know about him and his property at this point. The kidnappers could be at his place in no time. Eagle drove steadily, watching to make sure they weren't being followed. But he didn't see anything out of the ordinary. They drove up the long driveway, finding the dogs barking at the edge of the gates. As soon as they saw them, they switched from guard dogs to pets.

He unlocked the gate, got back in the truck, and parked near the house. He gave Issa a gentle shoulder shake and said, "Wake up, sweetie."

She bolted upright, fear on her face. When she saw him, she put her hands over her face, and whispered, "Jesus. You scared me."

"We're home."

She stared around in surprise. "I had no idea I had slept so long."

"It wasn't that long. But take it easy. We have some things to unload. I'll go back and lock the gates and check on the property." He turned to her. "I want you to stay in the truck."

She was in the process of opening the door, but she stopped and looked at him. "For how long?"

"Just until I can get a perimeter check."

She closed the door obediently. And sat there.

With the dogs on his heels, he checked the raptor pens and walked around the house and yard. He checked that the house security system was still on. Everything appeared normal. He gave her a thumbs-up, unlocked, and opened the door. Then he grabbed the boxes and carried them inside. On his second trip, he carried the clothes. He turned back to see her slowly making her way to the front door.

Inside, he dumped the three bags on her bed. "You might want to try on a few things."

She walked into the bedroom and closed the door. He put on coffee and turned to look around. With her out of sight, he went to his computer and brought up the security cameras he had installed.

He had several on the property. The first showed nothing. Nobody drove up to the gates; nobody entered the front door. But, as he went to the last camera at the back of the house, directed to the back of the property, he watched as a shadow slowly walked the outside of his interior fence line.

So they'd found him. They just hadn't figured out what to do yet.

CHAPTER 13

INSIDE HER BEDROOM, Issa felt like a little kid again. She dumped out all the clothes on the bed, stripped down, kicking off the overlarge pants and sweatshirt, and started with the underwear. The panties were a little loose, but it was nice to have them regardless. The bra sagged slightly in the front, but it was also doable.

She pulled on a pair of leggings, thinking maybe that would be the best fit and stared in dismay as they looked more like pants than skintight leggings. But they'd have to do. She found a pair of socks, already feeling the chill from losing the heavy clothing, and pulled them on. They came up over the pants. There was one particularly heavy sweatshirt. She pulled it on, laughing as it dropped past her hips.

"Well, it's better than what I was wearing but not by much." She took off that sweatshirt, grabbed a smaller one, and pulled it on. That was better. There was also a sweater. She pulled it on and smiled. "Still a vagabond look," she said to the empty room, "but it's much better than before."

Her feet ached. She took more painkillers and sat down on the bed, her feet propped up, and took off the labels and folded the clothing. She should go back out to the kitchen, but honestly her feet were killing her.

There was a hard knock on her door, then Eagle's head poked around the corner. He studied the clothes she had on and smiled. "You look better."

"I was thinking the same thing," she said, grinning. "It's a step in the right direction. Thanks again."

He held up a cup of coffee. "Do you want this?"

"Yes, please. Do you mind if I stay in here?"

"I was going to suggest you stay in bed and get those feet up."

"I hadn't realized how much they were hurting. I took an extra painkiller before we left, but ..." She shook her head.

"And you walked on them too much, so they'll be puffy and sore."

She nodded.

"Stay in bed, feet up, while I go deal with the animals." He scooped up the tags she'd taken off the clothing. "I'll get rid of these." He pointed to the dresser on the side. "All your clothes can go in there but don't worry about putting them away. When I come back, I'll give you a hand. I want you to stay off those feet."

Just like that he was gone.

She wasn't used to being told what to do and when to do it. She'd spent most of her adult life independent and alone. And, although there'd been relationships, the other men weren't like him. At least none she remembered. Maybe it was just that they all paled in comparison to Eagle. He was one of those big powerful all-encompassing kinds of personalities. When he was in a room, everyone else was dwarfed in size. And yet he had shown her nothing but kindness. And, of course, that capableness was what she loved about him. The sense of power inside and out was huge. It was also incredibly comforting.

Her nap on the ride home in the truck had helped, but

she was still fatigued. She curled up in bed, thinking she'd just rest.

When she woke up again, it was in dismay, realizing long shadows had already appeared outside. Had she slept the entire afternoon away? She got up, used the bathroom, and then slowly made her way to the outside patio door. That was when she realized it was not only late but a storm had moved in. Moving carefully, knowing she shouldn't be walking if she could help it, she walked out into the kitchen to see where Eagle was. There was no sign of him.

She frowned. His laptop was still up, as if he'd just stepped out. But where was he? How long had he been gone?

She sat down at the kitchen table and stared out the window, wondering how long he'd be. She turned her gaze to the laptop, wishing she could remember more of her life. She hadn't been too concerned before—happy to be in her safe bubble. But now that she saw his laptop, it just pulled at her to do a search of her name and to see what popped up. She stared at the screen and realized it was frozen with a time stamp on the bottom. Like a security feed.

She wasn't sure what she was looking at. There was a fence and a shadow. She bent forward, realizing a man was on the other side of this fence—and zoomed in for a better look. That profile was hard to mistake because she'd seen it before. It was one of the men who had kidnapped her.

EAGLE FOUND NO signs of the trespasser. Most people assumed his property was just inside the interior fence. But he had acres spread out as far as he could see.

He didn't want neighbors.

He didn't want trespassers either. And he sure as hell

didn't want intruders. He'd checked the pens. Everything was fine, although there was a distinct air of uncertainty among the birds.

Some were fretting and cawing; others just watched in wariness. The dogs at his side picked up the pace and spread out. There were miles to check. He stooped at the spot where he'd seen the intruder on the video camera. Now it was a matter of tracking him. But so far the man had just followed the interior fence line. He'd moved from side to side. Like a caged tiger on the outside, looking for a way in. Of course that was easy. If he wanted to, he could have gone over, under, or around the fence. Which meant something else stopped him from crossing it. And that was most likely timing, or he was unsure his quarry was inside the house.

Eagle needed to know where the guy had come from. The grass on the outside of the fence wasn't talking. There were no footprints in the sand and gravel on that section of land. But there were footprints on his side of the creek. Keeping to the grass, he tracked the footprints for several acres.

He stopped where the intruder had jumped over the creek. He could see his tracks on the other side. The good thing was there were tracks coming in *and* going out, so the man had left the way he came in. Eagle picked up the pace, almost running as he tracked his prey.

At the back of his property, in the farthest corner, he found a cigarette butt. He bagged it, then put it away in his pocket for safekeeping. He had zero tolerance for people who weren't mindful of the damage a forest fire could bring. In July, the state had burned badly as two out-of-control forest fires had swept across the land. This asshole needed to learn a lesson about leaving his cigarette butts on the ground. Eagle would gladly take on that job when he found him. And there was no doubt in Eagle's mind that he'd catch him. If not today, then soon.

The tracks ended at the road. A vehicle had been parked on the shoulder but was long gone. The intruder was probably on his way back with reinforcements.

Yet why? None of this made any sense. She'd already escaped. If she hadn't told them what they wanted to hear after three weeks or so of torture, surely they now realized she didn't have the information they wanted. So why worry about her now? She'd also been away long enough to tell her story. Shutting her up wouldn't stop anything she'd already put in motion. Although it would stop her from giving witness against them in a criminal court. Was that what this was all about?

Eagle wasn't too worried about justice at a trial. He didn't figure those men would make it that far. It was too damn bad she hadn't had a way to kill more of her captors before she left. It would have saved them all this trouble. But her priority had been getting away, and, given the condition she was in, he knew she wouldn't have survived another day. Something had given her the strength to take advantage of the moment.

Did the kidnappers follow her, either physically tracking her or via an online search of satellite images? The internet made life a lot easier for both the good guys and, unfortunately, the bad.

Eagle was pondering whether he should take a different route back when a truck came barreling toward him. He recognized the old white Ford as the brakes were slammed on, and Gray came to a screeching halt. He rolled down his window and called out, "Hey, what's the matter?"

"An intruder," Eagle snapped.

Gray's jaw dropped. "In the house?"

Eagle shook his head. "By the interior fence line, outside of the house."

"Oh, shit. You think they saw her?"

"No idea." He didn't say that they hadn't been home, so they couldn't have seen her because what he really didn't know and hadn't checked on the time stamp how long the man had been here. Neither had Eagle checked the earlier days to see if this was a second visit or a third. He nodded. "What are you doing here?"

Gray shrugged. "I came to make sure my patient was okay."

Eagle motioned to the cab. "How about you give me a ride back?"

Gray nodded, and Eagle walked around to the passenger side and hopped in, the dogs jumping into the back of the box at his command. It was only a five-minute drive to the front gates. He hopped out and unlocked the gates to let Gray in, then promptly locked the gates again.

When Gray got out, he asked, "Anybody tried to break through the gates?"

Eagle shook his head. "They're steel. Who would even try?"

"Anyone who doesn't know what they are made of might try to just drive right through."

"Not if they're trying for a silent approach," Eagle snapped.

But the thought had already occurred to him. The double-doored gate was on steel poles four feet into the ground with crossbeams. A pickup truck could do some serious damage to it, but it would also do some serious damage to the pickup. He doubted that an engine would survive a head-on collision with his gate. That was enough to make him happy.

He led Gray inside. There he saw Issa curled up on the couch, a blanket over her shoulders. Asleep.

Gray stopped beside Eagle, his expression softening. "At least she's walking."

"Doing too much walking," Eagle snapped. He walked over and put on the coffeepot. He was still on edge. He noticed the laptop was still up, showing the intruder at the fence line too. He closed the lid to not be questioned about it by Gray and walked over to check on Issa.

"Her color is much better," Gray announced. "I don't want to disturb her while she's sleeping."

Just then she bolted upright, shuddering with pain and panic. With her hand to her chest, she took big gulps of air. "You scared me."

"I didn't mean to wake you," Eagle said as he neared her. "How are you feeling?"

She pulled her knees up closer to her chest and murmured, "Cold."

He grabbed another blanket from the stack off on the side and tossed it to her. She smiled and tucked it up close to her neck.

"Were you always cold before you got hurt?" Gray asked.

She raised her gaze to him. Eagle couldn't help but notice the shuttered look on her face. She shook her head. "Not that I remember."

He nodded. "I'm Gray, by the way. The retired doctor who helped fix you up. Do you remember me?"

"Yes, slightly."

"Good. I came to check up on you. I need to look at

that head wound and check over the rest of you. You were pretty badly hurt, young lady."

"I'm doing much better." She relaxed. As if realizing there was no getting out of it, she slowly sat up, dropped the blankets, and said, "Maybe you could do it fast, so I can warm up again."

Eagle helped her out of her sweatshirt. She was wearing a sports bra and one strap had folded the bandage on her shoulder over. He should've helped her get dressed. Inside, he cursed himself. She needed help to do the simplest things as she was still injured. But she hadn't complained all day. He admired that.

STEFAN WOKE IN the morning. Instead of feeling rested and calm, his mind soared through the sky. It was frayed, unraveling outward. First he was in a jungle, and then the scene switched to a rain forest and thereafter to a mountain-top. He didn't know what in hell was going on, but he couldn't seem to ground himself to one reality. Like there was no ground. As if his silver life cord floated in the sky around him, disconnected from everything and yet ... connected to every bit of the world.

Birds flew at his side; tigers roamed below. He could hear the cry of other birds and other animals. They were one with him, and he was one with them, racing across the fields, climbing up the mountains, jumping from hillside to valley. He'd never seen anything like this. But layers and layers of different geographical areas overlaid each other as he stared in surprise. He glanced to the left to see the ocean and trees swimming together.

It made no sense. He sat up slowly and looked down at

his bed. Instead of the cloud he expected to see, he found a tree branch—big and thick, like from an ancient banyan tree. He reached down, so sure the branch was solid, and yet his hand went right through it. He touched where the bedpost should be, trying to keep his rational mind solid and forward thinking.

His mind knew the bedpost was there, but his eyes couldn't see it, and his hand couldn't find it. He stood and walked, only to find he was in the air. As he glanced down at the ocean, he swooped down lower, his feet now above the water. He frowned and sank lower. The water came to his knees. What bizarre magic was this? He turned around and realized, although it felt fantastic, he seemed on overload. Energy and sparks flew off him constantly.

This wasn't a good thing. More and more and more animals raced toward him. They whispered through him, around him—hiding him, lying on him, smothering him—and then suddenly he was gone.

"Stefan?" The voice came through the energy around him.

"Tabitha?"

"Yes. I'm here."

"Where's *here*?" he asked softly. "I feel like I no longer exist. That the only part of me that's real and true is the pieces that each of these animals carry with them."

"You're scaring me, Stefan. Remember to stay grounded."

"I think it's too late for that. I feel lost. I don't know what's happened."

"We have to get you back. Hold out your hand."

He stretched out what he thought was his hand. But, as he stared at it, he saw it was a wing. A big eagle's wing.

"Bizarre and yet so wonderful. It's glorious out here."

"Stefan!"

He struggled to return, listening to the voice.

"Follow my voice. Reach for me."

"Why?" he asked simply. "This is beautiful. Why change it?"

"Celina. Have you forgotten her?"

He tilted his face to the sun. "How can I ever forget her? She's the love of my life."

"Are you expecting her to live alone, to understand you chose this disassociation over her?"

"And yet there is this connection," he murmured, "to everything else." He struggled as he sorted through the different realities in front of him. But Celina's face forever in his heart slid into the forefront of his consciousness.

She laughed, reached up, and kissed him on the forehead. "Do what you must. Know that I'm always with you."

He smiled. "It's okay, Tabitha. Celina says it's okay to leave."

"No," Tabitha said in a stern voice.

He felt that tone. It was a shock, but it was bigger than that. It slipped through time; it slipped through whatever wormhole he was caught in. The animals disappeared. The world around him steadied. He opened his eyes to his bedroom, and standing over him was an ethereal form. He gazed at Tabitha for a long moment with a sense of disappointment and loss.

She smiled and whispered, "You can go back. Even visit with any and all of them. But you must remain grounded."

He whispered, "How is it you can spirit walk when you've never done it before?"

"Look a little more carefully," she whispered. "Now that you are back, I have to get to work." And she disappeared.

He studied the space where she had been and realized she had been held there by somebody he knew well. Then Dr. Maddy, one of his closest friends, was a help to psychics all around the world in too many ways to count. And she always kept a watchful eye on him. "Maddy?"

"Yes, I'm here, Stefan."

"What happened?" he asked as she materialized before him.

"I'm not sure," she admitted. "Your vitals are solid. However, your energy is thin. I think your psyche just got lost in the moment."

"But I was thinking that to be lost was a good thing," he murmured.

"Maybe it's time for a holiday. Leave some of these ugly cases behind and find a way to enjoy life in the physical form for once."

"It's Humbug," he said. "Humbug and Roash."

Her voice curious, Maddy asked, "And who are they?"

He smiled at her and chuckled. "Two birds with very strong wills. They are trying to get to somebody. But they're both injured. And they're drawing me in, drawing on my strength to get where they need to be."

She stared at him in fascination. "So maybe what you were doing was opening up your own energy soul so they could access what they needed without you having to participate?"

He studied her carefully. "It's never happened before."

This time her laugh ran free. "So what? Every day in our world, something new is shown to us. Hug Celina, and go back to sleep."

While he absorbed her words of wisdom, Dr. Maddy disappeared from his bedroom. He closed his eyes, wrapped his arms around the woman he loved and slept.

CHAPTER 14

SSA STARED AT the bullet hole as Gray checked it out. "It's ugly."

"That's also how you got this head injury," Gray added. "One shot hit you high in the shoulder and another just missed you, scraping alongside your head."

She frowned at the older man. "In other words, they missed twice?"

He gave her a half a grin. "You could look at it that way. You're one very lucky lady."

She thought about what she'd been through the last couple weeks. Then her gaze landed on Eagle standing protectively at her side, and she realized she really was lucky. Without Eagle, she'd have been lost. Probably forever.

The poking and prodding became worse as Gray went over her body, checking out each of her wounds.

Eagle helped her remove clothing and then redressed her. By the time she was fully clothed again, her teeth were chattering. He wrapped her in both blankets and held her. "Easy. It's shock." Eagle scooped her up and sat her down in the big armchair. She thanked him with a smile.

Still, she hadn't told him she knew who the man was she'd seen on the laptop. She didn't want to mention it while Gray was there.

Just then Gray brought a cup of coffee and placed it beside her. "Get this down. It will help."

She glanced at the mug, realized he'd put both cream and some kind of sweetener in it. She had watched him do it, but it hadn't registered the cup was for her. She'd heard sugar was good for shock, except she hated her coffee that way.

"So, will I live?" she asked in a laconic voice.

Gray nodded. "You're doing much better than when I saw you last. Have you remembered anything else?"

Instinctively her gaze went to Eagle. He gave a tiny half nod.

She smiled. "Just a little. Nothing major. I know my name is Issa McGuire, and I'm a biologist."

At that Gray's eyebrows shot up. "Really? Well, you two are well matched. Especially if you know anything about birds."

At that her heart froze. She'd checked for Roash earlier but hadn't seen any sign of him. Neither had he come back since they'd returned. Although she'd been sleeping, so maybe he was in the bedroom. She mentally searched for him, but there was no response. That was disheartening. Neither was there anything from Humbug, and that made her heart hurt. He hadn't been at the cabin. So where was he?

She huddled in the chair, drinking her coffee, while the two men discussed various events. Her mind was filled with worry for the birds. She closed her eyes and mentally sent out more signals, calling quietly, *Humbug, hear my voice. Come to me.* She strengthened her tone and commanded the bird to make his way toward her.

In the background she heard an odd screech. She glanced over at the men, but they didn't appear to notice.

She sank back down into the chair again, closed her eyes, and concentrated on sending message after message to Humbug. Then she switched to Roash. *Where are you? Come to me.*

Outside the long screech repeated. She tried to get to her feet, but Eagle was already up, a finger pointed toward her. "Stay. I'll go look."

He bolted to the door and looked from one side to the other. "Now what the devil made that racket?"

She shrugged. "One of the birds." But inside, her heart hammered. Which one had it been?

EAGLE STOOD ON the front porch. He'd grabbed his single shot rifle as he went out the door. It wasn't the most efficient but was deadly accurate. The dogs were beside him, both relaxed, neither one concerned about an intruder. He looked again and thought he heard the same screech. He walked around to the side of the house but found nothing there.

No birds were in the tall trees, and no signs of a large bird anywhere close could be seen. He thought he'd heard an eagle's call. It had an odd tone to it. Then again, everything was odd these days. Sometimes he couldn't trust what he thought he always knew. He walked around the house, making sure nothing was here. Then calling the dogs to heel, he went back inside.

He placed the rifle on the table and caught Issa's raspy breath as she saw it. He gave her a flat stare. "We have a lot of four-legged predators around here too."

She swallowed as her gaze lifted from the rifle. She put down the coffee cup and tucked deeper into the chair. "Did you see anything?"

He shook his head. He knew she was asking if he saw

signs of anyone other than what he expected.

Gray stood. "I better be heading out now. I just wanted to make sure you were doing okay, young lady."

"Thank you very much for looking in on me," she said formally.

Eagle walked Gray back out to his truck. "Is she really doing okay?" Eagle knew she was, but it was reassuring to know a professional could put his stamp of approval on her progress.

Gray slapped him on the shoulder. "She's doing better than I could possibly have imagined. I took a good solid look at that bullet hole, and it's healing very nicely. Almost too nicely," he muttered to himself as he got in his truck.

Eagle frowned. What the hell did that mean? But he didn't dare ask. He opened the gate for Gray.

Still, he'd seen her strange progress for himself. And Gray was right; she was healing very quickly. It could be because she was getting food and warmth, and she was safe, or because her body had a remarkable capacity to heal. Maybe she was not as badly injured as they'd first thought. At least that was an easier concept than thinking something unnatural was going on.

He waited until Gray pulled out, then he locked the gate behind him again. The sun had lowered on the horizon, sending an orange glow across the land. He headed to the pens, handed out food, set up the new batch of eggs in the incubator, checked on the injured, and continued into the house. The dogs needed feeding next.

He filled their bowls, added some leftovers from the night before, and poured some of the gravy he had left in the fridge over it all. They didn't always get something like that, but, when he could share, he did. He walked over and stood in front of Issa. "Gray has gone."

He tried not to see it, but it was hard to miss the whisper of relief that crossed her face. That he could understand. "He isn't one of the men who took you. I know that for sure."

She nodded, then motioned to the laptop. "The man you captured on the security camera is one of the men who *did* kidnap me. And, if he's found me here, you know he'll come back a second time."

Eagle stared at her for a long moment and then gave a clipped nod. "I'm counting on that."

"DID YOU FIND her?" The order came cool, quiet, and deadly.

Dylan nodded. "We're on it." He turned to look at the other men.

The boss barked, "No. Go alone."

Dylan looked at the boss, someone he'd come to regard as his son, and in a lower voice asked, "Why?"

"I don't want any security tripped. We have to make sure nothing goes wrong this time."

He shoved his hands in his jeans. "And if this rancher hobby farmer has brought in more men?"

The boss frowned and tilted his head. "Fine. Take one man. If the rancher has brought in more men than the two of you can handle, then come back and tell me. I'll assess from there."

Relieved, Dylan nodded. "On my way."

He headed outside, one of the new guys in tow, and hopped into the decrepit truck that came with the cabin. He had to twist the wires together under the dashboard for it to start. Then he drove out of the property. It probably wasn't a good thing his mind was looking for ways to escape the boss. It wouldn't have been so bad, but then the boss had kidnapped the little girl. That didn't sit right with Dylan. And what they'd done, ... well, that was just plain bad.

In his mind Issa would always be a little girl. That she'd grown into a beautiful young woman—one he'd tortured—was not something he'd been able to face. Just because no mirrors were around didn't mean he was capable of accepting what he'd done.

For some reason being in America had changed the boss. Dylan didn't like that. He liked certainties. He liked things he could count on. He needed to know white was always white, and black was always black. Apparently it no longer was. But what he did know was, until he found Issa and could confirm where she was, the boss would never let Dylan off the hook.

CHAPTER 15

ISSA STARED AT Eagle in horror. "You *want* them to attack?"

"An attack is always better than sitting and waiting. And better if they don't know exactly what or who they're attacking," he said. "I don't sit here and take bullets for anybody."

She slowly closed her mouth. "You have a plan?" she asked hopefully.

He shrugged. "I don't know that it's a plan exactly. But I'm not helpless."

She glanced around. "Do you have any place to hide? Any escape routes they wouldn't know about?"

"No, but I do have traps set all around the outside of the property. They won't get to us without us knowing."

"They got to the outside of the interior fence without us knowing," she pointed out. "So how can you say that?"

"Because I just set up a few more traps." His tone was cool as he showed her the cameras pointed at his latest additions.

That shut her up. At least for a moment. Then she shook her head. "I should leave. Just drop me in town and drive away."

"What good will that do? They will still come after you, no matter where you run to."

She winced. "Then what *can* I do?"

He crouched down in front of her. "You can go through your mother's boxes, so we know exactly what we're up against."

Her gaze widened. "I totally forgot." She struggled to her feet.

"No, none of that." He scooped her up and plunked her down on the kitchen chair. "Sit here. I'll get the boxes."

She glanced around but saw no sign of them. "Where did you put them?"

"In my office." He turned and walked away. When he returned a few minutes later, he carried both boxes.

She'd settled with her feet up on a second chair. He put the bigger box with the paperwork on a third chair beside her. The leather keepsake box he put down slightly midway on the big table.

"We'll start with the paperwork from your mother."

"Good. Because I'm not sure I'm ready to open the other one," she said shortly.

The cardboard box was full. At least a dozen brown manila envelopes were inside and a couple smaller envelopes, like to mail letters in. She stared at them for a long moment. But she never made a move to open them. He stepped forward and said in a low voice, "You want me to help?"

She nodded. "It would be a lot faster if you did."

He took everything out of the box, set the box off to the side, sorted the envelopes into a stack. He handed her an envelope and took the second one for himself.

She opened the first flap and gasped. "This is my birth certificate." Tears came to her eyes as she added in a hoarse whisper, "And my brothers'."

He stepped up behind her and read the names. "Well, at

least it's your name." He checked the rest of them. "Your three brothers were born twelve and fourteen and sixteen years ahead of you. Twelve years between you and the last one. That's a lot of years."

She nodded. "I know. I don't know if I was an accident or if they just kept trying for more."

Behind the birth certificates was her parents' wedding certificate.

"This one appears to be important family documents." She slowly went through them. "Here is my father's birth certificate. These are my brothers' and my mother's." She was drowned in data by the time she hit the middle of the file. "This is all very fascinating, but it really has nothing to do with my current issue," she said when she got to the end.

"No, but it's a huge gift. To have all that information. It means you can trace your family roots, and then it's your choice if you want to reconnect or not."

She sighed. "True enough. But not yet. It feels all too wrong." She put down the envelope and reached for the one in front of Eagle. "What's in this one?"

"I'm not sure," he said. "It looks like a ledger."

It was only one-quarter of the thickness of the envelope she had already gone through. There were maybe a dozen sheets of paper in it. On one column was a set of three letters. The second one contained a description, followed by three columns listing money, like a total and how much was paid out in a running total.

She frowned. "It's probably my dad's records."

"From smuggling?"

She nodded. "I know he paid the men after a shipment was sold."

She quickly flipped through the different sheets, seeing

nothing to change her opinion. When she got to the end, she shrugged and said, "All this information is more than twenty years old. I highly doubt it's got any relevance today."

She put the envelope on top of the others, and he handed her the first of them. She turned it over in her hands, frowning. "I'm surprised it's not labeled."

"You can go through and label them now," he said drily.

She shot him a look. "I know I'm taking my time. I'm just realizing how painful some of these memories are."

"I understand. I also understand we could be under an imminent attack, and it would help to have the answers these men are looking for."

She gave him a shuttered look and nodded. She opened the top envelope and pulled out its contents. It was everything to do with her brother Ethan. His school reports, records, copies of his immunizations. Basically a synopsis of the twenty-two-year-old's life, from a doting mother's perspective, although most of the information stopped when he finished school. Sniffling, Issa said, "My eldest brother's school records. I suspect there's one for each of us." She closed the envelope and put it aside on the tabletop, grabbing the next one. "Yes, this is for Sean, my middle brother." She closed it and went to the third one. "This is Liam's envelope." He was eighteen when he died. It hurt to look at the pictures from school and see the smiling face she could barely remember. She touched his face and shook her head. "How could he have been such a major part of my life for so long, and now it's almost impossible to remember who he was?"

"And the last one?"

She opened it up. "It's mine." Inside was a single picture of when she'd been a very young child. On her shoulder was a falcon. She sat back, and this time the tears would not be held back. *Hadrid.*

As she stared at her childhood photo, her fingers stroked the feathers of the only creature who understood who she was.

"HAVE YOU ALWAYS had an affinity for birds?" Eagle asked.

But she didn't look up. Instead, she seemed lost in the passage of time. Her finger slid down the feathers of the bird resting on her shoulder.

As he thought of the relationship he had seen between her and Roash, he could see she had a deep-rooted passion that had obviously started in childhood. "Was that your falcon?"

As she raised her gaze to meet his, he could see the tears sparkling over her beautiful blue eyes. "Yes. No." She shook her head. "It seems he was always a part of me."

"What happened to him?"

Her shoulders hunched. "When I lost my father and brothers, I also lost Hadrid. I don't know if he lived, died, was captured, or stolen away." She shook her head. "I'm pretty sure he's dead though."

"Why's that?"

She gave him a challenging stare. "Because I no longer feel him."

And that was at the heart of the matter. He pulled out a chair and sat down quietly beside her, but he didn't drop his gaze. But at least he was no longer looming over her. He kept the two of them linked as he searched for the truth. What he could see was that, as far as she was concerned, she spoke the truth. Whether she had actually felt the bird's life presence or not, he had no idea. He'd never felt such a thing with another person, let alone an animal. But, in her mind, she couldn't feel the falcon, so he didn't exist anymore.

"And do you feel that way about Roash?" he asked.

She nodded. "Yes, I felt him and Humbug both. Plus a couple others, but they weren't as strong." She sniffled slightly. "None are as strong as the bond I had with Hadrid."

He let out his breath slowly as his body sagged in the chair. "When you say *feel*, what do you mean?" He didn't know any other way to ask such a question except directly.

"I could feel him inside my head, chattering away at me when he was upset, when he was happy, and when he was in distress. I could also feel him in my heart. He was there when I woke up in the morning, and he was there when I went to sleep at night. When he soared in the sky, it was as if I was there with him." She wiped the tears from her eyes. "After he died, and we moved to America, there was nothing for so long. Yet I tried so hard. I called the birds all around me, looking for that same connection. I was like an amputee missing not just an arm but both legs. I was completely crippled. Maybe that's why I couldn't speak for so long. The voice in my mind had gone silent, so my own voice did too."

She dropped her gaze to stare down at the picture. She sniffled once and then again. Regaining control, she slowly placed the picture down and covered it with her hand, not to hide it, but as if she could see the images through her palm. When she raised her gaze again, some of the sadness had slipped back.

He could see her grief, but it wasn't as sharp.

"I joined the falconry club for that reason. I thought surely everybody else would have the same connections. My parents had told me to stop making up stories. My brothers used to laugh at me. But, in my heart of hearts, I knew what I had was real. So when I found out there were clubs with people dealing with the same birds, I was sure I'd found people like me."

"And did you?"

A ghost of a smile peeked out. She shook her head. "Just as there are men and their dogs, and old ladies and their cats, there were men and their birds. But nobody I spoke to had the kind of deep connection like I was talking about."

She gave a broken laugh. "Of course I was limited to who and what I could ask about without appearing to be crazy. I learned early that nobody appreciated me discussing my relationship with my falcon. They were quite happy to use it for their own purposes, but they certainly weren't open to acknowledging that such a bond was possible."

He latched onto the one word that he could understand. "*Use* it?"

She wrapped her arms around her chest as if once again cold.

But he figured it was more the chill of time and bad memories than the actual temperature of the room.

She gave a lopsided grin and said, "Can you see any other reason why a six-year-old would be a lookout for smugglers? A role I'd played since I was three."

His cup landed on the table with a *bang*. He leaned forward. "Are you saying the falcon was the lookout, and somehow he communicated to you what was going on, whether the men were safe or not?"

Her smile brightened. "Exactly. That's also the reason why my mother was inside the house during those times. I'm not sure she believed in what Hadrid did, but it gave her an excuse to stay inside."

He shook his head in disbelief. "That's a lot of trust to place on a trained bird."

"He didn't have any other use as far as my family was concerned, and they didn't like him. However, he was one of the reasons I could never be punished. My father and my mother both feared reprisals from Hadrid. His claws and talons were huge. If he hadn't been so useful, my father would've shot him."

She said it so starkly that Eagle didn't have a problem believing her. He sank back in his chair. "Well ..."

She chuckled. "Yes. We were a little rough around the edges. But the reason why I stayed safe was because of Hadrid. As long as he worked with me to keep the men safe, they understood his value. But, if he were to fail, then his existence would have been snuffed out instantly."

"Did he ever fail?"

She stared at him. Great big wells darkened her gaze as she turned inward. "My mother said he did. I don't see how he could have. But that night was dark and stormy. He was out flying, as always, searching, looking far below to see who was coming and who was not. I had directed him up the coastline and then back again, around the roads close to home. And he found nothing. He never did. I told my father that. And all went as planned. And then I don't know what happened. Somehow somebody found out what my dad was doing." Her voice was bleak and dry. "I could hear the gunfire, the shouting. And then there was nothing. Just silence." She took a deep breath. "And Hadrid never called me again."

"What did your mother do?"

Issa frowned. "I don't remember exactly. She was with Angus, a family friend, one of my dad's men. I was surprised to find him there, so I hid. I was scared, calling out, searching for Hadrid everywhere."

"Searching? Were you running from window to window to look for him?"

She snorted. "In my mind I was reaching out in every direction I had sent him, calling, beseeching him to come home. I couldn't live without him."

"And?"

She shook her head. "I never felt him again. I kept trying, unable to believe the truth. But the house filled with men. My mother snatched me up a few days later. We rushed away in the night to never return." She stared at Eagle. "The kidnappers knew me. They knew me from way back when. Most of the kidnappers were young, but one was way older. Although I never saw the boss, so I don't know about him."

"Maybe they were the same ages as your brothers back then?"

She shrugged. "How would I know? I barely remember my brothers as it is. Too many years were between us, and I was an oddity. I had a huge falcon as my guardian. That gave me almost a mythical supernatural presence. My brothers both hated Hadrid and were afraid of him. But my family received a certain reverence from everyone else, and they basked in the attention. But dare I fail ..." She got up, shifted her position, and sat down again. She looked to the coffeepot. "Could you get me another cup?"

He bounced to his feet, shaking his mind free of what she'd told him. He couldn't imagine how odd that would've been, or why the falcon would've latched himself onto her. That she could send him out and keep watch was surely just a coincidence. The men had been damn lucky to have operated under the eyes of the law for so long. At some point, of course, their luck was bound to run out. Then they would've blamed her and the bird. He shook his head, wondering about men, such as those in her family, as he picked up the coffeepot and brought it back. As he raised it to pour the liquid into her cup, there was a single gunshot, and the coffeepot exploded in his hand.

CHAPTER 16

ISSA FOUND HERSELF flat on the floor, covered in glass shards and ... Eagle. Her mind tried to process what had happened, when she realized Eagle was already up, at the window with a rifle in hand, studying the darkness outside. She could see the hole in the window by the shutter. The hot coffee had splattered over the table and the floor.

She quickly removed the paperwork from the dark liquid that even now spread across the surface. Shuffling her way to the stove, she grabbed several paper towels and quickly sopped up the wet mass.

Using more paper towels, she collected as much of the glass as she could, being careful to brush off both seats, the table, and all around where they'd been sitting.

She remained on the floor. She had no doubt who was outside. The trouble was, she still hadn't had a chance to go through the paperwork to know if it held the answers the kidnappers were looking for. She moved the bigger box underneath the table and put the envelopes she'd gone through back in it. While she kept a wary eye on Eagle at the window, she grabbed another envelope. It was on her father. She flipped through it quickly. But nothing worth killing over was revealed inside.

In the second-to-last large envelope were pages on her mother. Issa smiled, grateful to have at least that much information. One small envelope remained beside her. She opened it and pulled out pictures. They were all of her and Hadrid. There was a bill of sale and a name of the seller: Angus. He had sold Hadrid to her father. The pictures and envelope she tucked into her pocket. She'd do a lot to keep them. But she had yet to go through one big envelope.

She didn't even bother to ask questions as Eagle moved from window to window, checking outside. She was too intent on sorting the remnants of her life.

She remembered the security photo she'd seen on Eagle's computer. Had the shooter missed on purpose with his latest shot? Or did the bullet coming through the window glass deflect his aim? She almost felt the hair rise on her head as the bullet had passed so close that it could've killed her. Now under the table, half around the side of the couch, she didn't think she was in the line of fire.

But who was to say the shooter was alone? A half-dozen men could be ready to storm the house. She'd never held a gun in her life. She didn't even know the first thing about them.

She looked down at the pile of broken glass she'd collected, chose one long shard, and set it down beside her, just in case. Then she grabbed for the last envelope in the box, asking Eagle, "Did you see anything?"

"No, not yet. Are you okay?"

"I'm fine. Going through the last envelope of this box. Hoping for answers."

Just then one of the dogs came over to lick her face. Obviously, if they were doing that, the danger must have downgraded.

She opened the envelope but did not understand what she was looking at.

Until she got halfway through and realized it was the same information she'd glanced at when she took the boxes out of her mother's apartment. The sheets contained information on criminal charges, legal documents, and police reports. An investigation into her father's activities. She frowned when she saw the dates. Just months before he died.

How could her mother have gotten this information? And how serious were the charges against her father? Would somebody have killed him to stop him from saying something about somebody else? There was no damn time to go through it now in greater detail. She replaced the documents in the envelope, repacked it in the box, putting this packet on top.

As Eagle continued to keep watch, she reached for the smaller keepsake box. She pulled it to the floor beside her and flipped it open. The light was poor underneath the table, but she found another envelope—similar to the one that contained pictures of her with Hadrid.

Only these photos were of a different falcon with an older man. It was Angus. She didn't recognize the falcon. Birds often chose their own bonding partner. It didn't matter what the human said.

As she continued through a small stack of letters banded together, she saw death threats. Letters blaming Issa, blaming her bird, Hadrid, for the failure that night. She realized how many people knew of her and Hadrid. It was a small community, but everybody benefitted from the smuggling. And, with that colossal failure that led to so many deaths, the villagers' lives and way of living were all in danger.

Issa was shocked at the hatred expressed in those letters. She and her mother remained in Ireland only a few more days before bolting for America.

The villagers feared what they hadn't understood. There was admiration as long as things were going well. But, once that turned sour, the community needed to expunge her and Hadrid from their presence. Maybe her mother had left Ireland by choice. Maybe they'd been forced out. Issa had no idea. She quickly folded the letters back into their envelopes and put the elastic band back around them. Why had her mother kept these poisonous reminders? In the bottom of the box was one more envelope. She pulled it out to find several loose-leaf pages.

It was a letter her mother had written on the day her father had died.

> *It's my fault. Dear God in heaven, there can be no salvation for this. For the rest of my days I will know no peace for the part that I played in this travesty. My sons, all three of them, have died by my actions. My husband too, brutal and uncaring in the eyes of the law and in the eyes of God, yet my husband. He is also dead by my incompetence. I should have been watching over my family but was instead concerned with only myself. I know not how to make things right. I can only run and hide in shame and hope the world never finds out what I did.*

Tears filled Issa's eyes. She held the letter against her chest, feeling the sobs threatening to come out.

When she went to read the letter again, her tears started again. Unable to deal with the emotions at the moment, she quickly folded it and stuffed it inside her sports bra. She slipped her hand around the bottom of the box and found a key. She studied it for a long moment. It looked like a safe-deposit box key. Maybe it was older, something from her previous life. She had no way to know. Should she stuff that in her bra too? If she was captured, the key would be found on her body, and she'd be in real trouble then. She tried to remember all the questions the kidnappers had asked of her.

But, at the moment, her mind was too shocked to consider if anything she'd seen in these boxes was related to her kidnapping. She repacked the contents into the leather-bound keepsake box and hid it under the couch. And then unpacked all the envelopes about her brothers' lives and her father's and mother's lives from the bigger cardboard box. She tucked the little envelopes and the manila envelopes under the couch with the keepsake box and slid the now-empty cardboard box off to the side, as if it was just an empty box from bringing groceries home.

On her hands and knees, the shard of glass in her pocket, she peered around the side of the couch. "Eagle, are you here?"

"I'm behind you," Eagle said, his voice quiet. "Did you hide what you wanted to keep?"

She started, but of course he'd seen her. "It's all stuff I don't want to lose. I figured that fancier-looking keepsake box would look more important. So I hid it with my family's information from the other box."

"Good thinking. But it's probably better to hide them somewhere safe."

"Agreed, but where is that?"

After a long moment of silence, he said, "Good point."

"Which brings me back to the question I asked earlier. Do we have any way of getting out of here?"

"If we can reach the truck, we do."

Just then a huge loud, noxious ringing sounded out across the property, followed by several sharp splitting sounds and loud screams.

All leading to silence.

She started to tremble. "What was that?" she asked, her voice barely a whisper.

"My security system."

She buried her face against his chest and held on tight. Finally he relaxed his grip on her and said, "I have to go check."

She gave a broken laugh. "Check what? That they're not dead? Did you just kill all those men?"

"What men?" He tilted her chin up and said, "I only saw one man out there. Don't confuse this with the kidnappers."

She frowned. "How can you tell there was just one now?"

"I can't for sure until I look. But I only heard one man scream."

She let out a heavy breath and nodded. "Is it safe for you to check? What if they're waiting for you to step out the door?"

He gave her a grim smile. "I wasn't planning on letting anyone see me." He carefully shifted around the couch. "Stay here. I don't want to accidentally hurt you because you pop up where you don't belong." He tossed her a blanket. "Bundle up and stay warm."

She nodded. "Please come back."

"I plan on it." And with that he was gone.

She didn't hear which direction he left the cabin, and she hadn't gotten a chance to search or even explore the house fully. As she lay here, she realized she also hadn't seen Roash. She sent out a call to him. And heard his response. She smiled. At least he was alive. What about Humbug? And damn if she didn't get an answering flicker from Humbug too.

With her eyes closed, she sent out a search and probe, trying to see how far away Roash was. She had used a mental image of a map to show Hadrid so he would know where to search for her father's enemies and to give a warning if he saw anyone.

She'd send him a visual image of the coast and would have him soar up and over. She had seen images as he flew. The system had worked fine. Until that one night when she'd seen what she shouldn't have seen, and she'd had trouble getting Hadrid's images. Maybe that night of smuggling would have ended very differently, if she hadn't seen her mother in bed with Angus.

Something she hadn't ever told anyone.

But she knew. And Issa understood her mother's guilt now that Issa was an adult herself. But, dear God, the price she had paid, the price her brothers and father had paid, had been horrific.

Calming her mind, she tried to direct Roash to show her what he saw.

But it hadn't worked with him yet.

She'd never had another connection like the one she'd had with Hadrid. Roash had never been able to show her anything. All she could do was get an impression of where Roash and Humbug might be, two dots burning in the night. But ...

They weren't far apart. In fact, she wondered if Roash wasn't at Humbug's side. She sent out a series of questions, more emotional responses, searching, asking for Humbug. And she realized the two birds *were* together. And that was one hell of a good thing. Except Humbug couldn't fly far, and Roash's wing was also damaged.

She'd done what she could to give both birds enough energy to fly. She hadn't had much more to give them. In fact, she'd been using Roash's energy to heal her wounds. With Humbug responding, she sent him pulses of loving energy. Something she'd learned to do with Hadrid. Whenever he was fatigued from a long flight, she'd send him her energy mentally. As a small child, she'd had bundles of it. He seemed to do much better when she would open up her heart and surround him with love.

It'd been so easy back then. Now, as an adult, she felt like she was arguing with her own mind, her own belief system. She tried to figure out how to help the two birds. And all the while she couldn't stop thinking about Eagle outside, walking the perimeter, looking for intruders.

And possibly a man he might've killed. Or a man waiting to kill him.

While she couldn't help Eagle, what she could do was help Roash and Humbug. She opened up her heart, surrounded Roash with love and built a stream of energy between Roash and Humbug. If she helped Roash, maybe he could help Humbug. They were hurting, but they were both still mobile and fighting. She could sense them. Could hear their calls in her mind, in her heart. She caught another faint voice in the background. She strained to hear it and realized with a shock that it was Gillian.

The tiny saw-whet owl that used to sit on her fence post. Somehow Gillian had found Issa. As had the others.

Instantly she opened her heart a little more toward them all, sending more love in that direction. If the birds were looking for her, she was desperate to let them find her. She'd lost so much. She didn't want to lose any more. She was deep into sending out her loving energy when she suddenly realized birdcalls came at her from all directions.

Hundreds and hundreds of them.

She didn't understand what was going on, and she couldn't disconnect. She wouldn't anyway. Birds in the distance between her and Roash seemed to be calling out to her. Some crying, some rejoicing. As if the connection was new for them too. Confused and startled, yet open to the concept, Issa punched down all barriers to every hidden corner in her heart. If the birds wanted to connect, she'd do everything she could to let them.

The cries came in waves of noise, each distinct yet blended into an orchestra of joy.

She couldn't get sidetracked. She needed to help Roash and Humbug—to see what they saw. She needed Roash to send her images so she could see where he was, where Humbug was. She tried to tell Humbug to send her images, but Humbug was always sweet and silly. Not too interested in doing the work. Yet Roash had shown such promise in the beginning. Now it was as if he couldn't hear her. Or was too tired to function.

In frustration, she finally shut down, feeling her own energy draining. It was useless. What had been so natural at one point was now just impossible. A voice broke through her mind.

That's because you're trying too hard.

She sat up slowly and peered around the house. "Who said that?" Surely someone was here.

I did, the man said. *And, no, I'm not in your house. I'm in your mind.*

"Who are you?" It was almost like he floated on air around the edges, fuzzy. "There's no way you can be talking to me in my mind."

I'm Stefan. Tabitha is here with me too.

She frowned, recognizing the names. "You're the psychics?"

We are, Tabitha said. *With a penchant for helping those who are hurt and injured. In your case, and in my case, animals.*

"Can you feel Roash and Humbug? Gillian's out there too," Issa asked. "Can you help them?"

All we can do is bond our energy to yours to give you more strength so you can help them yourself…

She flung back the blankets, her mind rapidly trying to figure out how this would work. "I just tried, but I didn't have enough power," she said, knowing this was a bizarre conversation as she talked out loud to an empty room. "And Roash wasn't getting the message. Hadrid used to send me images of where he was flying. Roash doesn't seem capable of doing that. And Humbug is even worse," she cried out in despair, only partially realizing they mustn't have a clue who she was talking about. Not to mention they were talking in her mind, and she wasn't fazed in the least. It seemed so normal. Besides she'd do anything to help her friends.

A long moment of silence passed, and then Stefan chuckled. *It wasn't Hadrid sending you the images,* he said gently. *How could he have?*

His voice filled the room as if her mind was on a megastereo system. If she wasn't so desperate to get help for her birds, she knew she would think she was nuts. But she was willing to do anything to get her birds back.

That's a good thing, Stefan said. *Because you have to be willing to do anything. Like I said, it's not that Hadrid was sending you the images. He had accepted you in his consciousness, and you flew with him. You're the one who sent the messages to your father, saying that all was clear. Hadrid couldn't send pictures on that defining day where your life changed. And neither could you because your own mind was still locked on the images of what you'd seen in the house. You were so upset you couldn't connect with Hadrid. The bird was not at fault.*

She finished that thought for him. "I was," she said as the faint cry of intense pain sliced through her. "It's my fault they are all dead."

No, Stefan said harshly. *It was your mother's actions that led to that disaster. You were only six years old, bonded to a falcon in a way that most adults could never understand. I don't know how. I don't know where. All I can see is your energy. But you have to do what you must now, if you want to save Humbug. And please save him because his cries of distress are driving through my own consciousness. I can't track the owl. I just know he's in Colorado.*

"He's trying to fly," Issa said. "But his wings are damaged. He's an oversized baby. I'm trying to send him energy for the journey until he can reach me. I've been trying to send Roash that same energy too because I think he's flown to be with Humbug."

Silence came again, and then Stefan let out a long slow sigh. *Of course. That's why they tortured you. They tortured you so you would cry for help, and they could find the same falcon you had as a child, or another one equal to him, so they could use again what didn't belong to them.*

She started to sob. "They must have known my dad in Ireland. They figured, if they found me, they'd find the bird. Instead, I had broken birds. Not the majestic one of my childhood. There was more to it—I just don't know what."

But they knew that, if you didn't have another bonded fal-

con, they could force you to show them how you work with the falcon so that they could do it too. And, if you didn't show them how, they'd kill you trying. Never understanding it wasn't something they could force.

"Yes," she whispered, the truth and the pain slamming through her. "I don't dare be caught again."

You won't, Stefan whispered. *I will help.*

Tabitha's voice was already fading as she whispered, *So will I.*

"What about Eagle?" she asked. "Who'll help him? He's outside right now, searching the property for somebody who just shot at us. Who's going to help him?"

Then again came that same faint chuckle. And Stefan whispered, *You are.*

EAGLE STARED AT the bloodstains outside the fence, anger radiating from his shoulders outward. No way that asshole should've gotten up and walked away, not from the amount of blood here. That meant he wasn't alone. That also meant somebody was coming back. He turned to study the house and wondered if it was time to pull up stakes and leave.

But no way could he do that with all his responsibilities for the birds. Even if he opened the cages and let them go, most of them couldn't go anywhere. Between the broken and crippled legs, missing feet, busted wings, and many other things, the birds weren't capable of going far. That was why he was here doing what he was doing. Everyone needed a second chance at life.

And, as he considered Issa inside the house, he realized he felt the same way about her. But she was in too much danger here. Except it wasn't like he could put up a sign, saying she was no longer here, get the hell away. Because assholes were assholes, and they wouldn't give a damn. They'd burn the property to the ground just to make sure.

He followed the tracks back to the highway again, the bloody trail easy to see, particularly when he'd gotten to the fence. The injured man had rested against the fence, then climbed over—likely with help. Both sides of the wood were covered in fresh blood. That, in itself, would bring in more predators.

He'd be totally okay with that. He just wished that the four-legged predators would take out the two-legged ones. He had no trouble doing the job himself, but obviously his security needed a bit more work.

Returning to the house, he quickly reset the system.

Inside he found Issa sitting cross-legged on the couch, her hands palm up, like a yoga meditation pose. But her head had dropped to the back of the couch, and her gaze stared straight at the ceiling.

The hairs on the back of his neck lifted. She had exhibited the same behavior before. He carefully walked over and studied her gaze. He'd been racking his brain for a logical explanation since the first time he'd seen her like this. It was so bizarre and so otherworldly, so far off the state of normal that he had no idea how to deal with it.

And that same weirdness was happening all over again. If he could just accept that and move forward, it would help them all. The dogs lay down in front of her feet. He crept a little closer and stared down into Issa's wide-open gaze. Once again her eyes glowed. As if he could see blue skies twisted with midnight stars. A sense of timelessness.

He shook his head, crouched lower to see what she was staring at …

Something was going on above him. He knew it couldn't come from anything other than her, but, at the same time, there was just no reason for it to be here in the first place. He couldn't make out what he was seeing. ... His mind couldn't make sense of the weird sparkling ball of color up in the rafters of his ceiling. Was that a field? A lake? He didn't know what the hell was going on. He extended his hand to touch Issa, to have her wake up, and one of his dogs growled.

He turned to stare at Gunner, only to have Hatter step forward, an odd look in his eyes.

"Well, I'll be," Eagle said softly, frowning at the dog's behavior. "What's the matter, Hatter?" Eagle reached out again toward Issa, and again Hatter growled.

"You don't want me to touch her, is that it? I won't hurt her," he said incredulously, and he let his hand fall away. He stared at the dog. "What the hell?"

His phone rang. He pulled it quickly from his pocket, realizing the noise had disturbed Issa in a way. Her gaze was still locked on the ceiling above them, but her hands went limp in her lap.

"Hello?" he said in a low tone.

"You can't touch her when she's like this," Stefan said. "She's contacting Humbug and Roash."

Swallowing hard, Eagle pinched the bridge of his nose, straightened, and strode toward the front door, leaning against it. "You realize we had intruders tonight, right? She was busy hiding documents we took from her mother's house. I came back in from making sure nobody was around, only to find her sitting in this bizarre position." He threw out his left hand in frustration. "I go to touch her, and my dog growled at me. I raised that dog from a pup." He glared into the phone. "And, out of the blue, you call me again. What the hell is going on?"

"I suggest you take some time to study psychics, empaths, and realize that you have an incredibly strong one on your couch. Her skills *could* be limited to just birds, but the entire natural world will be affected by the rippling effect of what she can do. If your dog did that, the chances are he could see what you can't see, and he's bonded with her in some way."

"When the damn falcon returned, he was riding on my other dog's back," Eagle snarled. "That's when I found her nude in the long grass. She'd been tortured. Now she's being hunted. Do you know how far off the deep end I've gone here?" There was a long silence. The air buzzed around him.

"Yes, I do," Stefan said quietly. "I know you're not a big fan of the law, but it might be something to consider this time."

"Well, that's not going to happen. If I was to do that, I would've when she first arrived at my place."

"True, but these men, they won't stop," Stefan said carefully. "You might consider getting some help."

"I don't know why the hell I should believe you."

"You looked me up. You know I'm for real. I also do a ton of work for law enforcement. Hadrid, the falcon of Issa's childhood, is part of the reason Issa was held captive and tortured, I believe. These men won't stop until they get what they want."

"But it's dead, right?" Eagle asked cautiously.

"Yes, I believe it is dead. If they capture her once more, they'll take her underground, and you won't see her again. But something else is going on here—you need to be careful."

Eagle spun around and stared at the frail, gentle woman on his couch. "Nothing makes sense."

"You and I both know that underneath the surface of our pretty lifestyle there is a much tougher element. People go missing all the time. It's all about power, money, and, by no fault of her own, Issa's caught up in the middle of it."

"Does this have anything to do with her childhood?"

"I said it did," Stefan said testily.

"She brought home two boxes from her mother's place. Issa's place had been trashed, but the intruders missed these because she'd tucked them in a hidden root cellar," Eagle said quietly. "There's a lot of information about her family."

"You need to go over it. All of it. A lot more is going on than you can see from the surface."

"I can't see anything on the surface. Seems like everything is going on in the bloody atmosphere around me."

There was a space of silence yet again, and then Stefan chuckled. A warm approving chuckle. He said, "Now that is very true. If you have one job in this life, it's to keep her safe. She can keep many others safe, but she has no one to help her."

"What do you mean, she can keep others safe?"

Click.

He stared down at the damn phone and wanted to rage. He hit Redial, and the phone went to voice mail. "I don't know what the hell's going on," he said to the room, "but this is beyond me."

No, it's not, Stefan whispered in Eagle's mind. Then he disappeared leaving a void of truth.

It didn't matter what was going on. Eagle couldn't just up and leave this special woman unprotected. He couldn't let anyone hurt her ever again. As he turned to stare at the frail woman on his couch, he realized he was already in too deep. Even after his best efforts to keep his heart free and clear, she'd walked in and somehow walked out with a chunk of it. He'd gotten attached to this waif with her mythical skills. What the hell could *he* do to keep her safe?

"DYLAN, HOW BADLY hurt is the new guy?" the boss asked.

Dylan hunched his shoulders, then knelt closer. He stared down at the kid who was barely old enough to shave and said, "Bad enough he'll probably need surgery."

Dylan knew what would come next. And he couldn't do a damn thing about it. He sat back on his heels and waited. Sure enough, there was a shot, and the back of the kid's head splattered red across the blanket. He stood and shoved his fists deep into his pockets. He knew his life sucked when they were putting kids like this one out of their misery instead of giving them medical care, even though doing the job given them.

The kid had done everything right. But nobody had expected a security system like that. Even now Dylan wasn't sure what they'd run into. Was it bullets? He'd taken some bullets, but these were almost like darts, and one of them had hit a vital spot, and he bled really badly. But not any longer.

"Same place as last one?" he asked.

"You even need to ask?" the boss said. "What the hell is wrong with everyone? Is everybody over here incompetent?"

Dylan kept his mouth shut. He knew it was frustration causing the boss to boil. But he was dangerous right now. In fact, Dylan had never seen the boss more dangerous. Every day that this nightmare went on, things just got worse and worse. He was pretty damn sure the girl was there, and that was just making the job that much harder.

Dylan yanked the edge of the blanket, rolled up the kid as best he could, and then grabbed the last corner of the blanket, dragging the body to the front porch. It seemed like all Dylan did now was bury people. Young men who deserved a full chance at life. When had he had a change of heart? Or had he? Was it just a slow shift in time? Or too many men dead? Too many burials? Too many mothers who would never know the fates of their sons?

It wore on him.

Maybe it was just that slow weakening of his spirit, telling him that something was badly wrong in his world. And not only in his world but in everyone's.

Would the boss hire anybody else? He'd killed the last several. Dylan just knew that the next guy would get a bullet one way or another too. Likely before this was all over, Dylan would see one with his name on it as well. He didn't have a whole lot he was proud of in his life. But he hadn't been ashamed of anything—until these last few months.

He put his thoughts behind him and dragged the kid out to the front, then went for the tractor. But, in the back of his mind, he wondered what the hell he would do. Was there anything he could do? Or was he just going to wait until that last bullet found him?

CHAPTER 17

ISSA OPENED HER eyes, her mind swirling with images and thoughts and feelings. But at the center of all of it was a chill. She held up her hand and saw her white skin and blue veins. She could hardly feel her feet.

Almost instantly Eagle bent down, picked her up, swore at how cold she was to the touch, and whispered, "I don't know what you keep doing to yourself, but, whatever it is, it seems to suck the warmth right out of your bones."

Her teeth chattered. She agreed but couldn't quite get the words out.

"Don't talk," he whispered. He carried her back into the bedroom and tucked her under the covers. "I'll make you a hot cup of tea. Try to warm up."

He raced into the kitchen, leaving her where she lay. The chattering of her teeth got worse. But she didn't understand why she was so cold. She had just been sitting on the couch. He'd been the one outside, and she hadn't even asked him if he had found anything. Vaguely she remembered the screams in her head.

"You killed someone," she whispered. But he wasn't close enough to hear.

Maybe she needed a hot bath. That might take the chill away from her soul. But she doubted it. Her mind was caught up in images from both her past and present. Stefan was there on the edges. He seemed to come from a more advanced belief system than she had.

It was hard to imagine what he was capable of. She couldn't even remember how her relationship with Hadrid had developed. Or what she'd done to make it so close. She hadn't been able to duplicate it in all the years since either. What she had with Roash was like water to rich cream. Hadrid had bonded to her in a way she'd never understood and hadn't even tried to understand. She'd just accepted it.

She froze at that. Was that what Stefan meant? To not try so hard? Just to accept?

At the same time, memories of her mother in bed with another man while Issa stood guard all alone for her father and brothers consumed her. Had her mother loved Angus? Or had it been a way to get back at her husband? Or maybe it was a few warm moments in a cold lifetime. Either way, it added to Issa's confused feelings. She'd had a civil relationship with her mother, but it certainly hadn't been a loving relationship—at least not on her mother's side. How sad was that? They could've been so much more. It was almost as if, every time her mother saw Issa, her mother was reminded of her own failures. She'd complained bitterly about the lack of time Issa spent with her, but, when Issa was with her mother, they hadn't even spent it together. Like her mother had used guilt to keep Issa close just to keep punishing her.

For Issa, every time she saw her mother, she was reminded of everything she'd lost. And at the top of that list, right or wrong, was Hadrid.

EAGLE MADE A cup of tea, carried it carefully into her room. He placed it on the night table. He could even hear her teeth chattering. He stood for a long moment and stared down at her. "Do you want a hot bath? Or do you want me to get in bed with you and hold you?"

She tried to answer, but nothing made it past the chattering.

He kicked off his shoes, walked around to the bed, crawled underneath the covers and wrapped her in his arms, pulling her tight against him. With his legs wrapped around hers fully, she was tucked into a fetal position, and he used his body heat to try to warm her. It amazed him to see just how cold she was—the chill seeping through her cheeks and neck.

"We'll try this for a moment," he murmured, letting his warm breath soak into her neck and face and icy cheeks. "If it doesn't work, we'll try a hot bath again."

She nodded and took his hand to pull it more fully around her. The chill of her fingers made him wince. What had sent her into shock? Could it have been her trances? He didn't know who to ask. He suspected Gray wouldn't have a clue. Neither would Annie. He closed his eyes and relaxed, trying to will her body to absorb his own heat, mentally surrounding her with big thermal blankets, the two of them in a cocoon against the world.

"I'm so sorry you've had such a miserable time," he whispered against her temple. "I'd have given anything for you not to have been through that."

He could feel her shoulders shaking, and, with so much chattering, he knew she couldn't talk.

"I can tell you that I tracked the blood back to the highway. I never saw a body. And I think whoever was hurt had a friend helping him."

She jerked in surprise.

"I doubt my security system killed anyone," he continued. "That doesn't mean his cohort didn't finish the job and bury him somewhere deep."

He didn't know if it was his body heat or his words, but she slowly stopped shaking.

Several minutes later, he said, "If you think you can sit up, let's get some warm tea into you."

With his help, she leaned against the headboard with the top blanket wrapped around her shoulders, the rest of the covers pulled up to her chest. Now out of the bed, he sat down on the opposite side and pulled the tea closer.

He took a sip and nodded. "It's perfect. See if you can get a couple sips down."

Her hands were still blue and, as long as he helped support the cup, it didn't shake too badly when she grasped it. She took one sip, gave a small smile, and took another big one. As her body slowly eased from her frostbite stage into just plain cold, she said, "I have no idea what just happened. I'll blame it on Stefan."

"Stefan? Did he call?"

She snorted. "If that's what you call it. I don't know what kind of psychic he is. I swear to God, he filled the room with his conversation. Or maybe it just felt like that. He was talking inside my mind—or something like that." She shook her head and leaned back, closing her eyes. "How is it possible he could do that?"

"This from the woman who can communicate with falcons."

Her gaze flew open, and she studied Eagle for a long moment. "That's normal. It's natural for me. It's all I've ever known."

He gave her a lopsided smile. "Sweetie, that's not normal

for anyone else."

She frowned and dropped her gaze to the cup in her hand. She gently swirled a finger around the rim of the cup. "It took me a long time to realize that. But for me ..."

"And maybe for Stefan, whatever it is he does, is normal for him."

"It was scary. Some of the stuff he had to say was even more so." She tilted her head to the side and said, "He brought up all kinds of memories from when I was little. And something I had always assumed I had done, Stefan completely flipped around to make me see I was doing something completely different. Something much more fantastic and bizarre. And that's why I don't really think he can be right. I told him Hadrid was sending me those images." She shook her head at the look on Eagle's face. "I'm sorry. I'm not making much sense."

"Explain," he said.

"I'm not even sure I can." She rubbed her temples. "I assumed I was always giving Hadrid suggestions about where to go. And he flew out and let me know if anything was wrong through images he sent me."

Eagle settled in to listen. His mind was still figuring out how she could even do that much.

She continued. "And then, when things blew up, everybody, myself included—not that I had much time to know or understand what was going on—assumed I was to blame. That I had either been making up this connection the whole time, and Hadrid and I really had no abilities, or somehow he'd been either distracted or just really hadn't seen the enemy when they arrived."

"By rights, no one should blame either of you," Eagle exclaimed.

"Sure, if you didn't understand how many times we'd done the same thing over and over again with no problem. So everyone assumed we were the perfect guardians for their illegal activities."

Eagle didn't want to stop the flow of her words, but he had so many questions to ask. "So, after it all happened, there was no way to prove to anyone what you had actually been doing?"

She nodded. "But what Stefan suggested was that I wasn't sending Hadrid out into any particular direction and wasn't showing him where to go, but that I was actually connecting with him on some level. ... That I was actually seeing the world below through him—seeing the world through his eyes."

Eagle sat back. He forcibly closed his mouth to stop his jaw from hanging open. "It's a fine distinction," he said awkwardly.

"But one with a very definite twist and outcome."

He tilted his head sideways and thought about that. "Of course, because, if you were somehow connecting with this falcon, seeing the world below through his eyes, you were the one making the decision as to whether your family was safe from danger."

"Exactly. In which case I'm the one who failed them. I always figured I had failed them, but that it was a shared responsibility between Hadrid and me. But, according to Stefan, if I'm the one up there, seeing through his eyes, then I am entirely at fault, not Hadrid. And that makes me feel shitty because, in a way, I'd been blaming Hadrid."

"And yet that night you didn't see anything, so how could you be responsible? You did your job." He took a deep breath. "That anyone could put a child in that position and then blame them when they failed, ... it's beyond belief."

"I shouldn't have failed." She stared at him steadily, then shook her head. In a low voice she continued, "It was my fault. ... I was distracted."

"And it was okay to be distracted. You were six years old." He knew they were coming to something crazy. "Distracted by what?"

She gave him a shuttered glance. "By my mother having sex with one of my father's men."

This time his jaw did drop. "Holy shit."

She nodded. "You see? I wasn't out there with Hadrid when I should have been. I was supposed to be looking out for the men below, but instead I was completely confused as to why my mother was in bed with someone other than my father."

He let out a deep breath. "Well, that changes things entirely."

"It does, and it doesn't," she said. "It's still my fault. I still was negligent in my duties. And my family paid for it."

He grasped her free hand and whispered, "I can say, without a doubt, sweetie, the only adult in this equation at fault is your mother. She was also posted as a lookout for the family. But because you and Hadrid were so good at it, she took the opportunity—probably every damn time—to have sex with this other man. When instead she should've been out there looking after you and her own husband and sons. But she left that on the shoulders of a six-year-old." He shook his head. "This was not your fault."

She burst into tears.

He quickly snatched her up, blankets and all, and pulled her onto his lap. There he cuddled her in his arms until she quieted. But, in his mind, all he could think of was how it was a damn good thing her mother was dead. Otherwise he'd be out there making her pay for what she'd done to her daughter.

Not to mention her husband and sons who had trusted her with their lives.

"SHIT," STEFAN ROARED. He stared at the beautiful painting in front of him. The one now marred by a huge owl's eye in the corner of the canvas. Always watching him, always glaring at him, waiting for him to do something.

"Dammit, Humbug, I told you that I'm feeding you and Roash as much energy as I can, along with Issa and Tabitha. We're moving you slowly, mile by mile, under your own power—or rather our power," he said in exasperation. "I don't know how else to help you two or her. I don't dare call the authorities. That's for them to do."

Of course the owl who was painted into his painting—an owl he didn't remember painting—stared back at him silently. That gaze never shifted as Stefan moved around the room. But that eye didn't belong in the painting. Stefan was working on something completely different. And every time he tried to complete one of his commissioned paintings, Humbug overtook Stefan's consciousness toward the end of the process. Thus, when Stefan came back to reality, an owl was painted in the corner of the painting.

For three days Stefan had tried six different paintings, but, as he stepped back to look at the finished work, he found a damn snowy owl painted into the corner. Not a whole owl but just a head, gazing unrelenting at him, as if crying out, *Help me, help her, help us.*

Stefan knew Roash was out there too. Figured he'd

probably start painting falcons at this rate. But, so far, he'd been blessed to have only one bird show up on his canvases.

He'd never had something like this happen before. Sure, he painted subconsciously all the time. But this was a conscious painting, one he was doing for a client. He'd painted away, thinking he was doing fine, how he was on track, but then he'd realize he had white on his paintbrush. As soon as he saw that, he knew. He'd turn, and there would be the snow owl with golden eyes. How could this owl have such control—such a strong will—that he could show up in Stefan's paintings like this?

He took another step back and shrugged. "At least I'm getting good at painting owls."

CHAPTER 18

I SSA WOKE UP feeling tired, exhausted, and broken in an odd way. With a start, she realized she wasn't even in bed. She was in Eagle's arms, her head on his chest. They were no longer in her bedroom but out in the living room on the couch. She shifted to look up at his face. "How long have I been asleep?"

"Not too long, half an hour." He motioned to the couch beside him. "I came out here to go through some of your papers but didn't want to leave you alone."

She yawned, wanting to lay her head back down against his chest. But it felt odd, now that she was awake. And then she realized she had to go to the bathroom. She slowly, carefully extricated herself from the blankets. And, with his help, finally managed to stand. She walked carefully back to the bedroom and into the bathroom. She'd warmed up, but now she was mobbed with fatigue.

She grabbed the sweater they'd bought at the secondhand store, tugged it on before she walked back out to the living room. Her feet were better every time she was on them. They still felt spongy and odd, but her mobility was much improved. She walked into the kitchen, spied the teakettle, and asked, "Do you mind if I put the kettle on?"

"Go ahead. How are the feet?"

"I was just thinking about that," she said as she picked

up the kettle and walked to the sink, filling it with water. "They feel much better actually. Still tender but not quite so clunky. More like my real feet instead of stumps stuck to the end of my legs."

"Good," he said, but his voice was distracted.

She put the kettle back on the stove and turned on the burner. She didn't know where the teabags were. She opened a couple drawers, found them, grabbed a second cup rather than walking all the way back to her bedroom, and then saw a teapot. She decided she'd make a cup for him, and, if he didn't want any, she'd have two. She placed the teabags into the pot and turned, watching him as he went through the papers in one of the files.

"Did you find anything interesting?"

"I found lots that's interesting," he said, turning his attention from the documents in his hands to look at her. "I don't know how relevant any of it is to you in the present though. Your father was a criminal with a record and was facing charges that would put him away for a long time."

She frowned. "I saw something in there about criminal charges, but I couldn't deal with reading it at the time." She walked to where he sat, her arms wrapped around her chest. "What kind of charges?"

He stared at her quietly. "Attempted murder."

She closed her eyes and swayed on her feet. "Seriously?"

"Yeah. I'm sorry."

His voice was sympathetic, but, at the same time, there was nothing anybody could do. It was a long time ago. "Does it say who he supposedly tried to murder?"

"Angus McKinley," he said.

She frowned and walked around the side of the couch to stare at Eagle. "I found my mother having sex with Angus that night. My dad must have learned of it earlier, and that's why my dad tried to kill him. Even so, my mother didn't stop seeing Angus." Issa rubbed at her temples. "There was a bill of sale from Angus. For Hadrid."

"Really? Your falcon?"

"Yeah." She bent down and pulled out the envelopes full of papers. She came to the one she was looking for, the manila envelope with a mix of documents. "I think it's in here. In a smaller envelope with pictures. It would be in there." Then she remembered where she'd placed them. "Oh." She reached into her pocket and pulled out the folded envelope. "I didn't want to lose it."

He held out his hand.

She said, "No, let's put them on the coffee table." They leaned over, and she spread out the photos. She pointed to one of the men with a big red beard. She tapped it and said, "That's Angus."

"And all these others?"

She spread them out. "I think those are the birds he worked with. Hadrid was his," she said with conviction. "I think my father wanted one for himself." Again she lifted her face to stare off in the distance, trying to remember. Trying to extract those little tidbits of memory from so long ago.

"That would cause a kerfuffle, if Hadrid bonded to you instead of your father." Eagle pulled out the bill of sale. "Pretty darn sure no father would purchase a falcon for a small child. So either he had purchased it for himself or one of your brothers bought Hadrid."

She nodded. "Or my father purchased Hadrid for my brothers, but the falcon bonded with me instead. I don't remember a day when that falcon wasn't mine."

He nodded. "That would have caused trouble within the

family unit."

She winced. "Maybe. Again I don't remember much about the rest of the family."

He turned to look at her. "Any chance your father wasn't your father?"

She stared at him and then finally understood what he was saying. Her eyes grew as she considered the implications. "I don't know," she said quietly, her heart slamming against her chest. "It's a little ugly to think about."

"Your mother was obviously having an affair," he said quietly. "You saw them. What are the chances the relationship had been going on for so long that he could've been, potentially, your father?"

She motioned to the papers that surrounded them. "I doubt there's anything in here to give us a definitive answer, but we can look. Besides, what difference does any of that make now?"

"The men who kidnapped you knew you back then. And that means we need to know why."

Her shoulders sagged. "I know."

Together they sorted through the paperwork, once again looking for any clues that gave an indication as to what was going on. They found nothing else bearing the name of Angus McKinley or any other Angus for that matter.

"Take a look at my mother's envelope. A lot of information was in there." She glanced at him. "Do you have a scanner, just in case we lose all this, so we can make a digital copy?"

He turned to look at her in surprise. "Yes, I do. That's an excellent idea." He gathered up the envelopes in front of him, while she collected the photos and the bill of sale for Hadrid. Together they walked into the office where he scanned every item in the first envelope.

"I'll get the rest." She walked back and retrieved the keepsake box. "Considering somebody is after me and potentially after this material, I would very much like a copy no matter what happens to the originals."

He nodded. "A lot of paperwork is here," he said. "Bring the tea in too." He stopped and looked at her. "Or you handle the machine, and I'll get the tea. Save wear and tear on your feet."

She shrugged and nodded. "Sure, that works."

She looked at the little scanner, took out the piece of paper, and replaced it with another one. They were sending everything to his main computer desktop into the scanner folder. She'd have to rename everything and file them later. At the moment she was much more concerned with just preserving a copy. As each page went in and came out, she sorted them into files. The piles started to make sense. For whatever reason her mother had considered all these documents worth keeping. Now if only Issa understood why.

After bringing tea for her, Eagle checked both boxes carefully. She watched as he slowly opened up the bottom of the cardboard box, and a piece of paper folded several times fell out. He handed it to her.

She unfolded it and said, "It's a handwritten copy of my father's will. He'd left everything to his sons. Not to his wife or his daughter." She frowned at the piece of paper. "How does that make any sense?"

"Maybe he knew she was cheating on him? Or maybe he knew you weren't his?" He turned to look at her. "Did you look like your brothers?"

She frowned. "My hair was more auburn, more reddish. Theirs was brown with a bit of red. My mother had fairly red hair."

He nodded. "We'll have to look up some of the family members, find photos of the three brothers. In their files, were there photos?"

She nodded. "In each of my brothers' files there is at least one."

Eagle went through the boys' information. And, indeed, a couple photos were inside each envelope. He opened her father's envelope and found a photo. He showed it to her.

She looked at it. "Yes, that's him." She shook her head. "I don't look anything like him."

He held it up against her face and shrugged. "Could be family."

She motioned to the box. "Oh, there was also a key in the bottom of that one."

She fished into her bra and brought it up. He stared at her chest. "Anything else in there?"

"Nothing you haven't seen before."

He grinned, his face lightening. "Believe me. I haven't forgotten."

The suggestiveness of his tone and the warm look in his eyes had the heat rising up her neck. She turned her back on him. "I have to gain twenty pounds to have any sex appeal."

He leaned forward, whispering against her ear. "There might not be very much of you, but what there is, is very delicious."

Instantly heat washed the rest of the way up her face, and she could feel her cheeks turning hot. "I blush extremely easily. So I know my cheeks are bright pink right now."

His laughter rolled free. "Here. Sit down and go through your mother's envelope while I scan. We need to track this key to the lock it belongs to. The answers have to be somewhere."

It was a steady toil to finish. It took Eagle over two hours to get every document scanned, while Issa slowly went through the physical documents on her mother. Then Issa switched to renaming the files on his computer and sorting through them. They paused at an envelope of old pictures. The images were of jewelry. Although poor-quality photos, each snapshot appeared to be of the same thing: an expensive heavily jeweled necklace. There were no identifying marks or notes on the back of the photos.

He scanned them in anyway. Afterward he moved the boxes and their contents to her room.

As long as the scans were saved into cloud storage somewhere, she'd know how to find them. Even if the kidnappers stole the computer along with the boxes, she'd have a copy. It was her heritage—what little of it there was.

By the time they were done, she was exhausted. Her mother's envelope still sat clutched in her fingers. But she hadn't looked at it.

Some things she just didn't have the energy for—and that had nothing to do with her physical fatigue.

AFTER HE GOT Issa into her bed for the night, Eagle picked up his rifle and stepped outside. He'd finished the scanning and had transferred everything to his off-site storage. He had taken the precaution of moving all the scans onto a flash drive as well. He placed it in an empty coffee canister he had been using for spare change.

Not that he didn't trust off-site storage, but … he didn't trust people. This way he had a backup of the backup. And the papers had been filed off to the side. Bits and pieces of the information he'd read tonight slipped through his brain. Her father had a criminal record. He had been involved in criminal activities. He was being investigated for the attempted murder of Angus McKinley.

How much did any of it matter today? Did any of it have to do with Issa? As far as he could see, her life was uneventful from the time she had arrived in the States. He had read the doctors' reports for Issa's psychological testing, stating she'd been traumatized by some unknown event. But the doctors surmised it was a combination of the loss of her family and the move to America. Her school marks were listed. She had essentially failed her earlier grades but had been moved ahead regardless.

Eagle wondered about her mother. She didn't keep any of Issa's grades from the higher levels where Issa had done well enough to get into college. There she'd won the president's award for top marks in her graduating year. That was no small feat. She'd been on the dean's list every year she was in the university. Again no small feat. So she'd finally adapted and charged forward.

He could see that in her. A part of her was still traumatized from that defining event, but she had clearly blocked it out as much as she could. Her accelerated physical healing from her torture continued to surprise him. It was like so much else about her—too good to be true.

Her feet might not feel like blocks of wood anymore, but also all those little cuts had closed up and healed so well, and the bruises on her torso were gone. In five days' time instead of the ten he had expected for her feet alone.

He was pretty damn sure, if he brought Annie's X-ray machine back, he'd find Issa's cracks and fractures to her bones were eighty percent healed. In the same five days. How did that happen? Particularly when her body was so low in body fat—no energy stores in reserve—so scrawny that it must completely utilize every ounce of energy she had available just to maintain a survival level: to keep her breathing, her blood pumping, her brain working. In cases like that, survival trumped healing, slowing to the point of not being able to heal at all. Infections would fester; breaks just couldn't mend. But, in her case, she had charged ahead.

It bothered him. Not on a *hey, this is bizarre* level but a *hey, this is wonderful* level. He didn't know what to make of her.

And then there was the intruder last night, the blood trail he'd left. When Issa had gone to bed, he'd sent out more texts to several guys from his old unit. People he could count on; people he could trust.

He hadn't heard back from anybody—which was a little unusual—but, given everyone had lives of their own, maybe not. He sat with the rifle across his knees on the front porch steps, nothing moving except for his gaze as he slowly let the darkness seep in. One of the first things he'd done when he had moved here was memorize the horizon, the shadows, the shapes.

Over the years the shapes had grown, dropped, changed, but he had always noted the differences. When he'd been in the military, keeping track of the shadows had kept him alive. He had no problems with the bears, the wolves, or even the badgers around here. Like him, they were just out living as they were meant to.

It was the two-legged assholes he had a problem with. He checked his watch and realized it was only eight p.m. With Issa being awake so much and moving around more now, as much as she could, she had crashed early. He knew, in a few more days, she'd be frothing at the bit to return to her place. The thing was, it wasn't fit to live in, what with all the damage the kidnappers had done. It wasn't safe to live there either, not until the kidnappers were caught or killed. Plus it wouldn't fit who she was now. Not after what she'd been through. At least not without a decent security system. Somehow he also felt it had been her private place to get away from her mother. With her mother gone, Issa probably needed something different. Besides he didn't want her to leave. She belonged here. She probably belonged here with his raptors more than he did.

A noise in the distance had him tilting his head to listen closely.

When the engine shifted, he knew somebody had taken the turn onto his driveway. Bright headlights shone in the darkness. He watched as a second vehicle came behind the first. One he might handle; two was another story. He got up and walked into the living room and shut off the lights. Then he slipped to the side, rifle at hand, dogs at his heels. Until he knew who was out there, nobody was coming onto his place. The first truck pulled up to the gate. The windows were rolled down, and a familiar face turned to look at the security feature.

"Eagle, it's me, Tiger." Tiger's voice was faint, and yet it moved across the yard.

Eagle's face lit up with joy. As he headed toward his former teammate from the unit back in the military, the second vehicle pulled up with a honk.

When Tiger looked in the rearview mirror and frowned and didn't get out, Eagle froze. As Tiger sat and waited with his lights shining through the locked gate, Eagle could see the sheriff markings on the car from where he stood.

The engine turned off on the official county car. The driver's door opened, and a deputy stepped out. He stood, looking up at the truck in front, and yelled out, "Are you going to drive into the yard?"

Tiger yelled back, "Can't. The gates are locked."

As Eagle watched, another deputy got out of the passenger side. "Any idea where the owner is?"

Tiger shook his head. "I just came unannounced. No idea."

The two uniformed men walked up to the gate and stared through it. The gate was built in such a way they couldn't slip through it; Eagle had made sure of that. And they'd have to be pretty damn skinny to slide underneath the bar at the bottom.

Deciding this was the best time to have a talk with the deputies, Eagle walked toward them, carrying the rifle loosely in his hand. The two froze at the sight of him.

One looked at the weapon in Eagle's hand and said, "You got a license for that?"

Tiger sniggered behind them.

Eagle's face was cold and his voice cutting. "Yes. Do you have one for yours?"

The first deputy frowned at him. "We just want to ask you some questions."

"Go ahead. Ask."

"You going to let us in?"

"Why can't you ask questions where you're standing?"

Eagle took several more steps forward and stood in front of the headlights so the deputies could see him. He hoped they saw the glint in his eye that said he didn't give a damn who they were. They weren't coming on his property without a warrant. They were already too far in on his acreage for his comfort.

"State your business," he said calmly.

The two deputies looked at each other, and one said, "An injured unconscious man was picked up earlier today just down the road a few miles from your place. Unfortunately I got word on the drive over that he has succumbed to his injuries."

Eagle kept his face completely blank as he said, "And?"

"We think he came from your place," the first man said.

"There's a lot of acreage here. Somebody could have dumped him on the highway and taken off, hoping he'd die before he could tell what had befallen him," Eagle said drily. "I haven't seen anyone here." At least he could say that honestly.

The deputy nodded. "That could be. The nights are getting too cold for games like that."

"It's not that cold yet," Eagle said calmly.

The deputies glanced around, seeing the raptor cages. "Anybody ever give you any trouble over your raptor center?"

Eagle gave him a thin razor-sharp smile. "Never."

The two officers glared at him. "Make sure you stay on the right side of the law," the second deputy said with more bravado than steely determination. "We can shut you down."

Eagle's gaze slid toward him. The younger man involuntarily backed up a step.

In a low voice, Eagle said, "I'm well within my rights. Are you?"

"We don't want no trouble. We're just trying to find out where this man came from."

"Now that you brought it up, I want to know too." He turned to glance around at the pens. "I haven't checked them tonight. Always do a check before bed. But normally, if there's an intruder, the birds let me know."

Just then one of the big eagles named Borgan screeched. Eagle thought to himself the bird was grandstanding more than anything. He didn't like strangers.

"Like that?" the deputy asked.

"Something like that, only two hundred times worse. I do have several hundred birds here."

The two men nodded. "You didn't hear anything disturbing them in the last twenty-four hours or so?"

Eagle tilted his head as if thinking. "A couple coyotes came through. Normally my dogs chase them away, but the dogs were in the house. Once I opened the door, they took care of them."

"Did you kill them?"

Once again Eagle stared at the younger deputy. "No, we don't kill senselessly here. The coyotes just needed a reminder there were better places for them to go hunting," he said gently.

The men nodded, and the younger one said, "Well, if you hear anything, please call the sheriff's office."

Eagle watched as they both walked back to their car. It was obvious they didn't want to go, but they had no legal reason to stay. They backed the vehicle out to where the road widened slightly and turned around, headed down to the highway. Eagle waited until he heard the engine slow as it approached the crossroads, then gunned as it went around the corner.

He walked over and unlocked the gates. The entire time the deputies were here, Tiger hadn't said a word. Neither had Panther, who sat beside him. With the gates wide open, Tiger drove forward and parked on the side of the house. He shut down the headlights, opened the truck door, and hopped out. The two men embraced briefly.

"Sounds like you got bigger trouble than you let on," Panther said quietly behind him.

He turned to greet the huge black man who had also been part of his unit. Panther was born as Peter. As soon as he could, he would only answer to the nickname Panther. It suited him. "It's good to see you two. It was just a text, you know?"

Two sets of teeth flashed in the darkness. "We were bored," Tiger said. "And you obviously needed our help."

"Now that you're here, you mind walking with me while I check the fences and the pens?"

"Did you hear or see the man they were talking about?"

"I didn't check that close."

Tiger snorted. "You haven't changed a bit."

"You might be surprised." While the three of them walked the fence line, he brought them up to date on the mess his life had become.

"A woman all the way up here?" Tiger asked in surprise.

"And she'd been tortured," Eagle added quietly. "Not just a little bit. But systematically over weeks. Bruises on top of bruises on top of bruises. Tiny slices on the soles of her feet so she couldn't run. Broken bones. You know the drill."

"Jesus Christ," Panther whispered, the oath slipping out with more severity than Eagle had heard from him in a long time. But, if there was one thing none of the men in his circle would accept, it was abuse of anyone, particularly a defenseless woman.

"Where is she now?"

"Hopefully sleeping."

As they walked toward the house, Panther pointed up to the sky. "What the hell's going on?"

Eagle stopped and looked at the roof along the front of his house. Every inch of the edge was covered in birds. All sizes. The three men eyed the birds carefully. "The real question is, will they let us go in the house?" Eagle said.

"Man, there is more stuff here you need to be telling us about." Panther took several steps forward. Two of the larger birds spread out their wings as if about to take flight. Panther froze. "Are they going to attack me?" he asked, a note of incredulity in his voice.

"No idea." Eagle walked toward the front of his house, the dogs at his side, and his friends behind them. As he walked to the base of the porch steps he called out to the birds, "They are friends. They will help protect her. They aren't here to hurt her."

"Dude, you talking to the birds?" Tiger whispered. "I know you love them and all …"

Panther snickered. "On the other hand, if it works, I am all for it."

Eagle took another step. Every pair of eyes turned his way. He called out, "Issa, are you awake?"

The front door opened, and she stepped out, a blanket wrapped all around her. Moving silently into the night, she walked to the top of the steps. Instantly the birds quieted above her. "Good evening, gentlemen."

Panther, his voice low said, "Ma'am, I'm Panther, and this is Tiger."

A glimmer of a smile whispered across her face. "And he's Eagle. So does that mean there is a Hawk as well?"

That got a laugh out of them all. "Indeed, there is. He just happens to be off in Europe right now."

She asked, "Are you all coming in?"

Eagle motioned to the roof and said, "Maybe you should come here and see this."

Curiously she walked toward him. Moving carefully, she stepped down to the grass. Eagle watched a grimace cross her face as she turned and looked up, seeing the birds. She gasped; then her laughter rolled out. She dropped the blanket and opened her arms. Instantly the birds rose in the sky and twirled around her head.

The men backed away as the birds came down, swooping over her hands, not to scare her but almost in greeting. Issa stroked, touched those that hovered close enough. When the huge golden eagle came down toward her, the three men backed up even farther.

But she opened her arms wide and gently wrapped them around his huge body. He clung to her forearm and then dropped his head against her cheek. And she stayed like that for a long moment.

Eagle was dumbstruck. But it was nothing compared to what his friends were. He watched as she completely tamed the birds of prey around her. Behind him, he heard his friends whisper, "We really have to talk. Who ... and what ... the hell is she?"

And he realized he truly had no idea.

INTERESTING. TWO DEPUTIES at the gate and another truck arriving. That was the most activity he'd seen in days. Dylan shifted his position. He'd spent so much time here the birds just watched him. He'd never done anything to hurt them, and as such, they accepted his presence. He was counting on that.

As an alarm, having the birds around was a hell of a dynamic system. He looked through the binoculars, the night glasses giving a nongreen hue to the men on this side of the fence. But it looked like two deputies and two unidentified men in a large pickup. The same damn man they'd been tracking appeared on the other side of the fence. Dylan had finally gotten the big man's name. Eagle Saunders.

The owner walked over to the gate. He appeared to know the men in the truck. When the deputies came up to the gate to talk to Eagle, he didn't give an inch. Dylan watched his body language, clearly understanding that this Eagle didn't have much respect for law enforcement. Dylan could understand that. He didn't either. He operated in the shadows.

Law enforcement was for people who walked in the light. People in the dark never needed them. And people in the light believed that law enforcement could protect them. They didn't realize how much those who lived in the dark didn't give a shit about the law.

The deputies were an irritant more than anything else. Dylan watched with interest as the conversation continued. Then the deputies got into their vehicle and took off. Eagle turned to the driver of the truck, opened the gate, and waited until the truck passed through. Dylan thought he caught a glimpse of somebody else in the house.

But the truck drove past just then. He watched as Eagle closed the gate and locked it. Then Dylan looked up and saw the sky turn dark.

With the flapping of wings, it was almost impossible to see anything. He swore he could hear somebody. But the sound was too far away. Just when he thought he saw someone on the porch, the men moved into his view. He swore out loud. "Almost as if Mother Nature herself was protecting somebody."

But he couldn't go home if he didn't have proof she was

here. At this point, he was almost ready to storm the house, and, if she was there, good. They could take her. And, if she wasn't there, just kill everybody anyway so they could move on.

But this was his best shot. Dylan and the boys had heard rumors. Rumors that locals had been unwilling to confirm. And bribery only went so far. Somebody in town had mentioned X-ray equipment, and another had mentioned a doctor. But none of that confirmed Issa was here. This was a long way for her to have traveled in her condition. Unless somebody actually drove her this far and dropped her on the road. … That would be some kind of an asshole move.

Being one of the guys who had slowly sliced and tortured her young body, he wasn't any better. In fact, he was much worse.

The poison of evil inside was taking over who he was. He'd always been able to hold himself tall against the nasty evilness of his boss. Yet Dylan had done the man's bidding. But that had been okay because that had been his job, and he'd believed in the cause. Everything in his world easily fit into his black-and-white rulebook.

When you kidnapped a young woman and did the things to her they had … He'd crossed into the zone of winter darkness where he'd known he'd done wrong but was too frozen to stop himself.

And there was no forgiveness for that. Plus she was family, which just made it that much more horrific. She was the innocent one.

Still Dylan had one of the new guys the boss had hired to watch over the place. If the kid was smart, he'd sit on her and leave the raptor center alone. Dylan respected the birds, but he doubted the new kid would.

CHAPTER 19

ISSA HEARD THE men's shocked exclamation behind her. She understood their confusion. For the first time in twenty years she felt ... normal. As if she'd thrown off a restrictive costume and was back to herself. She didn't want to go back inside. But, with the most recent gunshot attack, she was compelled to. Inside she walked straight to the nearest window and opened it. Instantly several birds flew in. She laughed like a child. She held out her arms, and a small songbird landed on her fingers. She crooned gently to it as she stroked the beautiful feathers along its back.

"It's late, little one. Why are you not tucked away safe for the night?"

It hadn't escaped her that many of the raptors flying around would've taken the songbird as a tiny morsel for their breakfast. The bird chirped, walked up her arm, and settled against her neck. Issa closed her eyes and rejoiced. A call came from another bird flying above her. She opened her eyes to see what appeared to be a mourning dove. She raised an eyebrow and held up a hand. He landed on the back of her wrist. She brought it down so she could look at it closer. At the same time, the songbird stroked her soft cheeks.

"Aren't you special, little one," she murmured. The mourning dove walked back and forth along her forearm. Not upset or agitated. Looking to get comfortable. He walked up her sleeve to her other shoulder and sat there.

"This is all fine and dandy, guys, but the rides will be over very soon."

The mourning dove trilled in her ear.

She smiled, gently stroking its soft gray feathers.

The eagle she'd been holding outside walked into the room and stood on the back of the couch. Huge and majestic, his golden gaze stared at her. Unflinching, he felt secure. She'd never seen anything like it. She walked over to sit beside him.

The little songbird remained nestled against her neck. It was so tiny. The eagle continued to stare at her, his wings folded back, but the fascination in his gaze was reflected in her own, she knew. This was such a magical moment. She gently stroked the long head and chest, his beautiful dark and yellow feathers a wonderful attraction in the room. But he wasn't alone.

There were crows and magpies and other songbirds, sparrows and chickadees, not just the raptors, which were what she had thought would potentially be attracted to her. When a barn owl hopped up onto her knee and twisted his head around to look at her, she chuckled in delight. "And what's your name?"

It made a tiny sound, but, in her mind, he had answered her.

"How can you be called Rubiks?" she asked with a tiny laugh. "You're mostly one color—brown. A Rubik's Cube is full of colors."

This time there was no answer. But he continued to fix his gaze on her. She stared at them all in wonder. And finally she turned to the three men in the middle of the living room, shock and bewilderment on their faces. The two new arrivals were just as big as Eagle and just as dumbfounded. She'd loved it when Panther opened his mouth and flashed his gold tooth. But right now, none of the men were smiling. They stared at her like she'd grown two heads right in front of them.

"I guess you want me to explain?" she asked in a small voice.

Eagle stared at her. "*Can* you explain this?"

"I don't know that I can. But this happened to me when I was a child. I forgot until now. But I would go outside, and the birds would come to me. I'd play on the swing, and the birds would collect around me. They'd land on my shoulders, on my hands, on my legs. If I had a glass with water, they'd sit on the glass, and, if there was a table, they would perch beside me."

"What did your family think?"

"Honestly I think they thought I was crazy. Among the other kids, I was a fascination, and some of them really looked up to me." She gave a lopsided smile. "My brothers on the other hand, I think they were jealous. The youngest one, Liam, would chase away the birds. But I don't think he did so to protect me. It was more because he didn't want the evidence that I could do something he couldn't."

Eagle crossed his arms over his chest, his gaze going from bird to bird.

She stood and walked closer to him, the owl now on her palm. "Liam was always angry." She extended her arm with the little owl on it. He hopped onto Eagle's forearm and nestled up against his sweater.

Eagle froze. "I handle birds all day long," he said. "And most of them don't want to be touched." He nodded toward the little owl. "What did you do to him?"

"I told him that you were a friend," she said gently. "And that you wouldn't hurt him."

She turned her gaze to the two huge men standing behind Eagle. Panther stared at her in fascination.

Tiger, on the other hand, stared at her in shock. "Dear God, can you talk to animals too?"

She shrugged. "Maybe. It's not like I use words though. For whatever reason, I've always had an affinity for feathers. Maybe that's what I had with Hadrid."

"Who's Hadrid?" Panther asked.

Rather than answering, she let Eagle give the explanations. She walked around the room, gently stroking and greeting each of the birds that had come in. And then, unable to stop herself, she walked to the front door and stepped back out.

Hundreds of birds flew near the fence, on the rooftop, and the deck. She cried out in joy. A part of her world had finally come back. A sense of remembrance, a sense of homecoming she'd never thought to have again. She'd searched long and wide for a connection with another bird like she'd had with Hadrid. And here was one of those events in her childhood, so connected to Hadrid that it had been commonplace, and yet, since she'd lost him, she'd lost these experiences, these connections too.

She called out to them, her voice imitating, picking up the different sounds as she cooed and cawed, sending cries into the air. More and more birds arrived. She turned and danced in a circle with her arms wide. Her head back, she let out an odd sound from deep within her gut. Sounds she'd heard many times before but not in the last twenty years. When she finally fell silent, she let her eyes drift closed, and just stood there, feeling the love, feeling the connection.

Long bottled up emotions welled up, bringing tears to her eyes.

A small bird landed on her arm, walking up to her shoulder where it hunkered down and cuddled close. When it trilled in her ear, the tears dripped down her cheeks. *Gillian.* The little saw-whet owl had found her again.

When she opened her eyes again, the men stood in front of her. She stared up at Eagle, knowing he could see the tears coursing down her cheeks, and she whispered, "There's such a bond, a sense of love and connection with these birds that, as a child, it was way stronger than my connection to my mother. Or my father. And definitely not with my brothers. As if I was hatched and not born. As if I was meant to be a bird myself. And yet God made a mistake and plunked me way down in this awkward human form."

Eagle's gaze shifted to her shoulder.

She smiled. "The little owl is Gillian. She lived with me at my cabin," Through the tears, her smile deepened as she added, "Isn't that wonderful?"

He looked at her and nodded. "It's just too unbelievable."

"I know," she whispered. "I *do* know. When I was a child, this is what I had. They were my friends. They were my confidants. In so many ways, they were my family. Nobody else understood me. Nobody understood a damn thing. But I always knew when somebody was being mean to a bird. I always knew when someone was coming because the birds would let me know. I would hear their wings as they flew. When a tree rustled, I could tell what bird it was. I didn't know the names, certainly didn't know all the proper terms, but I could tell their colors, their size, if they were ones I had seen before many times, or if they were new," she added, her voice soft. "I never went to school in Ireland. Maybe because I wasn't allowed to. Because they didn't think I'd fit in."

"I can't imagine that you would have," Tiger said. "Children are inherently mean. If you come to school with twenty birds in tow, the teachers would have had a lot to say to you, and none of it would've been nice. And, depending on where you lived, if there were any kinds of fears or beliefs that you were more demon than angel, it would've been much worse for you. Everyone instinctively is afraid of what they don't understand."

"You said you didn't have the same connection with your mother?" Eagle asked. "Did that start in infancy?"

Her eyes widened. "I don't know." She let her gaze return to the front door. "Did you see any baby pictures of me?"

He shook his head. "No, I didn't. But it makes me wonder why. And how this"—he waved his arms at the birds surrounding them—"could've come to pass. Did she have anything to do with you or did she avoid you?"

"Nothing to do with me. Avoided me every moment she could. Maybe she didn't want me. Didn't want another pregnancy. Once we moved here, she was different—then I was too."

"Your birth certificate has your father's name, not Angus's."

She laughed. "No way she could list anyone else. My father would have killed her," she said simply. "I was something unique for him to hold up to his friends, to show them what I could do. I think he's the one that fostered a love for me and maybe even over my mother's wishes."

"They fought all the time?"

She stilled and tried to glance back into her past. "There was yelling. I never understood if he yelled at my brothers or if he was always yelling at my mother." She stopped for a moment, then nodded. "No, they often fought. Mealtimes were terrible." She frowned. "That's why I spent so much time with the birds."

"Your birds made it a happy, unique time in your life," Panther said.

Her gaze hardened as she turned to look at the two men. "And I was just six when I lost it all. Until *this* moment. These last few years I slowly started finding this part of myself again through Roash and Humbug. Roash came out of the sky, circled, and slowly flew down to me. Instinctively I held up my wrist, and he landed on my forearm. In the beginning with Roash and Humbug, there was a bit of a connection, but nothing like now. Big doors shutting away that part of my life have reopened. I couldn't be happier."

She tilted her face to the sky and smiled, her eyes closing naturally as the birds' cries rose up around her. "And now I feel like me again."

INSIDE, EAGLE DIDN'T know what to say. The evidence was all around him. In the past he may not have believed in anything he couldn't see or touch, but right now a tiny owl perched on his forearm. And it looked to have made itself right at home. In fact, it really liked his gray wool sweater. He'd thrown it on earlier when he'd gone out to stand guard, and this little owl leaned into it every once in a while, rubbing his head back and forth. That the owl was called Rubiks made his heart cheer. It was adorable. He respected and loved the birds in his care. But he sure as hell hadn't become friends with them like she had. He glanced at Panther and Tiger.

He knew his friends. They had decades of military experience behind them, just like he had, and they were as dumbfounded as he was now. They stared at him—expecting him to explain. He shook his head. "I don't know what to say."

Panther turned to her. "Ma'am, you are the damnedest thing …"

Her lips widened into a big fat grin. With a trill of laughter, she said, "Thank you."

She was like a small child who somebody gave one of the biggest and best gifts to.

Panther walked to the big living room window. It was still wide open, and the birds flew in and out. He watched the species swirl around him, come in, and then swirl back out again as if checking on the inside of the house, making sure all was well, only to leave again. Panther turned to stare at Tiger and then Eagle. "Is this for real, or are we on some bizarre drug trip?"

Eagle nodded. "It sure as hell is for real."

Tiger said, "And this is exactly why somebody's after her." He shook his head. "Man, you cannot let that happen."

"Too late. They are already looking for me." She gasped and turned pale. "That's it. Now I remember."

Eagle reached her side in seconds. "What are you talking about?"

"Trauma. My original connection to Hadrid. It came from trauma. I was stuck. I fell off the craggy cliffs into a crevice. I had screamed and cried for help, but nobody heard me. My leg was broken, and I was violently ill from the pain. Nobody came." Her voice was dark, the chill in her eyes bleak.

Eagle gently patted her shoulder. "Why would you even be alone?"

She slowly turned her gaze his way and said, "My mother. She told me to go and play. She was busy."

His lip curled. "With her lover?"

"It was a man. But I don't remember if it was Angus or not," she said quietly. She shook her head. "I was so very young. I remember I fell once and sprained my ankle. They took X-rays. The old break showed up."

"What did your mother say to the doctor?" he asked, his tone dark.

"She said I broke it by being foolish."

Panther stepped toward her. "Was she always so harsh?"

"Always," Issa said flatly. "You had to know her. She wasn't very warm or caring."

"I can see that," Tiger said with a half a snarl. "She doesn't sound like a loving mother at all."

"Go back to what you were talking about, when you said *trauma*," Eagle said, getting the conversation back on track. "What did that mean?"

"Hadrid found me. Hadrid led my father to me. Hadrid had a leg band telling us it was one of Angus's birds. Hadrid had already bonded to me. Angus knew that there was no point in arguing and sold him to my father."

"So you were crying out for someone to help, and the bird comes?" Panther asked in disbelief. "How does that happen?"

She turned her gaze his way. "No one else would listen to me," she said softly. "My father and brothers didn't care. My mother obviously didn't care." She shrugged. "Apparently my cries connected with Hadrid—who did care."

At their snorts of disbelief she gave a half smile. "My family was many things, but I was the odd one out. I was a girl, not my father's favorite son. And I was so much less than anybody else. I was a liability to them. Until I found a way not to become a liability."

"Was your fall an accident?"

She nodded. "Yes. But, after I had the broken leg, I used to sit on the cliffs and watch my family below. We were above Smugglers Cove. I could see boats. I had one of those long telescope things to look through. My father would leave my mother and me as a lookout. It was more of a joke, to include me, but my mother would leave it to me anyway."

"Did your father know it was just you?" He watched as her gaze turned inward.

Then she said softly, "I think he suspected I was alone."

The men shook their heads. "Not sure I think much of your family," Tiger said. He turned to the kitchen. "I'm making some coffee."

"To hell with coffee. Is there anything stronger around here?" Panther snarled. "Just the thought of her family makes me want to puke. And, if I'm not doing that, I want a couple good stiff drinks."

A sharp crack sounded. Something hit the window as Panther walked toward Tiger. He hit the ground as Tiger hit the lights. Eagle tackled Issa and flattened her onto the couch. She cried out in his arms. His head was close to hers as he whispered, "Stay down."

She gazed at him and whispered, "Was that a gunshot?"

He nodded.

She struggled to get out of his arms. "Did Panther get shot? We have to help him."

He clapped a hand over her mouth. She nodded in understanding. He released her, slipped around the couch, and headed for Panther. Only he was already gone. Relieved to see he wasn't badly hurt, Eagle took a quick look to find both men taking positions at the windows. "Panther?"

"Just a graze."

Eagle doubted it. But Panther was one hell of a big man, and it would take a lot for him to admit he was hurt. With his gaze adjusted to the darkness, he gave Panther a quick look over. There appeared to be blood on his shoulder and upper arm. But he was using his arm. The three men looked at each other.

"Sharpshooter?" Tiger asked.

"Must be."

"Security system is still intact," Eagle said. "It got a good workout yesterday."

"Our weapons are in the truck," Tiger said. "We will have a hard time getting to them from the back door of your house."

"There is a window and glass deck door in the spare room. You can go out that way. But you don't have to go anywhere. Every room has a rifle at every window."

The men looked around, and, almost with cheers at the sight, they picked up the rifles. "Fully locked and loaded?"

"The only way to keep 'em," Eagle bit out.

He could hear the gasp of surprise from Issa at his side. He glanced at her and raised an eyebrow.

"Can you teach me how to shoot?"

"I can do that. Later."

"I'm not much of a fan of being a sitting duck," Panther said. "I suggest Tiger and I head out and locate where these assholes are. You stay here, look after Issa."

Eagle struggled with the concept. But it wasn't just Issa,

it was also the birds.

"They can't. It's too dangerous," Issa said.

"They know the property as well as I do," Eagle said in a low voice.

"They do?" Issa asked.

He nodded. "They helped build the security system."

The two men went through Issa's bedroom and slipped out the back. Issa shifted on the couch, staring in the direction the men left from.

Eagle walked back to her. "They will see if anybody is out there."

"Yes, but you don't want to look after me. You should go with them."

He gave a small snort. "I'm not leaving you."

She nodded. "How about I just hide? You check the property and make sure the animals are safe."

He shook his head. "Not happening."

"I have the birds." She placed a finger on his lips. "This isn't the time to worry about me," she whispered.

"It's only about you. These men are here to help you. Nobody gets to you, do you hear me?"

He watched her eyes glisten with tears. But she nodded. "I get you." Then she did something that completely shocked him. She slid her fingers across his cheek, grabbed him by the ears, and pulled him down. Just before their lips connected, she whispered, "Thank you."

And she kissed him. It was not a light thank-you kiss, but a deep searingly passionate kiss that reached inside his loins and yanked at him hard.

When she released him, he was still locked in the trance of her spell. He shook his head. "Lady, you pack a mean punch."

"We all have our weapons."

He stared at her for a long moment.

"What did I say?"

He glanced at the window, then down at her. "You do have some unusual ones. It occurs to me, can you find out if a predator is out there, like you did with Hadrid?"

She raised her eyebrows and shook her head. "I just learned minutes ago that these birds and I can communicate on some level. But to send them out, like scouts? Have them report back? That's a lot to ask for—from them and me. I've been sending messages to Humbug and Roash, but we've learned that over the last several months." She paused, pursed her lips. "Humbug isn't flying well."

"I thought Humbug was incapable of flying in the first place, other than two-foot jumps." He studied her. "How did he manage that?"

She stared up at him. "I don't know. I'm not this person with magical powers," she snapped. "Maybe Stefan had something to do with it."

"Yeah, that Stefan guy again." He shook his head. "We need to talk to him."

"Tomorrow. And maybe Tabitha. She's connected to Humbug. Maybe they can feed him enough energy so he can make his way here."

He gave her a sidelong look. "You do realize how bizarre that sounds?"

Her lips twitched, and her eyes glowed with mystery as she motioned to the ceiling above them. "And this isn't weird?"

He crouched down and turned to look at all the birds. "Okay, so this is beyond weird. What you're talking about, other people remotely feeding a bird energy—whatever the hell that means—and helping to direct it to this place ..."

A cry sounded outside. Eagle raced to the window and peered out.

"That was a bird cry," Issa said. "Not human."

He turned to look at her. "Are you willing to bet on that?"

She stared at him steadily for a long moment and then nodded. "I think the human cry might come soon."

His brow furrowed as he stared at her in confusion. And, sure enough, screams split the air. Human screams.

He raced out and froze. "Wait here," he said. And then the cries shut off suddenly. "Jesus." He slipped out the front door to his security fence line. He stared into the darkness, but nothing was ahead of him. A human cry from the left caught his attention.

He quickly responded. The cry hadn't sounded like Panther or Tiger. That meant somebody else was on the property. He didn't dare leave Issa unprotected for long. He sent out a call, letting both men know where he was. The call was answered from up ahead.

He tracked his men to the raptor pens to find them kneeling over a man on the ground. Pulling out his phone, he used the flashlight to check the man over. He appeared to still be breathing but not for very long. As the flashlight climbed higher up his face—one Eagle didn't recognize—the men at his side gasped.

"I'm pretty sure the sheriff won't have too much trouble figuring out what happened to him." The flashlight illuminated the hideous details.

The man's eyes had been scratched out.

CHAPTER 20

ISSA WAITED IN the darkness for the men to come back. She'd watched Eagle head toward the pens. When would those assholes give up? Would they ever? She was putting them all in danger by staying here. But where would she go? And if she was truthful, she'd admit she didn't want to leave Eagle.

After all she'd laid on him today, she'd probably shocked him. The kiss most of all. He was the kind of guy who would like to be in control. And she hadn't given him an option. But she figured, if she didn't show him how she felt soon, then he would never make a move. She slipped to her bedroom and wondered at the sensibility of packing up and walking out. Would Eagle come after her? *Yes.* Would the assholes? *Yes.*

So he and she would remain in danger regardless.

Plus she didn't have anything to carry her new belongings in. Then the fact that she couldn't walk very far. Plus Eagle had his land peppered with booby traps. She wasn't likely to get off the property at this rate. She sat on the side of the bed and rubbed her head. Her temples were pounding. The window was open, letting the birds move in and out.

Fragments of images slammed into her head once again. Bits and pieces. She could hear voices outside, but there appeared to be voices inside too. The pain was killing her. There was just no stopping it. The bird cries and the voices, memories from her childhood. She didn't dare turn on a light until she was told it was okay. The last thing she wanted to do was bring attention to herself. That would cause Eagle more complications. But, as she stared down at the boxes, she realized she really needed to spend more time here.

"You okay?"

She lifted her gaze to see Eagle standing in the doorway. She nodded. "My head is hurting. Maybe if I just lie down." She waved at the bed. "Unless there is something I can do?"

He shook his head. "No, it's all taken care of. We didn't see anyone."

She frowned. "You're covered in blood, so obviously you're lying to me. Is he dead?"

He shook his head. "No. We called an ambulance."

"Did your security system get him?"

He snorted. "No, but yours did." And he turned. "I'm going to clean Panther's wound. It's not bad, but he needs a clean bandage. If you feel like it, come join us. But, if you aren't feeling well, stay where you are."

"I was thinking about leaving," she called out. "Do you have an old duffel bag or anything I could pack my clothing in?"

Silence.

She frowned. Had he not heard her?

He turned back, pulled her into his arms, and kissed her with a rage. Like he was angry that he wanted her. Angry she'd come into his life. Or maybe just angry she was talking about leaving. When he lifted his head, she murmured at the loss of his touch.

He lowered his head again, and this time his lips were gentle, soothing as they lightly stroked her ravaged mouth. "I'm sorry. I didn't mean to be so rough."

"It's okay," she whispered.

"No, it's not okay. But I want you. I want you so damn bad. It makes me angry to hear you talk about walking out. You aren't going anywhere." He laid her down on the bed, turned, and left her room. "So stop acting or talking like you're going to. Not gonna happen."

HE STORMED FROM the room, more pissed than he could remember being in a long time. And hurt that she'd even think about leaving him. Didn't she realize she belonged here with him and his birds and his dogs?

Tiger stepped inside and studied him. "You didn't mention how badly she's got you tied up in knots."

"Nothing to mention," he snapped.

In the darkness behind Tiger, Panther's grin flashed white. Eagle glared at his friends, but they just gave him fat smiles in return.

"Are you going to stand there all night?" he growled. "Or help me figure this out?"

"We're here, aren't we?"

He went to the kitchen and pulled out his first aid kit. "Panther, let's clean that up."

"Nope, all good."

But his drawl had deepened, with just enough stillness to his tone that Eagle knew Panther was lying. "I'm just about in the right mood to fight you over this, so why don't you do both of us a favor and sit."

Tiger pulled out a chair, flipped it around, and pointed.

Panther glared. Eagle stared silently back. Like hell he'd give in. He was up for the fight if Panther wanted one. In fact, Eagle would welcome it.

Anger and outrage warred inside. Somehow she was planning to leave. Almost escape. How was he supposed to feel about that?

"We aren't trying to interfere," Tiger said quietly. "But it was pretty obvious she was looking to leave."

Eagle turned his glare to Tiger. Warning his friend not to go there.

But they'd been buddies for years. Inasmuch as Tiger was right, Eagle shouldn't take it out on him. Tiger grinned, flashing white teeth that lit the room on fire. It had always been like that. He'd flash a smile, and things cooled instantly. Eagle wished he was more like that. The truth of the matter was, he burned a little slower and rose a little higher and took a little longer to cool down afterward. And, just like that, his temper eased back.

He gave a clipped nod. "She doesn't know how dangerous it is. But it still is irritating." He ran his fingers through his hair.

"Will she stay in there now, or will she escape through the back door?"

Eagle gave Tiger a startled look, turned, and bolted toward the bedroom. She was curled up in bed, her secondhand clothes stuffed in a plastic bag on the floor beside her. Leaving would be suicide right now. Surely she had enough sense to know that.

"I won't leave," she said, her small voice coming from the bed.

He heard the tears clogging her throat. He bowed his head, feeling like a heel. He sat down beside her, but she wouldn't have it. Her face was buried in the pillow, her hair covering her gentle features. Swearing softly, he stood, pulled the blankets off her, and tugged her into his arms. He didn't know why he kept doing this. But he could no longer stop.

"I'm sorry," he whispered. "I didn't need to be so harsh. You've had a lot of rough treatment from those men. I don't want to add to that."

She sniffled, a hand wiping her face like a child.

He smiled and brushed her hair back off her forehead. His eyes automatically noted the colorful rings on her cheeks, under her eyelids. "You're doing better but not that good yet."

She nodded. "I know. But I was hoping my anger might get me out the door, out to the gate. I'm not sure how far I could go from there," she admitted.

He chuckled. "I need to dress Panther's injury. I am counting on you to stay here."

She tilted her head back, her gaze curious. "On one condition."

He frowned. "I don't like bargaining."

She gave him a glimmer of a smile. "Can you give me another kiss?"

His jaw dropped. The face of the woman who sounded like a lost child now bloomed into a big wide grin. "Okay, it's a bargain." And so very gently he leaned down, tilted her chin up, and kissed her. Her lips were so damn sweet. Almost fragile and yet not. Nobody who survived what she had would be considered fragile.

Just as he pulled away, she reached around his neck and tugged him down toward her. This time she was kissing him. And suddenly he was ravaging her mouth. His body shook. They weren't there yet. But they would be. When she healed.

And that reminder was enough to cool his ardor.

He broke them apart, breathing hard, and whispered, "This is so not the time or place, and you're not healthy enough for that yet," he said with regret.

A grin flashed across her face, and he swore he saw a dimple. Where the hell had that come from?

She slipped off his lap, back under the blankets, and whispered, "Good night. And sweet dreams."

He snorted. "You might have sweet dreams. Not me. Mine will be damn hot." He got up and walked out. As he headed to the kitchen, he thought he heard a light chuckle from Tiger. Eagle was grinning like a madman when he got to Panther.

Panther said, "I don't know what kind of magic that girl has, but she's working it on you so very easily."

"It has just been a little too long," Eagle muttered. He slammed the first-aid stuff back on the table. "Let's take care of that."

With Panther sitting quietly, Eagle cleaned and washed the wound. "You need a couple stitches."

Panther shrugged his massive shoulders. "Don't bother."

"You know as well as I do that wounds heal faster when pinched together."

While he worked, the two men talked. "What's next?"

"I need to track down the lock that key fits."

"Don't forget my dad's a locksmith. If there's something to learn about that key, he'd be the one to ask," Panther said.

"Shit, I forgot about that." Eagle finished, cleaning up the mess.

"Let's take a picture of it and send it to him."

He stopped, turned, and looked at Panther. "Pop knows how to use a computer?"

"Does he ever," Panther said proudly. "He's learned to do all kinds of stuff. Scary actually."

Tiger snorted. "You're not kidding. He's always wanting at my computer so he can overclock my stuff." He shook his head. "I don't let him go anywhere close to my electronics."

"However, some of that shit he did was pretty cool. He hooked his TV up to some kind of satellite box, then ran the wires to his computer, and he tapped into some archaic VCR system."

Eagle laughed. "He was always good at inventing things, wasn't he?" He retrieved the key, putting it on the table. "You guys recognize this?"

The two men studied the key, picked it up, felt the weight of it, and shrugged. "Could be for a safe-deposit box, but it would have to be an old one."

"It might be a safe-deposit strongbox," Panther said. "I've spent a lifetime around keys." He took a picture and sent it to his father. "The old man might take a while though."

But he was wrong. Less than two minutes later, Panther's phone rang. He looked down in surprise. "Pop, what are you still doing up?"

"Cleaning up your ma's laptop. Damn thing's a pain in the ass because it's not meant to be upgraded. She gave me some trouble, but I got her done."

Horrified, Panther stared down at the phone he held out in front of him so everyone could hear the conversation. "Pop, does Mom know what you did?"

"Not yet. Getting it back together again before she gets up in the morning. Don't you tell her, son."

They all knew Pop, as they had learned to call him years ago. He was getting in and out of trouble on a daily basis.

They were pretty damn sure that Mom, as they called her, was fully prepared for every new mess he created.

"The key you asked me about? You know what that is?"

"Safe-deposit box or strongbox? Right?"

"Yes. That deposit key is from a foreign bank."

"Can we tell what bank?" Eagle stepped into the conversation.

"Eagle? Is that you? You in trouble again, young boy?"

Eagle winced. "What do you mean, *again*? It isn't me that's in trouble." He looked over at Issa lying helplessly in the bed in his spare room. It wasn't exactly something he wanted to explain to anyone, particularly not over the phone.

"You're in trouble though. Do you have a way to track down what country?"

Eagle nodded. "Ireland."

"So what did you bother me for? It's a pretty damn old key. Doesn't mean anybody still has the box. You know that, right?"

"So it could be a strongbox then too?"

"I reckon." After that Pop rang off.

The three men stared at each other, frowning.

Eagle turned his gaze toward the bedroom again to check on Issa's position. No sign she'd moved since he had walked out. "We have the two boxes retrieved from her place. I didn't see anything in them referencing a key. We scanned it all as fast as we could, just in case they were stolen. But we still have the paper copies."

"Then bring them out. With the three of us, we'll get through them faster."

Trying not to disturb Issa, he quietly brought out the box with all the paperwork and then the keepsake box.

Panther suggested, "Let's take a thorough look, then

pack and seal it, so we don't need to go through it again."

Eagle opened the keepsake box obediently, sorry it showed wear from sheer age plus from their unpacking of its contents. The lid was slightly damaged and part of the inside tray fell apart, displaying a piece of paper.

"Damn. I feel like she should be the one to look at this."

"Hell no. She's sleeping." Tiger shook his head. "We're watching over her. The sooner we find out what the hell's going on, the better. We could wait hours for Sleeping Beauty to wake up."

Eagle admitted they had a point. He pulled it out and took a look. "It's a letter from her mother. It talks about bank accounts and, yes, a safe-deposit box," he said quietly. "Let me scan this in the computer."

The note started with an apology.

I'm sorry, Issa. I never did right by you. I've tried to in the end, but you were so very different than the rest of my children. Maybe because you had a different side. Every time I saw you, it was a reminder of the life I'd never have. I loved Angus. But I was married to your da. And he would never have let me go. Angus wanted me to leave with him. And, to this day, I don't know if Angus had something to do with your da's death, as I suspect. It all happened so fast. I don't think the truth will ever be known. Your da didn't know about me and Angus for a long time. Until he caught us. That's why he beat Angus, almost killing him. And we stopped for a while.

What you don't know is that there's money for you ... and a few other things that are very special. After all, there is no one else left in the family to receive it. I didn't dare touch it. It's blood money. Some from

Da. Some from Angus. I loved both men and lost them both. There is no forgiveness for that. For the longest time I figured there was no forgiveness for you either. That there must be something evil in your spirit because the birds would talk to you. When we came to America, you were still so shocked, still in such pain, and couldn't talk. I realized you were really what you've always been—just an innocent child—but I couldn't change how I felt. And for that I know you must hate me too. Still maybe the money will help make up for it. It's in Ireland. I don't dare go back and retrieve it. There could be men waiting for me—and now you. I don't know how many years it'll take before this will blow over. I left as soon as I could. After all, there was nothing to keep me there. Even now I don't know the truth of what happened that night. Maybe it's for the best.

The key for the safe-deposit box is in here too. It's for the bank where your da kept everything. There are account numbers and the safe-deposit box number written on the back of this letter. And then there is an old keepsake box I left at your favorite place—a duplicate of the one I had at home. The address is on the back too. Once you open up the box, you will open up so much more than you really want to know. Part of me wants you to walk away and leave it. Just like I did. You're strong. You're educated. You're capable. You don't need the pain that will come by going back. But the other part of me says you have as much right to it as anyone. Maybe it's time for the truth to come out anyway. What we know of the truth anyway. Know that I love you, even though I never showed you.

Your mother

CHAPTER 21

S HE WOKE WHEN she heard the voices talking about the keepsake box and something about a letter. When she heard the letter being read out loud, tears came to her eyes. She threw back the blankets, sat up, and walked softly into the kitchen. She wrapped her arms around her chest and whispered, "Do you think she loved me at all?"

The men turned to see her, guilt written on their faces.

She waved a hand dismissively. "You were right to read it. I could've slept for hours." She reached for the letter. Eagle gave it to her and went back to inspecting the box. She knew he would dismantle it panel by panel. She studied the bank information. "None of this means anything to me."

"It doesn't matter. All the information is there." He glanced at her. "Do you have a passport?"

She frowned. "It's in my own safe-deposit box at the bank. I had no security at my cabin. I didn't know where else to keep things like that."

"How do you feel about a road trip?"

She dropped down on the closest kitchen chair. "Are you talking about going to Ireland?"

Eagle nodded. "We have to get to the bottom of this."

"Even though she wanted me to leave it alone?"

He crossed his arms. "Good point. It is your decision, not mine."

Panther said, "Some things are meant to be left alone."

"But all of it would've been twenty years ago, and how much more pain could there be now? I already know my father was a criminal and that he might not even be my father." She took a deep breath. "The biggest problem with not going is always wondering …"

The men waited and nodded.

She looked from one to the other. "All of us?"

Panther shook his head. "Nope. We'd stay here and look after the place, take care of the birds. We've done it lots of times in the past. You and Eagle need to go. And you need to go fast."

"Unless you don't feel like you're capable physically. I suspect that what you were being tortured for was the information in these boxes."

Startled, she glanced down at the letter. "Do you think so?"

"They were looking for something at your cabin, remember?" Eagle said quietly.

"Yes, they were. And they were talking about my childhood." She frowned. "But I don't think I want to get the Irish authorities involved …"

"I have friends over there." Eagle turned to look at Panther and Tiger. "Do we still have a couple men in Ireland?"

"Jonah is in Ireland," Panther said. "You know he would be more than happy to help."

"Can he look into this for me?" Issa asked. "Then I wouldn't have to go."

The men turned long thoughtful stares at her.

She flushed. "I guess I'm scared," she whispered. "I don't want to be caught again, and I don't have a clue what to do with this stuff."

"It's always better to face these things head-on," Eagle said.

She shuddered, realizing that really was the best way. She gave a quick nod. "How long do we need? How quickly can we leave? I don't want to be away from my friends. I'm still trying to heal and help Roash and Humbug. Then there are the men here causing trouble."

"We can be there by noon tomorrow," Eagle said. "At least in England, then on to Ireland. It depends on how far away this place is. So it's possible we can be home in three days."

Her gaze widened. "And Humbug?"

He stared at her gently, and she knew what he was thinking. He had no proof Humbug was even alive. That she was able to help him. "Can you tell me exactly where Humbug is?"

"No." She shook her head. "You go."

"Without you?"

She stared at him steadily. "I'm not well enough to fly. You know that. I need to be here for Humbug, and I trust you. You can bring back whatever is in the safe-deposit box and in the house. That's the best answer." She got up and hobbled her way to bed. "I'm going back to sleep."

In her room she clutched the letter from her mother in her hand. She sat down on the bed and tucked under the blankets. She folded the letter and put it on the night table. Closing her eyes, she fell asleep.

When she woke up the next morning, the sun shone into her room. She sat up, listening to the silence of the empty house, and slipped out to the bathroom. She didn't want to leave here. Not to go home and not to go to Ireland. But this was Eagle's home. Had he left for Ireland already? She closed her eyes and searched for him mentally.

And found him. She frowned, walked out the back door, stood on the little deck, and stared. He was across the yard at the pens. He raised a hand in greeting and carried on. She smiled as the birds came to greet her. Some were on the roof above; some flew in the sky.

So many were lined up on the railing beside her. This was why she couldn't leave. She knew they didn't need her— she needed them. She stroked the beautiful feathers of the few closest to her.

Eagle asked, "How do you feel?"

"Good," she said in a determined voice, afraid he would try to persuade her to go to Ireland. "I don't want to go to Ireland," she said in a firm voice. "My decision is final."

He gave a clipped nod and said, "Good. Panther and Tiger went for us instead."

"They what?" she exclaimed in both horror and relief.

He shrugged. "I trust them with my life. I have many times. They've already left to catch the plane." He glanced down at his watch. "When they hit Ireland, I'll let you know. And then it's a quick hop to the bank and to the address we have." He gave her a smile. "If you want to, you can put on some coffee. I found an old carafe that fits." With that he turned and headed back toward the birds.

Leaving her standing, staring after him.

HE COULD FEEL her gaze following him every step he took away from her. He knew he'd startled her. But he also knew she was relieved. So was he. It was one thing to take her when she was healthy and fit. It was another thing entirely when she was still recovering. And he had meant it when he'd said he trusted Panther and Tiger with his life—he had done so many times. They'd gone on many missions together for years. They had a network of men throughout the world to call on if they needed to.

He went back to the incubators and checked on the timing of the different units. Recording his notes on the big clipboard to the side, he shuffled feedbags and opened up the freezers. He was due to get more fish in soon. He hoped he had enough to get through this nightmare. The fisheries often dropped off crates of frozen fish for him—usually an illegal catch that had been confiscated.

He opened up a bundle of fish, took up his ax, and chopped up several chunks on the big board he kept on the ground. He'd leave them to thaw while he carried on feeding the others.

By the time he came back, the fish had thawed nicely in a pool of juices. He divvied up portions and carried them out to the eagles. After they were fed, he grabbed his big heavy metal rake and cleaned up the base of the pens. With that done, he dumped the load, set the rake in the wheelbarrow, and parked both beside the pens.

He stopped for a moment, staring at the long driveway, then headed back inside. When he stepped through the door, Issa was curled up on the couch, a cup in her hand, studying him.

He stopped and stared, feeling a sense of rightness he hadn't known before. A woman had never lived here with him. This house had missed a woman's touch. And it was funny just how much that touch happened on a natural basis.

The kitchen table he usually covered with discarded newspapers had been cleaned off, the sugar and cream bowls at the center. Underneath them was some kind of checkered cloth. He didn't know where she'd gotten it. She studied him for a long moment. He smiled and carried on to the coffeepot. "Did you leave me any?"

"Of course," she answered smoothly. "How often do you go into town?"

He poured his cup, turned to look at her, and said, "What do you need?"

"I don't need anything." She shook her head. "Roash and Humbug. I can sense them. But I don't know where they are."

"Can you call them?"

She shrugged. "I have been. It's as if something's between them and me."

"What does that mean?"

"Don't you think if I knew, I would have found a way to get past it?" she said in frustration.

"Call Stefan?"

Her jaw dropped. "Make a long-distance call to a stranger?"

"Unless you have another way?"

He eyed her over the rim of his cup as he took a sip of the hot brew, loving the fact she'd very quickly picked up on how he liked his coffee. It was stronger than most people could stomach, but it was about the only way he could handle it. Otherwise it just tasted like dishwater to him. "I wouldn't mind talking to him myself."

Instantly the phone rang.

Eagle stared at it, like a bomb ready to go off. It sat nearby on the kitchen table. "That's going to be him, right?"

She snorted. "You're asking me?"

He strode forward, snatched the phone off the table, and

answered, "Hello."

"Yes, it's me," Stefan said. "It would be a lot easier if I could talk to you in other ways. Put the phone on Speaker please."

There was just enough of an order in his words to get Eagle's back up. But still, the man had either heard the conversation or heard something. And, if he could help Issa, Eagle didn't want to antagonize him.

"Very smart," Stefan murmured. "Know this. I have no intention of hurting her or any of the birds on the property or those on their way to her."

"I hope a lot more aren't coming this way. I don't have enough feed for too many more."

"Let's hope you have room for these two," Stefan said, fatigue pulling in his voice. Now with the phone on Speaker, his voice filled the room, his tone harsher as it echoed off the walls.

"Stefan?" Issa asked in disbelief.

"Yes, it's me. I don't normally listen in on conversations," he said. "But you've got a bloody highway between you and the birds. So when I hear you say there's like cotton batten between you and them, it's a little irritating. Because it's not by their choice. When you were a child, there was nothing between you and Hadrid. Communication was clear, concise, and you were in control. But you were in control naturally and followed what you needed to do, knowing you were in the right, and knowing you could do it. There was never any question. But now that you're an adult, and you've missed all those years in between, you're questioning everything. You keep searching for the same connection, but you're searching in all the wrong places." His voice was full of exasperation. "Because the only place you should look for something like this is inside yourself."

Dumbfounded, Issa could only stare at Eagle.

In the meantime, Eagle said, "While you're on the line, can I ask you something? She does this one thing that's really freaky. I don't know, otherworldly. It's like she's in a trance. I've seen it twice now, and it just freaks the hell out of me."

Stefan's tone was sharp when he snapped, "Please explain."

Issa said, "Yes, explain. You never mentioned that to me before."

Eagle took a moment, gathering his thoughts. "Twice I came upon her, once in the bed and once on the couch. I thought she was asleep, except her eyes were wide open. When I checked to see if she was okay, it was like she was in a trance, and, when I looked deep into her eyes, I didn't see her eyes anymore."

"What do you mean, you don't see her eyes anymore?" Stefan asked curiously. "That's a fascinating observation."

"It's as if her eyes, the iris itself, had become like a galaxy. I don't see planets obviously, but I see light dots of colors. Yet there is no pupil, no iris, and no longer any white of her eyes." He heard Issa's shocked gasp. "More than that, it's almost like I can see images outside of her eyes." He fumbled to a stop. "Forget that. That just sounds too stupid."

"Actually it sounds very logical. You need to tell me more."

"*Logical?* How the hell does that work?" He tried again. "Think about a megaphone. Where the small end is against her mouth and the large end is a foot or two away. At the large end, it's like there are images—colors—something showing. As I was watching, I could see bits and pieces moving in the air. When I tried to look from the same position she was in, it was clearer. I could see part of the sky, lakes, fields. When I moved back, it was like a disturbance in the air, but ..." He stopped, stumped for words.

"Did you see the same thing when she was on the couch as when she was in the bed?"

"Sort of. Her face was almost trancelike but with a sense of animation or life that set it apart from her being unconscious. Something was going on—but I couldn't understand what. There was also a kind of buzz in the air. The first time I wondered if it was from the electrical lines outside. Sometimes in cold weather you can hear a buzz off them." Eagle shook his head. "I'm just not sure how to describe it. When she was on the couch, there were a lot of noises outside, and I couldn't really hear any buzz that time."

"The noise makes sense too," Stefan said. "That's the energy crackling. She's connecting on a feral level to something else. The thing is, what else is she connecting to?"

"Hey, I'm here too, you guys—remember?"

It was Eagle's turn to snort. "Oh, and here I just thought you were struck dumb," he said.

She glared at him and stared at the phone. "Stefan, what does any of that mean?"

"It goes back to the same issue. What you did as a child was normal and natural. But it was taken away from you when you were so young, and you grew up with all that distrust, disbelief, and told yourself everything was not true, that it was just a childish memory. If that makes any sense," he said humorously. "A lot of this work is trust-based. You have to have faith. And, as we grow older, we're sucked into mainstream thinking. Which is why it makes sense that this is happening when you're in a deep subconscious state.

Because, inside your soul, your subconscious knows what is true, and it's probably been doing this all along. Or something has triggered this reaction, and it's happening now, whereas it wasn't before."

Eagle frowned. "She's had nothing but traumatic events. First off her mother died unexpectedly. Less than a week later she was kidnapped and systematically tortured for weeks. I found her outside my inner yard, broken and bleeding and sporting a bullet hole."

They both heard Stefan suck in his breath, something changing in the atmosphere. Eagle looked at Issa, who sat staring at the phone oddly.

As Stefan spoke, his voice changed, becoming deeper, almost disembodied. "Yes. This is your childhood once again. You need to think about what happened when you connected with Hadrid," he said. "I don't know if it has anything to do with Ireland and the trip somebody is taking on your behalf. You need to understand why the kidnappers were putting you under the stressors they were."

His voice returned to normal, and he said, "I have to leave now. Keep calling for Humbug." And he hung up.

It took a long moment to break the trance from his call. Issa settled back on the couch and said, "Stressors?"

"Meaning some form of stress applied to get a result or a desired outcome," Eagle said quietly. He walked around the couch, filled his cup with more warm brew, and returned to her side. He studied her for a long moment. "I'm afraid I might have an idea what he was talking about."

She frowned. "Glad you do, because I sure as hell don't."

"Think back to when you were a child and you first met Hadrid. The relief that something, someone appeared to care."

She started to shake her head. "I can't remember that long ago."

Eagle stared in shock as she moved from a wakefulness to a trancelike state, as her eyes once again glowed with an otherworldly light. He grabbed his phone and took a picture, though he didn't think there was anything large enough for anyone to see. He took several and then realized he was wasting his time trying to get proof of this happening.

He spoke quietly. "Look back into your history. Remember when you were a child stuck in a crevice, and Hadrid came to rescue you. See what the stressors were at that time. See what the outcome was at that time. Bring back all those memories to the present day."

He kept repeating the same thing over and over again. He had no idea if she heard him, would respond to his positive suggestions or not, but, if Stefan had said something in her childhood related to her kidnapping, then they needed to find out more. That Stefan had even called and understood the conversations or knew that somebody had gone to Ireland on her behalf was all just a little too much to take in. But Eagle was nothing if not adaptable. As he'd proven since she'd arrived.

Suddenly she grasped his hand. "Call them. They're in trouble. Now."

He stared at her. She blinked and suddenly it was her again.

She leaned forward urgently and said, "Call Panther and Tiger. They are walking into trouble. You have to warn them."

He stood back up, pulled up Tiger's number, and called him. Tiger answered after several rings. "What's up, man? We just arrived."

"Yeah. I don't know that there is any point in me calling you, but, according to Issa, you're walking into some kind of trouble. She insisted I call and warn you."

"What? Did you just tell her that we left?" He chuckled.

"No. That was hours ago. She just went into a weird trancelike state, snapped out of it, saying I had to warn you and fast."

He heard Tiger take a long deep breath. "Jesus, she's weird."

"Yes, but no doubt something is going on. So watch your back."

"I'm watching my back and my front."

Eagle could hear the laughter in his voice.

But then he sobered and said, "You know we're always careful, right? Thanks for the heads-up." He hung up.

Eagle glanced at her and said, "I've done all I can."

She gave him the saddest smile he'd ever seen, then she said, "I don't think it'll be enough."

STEFAN CARRIED HIS mug of tea onto the deck and sat down. He was grateful for something. There was one chair not covered in bird droppings. He stared at his deck and shook his head. "The unexpected negatives of having birds around," he muttered.

Celina came around from behind him, holding her own mug of tea, and said, "I see a good night's rest didn't help."

"How can anything help? I'm completely sidetracked by an owl," he said in disgust. "Serial killers out there don't have half the connecting power of this thing."

"Did you ever figure out why the connection to the owl is so strong?"

Stefan shook his head. "No," he said shortly and sighed. "I didn't mean to snap. Lack of sleep and now nine canvases have an owl on them."

She grinned, then started to laugh. He opened his arms, and she sat down in his lap. "Maybe there's a market for owl paintings?" she asked with a note of humor.

Stefan shrugged. "No way to know. I'm just not sure how many more canvases I'm willing to sacrifice to the cause."

"Is it moving you any closer to an answer?"

"No. I'm still feeling Humbug. He's still moving cross-country but isn't going very far or very fast. Roash is with him, and that's all I know."

"It's a few hundred miles, is it not?"

"No, not that far."

"Any way for you to ..." She stopped and frowned. "I don't know, maybe teleport him physically?"

Stefan stared at her, and his jaw dropped. He started to laugh. "You mean, actually move them through energy to where he needs to be?"

She gave him a sheepish smile. "I know it sounds foolish, but it just occurred to me that, if it was possible, then this would be over a lot faster. Obviously he's heading to where Issa is. He's only going a mile or two or three a day, so can you do anything to speed this up?"

"Yesterday he managed four," Stefan said grudgingly. "He's almost halfway now."

He leaned his head back and smiled as she gently stroked his cheek. "So what you're trying to do is give him enough energy so he can do this on his own?" Her eyes smiled in comprehension.

He felt his heart melting as he realized once again how

lucky he was. Would anybody else understand him the way she did? When her lips gently stroked his forehead, he crushed her to him. Be damned with the tea. He'd give up a world of half-lived lifetimes for this moment of completeness.

"Did I ever tell you," she whispered, "how much I love your heart?"

He tilted his head back and looked up at her. "Just my heart?" he teased.

She stroked his nose. "All of you. But of all the people I know in this world, you're the only one who is driven by his heart."

He shook his head. "There are lots of us. Maddy's another one for sure."

She nodded. "But I don't know them like I know you. I don't see the purity, the strength, the compassion in their hearts, the same as I do in yours. I know they have the same elements as you. But I love *you*," she said with a smile.

He went to answer her, but a pain struck behind his eyes. Gasping, he straightened his arms, automatically wrapping around to hold her so she didn't fall off.

"What's wrong?" she asked. "What just happened?"

"It's Humbug," he groaned. "He made a crappy landing. Now he is hurting again."

She smiled gently. "Then you know what you need to do."

He opened his gaze and glared at her. "How many women tell their men to take a moment and help an owl? Especially one that's too stupid to land on its own?"

The words were hardly out of his mouth when her fingers stroked across his lips, and she whispered, "Not too stupid. Too tired. Undefeated. So determined to reunite with Issa that he'll do anything he can to get there. And with your help."

"And Tabitha's," Stefan added. "We can't forget she's doing the same thing I am, every day, every night."

Celina nodded her head. "And with Tabitha's help." She leaned over and wrapped her arms around him. "And I love you all the more for it."

Stefan hugged her tight. He was a fool. But it was the only way he knew how to be.

DYLAN RACED INTO the front yard. The truck doors slammed behind him as the others got out. The time was tight. Whatever the hell was going on was going on fast. And he had a rough idea what it was.

The boss's head jerked to the side as soon as Dylan burst through the doors. "What's changed?"

"The two men left. Went to the airport. With their IDs, we tracked them. They're flying into Dublin."

The boss's face lit up. "Finally," he said. He started to move his fingers—snapping—as his mind worked his way through the logistics of his next step.

Dylan watched. He'd seen it happen many times before. The boss'd be quiet for a while, and then, all of a sudden, he'd come up with a plan. Generally it was a good plan. Lately it was more violent.

Dylan waited quietly, the others coming in behind him. He put his arm up to stop them from bursting into the room and held his finger to his lips. He kept trying to teach the new guys, but they were too slow getting a message. But then they didn't have twenty-plus years of loyalty behind them. And the new guys were getting stupider by the day. He couldn't believe one had been attacked by the birds. He'd told the boss what had happened to the kid but not the other men, in case they spooked.

He needed them to the ugly finish line. And couldn't afford to lose any more men.

Finally the boss turned and said, "Get ahold of Ronnie and Gorham. Have them track the two men from the airport. See where they're headed. And tell the network they're coming. The only reason for these two men to go there is if she said something. We need to know what it is they are going after."

"Or who." Dylan nodded.

The boss frowned and continued snapping his fingers harder. Again and again and again. He stopped, turned, and stared at Dylan. "I'm not comfortable if one of us isn't there."

Dylan inclined his head. And waited.

The boss resumed his snapping, then stopped abruptly. "Is there anyone else we could call on over there?" He turned and glared at Dylan. "I mean, someone we can trust."

That's where the clincher was. Loyalty was down. People they could trust were thin on the ground. Dylan considered everybody they'd sent in the past. "I'm not sure. It's a risk."

The boss's frown deepened. "The owner and the girl—are they still at the house?"

"Yes." Dylan nodded.

The boss turned.

That same creepy smile washed over his face, and Dylan knew things were about to get violent.

"Then find a way to force those two to go to Ireland as well." The boss frowned, resumed his snapping but at a much slower pace. "Why wouldn't they have gone in the first place? They should've been the ones who left. How is it that these men are so trustworthy they would send them on something like this?"

"We don't know exactly what they know."

The boss nodded. He stared off in the distance. "It has to be connected. There is no such thing as coincidence." He started snapping again. Faster. "No, we have to make sure they go. Nothing else will work. She might try to get out of it. That's not going to happen."

Dylan took a deep breath. "She might not be well enough to travel."

The boss stopped, turned, and glared at him. Dylan refused to back down. They'd shot her, cut her, burned her, and beaten the shit out of her. Even Wonder Woman would need a week or two to recover. But that didn't mean she wasn't capable of getting on a plane. He knew that the man, Eagle, would make sure she was safe. So whatever they did to force the two to make the trip would have to be enough to shake him.

So it would have to be big—and nasty.

CHAPTER 22

T HE NEXT SEVERAL days went by quietly. Knowing some kind of time crunch raced toward them, Issa did everything she could to heal. She minimized all activity. She slept. She took long hot soaks, and, with the passage of time, she grew stronger and stronger. She knew she was healing faster than most people. Necessity was part of it, then so was her relationship to the birds around her. She'd always reached out for her birds when ill and gained strength from them. She'd done it subconsciously in the beginning, but now it was conscious. She knew the birds had willingly allowed her to use their life force, as she called it, but she had to do it carefully. Roash had been shot as well by the kidnappers, thankfully they had been lousy marksmen. But, by taking small amounts each time from him and Humbug, and any others she could mentally call out to, she'd lived long enough to escape her kidnappers.

And it was due to her birds. Only she had thought of it as a natural balance.

Until she'd spoken to Stefan. And connected the dots. Other people didn't do what she did. She didn't know if that made her a psychic or a sensitive, but it made her different from the rest of the world. Again. Yet she couldn't be upset about it. That relationship with her feathered friends had saved her life.

As she gained strength, as she could do more, Eagle let her. He worked with the birds outside, something she'd still avoided doing. She was afraid they were still being watched. She no longer had that same sensation but couldn't forget the possibility.

On the third day after Tiger and Panther left, Eagle walked inside carrying a small box. She glanced at him and said, "Did that just arrive?"

"Special delivery."

"All the way out here?"

He glanced at her and nodded. "The driver had been paid extra."

If that hadn't given her enough of an inkling, the hard tone in his voice would have. She got up very slowly, staring at the box, fear rippling through her. "That's not good then, is it?"

"I'm thinking it's not good at all." Eagle walked to the kitchen table, put the box down, grabbed a knife, and slowly opened the packaging. It was smaller than the size of a book and a little bit thicker. When it was open, he pulled out some of the packing paper and found a note. "No substitutions," he said. He turned the letter so she could see it.

She stared at it and knew. "Please tell me they didn't kill them."

He shot her a hard look and said, "Those men won't die easily."

With her heart in her throat she watched as he pulled out an even smaller box the size of a matchbook. And she just knew. She turned away. "I can't look." She heard the sound of the box being opened, and then he sucked back his breath. She shuddered. "What is it?"

"A tooth. A tooth covered with gold."

She clapped her hand over her mouth, her gaze huge as she stared at him. "Panther's?"

He nodded, his face grim. "Panther's favorite tooth. No way in hell they would've gotten that out of him unless he was either unconscious, dead, or pinned to the ground by a good half-dozen men." He stared down at the box, pulling out his phone. He dialed Panther's cell number. No answer. He dialed Tiger next. Still no answer. "We're leaving." He glanced at her. "A half hour ago."

She nodded. "I'll pack."

No substitutions meant she had to go. She had to put Panther and Tiger ahead of her birds. She wished she could drive around and try to find Humbug and Roash, but it was a big world out there, and all she ever saw of them was in heavily treed areas. It would be impossible to find them.

She'd hoped Stefan could track them but apparently not. She also figured, with her connection to them, she should be able to, ... but, no matter how hard she tried, even with sending them energy, she hadn't received any images of where they were.

Stefan's previous words whispered in her head. That she'd been the one flying with Hadrid. She'd been up there with him. Looking and seeing everything for herself. If that was true, she could do that with Humbug and see the world from his eyes—and maybe find out where he was.

But it took energy. And lots of it. Something she didn't have. It was all she could do to get through a day on her own two feet. This trip would finish her. But she had to go. She couldn't let anything happen to those two men because of her.

And she also knew Eagle wouldn't let her go alone. He would go after those who went after his friends. She sent

Roash and Humbug as much energy and encouragement as she could. From now on they'd have to do with a little less of her energy. It had nothing to do with distance and everything to do with resources.

Not true. There is enough energy for all of us. Just reach out, Stefan murmured in her head. *It takes a little practice, then suddenly all the energy you ever need is there and available for you.*

She opened her mouth to answer him, but he was gone as soon as he arrived. She pondered his words as she quickly threw together her few things. What would it take to communicate like he did? But with her birds? Or was that what she was already doing?

She was grateful for the last couple days as she'd gained that much more strength. Her shoulder was still sore, her torso still achy, some of the cuts—especially on her feet— were not quite healed, but, by and large, she was fine. Although she did get tired fast. She made the bed and went back to the kitchen to find Eagle on the phone.

She had to get her passport and money from the bank in town. She wasn't sure how soon they would leave, but she knew she needed food. Checking the contents in the fridge, she made several sandwiches and waited until Eagle was finished with his call.

He put his phone away. "Gray's coming, and one of the guys who helps unload the feed will join him. They'll look after the birds for three days. That's as long as we've got."

"Hopefully we won't need that," she said quietly. "I'm so sorry."

He shook his head. "You don't have anything to be sorry about. But these assholes, they'll be sorry." He downed his sandwich in four bites. "We're leaving in thirty minutes."

"I have to stop by the bank to get my passport. And I need money."

He nodded formally. "We'll hit the bank on our way."

He glanced at the bags on the kitchen chair. "I see you found the bags. Are you packed and ready to go?"

She nodded as she took a bite of her sandwich.

"Good, I'll be back in five."

EAGLE WANTED TO believe his friends would be fine. But he'd lost so many in Iraq and Afghanistan, he had no intention of losing these two guys. They'd survived some of the worst missions anybody should be forced to endure. To think he might've sent them into this kind of danger made his gut churn.

At the same time it just made him angry. Those men would pay for this.

In his bedroom he pulled out the contact list that he hadn't looked at in years. They were all good men. And he knew that, if they'd made a similar request of him as he was about to make of them, he'd have dropped everything and gone to help too. At the top of his list was Hawk. Right now he needed him with them in Ireland—if he could free himself of whatever else was going on. A text wasn't going to do it. He sent a quick message, asking, "Can I call?"

The response came instantly. "You damn well better."

He got up, walked into the master bedroom, closed the door, and called. When his friend answered, he filled him in on the case.

Hawk being Hawk and very short on words, waited until Eagle was completely done and then said, "What kind of a shitstorm are you in now?"

"It's Tiger and Panther that I'm worried about. I can't go over there and leave her here. It's her they want."

"I'm with you on that," Hawk said in a hard voice. "I have men I can call on. Two of them are in England. They'll have no trouble getting over there. I'll have to track a third one down. I'll figure out if we need more. Any idea how many assholes we're facing in Ireland?"

"I don't know," Eagle said. "The men who tortured her were here in Colorado. They snatched her on the other side of Denver."

"Did she ever give you a location as to where she was held?"

"No, no idea."

"Well, she had to come from somewhere," Hawk said in exasperation. "You still living alone and away from everyone?"

"Well, I was," he snapped. "You can see how well that worked."

"Yeah, life's like that." Hawk's laughter rolled free. "I'll meet you at the airport."

Like that, Hawk hung up.

Eagle's mind raced as he tried to come up with a plan that would keep them all safe and find out whatever the hell was going on and get them back home again. He walked to the kitchen to find Issa sitting at the table, hugging a cup of tea.

He stopped and realized just how alone she really was. She didn't have a network of soldiers to call on like he did. The men he knew were the best there ever were. If anybody would help save her life, it would be him and the guys. The thing was, he was okay with that. If there was one more battle, one more underdog that needed saving, he was up for it. Especially if he was saving *her*.

DYLAN ANSWERED HIS phone and said, "They've taken the bait."

The boss chuckled, his voice dark, deep. "Of course they did. Now to make sure we intercept them on the other end. No mistakes. This has been going on for too damn long. I want it finished now."

"I'm on my way back. We should be able to catch a flight today."

"I'll be ready."

Watching the cloud of dust disappear as Eagle and Issa drove away, Dylan moved steadily, retreating through the trees back to where he'd parked his vehicle off the road. He and the boss had to move fast now. He didn't want to be on the same flight as Eagle and the girl. But Dylan couldn't afford to be too much later behind them.

This was where things got dicey. He had to keep everybody happy—and keep himself alive.

CHAPTER 23

ISSA WOULD'VE ENJOYED the flight if it had been for any other reason. She struggled to get comfortable in the narrow hard seat. Her body was still too lean and got sore from sitting for a long time. Eagle reached out, his palm open. She smiled and slid her hand into his.

To know she wasn't alone, to know he was there for her, even if only for this trip, gave her immeasurable comfort. She knew he was worried about his friends. He wanted somebody to pound. To blame. So did she. She was terrified of not being in time to save them. She had no way to know what they would find. Part of her knew this could be the end of her young life. At the same time, she wondered how much of any of this her mother had known about. Were there more secrets Issa hadn't found? Were there more answers her mother had deliberately withheld from her? Had her mother been more involved in either her father's or her brothers' deaths?

And why should any of it matter twenty years later? But she knew hatred never rested. It festered deep inside. Sometimes the only way for others to heal was for the truth to come out. She refused to be held accountable for any actions when she'd been a young child. She had struggled enough to heal and to move forward herself, which was a big deal for a six-year-old. She had no idea how her mother had accomplished that.

It had taken a long time for Issa and her mother to even have much of a relationship. Whether that had just been her mother's reserved nature—or the fact that inside Issa blamed her mother for taking Issa away from everything—Issa didn't know. It had improved. Not like any normal mother-daughter relationship she'd seen around her, but it had been okay. She leaned her head back and asked quietly, "Do you think my mother knew?"

"She knew more than she told you, but, whether what she knew played a critical role or not, there is no way to know yet."

She stared out the window at the endless sky beside her. "I wonder if I'll come for a holiday."

"I doubt after this you will. Unless you need to come back to heal."

She shook her head. "I need to heal at home. With the birds. Where my life is."

"What are you planning on doing for a job when you are strong enough?"

"I'll apply for grants to do research on endangered species in our area," she said quietly. "All I've ever wanted was to help the birds."

He squeezed her fingers gently.

"How did you get started with the raptor center?"

"The usual way," he said. "Somebody brought me an injured bird they thought I could help."

That startled a laugh out of her. "And, two hundred birds later, you're still helping out?"

"Two hundred birds later, and now I know how to do it easily." He cracked a smile.

Just then the pilot's voice came on, saying they were

landing.

She buckled her seat belt and clasped her hands together. "Will they be waiting for us at the airport?"

He never questioned who *they* were. "Quite likely they will. If not when we first arrive, when we least expect it."

She took a shaky breath.

"Issa, the truth is, they're watching us. When they think they can snatch us, they will try." He again squeezed her hands reassuringly. "If not, I imagine they will wait until we get to your old homestead and just see what it is we're here for."

"The trouble is, I don't even know myself."

WITH AS LITTLE as he knew, Eagle would give rein to the fury on the people who'd hurt his friends, but he did his best to hide it from her. He tried not to take his temper out on her. She sat beside him on the plane, her fingers locked together, her knuckles white. He didn't know if it was the strain of the situation or the pain eating at her, but her face was pale, her lips pinched.

He leaned over and whispered, "Do you need a pain pill?"

She shook her head. "No. I'd like a baseball bat and the men who did this to Panther."

He sat back in surprise and studied her features. She turned to look at him, and he recognized the glare. She hurt for Panther. She was angry somebody would do something like this to somebody she knew. And, in some way, she was affronted at the human race for being so low. She had a lot to learn about humanity. But she'd had some pretty rough lessons this last month. He was afraid some ugly ones were up ahead too.

As the crowd moved forward, exiting the plane, he tucked her arm into his so he wouldn't lose her. It would be way too easy to grab her here, move her down the hall out of his sight. He'd have a hell of a time finding out where they'd taken her. He bent down and whispered, "Stay close to me. Hang on to me at all times."

She gave a hard, jerky nod, not answering verbally. They only had carry-on luggage, so clearing through customs was fast.

Outside, instead of a bright sunny day, they were met by a dark gray fog with a rainy appearance to the sky. She stopped and studied the area, raised her nose and sniffed. "This should feel like coming home in some ways. But it doesn't," she admitted.

"No reason you should feel anything here."

He motioned toward the side of the airport where the rental vehicles were. He walked over, recognizing the profile of someone leaning casually against the gate. As they got closer, Hawk turned and walked to a rental car, opened the driver's door and unlocked the rest.

Eagle opened the rear passenger door and told Issa, "Get in. I'll sit in the back with you."

She looked at the driver and back at Eagle and got in without a word. As soon as they were buckled in, Hawk pulled the vehicle out of the airport. In a low voice, Eagle asked, "Any word?"

Hawk shook his head. "You?" He glanced in the rear-view mirror to catch Eagle's gaze.

Eagle shook his head. "No, nothing."

"Back to her property then?"

Eagle nodded. "Yes. What does the lay of the land look

like?"

"Remote, craggy, a smugglers' paradise," he said too succinctly. "Not much has changed from when she lived there as a child."

"The house is still there?" she asked in astonishment.

Eagle turned to look at her. "Is there any reason why the house wouldn't be there?"

She shrugged. "For some reason I assumed it was gone. It's not my house. It was my father's house." She leaned forward. "I'm Issa, by the way."

He tilted his hat with two fingers. "Nice to meet you. I'm Hawk."

Eagle watched the interchange quietly. He knew Panther and Tiger had approved of Issa. But Hawk in his own way just gave his approval too.

She whispered, "Are you sure it's safe?"

"Safe in what way?" Eagle asked. "Safe as in, can we trust him? Safe as in, to go to your old house?"

She glared at him. "Of course it's safe to trust Hawk. He's our friend, but is it safe to bring him into this mess?" she asked. "Panther and Tiger are in trouble because of me. I don't want anybody else to get hurt."

Hawk snorted in the front seat. Eagle studied her quietly, a small smile playing at the corner of his mouth. "All three men would be gratified to hear you say that. And they'd also be incredibly insulted if you tried to stop them from going for the action."

She sat back. "You know that whole alpha-male thing can only go so far. They've got Panther. Remember—I want a baseball bat and also a chance at those who hurt him too."

Eagle chuckled. "I forgot you're such a spitfire. You were broken when I found you. That personality of yours wasn't shining through. But I have to admit, these last few days ...”

She glared at him. “I didn't know if it was safe to be around you either. From the moment I woke up, I was figuring out how to escape. It didn't take me long to understand that not only could I trust you but you aren't like anybody else I know.” She shrugged. “Of course Gray worried me.”

Eagle settled back. “Right, his accent. Gray is harmless.”

“Is he though?” Hawk asked from the front seat. “He might stitch a mean seam, but it sure hurts.”

“That's true for anyone who wouldn't take painkillers.”

“You promised me bourbon. Who knew the stuff you had was weak as shit. I felt every stitch he put in me.”

Eagle shook his head, a smile on his face. “Those were the good old days.”

“You know what good old days are?” Issa asked beside him. “I used to think my life came in parts. Part five was when I woke up in your house. But somehow it switched into part six. Part six is whatever nightmare this is.”

He turned to study her. “That's an odd way to look at your life.”

“My life has had very clear stop and start times. That's all I meant by it.”

“Just so long as part seven is good, none of what happens in part six will ultimately matter.”

“It will matter if somebody gets hurt.” She shook her head and wouldn't continue.

He gently tucked her up close to him.

They pulled into the small town. Memories stirred in the deep recesses of her mind. She sat up and looked around. “Shouldn't people be on the roads?”

“It's seven in the evening here. People are at home or at

the pub—where we have rooms for the night."

"Are we going there now?"

Hawk shook his head. "No. We're taking a rendezvous down to the address on your mom's letter. Your old home."

She winced. "I really wish that woman was alive and here right now."

"In fact, her death is likely what precipitated all this," Eagle said.

She twisted in her seat to better look at him. "What are you talking about?"

"Just think about it. Everything was going along like normal until she died."

"Yes, but how would anybody know?" She stared at him, confusion in her eyes. "Everybody here in Ireland probably thought she was already dead."

"You don't know what she might have set up," Eagle said. "She was married to a smuggler for a long time. She was heavily involved in that side of the business. She might have had other dealings you are unaware of. Other connections she kept in touch with."

CHAPTER 24

"L IKE WHAT?" Issa challenged, not sure she was ready for more family hits.

But Eagle was never somebody to back off. He watched her quietly. "A mother who may very well have had something to do with either her husband's or her sons' deaths."

It was delivered in a flat tone, like he had left no room for frills or niceties. She sank back in her seat, remembering what she'd learned so far, how she had even had these thoughts too, and said, "Oh."

She turned to stare moodily out the window. It was as if she visited a foreign country, without the joy of being on holiday. Foreboding filled her; resentment rode on her back. She didn't want to be here. She didn't want to be dealing with this. But, at the same time, she was incredibly afraid for Panther. If they'd taken his tooth, what else had they taken? And what had they done to Tiger too?

She remembered her father's men had been nothing if not direct. They had lived by a strong code, and they were just as likely to jump each other if one broke the code. But, in their own way, they were honest. It was hard to believe any one of them would've done this to Panther.

If her mother had known the details of the smuggling operation or the men involved, she hadn't cared to divulge any of those. Issa had tried having those conversations with her mother for years, for decades, but she'd just shut down. "Any time I asked about my history, about my family, about Ireland, my mother wouldn't talk to me for days."

"Did she ever tell you about your brothers?"

"She never mentioned them. Like that part of her life was a hundred percent over, never to be reopened."

Hawk gave a low whistle. "That's pretty hard to do. If you loved your children, it's automatic to talk about them. I know they all died at the same time, but it's almost instinctive to bring them into a conversation. It gives them life, keeps the memories alive."

"I think that is what she didn't want," Issa said. "She didn't want to remember them. It was as if she was glad they were gone." Issa shook her head. "For all I know I was supposed to die too."

"Why do you say that?" Eagle asked.

She turned to look at him. "That night a hell of a storm blew in. She never once came and checked on me. At the time I knew it was because I had a job to do. I was expected to do it no matter what. But it was hard to stay out there in the darkness. If it wasn't for Hadrid, I don't think I would've survived."

"As in, you might've died out there," Eagle asked, "or, as in, it was a terrible night, and you were lonely and cold and miserable?"

"The second. I was sitting on the edge of a cliff, and I had to walk home in the dark. Let me just say that, if I ever have a child, I will never let them go alone out on the edge of a cliff in the dark and ugly weather. I don't think my safety was ever part of my mother's thoughts."

They continued for another ten minutes in silence. The country was harsher than she'd expected. Craggy rocks, hilly sides, green on top, brown on the bottom. Water, so much water in this corner of the world. Then she remembered her father had a boat. Used to move goods up and down the coastline. "I wonder what happened to his boat."

She explained further to the two men. "I don't remember seeing any deeds of ownership to the house or boat or any vehicles in my mother's papers."

"But you don't know if they're in the safe-deposit box or whatever else we came here for."

"No." She turned to look at him with a half smile. "Did it ever occur to you how much my world has been impacted by those first two boxes?"

He nodded. "Your world has been one of secrets, misinformation, double dealings, and treachery. Time to clean out the secrets and the poison, so you can move forward as a whole person and leave all that baggage behind."

She studied him carefully. Then stroked his cheek. "That sounds perfect."

The vehicle slowed and turned into a driveway, which climbed and twisted and climbed some more. When it finally came to a stop, the headlights showed a ramshackle house sitting on top of the hill. She was riveted.

"This is it," she said. "This is where I lived." She opened the car door and stepped out. She walked around to the side, both men rushing to catch up with her as she headed toward the building.

She stood in front and stared, memories cascading through her mind. Liam and Sean running through the house, always busy, always on the go. Her father, Rory, telling the lads to behave. Her mother silent at the stove. Issa frowned. Had her mother always been so quiet? Issa didn't understand. Even now she didn't understand who her mother really was. The mystery was less about Issa and more about her mother.

Issa slowly approached the building. It was in a sad state of disrepair. At the top front step the door was propped open with a rock. She stopped and turned to look around. Some of the fog had lifted. Clouds let the blue sky peek through. And she could see for miles. That she remembered. She didn't want to go into the house. She stood, staring, realizing how much of her life here she had spent outdoors. On the crags, sitting and watching, always staring upward and outward.

Eagle stepped in front of her, his gaze direct and clear. "You okay?"

She gave him the briefest of smiles. "I will be. Thank you for bringing me."

He studied her for a long moment and gave a clipped nod. "I'll go in first. You stay here."

Before she could argue he disappeared into her cabin leaving her with Hawk. When he returned a few minutes later he said, "Let's go. I want to make sure we get home as fast as possible."

On that note she slipped past him and stepped inside. She didn't have good memories or bad memories of this place. She had disconnected memories that made no sense. In a family of mostly men and being so much younger than the rest, she hadn't found a place for herself easily. Yet she hadn't felt the back side of her father's hand either. She somehow felt he loved her, but she didn't have memories of him carrying her on his shoulders or of his laughter. She did remember his big booming voice. The hard edge to it. There had been a constant stream of people through the house. And he ruled whatever clan he had with an iron fist. But he also held the respect of everyone around. She remembered that. Nobody seemed to argue with him in the house. They came; they spoke and then left. She used to sit up in the crags just over the side of the house and watch people come and go.

She wandered through the small living room, the kitchen, both rooms barely recognizable. Certainly not habitable. "Nobody has lived here since we left, I assume."

"Not that I could find," Hawk said.

She crossed to the kitchen window where she used to see her mother standing at the counter, either cooking or washing. And she stared out at what her mother must've stared at for many years. "I wonder if she was ever happy."

"It doesn't sound like she was. Hopefully when she was younger."

Issa turned and studied the walls. "Are we expecting to find the other keepsake box here?"

"I'm hoping you can tell us that." Eagle stood at the doorway, watching her. "She mentioned a deposit box, bank accounts, and the duplicate keepsake box. But finding that last one might be a challenge."

She shrugged. "Who knows? Depending on where she left it, it might have been thrown away a long time ago. What's treasure to one is garbage to another."

She wandered through the downstairs to her parents' bedroom—the ceiling tiles hanging now, holes in the walls, floorboards scuffed and ruined. She gave it a quick glance, then turned and headed for the stairs. The two men followed silently behind her. There was no light, and it was hard to see. Hawk turned on a flashlight and handed it to her.

She took it gratefully and led the way.

"My brothers had the larger bedrooms." She walked into

the first and took a quick glance around, then headed into Liam's. Her eldest brother, Ethan, hadn't been here very often, and, when he was, he bunked with Liam.

Hers was a much smaller room, and, as she stepped inside, waves of remembrance washed over her. "This was mine. I used to sit for hours at a time here, staring out the window." The window was small, at the peak of the roof. The room was made even smaller with the slanted ceiling, so she could barely stand upright. But, as a child, it would've been fine. There was still some kind of a blanket on the floor. She stared at it and wondered. She walked over and picked it up. She smiled. "Hadrid would've been after this in a heartbeat."

"Any chance Hadrid's alive?" Eagle asked, his voice low and quiet.

She shook her head. "I don't think so. I've spent the last twenty years wondering that. Some falcons live a long time. But I never felt him after that day. I'm pretty sure he was shot and killed."

Only silence came from the men as she stood for a long moment in the small room. Finally she said, "I have no idea about this keepsake box."

"What was your favorite place?"

She frowned. "I don't remember having just one. I had several, depending on the circumstances. Figures that there'd only be a vague reference to the location. Then that was my mother."

She studied her room. This hadn't been her favorite place. She turned, gave her brothers' rooms one more quick cursory look, and then walked down the stairs. She headed outside to the crevice where she used to sit all the time, watching the comings and goings in the house below.

Her mother had to call her over and over again to get her inside. At the time it seemed natural. Normal. Now she wondered why a young child preferred to be outside in the elements rather than inside the family home.

When she got to the spot where she used to sit, she turned and crouched to see what the view was like when she'd been smaller. It was just as wild and wonderful and mysterious as it had been back then. But it had been all she knew.

"Where did you used to sit? Where was your favorite spot here?"

She shot him a hooded gaze. "If she was talking about my favorite place, chances are she was being sarcastic and talking about the one place I loved and yet hated."

Hawk's brows raised. "And yet she was your mother?"

She gave him a silent nod and turned, heading to the spot where she'd fallen into the crevice. She didn't know why anything would be in there. But, in a way, it was also her favorite spot because it was where she had connected with Hadrid. It took a good five minutes at a strong pace to get there. She looked down, realizing it was not that big after all. For a child, yes; for an adult, no. But she'd fallen with her leg caught between the rocks and had not been able to move.

"I fell down here," she said, motioning toward the opening along the cliff edge. "But, as you can see, nothing is hidden here."

Hawk and Eagle moved forward. Hawk jumped down so he could sit in the spot where she would've fallen and study the crevice. He used a flashlight to shine deep inside to see if anything could've been wedged in. He shook his head. "I don't see anything." He moved toward the opening of the fissure.

"Be careful," she warned. "It's slippery. That's a long way down."

Eagle jumped down behind him to take a look himself. "How old were you when you were in here?"

"Four?" she said. "I fell in, and I couldn't get out again."

"That's a pretty bad fall for a child so young. What about your parents?" Hawk asked. "Where were they?"

Eagle answered for her. "She was alone most of her childhood. It took hours for anybody to find her."

Hawk shook his head. "You were pretty young to be left alone."

"Not in my family. It was only the fittest who survived," she said shortly.

She turned and studied the area, but her mind wasn't connecting with her mother's words and what they meant. She turned to look back at the house, trying to remember what she would've done, where she would've been the happiest. As she stood here, she thought she saw movement coming up the road. She crouched and whispered, "We have company."

EAGLE WRAPPED HIS arm around her shoulders and studied the new arrivals. They were still a long way off, but he could see two men. Both of them carried long rifles. He glanced at Hawk. He nodded, hopped up, and disappeared into the mist.

Beside them he could feel Issa shiver. "Take it easy. We were expecting this. We were just hoping to find something first. They will want to know what it is you know."

"But I don't know anything."

He could hear the truth in her voice and the urgency,

and knew how close she was to breaking. She'd already been traumatized once. Coming home wasn't exactly a pleasant experience either. But to be captured now would be an entirely different story.

Still they had no reason to think these particular men were involved.

He grabbed her hand, and together they slowly walked back down. What he didn't want was be taken by surprise. As he approached the house, he called out, "Hello, what can we do for you?"

Slowly the two figures separated from the wall of the house and stood cradling the weapons across their bodies. One was an old man. "What are you doing here? This is private property."

Eagle nodded in understanding. "True enough. I brought Issa home to see her old house."

At her name the two men froze and then turned their gazes on her. "Issa?"

She stopped and stared at them, as if searching to remember who they were. "Yes," she said quietly. "My mother took me to America not long after everything blew up. This is the first time I've come back to Ireland."

The two men looked at each other and then at her. "You know people have been looking for you for years, don't you?"

She shook her head. "No, I had no idea. Why?"

The older man stepped forward. "Do you remember me?"

She moved closer so the flashlight would give her more light to discern his face. Then she said, "I'm sorry, no."

He nodded. "It's okay, lass. You were young, just a little thing when you left. I'm actually your uncle. Your father was my brother."

She gasped. "I have family?"

A pained look crossed his features. "Didn't you know?"

She shook her head. "No. My mother said nobody was left. It was just her and me."

He scratched his forehead as if perplexed. "I don't know why she'd do that. You have plenty of family here. Your father was my eldest brother. We have two sisters. You've got cousins galore."

She stared at him. "Then why would my mother tell me they were all gone?"

"She probably just didn't want you to remember the old country," the other man said. "It was a painful time for her. It was probably much easier for her to walk away and forget it all."

Issa nodded.

Eagle watched the exchange, and, although he had worried when he saw the men with the rifles, there was nothing aggressive about their stances. In fact, they looked delighted to see her. "Have other people been hanging around the house?" he asked.

The men shook their heads. "No one's been here since. After my brother died, everything went to your mother. But she'd lost three sons and her husband, then disappeared."

Eagle could understand that. So many people put credence in a house being a home, but *home* was being where your family was. And after Issa's mom had lost most of her family, she likely felt nothing was left for her here. He put an arm around Issa and told the men, "We're staying above the pub. We're only here for a couple days."

Her uncle chuckled. "That should make you happy. It was your favorite place."

Hearing the phrase from the letters again, she asked slowly, "It was?"

He nodded. "There's a little alcove at the top of the stairs. You used to sit in there all the time and wait for your brothers and your father to be done. Your mother was never there. At least not often."

They slowly wandered back to the vehicle. Her uncle stopped and said, "It would be nice if you could stop by our house to see the rest of the family, although we're often at the pub too. We never knew what happened to you."

She smiled at him warmly. "Absolutely. I had no idea anybody was left."

He nodded bashfully. "Now that you know, it would be nice if you would not be such a stranger."

Eagle considered himself a good judge of character. But these two men left him cold. He couldn't decide if they were truly happy to see her or if they had ulterior motives. Their explanation for checking out the property made sense. In any small town anywhere in the world, you'd find a similar attitude with the locals. Strangers poking around on a property that had been empty for a long time usually meant trouble.

Maybe there really was no treasure here. The area was quite depressed. It was hard to say what the economic times were like back then, but he doubted they were any better. Had the smuggling stopped? Maybe a new leader had stepped forward.

The men nodded their heads and slowly started back. But the behavior of the younger man concerned Eagle more. Tall, strong, physically active, almost like a farmhand would be built, there'd been a speculative interest in his gaze. Whether that was at Issa herself for being a beautiful young woman or for her interest in whatever was going on here, there was no doubt her arrival had caused a stir.

And would become that much more when they went to the pub. There was still no sign of Hawk. He'd stepped into the shadows and stayed there. He was very good at that.

Issa walked toward him, looped her arm through his, and said, "We can leave now."

He slanted her a sideways look. "Are you ready?"

"Yes." In a low voice she said, "I thought for sure they would have something to say about Panther and Tiger."

"I'm not sure those men are involved."

"I hope not. They're family."

"But are they?" He squeezed her hand against his body and walked back to the car.

The men were down the road, and they'd have to drive past them. And Eagle didn't want them to see Hawk. On the other hand, Hawk may have already walked to the pub.

At the car she stopped and asked, "What about Hawk?"

"You never have to worry about Hawk," Hawk said from behind her. He glanced at Eagle. "You drive. I'll crouch down in the back as we pass them."

Eagle nodded.

With him and Issa in the front, and Hawk stretched out in the back, Eagle slowly drove down the road, passing the two men with a hand wave, and carried on to the pub. He didn't know whether the word had already passed around that Issa was here or if it was normal for the pub to already be bustling by the time they walked in. A staircase going up led to their rooms, letting them avoid the center of activity.

Upstairs Eagle said to her, "Does any of this seem familiar?"

She shrugged. "Not this part. But the alcove is. I remember sitting here, while my dad drank."

"Was it big enough to hide anything inside it?" Hawk asked.

"I wouldn't have thought so. Yet it was big enough to hide me most of the time."

"Any other way to get to it?"

She frowned and thought about it. "I think so. There was a bathroom up top. One of the reasons why I could stay there. Any time I needed, I could go to the washroom."

"Can you get to that alcove without going through the pub?"

She turned her gaze on him. "Is that an issue?"

"It would be nice to not have everybody see what we're doing."

Understanding dawned. She stepped out in the hallway and took a look. "I used to run up and down this hall all the time." She led them to the far back wall and a second staircase. "This is the one the staff uses." She walked down a few steps, and there was a small landing. She stepped off to the side of it—a space the size of a broom closet. "This is where I stayed all the time."

She bent down and peered through the lattice work. She pointed out the noisy pub below. "My dad sat below me. And I was up here."

"Did you have Hadrid with you?" he asked in a low voice.

She shook her head. "No, Hadrid stayed outside."

"And did he give warnings?"

She nodded. "Of course. That's what his job was. It was to keep watch all the time."

"And you weren't down there in the main part of the pub because you were the lookout while your dad was meeting with some people?"

She nodded. "He often held his business while I was here. This is where he conducted his meetings." She bent down lower, her fingers tracing scratches she'd made a long time ago. "I wrote my name here. See?"

He peered closer, and, sure enough, in the wood was her name. "What did you scratch it with?"

She frowned. "I'm not sure. Maybe a nail."

He watched her work on her memories, dredging up fragments that were so close and yet so far away. He understood how frustrating it must be. "It was a long time ago. Don't worry about it." He studied the area, his fingers gently tapping along the walls. "Interesting. Could you have hidden something here?"

She shrugged. "I don't know what. It's a pretty small space."

"What about any of the places up and down the hall? Did you ever go to any of the bedrooms? Or a closet?"

She turned to the closet a few steps up. "That holds the bedding for the guestrooms. I used to go in there and sleep," she admitted. "But they didn't like it when I did that."

Hawk, standing at the top of the stairs, gave her a hard look, turned, and studied the closet beside him. He opened the door and said, "Where did you sleep?"

She pointed to the bottom. "I used to tuck in the back on the floor. It's deep enough I could stretch out and sleep."

He squatted down and then started to stand, only froze. Returning to his hands and knees, he pulled out a keepsake box she recognized. It matched the one she had at home. She watched as Hawk backed out slowly.

She gasped. "I know that box. I used to leave notes in there for my friend."

Hawk straightened and closed the door, taking the box with him, while Eagle motioned her back up the stairs. "To the room, now."

Safely inside her and Eagle's room, the three of them stared at the box.

"Surely this couldn't have been there the whole time?" she said.

"It was in the very back with other larger cardboard boxes. I only noticed it because I recognized the corner as similar to the picture Eagle sent me."

STEFAN SAT CROSS-LEGGED on the floor, a blank canvas in front of him. Not on an easel but flat on the floor. He took a deep breath and waited for the energy inside him to calm. He had no idea what he was supposed to paint. He only knew he had a persistent sensation that something was happening. Something bad. And he was supposed to do something about it. But he could help only so many people in the world. His ever-expanding network of skilled energy workers around the world was a miracle in itself. But—as the network increased in size, as they sent out messages far and wide—they got far more responses than they ever thought they'd get.

And it was taxing all of their energies, which he knew was foolish because the universe was full of energy. He should be able to tap into Mother Earth's core at any time. But, at the moment, something was making extra strong demands. He didn't know what. He sat for a long moment and then watched as his right hand reached once again for the black pencil.

He groaned. "Humbug, is that you? What's changed?"

But a different cry was in his ear.

He twisted his head to look out the window. He could see the huge wingspan of a large falcon. But even as he watched the bird out the window, it faded and blended into the window, then separated. From that he could only assume the bird was dead, leaving behind a strong spirit here. Some people referred to these animals as spirit animals. Strong guardians over their human companions. Not companions in the real sense of the word but watching over those connected to them.

Like a psyche trying to return to its living, breathing form.

It reminded Stefan of his earlier experience, his first flight with the animals—or his first flight through a bird's eye view. What a powerful event that had been. So powerful that his psyche willingly wanted to leave his body behind. Permanently. If it hadn't been for Maddy, Tabitha, and his beloved Celina … He shook his head. *Stay in the present moment, Stefan.*

Of course it would be a bird. Everything in his world right now was birds. Feathers were everywhere inside and outside of his house. He could barely take a step without finding yet another one. Celina just smiled and kept sweeping them up. He wasn't quite so generous. But, at the same time, he knew they were signs. Messages. And he was obviously not getting it. Even though the birds were revealing more breadcrumbs for him to follow.

As he went to draw the owl once again, his hand stopped. Surprised, he realized something else was going on here. He closed his eyes, tilted his head down, and sent out a whisper. "Tell me what you need. Show me what you need." Then his hand took off, sketching like a madman across the two-foot-by-two-foot canvas in front of him.

He kept his eyes closed, knowing something special was happening. There was a sense of urgency. A sense of panic. He could feel the birds outside alighting, more agitated, their vocals louder, stronger. It was hard to know what was going on. And yet he knew that, if he pushed it, if he opened his eyes and interfered in the process, he'd break the spell, and he'd have to start over again.

Accepting that, he sank deeper into the trance.

He barely heard the door open or his wife approaching, but, when she sat beside him, not touching, just sitting close to him, her whisper was audible. "My God, Stefan."

Finally his hand dropped. Sore, fatigued, the inside of him squished flat, like run through some kind of a wringer washing machine, he felt a sense of exhaustion both for himself and whoever sent the message. He opened his eyes, and one of the most incredible wildlife pictures sat before him.

In black charcoal on the white canvas was a beautiful falcon soaring high above a craggy cliff. And yet at the same time, in the top corner was, once again, a very small faint owl's head. Humbug overlooked the whole process, and yet this falcon, the same spirit falcon that he'd seen earlier, soared across his canvas. So majestic, Stefan swallowed. He didn't understand what was going on, but he did know one thing. He would keep this drawing.

Celina slipped her hand into his. "He's dead, isn't he?"

"I don't think so. But, if he is, he's got a very strong message to give."

"How can you tell?"

"Look at his feet." And, indeed, dangling from his talons were jewels, long strands of brightly colored jewels.

"Necklaces?" She stared at the canvas for a long moment and said in bewilderment, "I don't understand."

Stefan sighed. "Neither do I."

CHAPTER 25

ISSA CIRCLED THE duplicate keepsake box warily. "You sent him pictures of the two boxes we got from my place?"

Eagle nodded. "The small one was very distinctive. Your mother said it was a matched set. Panther and Tiger have copies as well."

Squatting, she tried to open the box, but it was locked. There was a small keyhole. She held out her hand for the key. Eagle stared at her. "How do you know I didn't give it to Panther?"

She shot him a look and said, "I'm pretty sure Panther would have had his father cut a spare."

He smiled and pulled out the key. "He did, indeed. They swung by his place on the way to the airport and sent this one back to me. This is hardly a safe. He said it belonged to a safe."

"This is actually a strongbox."

She put the key inside and turned. It didn't open. She studied it for a long moment, shaking her head. "And I thought this would be it."

She turned to Eagle. "Hawk is right. Panther's father said a safe. This isn't a safe." Then she stood and swore softly. "When you asked if I would've hidden anything down there, ... well, I didn't hide it. But I found a key behind the wood. I used to play with it all the time. But I didn't hide it originally. I found it."

Silently, she led Eagle back to the little alcove. She crouched down, slipped her fingers behind one of the slats, and pulled out the key. She held it up. With his fingers to his lips, they raced back to the bedroom. She walked in, holding the key out to Hawk.

He shook his head. "This is just too bizarre."

He positioned himself between the door and Issa. She sat down on the bed, put the key into the box, and, indeed, it opened. Inside were several velvet bags, stacks of money, and more envelopes—probably containing documents.

She picked up the cash. "Well, this answers that question. It's a miracle over all these years no one found it and emptied it."

Eagle picked up one of the velvet bags and opened it carefully. Out fell a beautiful jeweled necklace.

She stared at it. "Now that's not good."

"Why?" Hawk asked.

"My mother had a picture of this. I said how beautiful it was, and she said it was a piece of the devil's work." She shook her head. "Didn't you see the pictures of this in her files that we scanned?"

Eagle nodded. "Yes. I sent them off to an appraiser to see if he knew who and what the pieces were. But I haven't heard back yet."

"There were three or four pictures." Issa pointed to the velvet bags. "What do you want to bet …? Let's find out for sure." She carefully opened a second velvet bag to find another extremely rare and extremely valuable-looking necklace with long strands of sapphires—dark midnight-blue sapphires. She fingered them gently. "So beautiful."

"What a waste."

"They were sitting here in a box all these years." She opened the other two velvet bags to find similar necklaces. One was some kind of silver, although she thought it was possibly platinum, with tiny diamonds on what appeared to be a spider's web of a necklace. In a low voice she said, "These are very valuable, aren't they?"

"I'm afraid so." Eagle carefully packed them up, placed them on the bed behind the box, put the envelopes off to one side, and found the whole bottom underneath was layered with cash.

"Why would your mother have taken the other box and left this one behind?" Hawk asked in a low voice. "Or did she grab the wrong one by mistake?"

"She said it was blood money," Issa said. "Part of the devil's work."

"Did she become religious after she left here?"

"Not that I know of. But she never would talk about this time of her life. I don't know how much of it she was ashamed of versus how much was just too painful to talk about."

Eagle took out the bills and found nothing else underneath, so he repackaged everything but the envelopes. "Let's see what these are." Opening the topmost envelope, he pulled out paperwork. "The top one is another copy of an old will of your father's. He left everything to his three sons. Nothing to his wife and daughter. But the will was dated ten years after his last son was born. In a court of law, that inheritance would pass to the unborn daughter."

"Or he knew I wasn't his daughter and didn't bother to revise it after I was born," she said in a low voice. "Maybe all those relatives aren't my relatives."

Eagle grabbed the second envelope, opened it, and

pulled out more documents. "It's your mother's old will. It leaves everything to her husband, nothing to anyone else."

"Well, in that case, I don't know what will happen to her estate."

"When you closed her estate, was there another will?"

"Yes. It was with the lawyers. She left everything to me." She tapped the paperwork in his hands. "Her husband died and her sons died before her. I was her only living relative, so by rights it comes to me anyway. Should we bring the local police in on this?"

The two men turned and studied her. "It could open a huge kettle of fish, you know?"

She turned to look at Hawk. "Personally I don't care about any of these valuables. Panther already lost a tooth. The last thing I want is for either of those men to die because of me. This is all old lies and old deceit. None of it belongs in my world."

Hawk looked at her with respect.

But Eagle was the voice of reason. "That may be the way for you. But I have a suspicion everyone around here will not agree. Deeds done twenty years ago are probably deeds they want settled quietly and swept away forever. They won't want the local police involved. Not to mention"—he nodded toward the box—"this is a fortune for those people. And likely the other reason you were kidnapped."

She glanced at the floor to see a small envelope. "Did you see this?"

He looked at it and frowned. "No. What is it?"

She opened it and pulled out a letter. "It's from Angus to my mother."

She read it aloud.

I always loved you. I understood your reasons for not leaving your husband. That you would have raised my daughter as his is too much to be believed. I was good enough for you to sleep with but not good enough for you to wed. Even at the beginning you were mine. But he had more than I had. If our situations were reversed, I would have had more and him less. But still I am poor because I don't have you. All these years you let me into your bed, yet you never let me into your heart. You know this weekend things have changed. He's no longer here. Even though he tried to kill me once, I had nothing to do with his death. I implore you to please don't walk away. Bring your daughter, my daughter, to me, and let's finally be together as we were always meant to be.

Your loving Angus

She sighed. "A note from our star-crossed lovers."

"Star-crossed lovebird," Hawk corrected. "I don't think your mother was as invested in that relationship as much as he was."

"In truth," Issa said quietly, "my mother wasn't invested in very much. I think she was basically happy with whoever would look after her. She didn't like confrontation. She didn't like strife. And she really didn't like hard work. Her life with my dad was just that. Angus was a light on the side for her. But I don't think she had any intention of walking away from the life she knew."

"I highly suggest we go into town tomorrow morning and talk to the police," Eagle said. "I know I'm the first to argue against that course of action, but, in this situation, too many angles, people, and cases are involved. And there's a time and a place … There's a good chance these jewels came from a well-publicized heist way back when. They should be returned to the rightful owners, correct?" Eagle glanced at his watch. "It's late now. Let's get some sleep. Tomorrow things might look brighter."

She looked at him. "You think we should go to the pub to meet everyone?"

"No, not yet. First off, we don't even know if they're your family."

She winced. "Good point." She waved at the box. "I don't feel like we can leave this here."

"We will return the box," Eagle said. "But it will be empty."

He quickly emptied the box and gave it back to Hawk with the key. Hawk disappeared out the door.

She motioned to the stuff on the bed. "How do we hide this?"

"I have room in my bag for all of it." He opened his duffel, removed some of his clothing, and placed the money on the bottom. The bags of jewelry he tucked into the side pockets. "I don't know what you want to do with the paperwork."

"None of it makes any sense," she said. "None of this is worth torturing me for, especially if they stole the money and the jewelry. Especially so if someone else had found the keepsake box and had just kept everything."

"And that's why we have to hit the bank to find out. We need to check out the safe-deposit box. Now get ready for bed. Hawk and I will stay up through the night on four-hour shifts. He's next door, and we'll be switching in and out. I need you to get some rest. You're still healing. We can't afford to have you get worse."

"And what about Panther? And Tiger?"

He leaned forward. "I have to trust that the men are keeping themselves alive. But, even if they aren't, there's very little we can do."

She bowed her head with a nod. "Well, tomorrow I want answers," she said quietly. "I've waited a long time. This is long enough." She got up and went into the bathroom to get ready.

HAWK RETURNED JUST then. Eagle went over the plans for the night.

"You think she's safe here?" Hawk asked.

"Honestly I'm not sure. If I thought I could spirit her back into town, hide her away in a different hotel, I would. We might still have to leave in the middle of the night. Do you have anybody you know in the local area or some nearby police department? Even Interpol might not be a bad idea. I'm pretty damn sure those gems will be on somebody's radar."

"You think that's what's behind this?"

"I don't know. But, when you talk money, and as many deaths as we know about, … either somebody wants what is in that box or wants to make sure it stays hidden."

Hawk nodded. "I'll send some messages, making sure we have somebody watching over us tonight and following us tomorrow."

"You do that. I'll take first watch."

Hawk left then.

Eagle sat down on the side of the bed. He went over the paperwork once again, searching for Angus's full name. Finding it, he sent out the name to several people who could help track him down.

Issa came back. Sleep was the best thing for her. She crawled under the covers, rolled over so her back was against him, and closed her eyes.

He gently stroked her shoulder and whispered, "Good night."

She mumbled a response, but he was grateful to hear it was sleep-blurred. It had been a devastating two days for her. He knew it would get a hell of a lot worse.

When his phone rang a few minutes later, he bounded off the bed and to the far side of the room so as not to disturb her. "What's up?"

"Angus is in jail, convicted on four counts of first-degree murder, killing four men of one family," his contact Charlie said quietly.

Eagle sent out a silent whistle. "I might have his daughter, who is also the remaining member of the family he killed."

"Now that would be very interesting. Angus had a lot of land. It was seized by the locals. Apparently he attempted to bring the police in on a father and his three sons' smuggling operation. The police were delayed. Plans went awry, and he ended up killing the family."

"Not quite. The wife and daughter survived. The daughter might possibly be the lover's—Angus's—daughter, though, so it's quite a love triangle."

There was a long whistle on the other end. "He's already served seventeen years of a life sentence."

"And he might very well be guilty. As far as I understand, one of the men he killed had been up on criminal charges against Angus himself."

"According to Angus's trial testimony, they were betrayed, but he doesn't know by whom. He was supposed to be outside on lookout. He heard shots and raced to the cove to find Rory McGuire already dying with a bullet to his chest. Two of McGuire's sons were dead, and another one was dying. The police arrived just in time to find Angus, the only one left standing, and charged him for the whole lot."

"Weren't there other men involved?"

"Yes. Two other men were killed by a different gun. I believe by Rory, the father. Actually I think four other men were killed. Several escaped and disappeared in the chaos. Apparently the men who escaped were also badly injured. The few that lived said Angus had come in and shot up the place."

"So, in other words, they were all Rory's men?"

"Yes, and that's what Angus's defense team said. But something was always fishy about his story. And he had no alibi. There were only dead men left standing—and Angus."

"Why was his story fishy?"

"He was supposed to be on the lookout. But, since he obviously didn't give them a warning, the others believed he'd been waiting for the opportunity to come in for the kill."

"When instead he was actually banging Rory's wife at the time."

"Really?"

"Yes, the daughter saw them."

Charlie snorted. "Wow. Angus did mention he was involved with another woman, but nobody could find her."

"No. She bolted for America. Walked away from everything with the daughter, Angus's daughter. But the mother died a month or so ago. The daughter was kidnapped and tortured for information she couldn't possibly hand over, and then two of my friends came over here to retrieve belongings left behind for her. They've been kidnapped. Now we're sitting here in a hotel room, figuring out what the hell's going on."

"Wow, when you get involved, you really get involved."

"I know, and I remember saying I wouldn't get involved in this kind of shit anymore," Eagle said. Charlie was yet another one of the men from his unit. Childhood friends, they'd known each other for decades. "But when it comes to your door, like she did in my case, and I believe the circumstances were beyond strange, you have to do something."

"Isn't that the truth? My brother, Duncan, remember him? He's in law enforcement in Dublin. I'll give him a quick call."

Charlie hung up, leaving Eagle to ponder this turn of events.

"What was that all about?" asked Issa, her sleepy voice beside him.

He winced and walked closer. "I'm so sorry. I tried not to disturb you."

"I'm not sleeping at all until this is over," she announced. "So tell me. What was that about?"

He sat down on the bed and said, "Apparently Angus is in jail." He quickly relayed the rest of the information.

"And my mother didn't come back and defend him? Seeing that she'd been with him at the time?"

"It may not have made any difference. If your dad had any idea where Angus really was, it makes sense he might've opened fire on him. In which case, Angus probably did shoot him. But how it ended up that he shot all three of your brothers, I don't know. But what we do know is that some people were there that night and lived to say that Angus did it."

She snorted. "Of course they did. My dad paid them all."

"Sure, but, if he was dead, who would pay?"

She frowned. "I don't know, but, in theory, they had the goods they'd smuggled in that night. Maybe dividing that up and taking Angus's share was enough. There were a lot of people in the house for the next couple days. Then suddenly we were gone."

"And did you leave during the day?"

She frowned, casting her mind back as she thought about it, then shook her head slowly. "No. She woke me up in the middle of the night, and we walked out." She turned her gaze toward the dark window. "We walked down the hillside to the road and into the pub. There we got a ride."

"Any idea who drove you?"

She looked up at him. "No."

"Well, she obviously had one person on her side."

"Or somebody she paid very well."

"As in money from that box? And how is it that nobody found the box? The money would have been easy to spend. The jewels not so much." He hated to see the fear and pain in her eyes.

"Haven't enough people suffered for whatever the hell went wrong twenty years ago?" she asked as she shook her head. "It's just too much." She rolled over and closed her eyes.

He frowned, helpless to ease her suffering. Seeing her shoulders shaking, he realized just how badly she was hurting. He put his phone down, lay on top of the covers, and wrapped himself around her. He slid his arm around her ribs and tucked her up close.

There was a catch in her breathing.

"It'll be okay," he murmured.

"How can you say that?" she whispered. "It's your friends hurting right now."

"Because I have faith in them. Panther is a serious badass, and, even if he's been tortured, it won't have been the first time, and it would just make him all that much more eager to get retaliation."

She sniffled.

He leaned over and kissed her cheek. "Sleep. It's the best thing for you."

She shook her head. "I can't shut off my mind. Needing sleep doesn't mean it's easy to come by."

He gently stroked her arms up and down, soothing the edges of her soul—hoping the comfort would help her to sleep. When finally she took a deep breath and let it out slowly, he smiled. "Do that a few more times," he urged.

Obediently she took a deep breath and let it out and repeated the action. Finally she sagged a little deeper into the mattress and whispered, "Thank you."

He shook his head. "How can you thank me? I haven't done anything."

"You came with me," she said simply. "I would not want to be here alone."

Just the thought of it filled him with rage. They would've picked her up at the airport and turned her into chopped liver again. He knew one thing: the men who had done this to her would have to answer to Eagle before this was over. He didn't know how all this played into one person, Issa, but somewhere, somehow it did. Eagle just didn't have all the pieces yet. All he wanted to do was get her home, back to his place, where she could rest and heal.

"I want this over with," she whispered in a raspy voice. "I want to go back home and have a normal life again."

He pulled her tighter against his chest and said calmly, "I'm not sure I can let you go home."

She snorted. "You've said that several times in one form or another. But, if push came to shove, you'd let me go."

"What if I said I didn't want you to go? That I wanted you to stay with me? To heal and stay at my house until we had a chance to get to know each other—like really get to know each other—and see if maybe something is here we wanted to nurture? What would you say to that?"

Slowly, ever-so-slowly, she rolled her head to look at him. He was once again amazed at her beautiful midnight-blue irises.

She gave him the sweetest smile and whispered, "I'd say, what the hell took you so long?"

He looked at her in surprise. "I've only known you for just over a week. I didn't want to push you."

"And yet, in many ways, I've known you forever," she said simply. She stroked his face, her hand slipping around his ear before she pinched it gently and tugged him toward her. "I'm pretty sure there are a lot of ways of getting to know each other."

And she kissed him. The minute her lips touched his, he was lost.

CHAPTER 26

S HE LET HER head fall back but kept her gaze on his. "Do we have time?" she whispered.

He smiled as he followed her down, his nose rubbing gently against hers. "Hawk won't come in unless I give the signal."

Her smile widened. "So does he already know?"

"He suspects."

She kissed the corner of his mouth. And then his chin. Her hands gently ran through his hair, almost massaging his scalp. When her fingers stroked the inside of his collar, she whispered, "You are wearing too many clothes."

He stared down at her. She placed her finger across his lips. "Do not ask me if I'm serious or if I'm sure or give me a second chance in any way. I'm sure what I want is you."

He lowered his head and kissed her. A kiss of promise, a kiss of passion, a kiss of so much more. She pulled her head back, pushed him up, and said firmly, "Clothes off now."

He gave a bark of laughter, hopped to his feet, and, while she watched, he stripped. Her blood heated as every inch of his skin showed up. He was a wonderful animal. He bore the scars of his past life and scratches from one of the birds. But he was muscle from top to bottom—toned, slim, lean, tanned. When he walked around the bed to her side, his erection standing at attention, she threw back the covers, shifting over to make room for him.

He stopped and shook his head. "Now you're wearing too many clothes."

She gave a shy smile and got to her knees. She lifted the heavy nightgown up over her head. She handed it to him. He tossed it to the side with his clothes. And they just stared at each other.

In a low voice she apologized, "I've got a little more flesh on me but not a lot. I'm sorry."

He tilted her chin up. She could feel the heat across the distance. "I wanted you when I first saw you," he whispered. "I could only hope you would heal and survive the torment that had been done to you. I'd never have touched you if it wasn't what you wanted. And even now I'm scared of hurting you," he admitted.

She smiled, lay back down on the bed, and opened her arms. "So maybe go a little easy the first time," she whispered. "And, if all goes well, we can to do it all over again."

He lay down on the bed beside her and gathered her in his arms. As if taking her at her word, he set about exploring and tasting every inch of her. Long slender strokes down her breasts, across her ribs, and over her flat stomach. She had healed so beautifully in such a short time. He knew her shoulder was still sore. But he kissed her gently on the scar, his fingers tangling in the bandage on her back. He shook his head, gently soothing with his tongue her sore muscles and tissues, only to slip down to a soft, small, plump breast, taking the nipple into his mouth and suckling it.

She cried out softly at the pulsation starting so deep and so low. He moved to the other one, licking the tip before taking it too in his mouth. She lay on her back, wondering at the joy coursing through her. Sensations rippled and poured as he soothed and stroked. She hadn't expected to find anyone willing to help her. But to find a savior who also might be willing to love her was a gift she'd never hoped to receive in this lifetime.

She'd always found comfort with her feathered friends, not understanding or connecting in any meaningful way with those of her own species. She'd had several relationships. Always looking for that same thing she had had with Hadrid. And never finding it.

When he slid his fingers over her hips, along her thighs, and down her knees, she shivered. Instantly he raised his head to look at her. "Are you cold?"

She tugged him down for a soul-searing kiss. When he lifted his head, his breathing raspy and hard, she whispered, "No. I'm empty, lonely. I need you."

She slid her arms around his neck and tugged him on top of her. Instantly the heat of his body surrounded her, filling her with his warmth, his heat, and his passion. Lord, she wanted him. As he stoked her fires, she released her own inner inhibitions and explored his beautiful body as he'd explored hers. When she grasped his erection in her hand, her fingers sliding gently over the sensitive tip, he groaned and rolled to his back, accepting everything she wanted to do.

He was such a miracle. She leaned down and kissed the tip, the soft smooth surface like velvet against her tongue. He caught his breath deep in his throat, his fingers grasping the sheets beside them. She stroked up and down, sliding to gently cup the two globes that fit perfectly in her hand.

"You're so magnificent," she whispered.

That startled a laugh out of him.

"No, I mean it," she protested. She slid her hand back

up and down, her fingers measuring, closing, squeezing gently as she explored the lower half of his body, her hands running down the inside of his thighs and calves, back up behind his knees, hearing him laugh as she caught a ticklish spot. She grinned and then sighed happily. When she sat up and stretched her knee over him, he reached out to help her.

Settling into position, she slowly lowered herself onto his shaft. She felt her body stretch past the point of comfort until she relaxed, her body accepting him, as if knowing how very well matched they truly were. When she finally settled deep against his thighs, resting for a moment to catch her breath at the sensation of being filled right to the heart of her, his groan was long and harsh. She watched the shudder ripple up and down his body.

And she realized just how much restraint he had placed on himself. She leaned forward, her hands going to his shoulders, and whispered, "I always did love a midnight ride."

His eyes opened, and their gazes locked. Slowly she started to ride, her hips rising, lowering, almost coming off on the next movement, and then slamming down again. Faster and faster she rode, arching her back, closing her eyes, and tilting her face to the ceiling. Her body and mind were one as she drove them both to the edge. She could feel the tension inside him, his fingers gripping her hips, slamming her down harder, faster, deeper, and the spring inside her uncoiled, sending nerve endings alive and screaming with joy outward. She shuddered, a long cry escaping. He roared, and his hips met hers, his hands holding her sealed against him, as his body shuddered and spewed deep inside her. She collapsed atop him, shaky, tired and overwhelmed by the moment. He pulled the covers back up and over her.

"I was supposed to do the work," he whispered.

Answering was almost beyond her. "And I should've let you," she whispered. "Because I think I'm too tired for more."

"Sleep," he whispered. "Sleep."

Her fingers gently stroked his cheek, her thumb crossing his bottom lip, and she whispered, "Now I think I can." And she let herself cross into the abyss that awaited her.

EAGLE WAITED FOR her to fall asleep. When he heard her deep rhythmical breathing, he slid out from under the covers, quickly dressed, opened one of the windows for fresh air, and checked his watch. He still had an hour before he was to change places with Hawk who kept watch outside.

So much was unknown to them right now. Eagle imagined Hawk moved through the area, checking it out.

That box had been hidden in the far back corner behind other boxes. Had no one been through that linen closet in all these years? How bizarre was that? He heard a board creak outside in the hall. He froze and then slid over to the door, his ear pressed against the side. With a tiny scratching sound at the doorknob, he responded by opening it. Hawk stood there. He had a hot coffee in his hand.

Eagle glanced at Hawk, then at the coffee. "Is that for me?"

"It's your turn to stay outside. I figured this would help." He thrust it into his hand. "Heard a lot of talk downstairs. The whispers are starting. The rumor is that it's Issa. I had a beer in the far corner. They seemed to forget I was there. Until I got up and walked through the room— then there was silence. I'll go catch four hours." Hawk tilted his head. "Good night."

He turned and disappeared into his room. Eagle sat back down again and thought about all the things they knew. He still awaited the appraisal on the jewelry. He checked in with both Gray and his assistant, Tony. The young kid answered the phone on the first ring. He updated Eagle on the birds. They'd been given yet another raptor, which Tony put into isolation and fed, but his wing might be damaged. Gray would take a look.

Eagle's heart slammed back home. It was where he should be, looking after the birds. They were his responsibility. Hopefully he and Issa would be done here in another day. But he suspected it would be at least two more before they could return. "We'll be home soon."

He hung up and called Gray. There was no answer. He left a voice message and hung up. Then he sent a text to the appraiser looking into the jewelry.

When his phone rang again, it was his appraiser. "I don't know what you've gotten into. That jewelry is very rare. It was stolen from a private collection. It belonged to an aristocrat who was well known for his screenplays and mad, crazy, love affairs with young girls. The robbery happened about twenty years ago. And the jewelry was never found, the robbers never caught."

"Ah. I am pretty sure I know where the jewelry is, but I don't know who'll get blamed for the robbery."

"Tell me what you know."

Eagle filled him in without telling him where the jewelry was.

"Everything's over in Ireland? You need to contact the local police to take it from there. This is huge."

"I'll contact you as soon as I know more."

"I can give you twenty-four hours, but that's it. This is a pretty major case you're talking about."

"Do you want the jewelry only, or do you want the people who stole it caught?" Eagle asked.

"Okay, twenty-four hours and I'll touch base again. But this is fascinating," the appraiser said. "It's a well-known unsolved case, so recovering anything will be big news."

"Did other items go missing at the same time?"

"I think smaller pieces of jewelry and gold coins as well as a bunch of artwork," he said. "It was assumed everything had been moved through England and dispersed into private collections around the world from there."

Eagle agreed. But he didn't want to give away too much information. After he hung up, he grabbed a notebook and started jotting down information. He texted Charlie for his brother's contact information. It was important to bring in law enforcement at this point. But he'd rather have someone he trusted to deal with. This was a hell of a puzzle that still didn't explain why Issa had been initially kidnapped. After all she was just six at the time this all went down. And her only part of her family's smuggling operation was to be one of its three lookouts, not counting Hadrid. Without finding her mother's boxes, Issa wouldn't know as much as she did now.

So what would the kidnappers want from Issa? And that was the part that really needed to be solved. She had to be safe while they figured this out and caught the kidnappers.

The only thing that was important to him was Issa.

STEFAN WOKE GENTLY. For that he was grateful. So often he was jerked from his sleep by a vision, by a need, by his own disturbed thoughts. But this time he woke to see the sun peeking over the hills on the far side, sending a warm golden ray across his window.

He smiled and settled deeper into the covers. If he didn't have to get up right now, there was no way he would. He'd lost a lot of sleep lately. Plus he was feeding the birds energy, helping them to find food and travel, definitely leaving him more sleep-deprived and low on energy. There had to be an easier way. He couldn't see the owl; he only knew it was there. And so was Roash. But something odd was going on between them.

He got a vision of Roash directing a mouse toward Humbug. He didn't know if Humbug was sick or too injured, but he refused to eat it. Roash cried, his call haunting and pained.

And Humbug's small chirps were almost the antithesis of what they should be. But he managed to fly a little farther. Roash kept close, helping Humbug, urging him. But every step, every take off, every landing required energy.

Stefan and Tabitha were both pouring love and healing energy into the two birds. Stefan could read Issa's energy pouring into them as well. Yet it was different looking—an unconscious connection she'd set up to function as needed but then didn't need to be active in the process. Stefan was completely blindsided by the fact that this owl occupied his mind and his energy. And in Issa's ability to take care of these animals on a spirit level that he'd never seen before.

But it was Humbug himself that blew Stefan away.

He still couldn't quite believe it. As he lay here, he heard a soft, gentle, almost cooing sound against his cheek. He stilled and waited. A soft feather brushed his cheek, followed by a small rustle on his shoulder.

And then the sensation was gone. He lay here for a long moment, a sappy smile on his face, wondering what his role in all of this was. And then it hit him. Maybe he wasn't just here to find the bad guys. Maybe he wasn't just here to save his friends. Maybe it was a reaffirmation that *all* animals deserved to live.

And that he had friends, way more than he knew, in way more species than he'd ever thought. It was an incredible lesson brought about by an unexpected source.

"Thanks, Humbug." He smiled, closed his eyes, and whispered, "If that's what this is all about, I'm good with that."

And he fell back asleep.

CHAPTER 27

A HAND GENTLY shook Issa awake. She bolted upright, clutching the blankets to her chest. She stared, blinking sleepily at Eagle leaning over her. His voice was low, urging, "Get up and get dressed. Now."

She didn't ask any questions. Her brain was slow to react, but her body was moving. She didn't know if Hawk had been here, if that was him shutting the door on his way out. But she threw on clothes, packed as fast as she could. She ran to the bathroom, used the facilities, brushed her teeth, and took a drink. She returned to find the hotel room empty, wondering if she'd dreamed it all and should have stayed in bed.

Just then the door opened. Eagle saw her, gave her an approving nod, and said, "Come on. Let's go." He grabbed the bags and ushered her ahead of him. Just as she was about to go out the door, he whispered, "Be silent."

Hawk was on the far side of the hall, waiting. She ran lightly toward him as Eagle brought up the rear. The stairs that led down to the pub also led back the other way to the outside. They quickly slipped out into the night. And she realized that, although the sky was light, the sun had yet to rise.

The men loaded the bags into the car. She slipped into the back seat. Hawk didn't turn the engine on, just pushed in the clutch, and the vehicle rolled down the slight hill on the road. When they were about to hit the main road, he turned the engine over, put the car in gear, released the clutch as he gave it gas, and the car surged forward. And yet they drove without lights. She sat still, figuring out what had happened.

Eagle turned to look at her and asked, "You okay?"

She nodded. "What happened?"

Hawk answered. "I woke up to voices outside my room, talking about bringing in reinforcements. They wanted to get answers from you, once and for all."

She gasped, sinking back in her seat. "Answers for what?"

Hawk shook his head. "I don't know. We're heading into the city to see the detective who is the brother of another friend of ours. And, if we get a chance, I thought you may want to see Angus."

"Is that a possibility?"

"Yes. He might be willing to talk to us."

She stared out the window, thinking how quickly her life had shifted. "It would be good, I guess. I had hoped to meet more of my family. The trouble is knowing who my family really is."

"Exactly," Eagle said. "And word travels fast, especially now they know about you. I don't trust them."

She cracked a smile in his direction. "That's because you like being in control, and this situation makes you uncomfortable," she said smoothly. "You were probably a bad-tempered child growing up too."

"Hey, that's not fair," he said mockingly. "I might've been a challenging child. But I wasn't bad."

She rolled her eyes at him and looked out the window.

"At least I had few hours' sleep."

"You actually had five. That's all we could give you. After Hawk heard the men, he came and got me. We did a quick look around the place to see what we were up against. That's when he brought the car around back, and I raced up to get you. Two, three, four, five, or even six guys—no problem. Twelve guys, maybe no problem. But six guys with guns, twelve guys with guns ..." Eagle shook his head. "No way."

"At least we could have gone down and picked up coffee on the way out."

Hawk gave a snort. "Maybe if the pub had been open, we could have ordered some to go, but that would have given us away. Nothing is open yet. We'll get to the city and have breakfast then."

"We have a drive to go yet," Eagle said to Issa. "So, if you can, close your eyes, and get some more sleep."

That she would like to do, but she didn't think it would be possible. Not to mention so much was going on in her head that didn't make any sense. She turned and looked at Eagle. "Did you bring all the stuff?"

He nodded. "It's possible it all came from a robbery in Paris twenty years ago. They're quite well-known pieces."

Her shoulders sagged. "I was hoping they weren't."

"What I don't know is why they were stuck in the back of that closet."

"Yeah, it was strange." She nodded. "I told my mom and dad about that spot. Not very many other people knew. I was friends for a while with one kid there when I was growing up. Arian. But I'm not sure his family thought I was a good influence on him. It was odd. He's the one that I exchanged notes with in the closet all the time."

The men didn't say anything.

She smiled at the memory. "Nothing major. Just a picture one day, a feather another, that kind of thing." She shrugged. "It was sweet. And made me smile."

"Who was that?"

"The pub owner's son, Arian," she said. "I never saw him again after we left—I never saw anyone from here after that." She frowned and shrugged. "So much of my history is from that part of my life, and most of it is almost impossible to remember. Just images, feelings, impressions, more than actual events."

"I'd say that's pretty normal, given the age you were."

She got caught up in the memories as they drove steadily toward the city. "I want to go back there later."

"Only if we have to," Hawk said.

When she didn't respond, Eagle turned to look at her. "Why do you want to go back?"

She sighed. "I feel like they need closure. As much as I do."

"Maybe they do. But that doesn't mean they will get it."

Close to forty minutes later they pulled into the city limits. Up ahead was a fast-food chain. Hawk pulled in and said, "I need a pit stop. I think we all could use some coffee."

When they'd all had a chance to use the single bathroom, they went to the counter and ordered coffee. A clock hung on the wall behind the counter. "What time does the station open?" Eagle asked Hawk.

"We've still got another hour. Probably half an hour on the road to find the address. Do you want to grab some breakfast here?"

"I was actually eyeing the muffins. Maybe that would do."

Hawk ordered six to go. Once they were back on the road, he divvied them up.

"You sure we weren't followed?" she asked.

"We weren't followed when we left, but it's pretty obvious we would've been heading toward the city. Maybe they put a tracker on the rental car. I don't know. Why? Have you seen anyone?"

"Honestly, these days all I do is look around and think I see someone."

"We are being followed in a sense. But it's our guys, not them."

She stared at Hawk, her jaw dropping. "You mean, you have somebody keeping an eye on us?"

"Of course. We never walk into a situation like this without backup."

She shook her head. "This is just too nuts."

"Says the daughter of a smuggler, the daughter of a woman who kept a lover on the side, whose entire male family died while on a job? Who knows what the hell is going on in the world? I still can't believe we found the jewelry and the money. You have to decide what you want to do about this."

"Do about it? What can I do?"

"The jewelry should be handed over. Hopefully it goes back to the proper owner, if these can be confirmed as the missing pieces. No way to know if the money was taken at the same time."

"Any idea how much there is?"

"Close to fifty grand USD."

She sank back. "My mother must have really hated that money to have left it here all these years. She worked at minimum wage jobs for most of her life and lived from paycheck to paycheck."

Finally they came to a large building built of stone. She stared at the forbidding-looking front and said, "This looks a little unnerving."

She hopped out of the car with her purse, noted that Eagle picked up his duffel, slung it over his shoulder, and reached out a hand. She slipped her hand into his, and together, with Hawk bringing up the rear, they walked in the front door.

Hawk said, "He should be waiting for us. Charlie set it up."

Several men stood off to one side of the counter.

Eagle identified himself and said he was meeting Detective Dennis Laslo.

The taller of the men smiled, walked over, and held out a hand. "That's me. Let's go to a private room." He led them to a small room where they all sat down. "This is quite a story you've got." He turned to look at Issa. "Are you Issa McGuire?"

She nodded. "As far as I know, I am. Although my father might not be who I thought he was."

"According to Eagle, that could be Angus." He studied her. "Do you want to see him?"

"Is he allowed visitors?"

"Oh, yes, he's been a model prisoner. He's still spouting his innocence. He doesn't know about you yet. But, if you'd like to see him, I'm sure you would brighten an old man's day."

She thought about that. Her mom had been in her fifties. Angus was likely in his sixties. And maybe that would be something she should do. If for nothing else, just to get closure.

"Yes, I would like that. If possible, I'd like to see him today."

IT WAS DIFFICULT to watch the play of emotions move across Issa's face. Eagle still held her hand gently in his. He loved that she'd moved her chair closer to his, that, at every opportunity, she was there right beside him. It had been a long time since he had had that sense of partnership. That sense of togetherness with someone. This felt right. He never thought he'd find a woman as addicted and hung up on birds as he was.

She could teach him so much, but that was for another time. He was still struggling with her abilities. He wasn't sure what to think of the Roash and Humbug issues. It didn't seem real. She could communicate in ways he'd only dreamed about.

Now watching her face at the thought of meeting Angus was almost painful. She'd buried her mother. The father she knew was in a grave, buried more than twenty years ago. Never thought to have a biological father alive. And to be the man she'd seen in bed with her mother.

The night that everything blew up. The night the four of them, three humans and one falcon, were all supposed to be watching, all of them derelict in their duties. But only one of them had an allowable excuse because she was a child.

He turned his gaze to the detective and said, "It would need to be today or at the very latest in the morning."

The detective nodded, opened the file in front of him, ran his finger down as if checking for Angus's location and a number. He picked up the phone and dialed. As they listened, he requested visiting hours. When he put down the phone, he said, "You're in luck. You can see him today."

Issa squeezed Eagle's fingers. He didn't know if it was in hope or in fear. But he knew Angus could be the one to give them the answers they needed.

They had other things they had to deal with first though.

The detective placed his forearms on the desk, clasped his hands together, and looked at her. "What do you know about the jewels?"

"Nothing," she said quietly. "I didn't know anything about them twenty years ago and just found pictures of them recently after my mother passed away. And well ..." She turned to look at Eagle.

He explained from there.

The detective raised an eyebrow, glancing from Eagle to Issa and back. "What do you want to do?"

"What's right. That means, handing them over," she said without hesitation.

Eagle smiled at her, loving her even more. And then froze at the thought. *Love?* Was that what this was? He shoved the thought down, reached into his bag, and pulled out one of the soft velvet bags.

The detective carefully poured out the necklace so everyone could take a closer look. Then he whistled. "Wow."

He picked it up, and they all stared at the emeralds shimmering in the light. He opened an envelope and showed Eagle and Issa the owner's photos of the four missing pieces of jewelry. The emerald necklace matched the one in the photo. Beautifully.

Issa said, "They'll need to be authenticated. And I'd like a receipt. If they aren't the ones stolen, I'd like them back."

The detective nodded. "Yes, that's fair. But, from the looks of it, I don't think there's any doubt these are the real gems."

Eagle spread out four large glossy photos, matching the ones in the detective's folder. Eagle reached down for the other velvet bags. Carefully he pulled out the necklaces and put them on the desk. All four necklaces matched the four glossy photos.

The detective said, "This cold case has been unsolved for over twenty years."

"It's still unsolved," Issa said. "All I can tell you is where these were found and what led us to them. And I know it probably had something to do with my family being wiped out twenty years ago."

The detective sobered. "You're right. This is not just about finding the stolen goods or capturing the men who did this. A great deal of human life was lost that night."

He picked up his phone and called somebody. Ten minutes later a rap came at the door, and it opened. The detective stood and said, "This is my supervisor. I'll write you that receipt. We'll go from there."

She nodded. "Is anything else missing?"

Both of the policemen turned to look at her. "Like what?"

Eagle smiled to himself as she gazed steadily at the men. "You showed us four photos, one of each of the four necklaces. Wasn't there other jewelry that went missing at the same time?"

The detective said, "Oh, that's a good question." He walked back to his folder and said, "Though we don't have any more photographs, besides the four necklaces, some old gold coins went missing. Just a few of them, along with a few smaller pieces of jewelry. Everything was stolen from the same private collection. The jewels were on display under what was supposed to be top security at the time. The thing is, the method of getting in and out was simple. Bribery and murder."

Issa turned pale at the word *murder*.

"The theft occurred during a big formal event. Politicians, movie stars, many private collectors were there. So the theft was well publicized." He raised his gaze and looked at her. "Did you find anything else?"

"Only Irish money," she said quietly. "And paperwork from my parents."

He nodded. "That's fine. We need the details on those, plus a statement from you, if you could, please."

Hawk asked, his voice harsh and amiable at the same time, "When will you get the jewels authenticated?"

"This morning hopefully but maybe not until tomorrow," the supervisor said. "We have a specialist who assists us on some investigations." He turned to look at Issa. "Are you going to see Angus?"

She stood. "Yes. Maybe he'll have some answers."

The two officers studied her, then glanced at the jewels. The detective asked, "Do you think he was involved?"

"I have no idea. My father—well, who I thought was my father—and my three brothers along with him were smugglers," she said quietly. "Maybe these were smuggled out of France weeks earlier." She shrugged. "I really have no way of knowing as I was six back then."

The detective said, "I have a time line here. The jewels were stolen in March, and your father died less than ten days later."

"In that case, it's likely all related. I don't know that my father ever left Ireland. Somebody else would've been responsible for bringing the jewels across the water."

The detective nodded. "That would make sense." He wrote a note down on the file. "Do you know how often he received shipments?"

"I have no way to know. Like I said, I was only six, and my mother and I left for America soon afterward," she said. "If we're done here, I'd really like to talk to Angus now."

The detective said, "And I'd like to hear what he has to say too. Let's get your statement. Then you can go to the prison."

"You could come with us," Issa offered.

The detective smiled. "If I thought it would do any good, I would. But I think your father will speak more freely if I'm not there."

Eagle agreed. "Then let's take care of the paperwork so we can be on our way."

CHAPTER 28

WALKING INTO THE prison was daunting. She'd never been in one before. She struggled not to look around as they walked through the hallways. They had a guard in front and more guards behind them. She appreciated everyone's concern, but, at the same time, she couldn't imagine how the men felt being locked up like this. Angus had been here for seventeen years? How horrible.

She was led into a room where she stopped. Angus already sat at the table; a guard stood off to the side. He seemed confused and bewildered as to why he was here. When he looked up at her arrival, he frowned, and then his eyes lit up. "Issa?"

She stood stock-still, overwhelmed once again by memories slamming into her. This man had given her gifts. He had helped her further train Hadrid. He was in the house, laughing and joking with her smiling mother. The only time Issa ever saw her mother smile was for Angus, this man in front of her.

Eagle slung an arm across her shoulder and gently hugged her. "Do you want to sit down?"

She cast him a sideways look and then forced herself to take several steps forward. Three chairs were on her side of the table. She appreciated having both Hawk and Eagle with her. She sat down, her gaze never leaving the man in front of her. The first words out of her mouth were not what she expected to ask. "Are you my father?"

A shadow crossed Angus's face. He settled back and said, "I have no way of knowing for sure."

She let .her breath out slowly in a long exhale. Her shoulders slumped. She had so hoped for answers.

"My DNA is on file," he said quietly. "I would very much like to get yours tested to see if it's possible."

"My mother told you that I might be yours?"

"Yes. But she was never far away from your father. Rory was a hard man. He told her often the only way she would leave him was in wooden box."

Issa's gaze widened at that news. But then her father ran a smuggling ring. He'd had to be tough about what was his. "But it's possible?"

Angus nodded. "Yes, it's possible. We were lovers for many years—until Rory caught us. For the longest time after that we stopped again, but I couldn't stay away from her. I knew, if he caught us a second time, he'd likely kill me. I loved her more than anything else in the world."

"My mother, did she love you too?"

His smile turned gentle, loving, as he said, "I want to believe she did. In my heart I think she did. But maybe I was just a light in an otherwise hard life."

"Why was her life hard?" She couldn't stop the questions about her family from flowing. She needed to ask about so much, but, at the same time, the little girl inside her looked for answers on a whole different level.

He explained about her parents' marriage way back when, how her father and he had been competing for her mother. Her father had won, and, for a time, she'd seemed happy. But then they grew apart. Her sons grew up, and life was hard.

"The law charged him with attempted murder?"

Angus nodded. "Aye. But I wouldn't press charges. He was right to do what he did. I was with his wife. Any other man would have done the same. I had no right being there. She was his. I was the one in the wrong."

"And yet that night, when it all went to hell, you were in bed with her."

His gaze widened as he stared at her. "Did you see us?"

She gave a solemn nod. "Which is why I've always felt guilty. I was so shocked by the sight that I didn't see what was happening in time to warn anyone below."

Sorrow crossed Angus's face. He reached a hand toward her.

She pulled back instantly.

Seeing the look on her face, he asked in astonishment, "Are you scared of me? I would never hurt you."

"And yet in a way you did. If I'm yours, you left me with an unhappy mother for decades, my first six years of life with a father and brothers who I barely knew and didn't really accept me." She shook her head. "If you're not my father, you were with my mother, inciting an already volatile situation, making my life much less than it could have been."

"I gave you Hadrid. He was my most prized falcon," he said. "Your father paid for him, but it wasn't nearly what he was worth. I had hoped to have him sire many more like him. But, after he bonded with you, I could do nothing with him."

"So then he was already of much less value," she said in a cool voice. It was hard to keep to an even tone. Both tears and laughter warred in her head. She wanted to get up and hug him, but, at the same time, she wanted to hit him.

He stared at her for a long moment. "It's hard to believe you're a grown woman. Have you done something with your life?"

"I'm a biologist," she replied. "And I'm still fascinated by birds."

He smiled. "Then giving you Hadrid was the right thing to do. For both you and the bird. When you have a lifelong love of animals, particularly one species, it's almost like dying to be without them." He raised his hands to the concrete walls around her. "My life here is nothing. I barely see the sun. No birds are in my life, and I have lost your mother." He turned to look at her. "She's dead, isn't she?"

"Yes, just over a month ago. That's when everything started. Let me explain what has happened after her death."

He fell silent as Issa went over the story, explaining how she had been kidnapped from her cabin after clearing out her mother's place, that she'd been held and tortured for weeks on end, and then she had managed to escape. And how Eagle came to find her. When she finally ran out of words, she raised her gaze to look upon Angus and saw tears in his eyes. She liked him that much more.

"I had nothing to do with it," he whispered, shaking his head. "No way any of us would do such a thing. It was against the code."

"One of the kidnappers talked about the code. He also talked about stressors. He asked a lot of questions about my childhood and where I hid *it*? But I have no idea what *it* was. I had no answers."

Angus's gaze narrowed, as if casting his mind back a lot of years. "*Stressors.* Now that's interesting. It's a term I used with the birds. Sometimes you have to force an animal into stress by adding stressors, so he comes to the point where he sees you as a good thing and the rest of the world as bad. In your case, being stuck in the crevice was your stressor. When you reached out, for whatever reason, in such a way, Hadrid found you. He responded to your cries. The stressor applied to you, unknowingly or not, brought the two of you together somehow. But it's not a term I would expect to hear very many people use."

"We're already thinking whoever kidnapped her was from here," Eagle said. "And quite likely from the group there the night her family died."

Angus settled back. "That night was one I wish to wipe out of my memory. I did not kill your father or your brothers," he said. He leaned forward. "Go home. You could be in danger here. You have to know I didn't kill your family. Somebody else did. And that person is still walking free."

"Can you at least answer me this? Is it possible my mother killed them?" She felt Eagle suck in his breath, his hand squeezing hers. And she realized she'd shocked him. She turned her gaze to him. "I have to know."

He nodded in understanding. They both turned to look at Angus. The shock on his face and his wildly shaking head gave his answer.

"No way. She wouldn't even leave him. There's no way she would kill him. And she lived for those boys. They were good young men, all of them. Strong and loyal. She would have done anything for them."

Relief bloomed in her heart. She realized she had needed to hear that answer. She took another shaky breath. "Good. Thank you for that."

He gazed at her and smiled gently. "You did love her, didn't you?"

"Of course. She was my mother. But she wasn't an easy woman to love."

"Isn't that right?"

Eagle said, "You've had twenty years to think about it. Who do you think killed her family?"

Hawk leaned forward to hear the answer better. And to look from one man to the other.

"First, what's your role in all of this, and what is your relationship to Issa?"

"I'm the one man who loves her. The man who protects her," Eagle said calmly.

She turned toward him, frowning.

Angus grinned. "He surprised you, didn't he, lass? That's good." He gazed over at Hawk. "And you. You have the look of a fighter on you. You both do."

Hawk gave a clipped nod. "Special Operations, military, fifteen years."

Angus nodded. "You're both on the right side of the law." It wasn't a question as much as a statement. Angus nodded again. "Figured so. Maybe that's the best way after all. Don't be on the wrong side of the law, like us here."

"*Us?*" She pounced. "Who were *us?*"

Eagle brought out his phone and hit the Video buttons. "I'm recording this. I need to do whatever I can to make sure Issa stays safe. And whoever those assholes are who kid-napped her, they will never capture her again."

"Before I start," Angus asked, "what will you do with the men when you find them?"

She watched as the two men measured each other.

Then Angus nodded in satisfaction. "Good. Hit them again for me too." He began to speak for the record now. "We ran a smuggling ring. There were five of us, plus Issa's three brothers. We'd been working together for a long time. Issa's father was the boss. We had long taken over the town. Nothing happened down there that our spies didn't let us know about. We were of the opinion everybody in that area was on our side. We had no idea, until some stuff started to go missing, that there was a problem. Then the coppers started showing up with really shitty timing. That was how we knew. We just didn't know who betrayed us. After Rory and I had the punch-out over your mother, I found out Rory thought maybe it was me. I convinced him that I was innocent, but I always wondered if he ever fully trusted me again." He shook his head. "I was one of the few who had an income outside of smuggling. We all did something else, but I ran a falconry that trained and sold them around the world."

He shrugged with a twinkle in his eyes. "Smuggling for me was a hobby, but for others it was a way of life."

"Did you find out who the mole was?"

Angus shook his head. "No, we never did. I was with your mother that night. When we realized something was wrong, we raced down to the cove and the shelter." He turned to look at Eagle. "There was a pier on the side of the cabin." He turned back to Issa and continued. "But I was supposed to be the lookout." He spoke with a broken voice. "I betrayed Rory twice that night. I couldn't resist the temptation to be with your mother. She was supposed to be with you, Issa, supposed to be on the lookout too, a backup in case you missed anything. But instead we all failed as lookouts that night."

"No," Eagle snapped. "This child and her bird did not fail. The adults failed her."

Angus winced. "You're right. I felt terrible that night.

339

Maier thought I had betrayed them as I was the only one left standing. Two others beside your family were dead as well. But their families were already racing toward us. Two others were injured. One of the injured, his family took him. They did their own doctoring as was common, and they disappeared from that part of the woods. The two dead men were tossed into a boat, and the boat was lit on fire."

"So that's what happened to my father's boat." She frowned. "I remember something about that now. Something about fuel leaking from the side of the tank."

Angus nodded. "That's quite true. There was a leak because we created it, but the men themselves were already dead."

"So, who else could there have been?"

"Briefly I too considered your mother, but then I realized she never would've done it. She was absolutely heartbroken. We had our contact on the French side. They used to come back and forth, but they had already left. Goods delivered as always. That was Pierre Montigue. He had his own smuggling crew on the French coast. How he got the stuff that night or any other night, I don't know. We didn't ask questions. We heard they did pickup and delivery. Some of the stuff we sold ourselves. Your father had connections in the city. A lot of the stuff was delivered in town. We were just one leg of the journey."

"There had to be somebody else." But the Frenchman's name was a big help. She watched as Hawk texted it to the detective.

Angus nodded. "I know. But I've been racking my brain all these years. I still have no idea."

She groaned. "What was in the shipment? Do you know?"

"I don't know, but it was more than just jewelry. There were casks. I don't know what they were full of, but I'd assumed French brandy."

She wasn't sure she believed him. Something in his voice had changed. She glanced at Eagle who returned her gaze. She gave an almost imperceptible shake of her head. He responded with a tiny nod.

But it was Hawk who snapped, "And that's when your story turns to shit. You're lying through your teeth. You know exactly what was in those casks."

Angus groaned. "Not many things in my life I felt bad about. Taking Rory's wife was something I could justify because I loved her so very much. But when we realized what was in the casks, it was more than any of us could deal with."

"What was it?"

"And how many casks were there?" Issa asked.

He sighed and stared off in the distance.

"You didn't say anything to anybody, even when you went to trial, did you?"

He shook his head. "No. I was a scapegoat. As long as I kept my mouth shut, I would live, and everyone else would survive. Twenty years have passed, and I don't really care anymore." He turned his gaze from one man to the other. "You will not understand."

Eagle crossed his arms over his chest and leaned back. "Tell us."

He groaned. "Issa, I would never have wanted you to know. But that shipment your father and brothers received were trafficked young girls."

She stared at him in horror. Eagle gripped her hands.

Angus rushed to say, "We never had a shipment like that before. I swear it. We didn't know what was in there when we started. But we heard one of them crying. They were supposed to be drugged for the entire journey, right up to being delivered. The shipment was headed for a house in Belfast."

"Oh, my God," Issa whispered in pain.

EAGLE WANTED TO take her out of that room and protect her from more horrific news. He asked, "How does that fit in with the jewels?"

Angus looked at him and whispered with shame in his voice, "They all came from the same house. They were supposed to go to a fancy house in the city. I don't know what happened to the girls. But this was big. This was way bigger than anything any of us had ever touched before. It was something we couldn't deal with. Your father refused. He wanted the girls to be released. One of them was crying, pleading to be taken back. She spoke French, so I didn't know what she said."

"Wait. You said when you walked in the meeting place, my brothers were on the ground already shot. So how do you know about the girls? How do you know my dad said he wouldn't do it?"

Angus winced. "Because I had just been outside. Initial shots were fired. I left Maier to collect Issa and shoo her back home, crossing paths with her as I left and raced down the hill to the pier where I snuck up on the shelter. That's when I heard them arguing. I saw the girls. But they started shooting again. And I stayed out of sight until it stopped. Then I went in."

"How many?"

He took a deep breath. "There were six girls."

Anger once again rose high up Eagle's throat. "This was a secret somebody would kill to keep. So when they refused to deal with the girls, some of the smugglers shot the other men who wouldn't go along with the human trafficking? Is that correct?"

Angus nodded. "I also was attacked from behind and was unconscious for a little while, but I survived. I heard men scrambling to get away, and I know the casks weren't there when I woke up. So they may have been taken elsewhere. And of course I was convicted of everything but trafficking. I kept my mouth shut about the girls so no one knew. I didn't know who brought them. I just knew they all came from a fancy house where the goods were retrieved from too."

Issa shook her head. "I found the jeweled necklaces. But good to know the girls came from the same place. Maybe the police can sort it out."

Angus opened his mouth. "What do you mean, you found the necklaces? I thought they were lost."

"Four stolen necklaces were in a keepsake box my mother told me to find. It had been stashed in the closet at the pub." Almost as an afterthought, Issa added, "There was also a lot of money and documents."

He sat and stared at her. "How is that possible? How would your mother have gotten them?"

"I don't know." Issa glanced at him quizzically. "You don't know anything about it?"

He shook his head. "No." Then he froze, as if stricken with horror.

Eagle tried to get him to answer the question. But he wasn't talking. Eagle realized Angus was caught in a never-ending nightmare, wondering what had gone so wrong that night. Who he'd covered up for all these years. And what that keepsake box might reveal.

"We turned the jewels over to the police," Issa said, her voice gaining strength again. "Maybe we can find the girls too."

Eagle squeezed her fingers and gave her a gentle glance. "I doubt it. That was a lot of years ago."

"Or at least stop this trafficking ring." She looked at him for a long moment, then turned her attention back to Angus. "Did my mother know about the jewels, the girls?"

"I hadn't thought so. But if you got the jewels …" And he fell silent once again. Suddenly he stood. "I'd like to return to my cell." And that was all he would say.

BACK OUTSIDE THE prison, Eagle opened his arms, and Issa stepped into them, grateful for his warmth and the steadfast nature of this man who refused to let anyone make him cower, no matter what the consequences.

"Hawk, we need to track down who else might've been there that day," he said over her head.

"None of this makes any sense in terms of why I was kidnapped," she whispered. "Unless they were after the jewels?"

"Maybe. Maybe the jewels and the money weren't enough. Maybe it was more about revenge, looking to find whoever betrayed them. One man was taken away. Injured, but he survived. His name was never brought up. Seems to me we need to track him down."

"Then we need Angus to tell us who else was there," Hawk said.

She glanced at the front of the prison and said, "I don't

think he will talk to us anymore. His memories have just been shattered all to hell."

"I gave him our phone numbers," Eagle said. "I told him that I would be in town for the rest of the evening, and, if there was ever a time for him to come clean, it was now. While you still have some respect for him."

Hawk nodded. "It's still early. Where do you want to go?" But it wasn't that early; it was past lunch.

"I think I need food," she said, fatigue evident in her voice.

Eagle agreed. He wrapped his arm around her shoulders. "Let's go find a restaurant. And then we'll call the detective. He probably has no idea this is so much more than what it started out to be."

"Is it wrong of me to feel grateful that my dad stood up? That he died, although doing something illegal, but he died for the right reason, to help protect those girls?"

"Not at all. It should help. Your father did everything he could. Once the situation turned ugly, he tried to step up."

Hawk's exclamation beside them caught their attention.

"Got it," Hawk said. "Charlie just texted me the list of names of who was on the cove that day that he got from his brother."

Eagle turned to look at him. "And?"

"One of Angus's known associates from way back when, the one never brought up in court cases, is the one who was picked up by his family members and whisked away up north. That was a Danny McNeil. There weren't any details about the family, but they had been part of the same smuggling clan for a long time."

"And do we know if he is alive or dead?"

"Not to mention how badly injured was he that night?"

Eagle glanced at Issa. "Would you recognize him if he'd been one of your kidnappers?"

She shrugged. "I don't know if I would. The head kidnapper, who they called 'the boss,' had lots of henchmen. He was always giving them instructions on what to do and how to do it. But I never actually saw him. And I didn't recognize his voice, other than the Irish accent." She frowned and shook her head. "I was blindfolded when I was originally taken there. When they took it off after several days, I saw the same gatekeepers. I never saw any sign of the boss man."

Hawk whistled. "Now that would've been good to know."

STEFAN WOKE TO the ring of the phone. He reached out his hand groggily, hit the button, and said, "Yes?"

An exhausted female voice filled the room. "Stefan, it's Tabitha. I did something I hadn't quite expected. But I think it worked."

"What did you do?"

"I connected with"—she took a deep breath—"a coyote. He allowed the birds on his back, and he's taking them several miles in the right direction. I'm not sure how far away they are from the actual property line. But I think they're pretty damn close."

Stefan bolted upright. "Humbug and Roash rode on the back of a coyote?"

"Yes. Now they are sitting on top of a fence post, resting, but they need cover. They still have a ways to go."

"It wasn't restful enough getting a ride?" He shook his head in disbelief. "Tabitha, even for you, that's pretty bizarre and miraculous."

She chuckled. "At the moment I'm just so exhausted from the effort of subduing the coyote's basic instincts. At the same time, I had to subdue both of the birds so they would actually be friendly enough to do this. But I have to admit, from now on, they need your help. At least until I rest."

"I'll check in on them and make sure they're hidden for a few hours. And then we'll see how we can get them the rest of the way."

"I hope so. I'm off to bed. I've been up all night with this. Now I need to recharge in a big way."

"Tabitha, thank you."

Her laughter rang free. "I live for stuff like this. You know that, Stefan."

She hung up, and he lay back down, a big smile on his face. He closed his eyes, and Humbug gently drifted a feather down on his cheek. "I know, Humbug. We're actually making this happen. Hold steady, buddy. We're almost there."

CHAPTER 29

"WHY? WHAT DIFFERENCE does it make if I saw the boss or not?" Issa asked in bewilderment. "I wasn't conscious much of the time either."

"They couldn't take the chance you could identify your kidnapper."

She turned to Eagle and blinked. "You're thinking he was somebody I might've recognized?"

Both Hawk and Eagle nodded. "That makes the most sense. It also makes sense that they knew to look for the jewels and the money."

"Revenge? Is that possible? After twenty years?"

"Do you know how badly injured Danny was, Hawk?"

Hawk shook his head. "No idea."

"Too bad. It would also help to know who else or what else he may have lost at that fight. You don't know how it impacted the rest of his life. Maybe he was unable to do anything again. For all you know, he's totally incapable of supporting himself, and his life is miserable, all because of whoever did this to him. And you could be the only living connection he has to the person who did this."

"Then why torture me?"

"Because he wanted to make sure you weren't protecting someone. He wanted to make sure you weren't trying to hide this person from him."

They were at the car by then. She slumped against the side of it. "I did hear voices that night before all hell broke loose. But I didn't recognize any of them. A lot of the men were young who worked for my father. One was old. But he wasn't that old." She tilted her head and thought about it. "He was small and was older than my mother."

"He might possibly have been somebody your mother knew. Maybe they were hoping she'd have bared her soul before dying and gave you all the details of what happened."

"Or, out of respect for her, they waited until she was gone," Hawk said. "I don't know these people, but everyone has a motivation for doing something in a particular way. It all seems to revolve around your mother and you."

"That's nothing new," she said in frustration. "None of this helps us find Panther or Tiger."

She watched the two men exchange glances. Just as Eagle was about to speak, his phone went off. He answered it with, "What's up?"

He spun and turned toward Hawk. At that moment Hawk's phone went off. Hawk pulled it out, checked the number, and glanced over at Eagle. He held it up for Eagle to see the screen.

She leaned over to take a look. It was Panther calling. She frowned. "I can't believe that."

Hawk shrugged. "Only one way to find out." He hit the Talk button and said, "Panther, what's up?"

Issa only heard one side of the conversations. She paced and waited. And just as the men sounded like they were getting off the phone, hers rang. She wiped tears out of her eyes to see a number she didn't know. Hesitantly she lifted the phone to her ear and said, "Hello?"

"It's Angus. You're looking for Danny McNeil," he said.

"He's the man who organized the shipment. He was older than your brothers. He was the one hurt and taken away. He might have answers for you."

"Any idea how I can find him?"

"Yeah. Barney from the pub. His brother-in-law is Danny's father. You be careful though. Not all the pub folks are on your side." And he hung up.

When she put down her phone, she found both men staring at her, but Eagle was now on another call. As soon as he was done, she raised her eyebrows and said, "That was Angus." She repeated his message.

Hawk nodded. "That aligns with the information I just got. But Panther didn't call me. It was one of my other men. He found Panther's phone—outside the pub."

She felt the color wash away from her cheeks. "Angus said Barney at the pub would know how to reach this other guy who is also his brother-in-law. But not to trust everyone at the pub because they weren't all on my side." She turned to Eagle. "Who were you talking to?

"The man who held you captive. He had Tiger's phone."

She took a deep breath. "Asshole. What did he want?"

"He wants us back at the pub."

"Then I suggest we let the detective know what the hell's going on and get back there fast," she said darkly. When only silence met her words, she stared at them in bewilderment. "What? Why are we stalling?"

"I don't want you to go back to the pub."

She crossed her arms over her chest. "It doesn't matter what you want. They have your friends, and I won't let the kidnappers hurt anybody else. If they want me, then let them tell me exactly what it is they're after. Because I sure as hell don't know."

Eagle hesitated.

She cut him off when he opened his mouth. "I didn't come all this way for you guys to rush to the rescue and leave me safe and sound back in town. That'll just get more men killed. Let's get the detective and whatever bloody team you have pulled together here. I don't care. But we're going back and getting to the bottom of this now." She glared at Eagle, than switched to look at Hawk. "You can't possibly want to leave your friends in trouble like this."

EAGLE WATCHED AS Hawk shrugged. "We already have men on-site. They're prepping to rescue our buddies now. We already told them that we're on the way."

"Yes, *we* are on the way," she said.

"Let me call the detective," Eagle said. He took a few steps away and filled him in on the latest info. They talked for at least ten minutes, while Hawk and Issa waited. When Eagle joined them, he said, "He's getting a team together. He needs at least twenty minutes."

"They've got ten." She snorted. "We'll head out but will take our time. They can catch up."

The men grinned.

"Too many people are involved," Hawk complained. "It's hard to keep any of them straight."

"And yet most are accounted for."

"Except the girls. No one made mention of the missing girls. The sex slave industry is alive and well in France unfortunately," Eagle said. "It's a huge market, and a huge issue for the police over there. The detective is also getting a team to track down the house here in Belfast."

"That was twenty years ago. They probably move the

girls around," Issa said. Still it warmed her heart to think they might find these poor women.

"Yes. It was twenty years ago for you too. Those women still have a right to some kind of a life if they haven't already gained their freedom. You also have to consider they might no longer be alive."

She nodded. "I hope the police can find them—and maybe have already. At the very least they might shut down the trafficking ring."

"The police will try. They'll have to backtrack the case to France and see if they can find records of the girls over there. Also where did the women go when everything blew up?"

"Don't forget not everyone died. For all anyone knows, the remaining smugglers who delivered them took charge of the cargo again and left."

"We won't ever know the details, will we?" she asked in a forlorn voice.

"No way to know at this moment."

The drive back was unsettling. The men discussed multiple options. They pretty much decided the kidnapper had to have been the man injured and spirited away. Too many people were involved, but so few had actual stakes in the process. Families of all the loved ones, yes, they would have an interest as well. But twenty years later it was hard to imagine the drive for revenge was quite the same.

"Any way I can get into the pub without being seen?" Issa asked.

"What good would that do? You were already there. As far as the pub owners know, you're still there. We paid for several nights, remember?"

She settled back. "Right, they don't know we left in the middle of the night."

"And it's not that late now. We could still be in our rooms."

"Jesus." She wrapped her arms around her belly and stared outside the car window. It was hard to stop the fear from taking over her senses. They were still a good fifteen minutes away from the pub when a vehicle pulled off a side street in front of them. At the same time, another one pulled up behind them. Hawk slowed down. She listened to Eagle swear. She glanced in front of them and behind.

"I gather this is a kidnapper's welcoming party?" She was proud her voice held no tremor. "The detective does understand how important it is to get here fast, right?"

"Oh, yeah. Hawk just texted him to let him know we're in a standard pincer move. With no place for us to get off the road. We have to go straight in with the escort."

And, sure enough, the vehicles stayed with them as they drove right to the pub. As they entered the parking lot, the first car drove to the far side exit and parked so they couldn't get out. Hawk drove in and took a spot as the vehicle behind them blocked their entrance too.

"Well, that answers that," she said, letting out her breath. "I guess it's showtime."

She got out of the vehicle and stopped for a long moment, staring up at the sky. Then she closed her eyes and sent out a call. In her mind her words were a whisper, but she added all the power she could, and she told the wind that they were in trouble and needed help. When she opened her eyes, the clouds moved closer. She had no idea if it had anything to do with her request. It was a game she'd played as a child. Something fun to make the evenings less lonely. She'd talked to the clouds, played with the wind, and laughed as she brought in clouds and wind and rays of sunshine at will. With the men, one on either side of her, she walked toward the back door of the pub.

The drivers of the other vehicles got out, leaning against the vehicles they had driven in. She smiled at them and waved. She felt Eagle start in surprise.

"What was that for?" he asked.

"There is nothing wrong with being friendly. You don't know what circumstance we're walking into."

They walked straight through to the pub, finding a man blocking every other option of exit. They were shepherded toward the main room. As she walked in, she pounded the bar gently and said, "It's mighty cold out there today. May I have a coffee please?" and she kept on walking, searching the room.

On the far side, her gaze landed on a bloody Panther and Tiger, seated at a large table, their backs to the wall. They were both pinned between two large men, seated on either side of them, surrounded by another six seated on the opposite side of the table before them. After the hot coffee was delivered to her, she walked straight over to the eight guards, her gaze going from one to the other, fury burning in her heart.

"Which one of you removed Panther's tooth?" she asked in a harsh voice.

The man nearest to Panther snorted and said, "What's it to you, bitch?"

Issa threw the hot coffee full in his face. He roared and bounded to his feet. He tried to flip the table to get at her, but the other men jumped up from the table to stop him.

She rocked on her heels, crossed her arms, and said, "So *this* is your code?"

She didn't know where her bravery came from, but she

remembered the words. Whenever her dad had been angry at the men, he'd asked that question.

All around her a hush fell.

Wiping his face, the man glared at her and sat back down.

She turned slowly, recognizing some of the faces she'd seen when she had first arrived and others she'd known from the past. "I don't know what this is all about or why you've tortured my friends. I don't know why you kidnapped me and tortured me. I don't know why we were shepherded here and given no other choice but to be in this room with you all. I don't know what you want. But I do know one thing. My dad would've been ashamed of each and every one of you."

Dead silence filled the hall.

EAGLE LET OUT a silent whistle. He'd never admired her more. When she had said she was a straight shooter, she had meant it. She brought out all the issues right at the moment, so they could deal with this right now. What she'd done to the man who had hurt Panther was something Eagle would never forget.

He'd figured they were all as good as dead right then. He'd seen the shock on Panther's face when she'd stood up for him. It wasn't something any of them were accustomed to seeing. They'd been fighting their own battles for a long time. But now they had a pint-size champion with uncharted skills.

Everybody in the room studied her warily. Having in-voked her dad, the leader of the smuggling group from twenty years ago, she'd also invoked memories that both haunted and hurt. This could go either way.

Eagle glanced at Hawk to see him staring at Issa with respect. Eagle understood the feeling.

Clouds moved in overhead, making the room even more dark and gloomy.

"Where is he?" she snapped. "Is he not man enough to show his face?"

Several of the men gasped and shuffled uneasily. And then she heard a sound. Eagle watched her face as the color slipped away from her cheeks. She took a deep breath, squared off her shoulders, and crossed her arms. And Eagle realized this was the asshole who'd kidnapped her.

There was a weird *click*, like a snap of fingers, but not quite. Two men in the hallway stepped out of the way, and slowly a wheelchair wended its way forward. Behind the boss, pushing the wheelchair was an older man. He looked to be mid-seventies but was probably a decade younger.

Issa stood strong and glared at the newcomers.

Eagle tried to keep watch on the newcomers too. They had eyes for no one else but Issa. When they were halfway across the room and only a few feet from her, the wheelchair-bound man said, "Where is it?"

She threw her arms wide and said, "Where is what? You tortured me for weeks, trying to find that same answer." She lifted her gaze from his and turned toward the old-timers in the room. "Did you know that's what he did? Did you know he kidnapped me after I returned home from cleaning out my mother's house? She had died only five days earlier. He threw me in the back of a truck, carried me to his lair, where he systematically sliced my skin, kicked me over and over in the same places, fractured multiple bones, burned my breasts with lit cigarettes, and withheld food and water for days on end. And left me without a blanket for the cold nights. And then, when I finally outwitted his men and escaped, I was shot twice. But I am here."

Her voice hardened. "I am here now, and the blood of my father runs through me. And I'll be damned if I'll take this kind of abuse anymore." She glared at the crippled man in front of her. "And, Liam, there is not a goddamn thing from you that I want."

Eagle straightened. "Liam? Your brother?" There was such a wealth of disgust in his voice that, when he turned to look at all the other men in the pub, at least twenty of them, not one would look him in the face. "This is the type of men you are? You do remember Issa was no more than a six-year-old child when she was here last? That she'd lost all three of her brothers—supposedly—and her father, and, twenty years later, just days after losing her mother, she was tortured for weeks on end. And you protect this man? You tortured my friends for his gains? I've walked this earth. I have served with good men. I have faced war, and I have faced assholes like you. How do any of you live with yourselves now?"

Liam opened his mouth and roared, "Stop this drivel."

"Drivel? Yeah, *honor, respect, a code to live by*—you would think that was drivel." Eagle turned his gaze back to Issa and said, "This is your show."

She tilted her head. "I know some of you were my father's friends. Some of you were his enemies. You feared him but were loyal as long as he was there to lead you and so long as you profited by his work. Some of you probably didn't like his stance when everything blew up. And maybe you even turned on him. For all I know maybe you even killed him."

At that, there was an angry stirring around her.

She snorted. "Don't bother telling me that you would never do that because, from all I've seen in the last few weeks, not one of you has any honor or any sense of morality left. I don't know what you're looking for. I never did." She looked down at Liam. "Did you have something to do with those girls being trafficked in those casks? Did you convince the others the casks were full of gold and jewels?"

He snorted. "You don't know what you're talking about."

But his gaze shifted.

She smiled a hard cold calculating smile. "In other words, you did. Were you the one who arranged it? Did you do it in Dad's name? Hoping he'd never find out, or hoping he wouldn't give a shit? So what were you hoping to find by kidnapping me? The jewels? The money?"

Several men bounded to their feet. "She lies."

"Really? Are you aware that those six casks held young French girls stolen from their families for the sex trade in Ireland? That's why my dad stood up and put his foot down. He was a smuggler, but he wasn't a sex trafficker. And he'd have no part in hurting young women. Remember the code? Remember women and children first? That's why he took the bullet. He died trying to do the right thing."

CHAPTER 30

"THE GOLD, YOU stupid bitch," her brother roared. "Where is the gold?"

Issa stared at her brother dumbfounded. "How the hell would I know?"

"Because the last time I saw you, you were stealing all the gold. They were old gold coins. They were rolled up in leather pouches. And he was taking them away one at a time." His voice increased in volume. "On your goddamn orders." And, as if a cork had been held in for way too long, then blew its top, he spilled words that seemed to have no end.

She could only stand in shock and horror as his vitriol rolled over her.

"Everything was you. Everything was you and that damn bird. Father was to buy a falcon for me. I'm the one who wanted to go into falconry. But, oh no, no, no. Somehow you and that stupid thing bonded. It became all about you. I never got anything I wanted. It was bad enough that he had his perfect two sons and the third one was just not old enough to be of any real value but was too young to be treated like anything other than a boy. I was still doing a man's job. But you were just a girl, and you got the incredibly expensive Hadrid. And he should've been mine."

He shook his head. "I didn't have anything to do with

the girls coming over. But I knew all about the gold. I knew all about the valuable cargo. And I was going to make sure I got some for myself. Da promised me that, if I wanted an education, I could have one. But he had also promised me a falcon. And we saw how well that worked out." His wrath and poisonous tone filled the room.

She shoved her hands in her pockets. "So you blamed a child because a bird preferred her?" she asked in disbelief. "If you knew anything about falconry, then you would know that the bird chose me. I didn't choose the bird." She settled into a wider stance and glared at her brother. "What kind of a life did I have? I spent all my time on a cliff, in the dark, alone. And I mean, *alone*. Nobody was there to work with me. Nobody was there to help me. To make me feel not so terrified. My life was nothing compared to yours. You at least got to go out—anytime, anywhere. You got an education. You got to go to school. I never did." She snorted. "I was necessary as a lookout."

"Bullshit," he roared. "You were never alone. You were mother's favorite."

She studied him, and, in a soft voice, she said, "You don't know, do you?"

He frowned, anger still riding him. He glared at her. "Don't know what?"

"Mother was never with me. She was always in the house, screwing Angus."

Gasps of shock rolled through the room. She tilted her head and nodded. "And it never came out at his trial because Mother never stood up for him. She never confessed what she'd done. You know he doesn't even know if I'm his child or Dad's?" she said in a conversational tone. She shrugged. "I guess it doesn't matter much now. But she never once spent time on the hillside with me. How do you think I fell in the crevice in the first place?"

He settled back and looked at her with disgust. "What?"

She nodded. "That's right. And even that night when everything blew up, I had been sick. I had a fever and a runny nose. I shouldn't have been out on the cliff side in that stormy weather. I should've been in a warm bed. I actually came back to the house to ask Mother to take my place, so I could be inside because I was cold. I couldn't get warm that night. I came to the house only to find her in bed with Angus. I shouldn't have been at the house at all, but I didn't go back out on the crags, so I hid before they saw me. Except Mother did. Angus didn't though. And then there were shouts and gunshots down below. Mother and Angus both bolted up, got dressed and raced down to the cliffs. Mother went down a different way after Angus, leaving me behind, but I went down too, much slower. Again, I was alone. You were always with the family. I was never with Mother. She had Angus."

He shook his head. "How dare you say those things about our mother?"

"I say those things because they are true."

Liam struggled with the truth. She understood how he felt.

"Every time you and Dad were out and Mother was alone, Angus was there." She shook her head. "You've held an idealized view of your mother. And I held an idealized view of my father. Because I already knew what my mother was. I loved her anyway," she said clearly. "Love is like that. You love them despite their faults, not just for the good things."

"Get to the part about the bloody falcon," somebody

roared. "Where's the gold we were promised?"

Issa turned to study them. "How is it you were all promised gold?"

"We're all part of it," Barney said, walking over from the bar. He handed her a second cup of coffee. "This one's on me as long as you don't throw it at anybody."

She accepted it. "That's if nobody else here deserves it. And when you say, you are all part of it, what does that mean?"

"Your da paid us all a little bit all the time. It helped put food on our tables, and we all knew there was a big score coming. We were all anticipating a much larger piece of the pie."

"And so, for twenty years, that hatred inside you festered, while you dreamed of something that never existed? Did you get a payoff from the girls? According to Angus, they weren't there when he regained consciousness. Did that make it worthwhile to kidnap me, beating, torturing me over four long weeks?"

Several of the men stepped back, and one said, "Look, we didn't have anything to do with that."

She studied them. "As long as you are associated with my brother, you are part of it. The same as you were part of the smuggling ring my father ran. You don't get to pick and choose the pieces you want. And then you say that nothing happened, but there were murders. Because my father and my two brothers were killed. And my brother here has murdered many more."

Liam snorted. "I didn't kill anyone."

"Ordering your men to murder is the same as having done the deed yourself. That you found it easier to keep your hands clean by ordering your henchmen to do it does not make your hands clean," she said, her voice harsh. "Not being in the same room where your men sliced my ankles and the soles of my feet, kicked me day after day after day, in my ribs and my kidneys, not to mention burning my breasts with lit cigarettes, does not make your hands clean."

"I was trying to bring the stressors back into your life so you would bring the damn bird back. With the added advantage, if you knew anything of the gold and jewels, you'd give up the information under torture," he said candidly.

She studied him for a long moment. "You thought I had Hadrid with me? And that, through your torturing, I would be forced to connect with him? And then what? You would have tied him down on a perch and interrogated a falcon? Did you think he had something to do with the gold?" She stared at him in disbelief. "That was twenty years ago. I never saw Hadrid after that day. He was like another part of me. I lost all three of my brothers, supposedly, my father, Angus, and Hadrid all at the same time. What I was left with was a mother who hated the sight of me. Oh, she came around a decade or so later, but I was a reminder of all she'd lost. And, while we lived here, I was a reminder of all she couldn't have. Angus wanted her to leave with him. But Dad was never one to let go of something that was his."

Several men muttered in the background, "Aye, he was like that."

"I assume one of you shot Hadrid?" she asked, her voice hard. But no one would answer or even look her in the eye. She turned her attention to her brother. She barely recognized this twisted vindictive man. He'd hated her so much … "Did you kill our father?" she asked Liam.

He shook his head. "I was trying hard to survive myself."

"So then who is buried in my brother's grave?"

His gaze fell to the floor. "Danny is."

"And his family, did they know too?"

He nodded. "Danny was already dead. His folks took me in because I was still alive, and, if they couldn't save their own son, they could save Da's. They took me up north. They became my family as they nursed me back to health. But, at the same time, they wanted vengeance for their son's death."

"There isn't any vengeance to be had," she said. "I highly doubt anyone involved is left alive."

Liam shook his head. "No, nobody was left alive. But I needed that gold. It was there. So I told them you would know, that you had watched and ordered the falcon to hide the coins. That, if we were careful and bided our time, you would be the one to order the bird to show us."

She lifted her gaze to the old man behind Liam. He stared down at her brother. "And you?" she asked him. "Are you Danny's father? Barney's brother-in-law?"

He raised a tortured gaze to her and gave her a clipped nod. "I am. I'm Dylan."

"So, to appease your son's death, you help another in need, then you torture his innocent sister based on his twisted vengeance? That was okay by you? By your moral code? How is it you can look at yourself in the mirror?"

Danny's father said, "I started out believing it was just and right. But I lost that belief a while ago. For what we did to you, I have no excuse. I would say I was blinded, and I did not know how to get off the path I had traveled."

"And, if I were to approach Danny's mother and tell her of all you have done—or Danny's grandmother and tell her of all you have done—what do you think they would say?"

He closed his eyes in pain. "They would say it could not be true. That the man they knew would never have done something like this."

Just then Liam interrupted. "Oh, isn't this lovely. Dylan's been killing for me for years. There's no way out of this for him. Or for me. I need the gold. I can make a life for myself and have the surgery I need to walk again."

"What kind of surgery will let you walk again?" she asked quietly. "And I don't know what happened to the gold. I never saw any of it. Just like when you tortured me, I had no answers then, and I have none now. I doubt Hadrid is alive today. Even if he'd survived that night, he'd have died from old age."

"He was happy with you," Liam said bitterly. "He'd have done anything for you. You told him to hide the gold."

"He did do everything for me. I'm pretty damn sure he gave his life for me. Do you think that being outside that house alone at night as a little girl was safe? Did you see my old scars when you had me tortured? The scar from the bullet I took a long time ago?" She felt Eagle's shocked gaze. "I figure you must've done that. As you ordered Dylan to give me a matching one on the other side." But she didn't dare pull her gaze away from the snake in front of her.

EAGLE NOTED THE tension in the room was thick with angry murmurings. Outside a storm brewed to match the atmosphere brewing inside.

It was hard to tell if that communal anger was directed at Issa or her brother. So many lies, so much deceit had fallen on this small community.

She turned to look at him. "Is there enough?"

He took a moment to figure out what she meant, and then he knew.

She turned to the others who had spoken earlier. "How much do you think you were owed?"

One man finally spoke up. "Each two thousand."

She looked thoughtful for a long moment, then turned to Hawk and Eagle and said, "Please hand it out."

Eagle sat for a long moment, his arms crossed as he studied her. "You sure?"

She nodded. "My family always pays their debts. My dad wouldn't have wanted the villagers to suffer. I'll pay what was owed them, and, when I walk away from here, the five of us are free and clear."

Eagle shrugged. He wasn't sure how this would go down, but he knew exactly how much money was in his bag. He wasn't sure how many men she intended on paying though. He glanced at the window, not surprised to see the sky darkening with birds. Was that her doing? And was she creating the storm gathering out there too?

She turned to the first man who'd spoken up about the payment. "Line up all the men who are owed. Not one extra. My dad pays his debts even from the grave."

Of the twenty men in the room, seventeen lined up. The last two were the men who'd been guarding Panther and Tiger.

Eagle studied both of his friends' faces, catching the grins and the wicked glint in their eyes. And he realized neither were seriously hurt. They'd probably given as good as they got. He brought out two handfuls of cash, bundled in one thousand amounts, and handed them to her. Then he brought out four more handfuls.

When everyone but the last two men had been given

their money, Issa asked, "Were you the ones who hurt Tiger and Panther?" One still bore the hot coffee stains on his shirt.

The men exchanged glances, then looked at the money in Eagle's hands. One shrugged. "So what if we were?"

"My dad paid his debts. But he always gave a good beating when it was needed. But he never gave a beating when it wasn't. I'm in no position to give you what you deserve. But you will forfeit half of the money you are owed."

Both men started to protest. She took the money from Hawk, split it in half and gave each man half of that. Then she took two more bundles, walked over to Panther and Tiger and said, "I'm sorry. This does not in any way make up for what was done to you. But, on behalf of my dad, it would shame him from his grave to not offer you compensation."

Knowing the men would argue, she placed the money in front of them on the table and turned back to the other two who had beaten her friends. "If you ever lay a hand on any of us again, I will let them kill you."

The two men puffed up with a bluster. She waved her hand and said, "Stop. Any of these four men could cut you down in an instant. Even without guns. They are soldiers who fought for their country, for our country, and for anyone else who needed them. That you would treat them as you did is disgusting. That you did it on behalf of my twisted brother for his ill-gotten gains in his vengeful mind is beyond that. My dad would turn over in his grave if he had any idea."

She waved them over to the chairs in the far corner. "Now return what you took from Panther and Tiger, and go sit in the corner where you belong." The two men glared at her. She fisted her hands on her hips and said, "Now."

Both men handed over guns and a cell phone, then went to the far corner, and she turned to Barney. "Where is your son?"

One man stood. "That's me." His tone softened when he asked, "How are you doing, Issa?"

Her first natural smile broke free. She walked over and gave him a hug.

"I didn't even recognize you, Arian," she said in surprise. She held out her hand to Eagle and said, "Give me a full packet please." Without question he gave it to her. She handed it to her friend. "This is for you. Thank you for hiding mom's box in our old hiding place for me as she requested you to do."

His face lit up. "I had forgotten all about placing that treasure box in there."

"You did it though, didn't you?" She smiled. "Thank you."

She turned to face Barney who stared at his son and then at her, mystified.

She said, "In spite of everything that happened, when I was a child, your son and I were friends. And for that I'm forever grateful."

She turned to her brother. "I know nothing of any gold. I know nothing of what happened to it. But that you have killed and maimed in the name of the family to recover smuggled goods, all because you considered someone stealing from you as an injustice, is beyond me. You're the one who shot me, when I was just a child, because of your own hatred, your need to be the best, to act older, whatever it was that your twisted mind wanted to believe. You're nothing but a cold-blooded killer and a sad excuse of a human being."

Complete silence fell in the room once again.

Eagle watched in awe. Every man in that room was on her side now. And there wasn't one man who wasn't ashamed of his own behavior. Not the least of whom was Dylan.

She raised her eyes to Dylan and said, "It will be very hard for me to find any forgiveness in my heart for what you allowed those men to do to me. And the torture done by your own hand. I'm sorry that your son's life was cut short. But what happened that night was not my fault. It was not my other brothers' fault. Sometimes life is just a bitch. I can only surmise that the men who brought the girls heard the initial gunshots, turned their boat around, shot everyone involved with the smuggling, and took off with the casks. We hope the authorities can still follow the trails now and get to the bottom of this. Regardless if we know or not—we have to accept it and move on. Your method of moving on is unacceptable. To me and to everyone else in this room. And, if I were to find the gold, I would turn it in to the police—as I did this morning with the jewels stolen that same night. Or did you not know about the four magnificent jeweled necklaces my mother hid for me all those years ago?"

Her brother roared in anger.

"Shut up," she snapped. "You're nothing but a heartless thief. A low-class murdering dog. I will have nothing more to do with you." She motioned to Eagle and Hawk, and then to Tiger and Panther, before turning and walking toward the front door.

Eagle and Hawk looked at her and then at the men gathered here. They all stared at her brother.

"Don't you turn your back on me," Liam roared in frustrated anger. "Get back here, you bitch."

Issa turned to face him. "I don't take orders from you. Or have to take your abuse." She turned to Hawk and Eagle. "It's stuffy in here."

They looked at her, confused. Until Eagle walked over to the closest window and opened it. A bird flew in. Someone laughed. Issa opened the door behind her as Hawk quickly walked to the closest windows and opened them too.

The first bird was followed by dozens. Soaring, swooping, causing panic as everyone screamed, roared, and ducked.

Issa let out a sharp whistle; then commanded the birds to stop.

Instantly they all rose to the ceiling and sat on the rafters above, where the birds eyed the audience below.

"It *is* Issa!" someone in the back yelled. "Only she commands the birds."

Murmurs came from all around.

Liam glared at her. "I don't give a damn about your parlor tricks."

And he lifted a gun.

Eagle froze. *Shit.*

She lifted her gaze, seeing Panther and Tiger slowly creeping closer to Liam. With a hand up to stop them, she took a step toward her brother. And shook her head. "No, you cannot kill me."

His grin was a horrible thing to see.

He raised the gun higher. Eagle pulled his own out, seeing Tiger and Panther following his lead.

Several of the other men pushed back to line the walls. "Who'll stop me?" Liam sneered. "Not you. Your watchdogs? They might kill me, but they won't stop me from killing you first."

Eagle didn't dare take his eyes off the bastard. He'd be happy to shoot him right now.

Out of the corner of his eye, he caught sight of Issa's smile. What was she up to now?

He watched.

The room went silent.

Just as Liam started to move a finger, ... the birds attacked.

Not just one or two but dozens filled the air. Eagle couldn't see Liam to shoot. But neither could Liam see Issa to shoot her.

He could hear Liam roar, then suddenly, as if under a silent command, the birds rose once again, and a large hawk of some kind carried Liam's handgun in his talons.

Eagle's jaw dropped. He caught the same dumbfounded look on everyone else's face.

Except Issa. She grinned. Then chuckled. Seconds later she laughed uproariously. "Oh, Liam, if only you could see your face."

Spitting in fury, over the edge by her laughing at him, Liam yelled at Dylan, "Go get that bitch. It's time for her to learn a lesson."

But Dylan didn't move. He turned to stare at Issa's defiant form, and he said, "No. She's the daughter I wish I could have had but never did. If I'd but stayed with my wife, I might've been blessed yet again. But instead, I turned to a path of poison and let you guide me into a world I would never have gone to alone."

Liam sneered. "It's a fine time for you to be having second thoughts."

Dylan nodded. "That is so true. I am just as responsible for what you became as I am for what I became." His voice thickened. "I loved you like a son."

Eagle watched Dylan grab Liam's head, and, with a sharp snap, he broke Liam's neck. Eagle heard Issa at the doorway. He turned to watch, only to see her racing forward, her gaze on her brother. She stopped about ten feet away and bowed her head.

"It's not the end I would've chosen," she said in pain, "but it's probably the best way forward."

Dylan stared down at the man in front of him. "He did shoot you. I saw him. I just didn't want to believe it was on purpose. He also tried to shoot Hadrid. I believe he succeeded. The bird went down with the gold satchel in its claws. We looked that night but never again. I don't know how much gold may have been dropped. I don't know how much there ever was."

"Not much," she said wearily. "The real bounty was the girls."

Dylan shook his head. "Liam never told me about that."

"Of course not. Why would he? That knowledge would've made you understand why my dad died the way he did."

Dylan nodded. "It's a sad life and a sad way to finish. I wish it could've been so much better." The sound of sirens racing toward them filled the air. Dylan looked out a window and nodded. "It's time." He pulled a small handgun from his back pocket.

She took a step away from him.

He raised his gaze to her and said, "No, Issa. You have nothing further to worry about from me." He put the gun in his mouth and pulled the trigger.

CHAPTER 31

THEY WALKED THROUGH the airport into the Colorado sun. Finally home again. The trip back to his place was mostly silent. She had enough things to work through for a much longer span of time. One of the biggest things was, what would she do now?

Before leaving, they had visited Angus once again, bringing him up to date on what had happened. They'd also searched the cliffs for the gold. But found no sign of it. And no sign of Hadrid. In her heart of hearts she knew he had died that night. When that link had been lost between them, she'd known then. In many ways they'd both died that night. She was lucky to have been given a second chance.

The grief of revisiting everything was sharp yet again. But she dealt with it like she always had.

They also kept their promise to Gray. They were home after just three days. This time she came with four men, not just two. Panther and Tiger had been trying to return her money since she first gave it to them. It was a bit of a joke now.

When she walked outside and reached into her purse for her sunglasses, she found the money once again tucked inside. She sighed, picked up the money, turned, handed it to Eagle, and said, "Put this and what's left of the money you have in your bag toward the pens and the care of the birds."

He glanced at her and looked at the money in his hand. "You sure?"

She nodded. "I'm sure. Because now that we have access to the money in my mother's bank accounts, I won't run short for a while—if ever." It was more than expected and made her wonder all over again at her mother's choice to walk away from it all.

When they pulled up to the gates, Gray was with a kid waiting for them. She knew Eagle had been in contact with them the whole time. But she also saw another vehicle.

An older woman got out, turned to look at Eagle, and said, "There you are."

Eagle hopped from his truck. "Annie, what brings you here?"

"Apparently a couple birds will be here soon that need some help," she said testily. "Although, if the story is to be believed, it's a bit far-fetched."

STEFAN KNEW THIS was the place. He could feel vehicles, people, and energy up ahead—frazzled but razzed energy surrounded by an unbelievable wave of bird energy. But still, several miles stood between where the birds were and where they needed to be. And he wasn't sure at all what they would find when they got there. Humbug constantly urged Stefan and Roash on, as if some kind of homecoming was up ahead.

As Stefan stood in spirit form, studying the birds once again and the thick dense brush surrounding them, two dogs raced toward him. They sat down at his feet and stared up at him. Not at the birds but at him.

It was a joy of the natural order of things that many animals sensed his presence, even though he wasn't here in physical form. He bent down and placed a hand on each. Then he bowed his head and gently sent healing energy between the two. At his command, both birds climbed on board, each taking a dog to perch on.

Maybe the wounded birds could make this last leg of the journey on their own.

Then Humbug turned to look at Stefan, and he realized he needed to walk these last few miles with the animals.

So he walked at their sides, making sure they were both okay. And then the dogs' ears picked up as they heard the sound of a truck in the distance.

Stefan realized it really was a homecoming. This was it. Humbug was going home.

Stefan walked them close to the edge of the cages, took a look at the birds, the animals, the yard and realized how perfect a home this would be for Humbug. Several people got out of the vehicle that had just arrived.

He watched as Issa smiled, so breathtakingly beautiful he could feel it from where he stood. She caught sight of him and stopped. Then she took several hesitant steps toward him, her smile faltering, as if not understanding what she saw.

He smiled at her. "I'm delighted to finally meet you."

"And yet ... how is it I can see you? Know who you are? You are here but not here?" she said cautiously.

"Issa?" The big man walked around the vehicle, staring at her, then toward Stefan, a look of confusion on his face.

"Sometimes life is like that," Stefan said. "I come bearing gifts."

She smiled at him and said, "Thank you."

He motioned to the dogs, coming nearer.

Then she turned that direction and finally saw the dogs

and the exhausted birds riding on their backs.

She gasped, her arms flying open wide as she saw her birds. "Humbug!" she cried out, a sound of joy, relief, and love as she raced toward the tattered owl and falcon. "Roash!"

But it was Humbug's response that brought tears to Stefan's eyes—tears in his eyes in his human form, that is. Humbug's cry was not of welcome but of homecoming. A reconnecting to that last part of himself. That part was the other person in his world who was so important that he had crossed these many miles to get to her—even though injured and barely able to fly short distances.

Issa scooped him up off the dog's back and tucked the beautiful injured bird against her chest. In a breathtaking motion of love, Humbug curled into her neck, as if he never planned to leave.

For a long moment Stefan watched, knowing he'd been granted a blessing with this insight into a world he'd never seen before. As he started to back away, Humbug cooed in sorrow.

Stefan chuckled. "I'll come and visit, Humbug. But please, don't go on any more worldly journeys."

Humbug gave a trill of promise.

"One more thing before I go," Stefan said.

Issa just smiled at him, two birds in her arms now.

"You have a very strong spirit animal that worked hard to catch my attention."

"Hadrid?" she asked, awed.

"His connection to you remains. He's watching over you still."

Stefan closed his eyes and returned to his body, his bed, his world—hopeful now he could do his own paintings without Humbug appearing in the corners.

Stefan got up, happy and content as he walked to his studio. He looked at the pictures with Humbug and realized he wouldn't get rid of any of them. He would fill a wall with all of Humbug's pictures—in honor of one of the strangest journeys, strangest relationships, and strangest energy healings Stefan had ever participated in.

And one of the very best.

Laughing, he put up a clean white canvas, grabbed his paints, and got to work.

EAGLE WALKED UP to Issa, still holding Humbug and Roash, the dogs stretched out on the grass happily at their feet, and said, "So, do I get to meet the newest member of our family?"

She raised her gaze searchingly at his wording.

He smiled down at her and whispered, "How could we not be a family? We're already birds of a feather." And he grinned at his own joke.

She shook her head. "It could get pretty crazy at times," she warned.

He smiled. Then he gently wrapped his arms around her and both birds and held them close. "That's all right. I do crazy. Especially if that crazy is you."

This concludes Book 12 of Psychic Visions:
Eye of the Falcon.
Book 13 is available.

Itsy-Bitsy Spider

Book 13 of Psychic Visions Series

Buy this book at your favorite vendor.

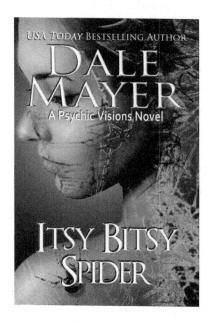

Psychic Vision Series

Tuesday's Child

Hide'n Go Seek

Maddy's Floor

Garden of Sorrow

Knock, Knock…

Rare Find

Eyes to the Soul

Now You See Her

Shattered

Into the Abyss

Seeds of Malice

Eye of the Falcon

Itsy-Bitsy Spider

Psychic Visions Books 1–3

Psychic Visions Books 4–6

Psychic Visions Books 7–9

Excerpt from Itsy-Bitsy Spider
Book 13 of the Psychic Visions Series

"HEY, QUEENIE, YOU'VE got a hell of a line outside your tent tonight," Booker called from the Ferris wheel station. "How come you didn't see that coming?" And out came his usual full-belly laugh at his own joke.

Queenie waved and smiled, as inside she groaned. Somehow this never seemed to get old. And the jokes never seemed to get better. At least with the people she worked with here. Then again she was working as a fortune teller at an amusement park. She had to expect a certain amount of ribbing.

Still, she did what she could, and, for that, she was grateful to have a job. She finished her ice cream, tossing the last portion of the cone into the garbage. All around her, the noise of the park and the smell of super sticky cotton candy filled the air.

She had to stay focused. This wasn't for her—this was for someone else. She stepped through the back entrance of her tent. After shrugging off her sweater, she picked up the huge headdress that went with the seer's role and placed it on her head. Her glass ball was under the table. She put it on the table in front of her. Then she pulled back her chair and sat down. This booth made money. Because of that, the owners paid to keep her. Not much money, however, but it was easy work, and she got cheap food and a free place to crash as a side benefit.

She'd been here for over a year now. The trouble was, before this job, she had had a similar one at another amusement park in another place. Before that was another amusement park in yet another place. She was footloose, yet a long way from being fancy-free. Life sucked. But it didn't matter because it was all for the right reason. She leaned across the table and opened the curtains that separated her from her customers. Close to six feet from the door, the line had formed, curling to the left. She smiled at the teenage girl standing in front and motioned for her to come forward.

The teen handed over her five-dollar bill. Queenie accepted it with a smile and asked, "What question can I answer for you today?"

"Will I get asked to prom this year?" She squealed out the question in a breathless voice.

Queenie chuckled inside. "Is there someone in your life already?"

The young woman shook her head. "Not yet. But I'm really hoping you say there will be soon."

"Let's find out." Queenie held out her left hand and said, "Place your hand in mine."

And then she waved her right hand around the glass ball. As soon as the young woman's hand connected with Queenie's, she smiled. Was there anything fresher than young love? She studied the ball, using it to formulate a story to tell the young woman. The ball was a prop for the people. She could see everything through her eyes right now. She said, "Somebody named Jake, by any chance?"

The young woman cried out again, as she gripped Queenie's hand like a lifeline and did a half jump in joy.

"Yes, that's him."

"Well then, you needn't worry," Queenie said gently, happy she could hand out the good news. "Because he's going to ask you to the prom."

The young woman dropped her hand and squealed again, jumped up and down, and then dashed out of the tent. Queenie smiled and dropped the money into the jar beside her.

"Next," she called out.

A man in a business suit walked in, carrying a briefcase.

She studied him and found nothing unnerving about him, but something was off. ... He appeared to be calm, maybe too calm. He sat down in front of her and said in a quiet voice, "I'm about to lose everything. Is there anything I can do to help myself?"

Now that was interesting. Rarely did people come with a question of what they could do to turn something around.

He handed over his money and said, "I know this is all fake but you have a certain reputation. ... I could really use some advice. A direction to look at? ... Something? Preferably good news," he said heavily. "I could really use a shot of good news right now."

Interested in spite of herself, Queenie held out her hand and said, "Place your hand in mine."

As soon as he did, tingles went up and down her back. Now she was very interested. Normally she was good at guessing the core character of a person. And nothing about him sent off her inner alarms. She waved her hand over the ball, as she tried to sort out the images coming through her. But all she could see were metal bars. And then she realized why he had lost his job. She glanced up at him and said, "Are you trying to find work?"

He shook his head sadly. "No. I thought everything was going great … but then …" His voice trailed away.

"But then?"

"Somebody blamed me for something." Pain and discouragement were in his voice.

She studied the bars in the ball and realized they were a jail cell. He was in grave danger of going to jail for the rest of his life. She frowned and looked at him. "Do you know somebody named Mike? Mike Marrow or Munro?" She frowned, trying to get the name clearer in her head.

He leaned forward. "Mike Munro, yes, he's my best friend."

She looked at him sadly. "He's not your best friend. He's the one who framed you. He's the one who's guilty."

The man stared at her in horror. He got to his feet and bolted from the tent.

She dropped his money into the jar. Next thing she knew, three little kids stood before her. They were laughing and giggling. One held up a five-dollar bill and placed it on the table. She could see the mom standing in the back. She smiled down at the kids and said, "What would you like to know?"

"What am I going to be when I grow up?"

She held her hand out to the first boy who wore a plaid shirt and cowboy boots.

He placed his hand in hers.

Instantly the answer flooded her mind. She chuckled. "You'll be a fireman."

He gasped and raced toward his mother. "Mommy, Mommy. She said I'm going to be a fireman."

Queenie smiled at the kid's excitement as a little girl stuck out her hand. "What about me?"

"You will work with animals, little one," she said softly, after seeing images of this girl as an adult caring for dogs and cats. "I don't know if it'll be as a vet or something else. But your path lies with animals."

The little girl dropped her hand, stepped away, and waited for the third child, a little boy, to step forward. He held out his hand and said, "What about me?"

But his voice was defiant, almost angry, as if he'd wanted to be the fireman, and he didn't like that his friend had that role. As soon as his hand touched hers, a shock coursed through her system. And then a strange cone appeared over his head. She swallowed hard at that sign and said instead, "Wow, you're really hard to read. I'm not sure I see anything."

"You don't have to. I'm going to be a policeman," he yelled. "I'm going to hunt down robbers."

He broke contact and raced away, past the adults at the entrance to the tent, and roared like a banshee.

She carefully eased her chair backward, and, using some of the antibacterial soap, washed the hand he'd held. It wouldn't change the fact the little boy would die—and sometime in the next three days.

She shuddered, hating that part of her talent. The last thing she wanted to know was who would die prematurely. But unfortunately these forces showed her a cone over those who had less than three days to live.

So far the cone hadn't been wrong. She'd seen enough of them to know. She sat back, sipping water from her bottle, trying to calm her nerves.

Out of the corner of her eye, she saw a spider walk across her table. She looked at it in fascination. The amusement park was definitely not the cleanest place, and certainly loads of food were here for rodents. But she hadn't seen much in the way of spiders. She wasn't afraid of them but neither did she like them. As far as she was concerned, if they left her alone, then she'd leave them alone.

This one didn't get the message.

It walked across her table, heading for the fortune-telling ball. She watched, wondering at the odd light around the bug. She saw auras all the time. Rarely around animals though. But the spider definitely glowed. She smiled at the oddity. "Where are you from?"

Something inside told her to pick it up. But she hesitated. Just because she wasn't killing the thing at first sight didn't mean she wanted it crawling all over her. The spider went up on its back legs, reaching out one of its front legs to touch the glass ball. A mist swirled deep inside the ball.

And those eyes ... How many eyes did spiders have?

The spider speared her with a look she found fascinating. She leaned forward, studying the bulbous critter carefully. Then, unable to help herself and yet cringing as she did so, she touched the spider. It scrabbled onto the back of her hand.

Instantly images assailed her.

Blood. A woman giving birth. A toddler—a boy. And a name flashing in neon inside her brain—a name she'd never forget. *Reese.*

Shuddering, she stared at the spider in horror. It stared at her. As if it knew her. As if it knew something about her.

She brushed it off her hand and onto the table and backed away, knocking her chair over in the process, staring at it in horror. "What do you know about Reese?"

Of course the spider didn't answer. How could it? But it gazed at her with that same knowing look. She shuddered.

Just then a large man stepped through the tent opening, dragging in a young boy with him. The man took one look at her and laughed. "Well, look at this. The fortune teller is scared of spiders."

He walked over, flicked the spider to the ground, and lifted his leg to step on it.

Before he could, she scooped it off to the side away from the man. "I'm not afraid of it," she said quietly. "And I don't kill anything unnecessarily."

He snorted. "You're a charlatan, just like all the rest of the idiots here."

"No, I'm not," she said warily. "What can I do for you?"

"Well, seeing as how I'm here, you might as well tell me the truth. I'm trying to acquire a piece of property. A pretty cabin on a lake. Will I get it or not?"

With a sneer he tossed a five-dollar bill on the table. Too many people were in her life with the same attitude. Most of the time she could ignore it. This man, however, … still it was her job.

She hated to reach out for his hand, but it was necessary, and his closed around hers, holding her tight. And once again images slammed into her. A mountain lake. A cabin with paths up and down to the lake.

And in the lake, a woman's face floated just beneath the surface.

Queenie broke contact and sat back down again, holding her hand against her chest, her nerve endings fried, her body already shuddering. She didn't know what the hell was happening. But something was wrong. She gazed at the man and said, "The property owner is dead." Her gut clenched. She should keep her mouth shut. She didn't need to start anything, …but she couldn't stop her visions or stop speaking of them. ... For some reason she saw a whole lot more than she'd like. Girding herself for his reaction, in a cold voice she added, "But then you already know that, ... don't you?"

He narrowed his gaze, a black thundercloud forming. "Bitch," he roared, storming out of the tent and dragging the little boy with him.

Not that it mattered. His face was emblazoned in her mind for a long time to come.

But the face from the lake would be there a lot longer. That poor woman had been murdered. And even now floated undetected in the chilly water.

Queenie spun around, grabbing her Closed sign, and hung it on the curtain that separated her from the front of her tent, then yanked the curtain closed.

She couldn't do any more of this tonight. She wasn't sure what was wrong, but, for some reason, her abilities were heightened to a new level right now. And it scraped along her nerve endings to the point she couldn't deal with anything. She returned to the table, dropped her headpiece there, and picked up her purse.

Instantly the spider raced up her arm and onto her shoulder. She shuddered and flicked it off. Only it returned to run up her pant leg instead. She danced around, trying to shake it off.

But it was too late.

She'd seen its visions.

Something it knew. Or rather *someone* it knew.

Then like a weird echo inside her brain, a tiny voice called out to her. "Mommy? Is that you? Where are you?"

But that couldn't be. Her son had been dead for many years—hadn't he?

Shaking at the unbelievable horror she didn't—couldn't—contemplate, but yet her heart and soul filled with hope, she pulled out her cell phone and the card she'd kept tucked in the back of the phone case for many years. Unable to trust herself to send a text, she dialed the number on the card.

"Hello."

Her heart slammed into her chest. She hadn't heard that voice in so very long. She'd loved it once, just as she'd loved the man. Then hated both as her life had been ripped to pieces, and he'd been unable to find her son—their son. Whether he knew it or not.

Finally she found her voice. "Kirk?"

A moment's pause followed. Then he said with a heavy sigh, "Hi, Queenie."

"I was just wondering, has there been any news?"

"No, nothing," he said without hesitation. "I'm sorry." As her silence lengthened, he asked sharply, "Why? Did something happen?"

She gave a strangled laugh and said, "Yes, but you won't believe me if I try to explain." And she hung up, sagging into the chair, tears burning the back of her eyes.

Itsy-Bitsy Spider

Author's Note

Thanks for reading. By now many of you have read my explanation of how I love to see **Star Ratings.** The only catch is that we as authors have no idea what you think of a book if it's not reviewed. And yes, **every book in a series needs reviews**. All it takes is a little as two words: Fun Story. Yep, that's all. So, if you enjoyed reading, please take a second to let others know you enjoyed.

For those of you who have not read a previous book and have no idea why we authors keep asking you as a reader to take a few minutes to leave even a two word review, here's more explanation of reviews in this crazy business.

Reviews (not just ratings) help authors qualify for advertising opportunities and help other readers make purchasing decisions. Without *triple digit* reviews, an author may miss out on valuable advertising opportunities. And with only "star ratings" the author has little chance of participating in certain promotions. Which means fewer sales offered to my favorite readers!

Another reason to take a minute and leave a review is that often a **few kind words left in a review can make a huge difference to an author and their muse.** Recently new to reviewing fans have left a few words after reading a similar letter and they were tonic to tired muse! LOL Seriously. Star ratings simply do not have the same impact to thank or encourage an author when the writing gets tough.

So please consider taking a moment to write even a handful of words. Writing a review only takes a few minutes of your time. It doesn't have to be a lengthy book report, just a few words expressing what you enjoyed most about the story. Here are a few tips of how to leave a review.

Please continue to rate the books as you read, but take an extra moment and pop over to the review section and leave a few words too!

Most of all – **Thank you** for reading. I look forward to hearing from you.

I love to hear from readers, and you can contact me at my website: www.dalemayer.com or at my Facebook author page. To be informed of new releases and special offers, sign up for my newsletter or follow me on BookBub. And if you are interested in joining Dale Mayer's Fan Club, here is the Facebook sign up page.
facebook.com/groups/402384989872660

Cheers,
Dale Mayer

Your Free Book Awaits!

KILL OR BE KILLED

Part of an elite SEAL team, Mason takes on the dangerous jobs no one else wants to do – or can do. When he's on a mission, he's focused and dedicated. When he's not, he plays as hard as he fights.

Until he meets a woman he can't have but can't forget. Software developer Tesla lost her brother in combat and has no intention of getting close to someone else in the military. Determined to save other US soldiers from a similar fate, she's created a program that could save lives. But other countries know about the program, and they won't stop until they get it – and get her.

Time is running out ... For her ... For him ... For them ...

DOWNLOAD a *complimentary* copy of MASON? Just tell me where to send it!

http://dalemayer.com/sealsmason/

Second Chances

Go ahead. Take Charge of your life. Move forward…if you can…

Changing her future means letting go of her past. Karina heads to a weekend seminar and discovers the speaker is the person she needs to move on from. But she soon realizes bigger issues are facing her…

Brian has moved on, at least he'd believed he had… until he sees Karina in his audience…and realizes he's been lying to himself.

Passion pulls them together, love binds them together, but a revengeful enemy determines to keep the two apart…and destroy them both.

Touched by Death
adult RS/thriller

Death had touched anthropologist Jade Hansen in Haiti once before, costing her an unborn child and perhaps her very sanity.

A year later, determined to face her own issues, she returns to Haiti with a mortuary team to recover the bodies of an American family from a mass grave. Visiting his brother after the quake, independent contractor Dane Carter puts his life on hold to help the sleepy town of Jacmel rebuild. But he finds it hard to like his brother's pregnant wife or her family. He wants to go home, until he meets Jade – and realizes what's missing in his own life. When the mortuary team begins work, it's as if malevolence has been released from the earth. Instead of laying her ghosts to rest, Jade finds herself confronting death and terror again.

And the man who unexpectedly awakens her heart – is right in the middle of it all.

About the Author

Dale Mayer is a USA Today bestselling author best known for her Psychic Visions and Family Blood Ties series. Her contemporary romances are raw and full of passion and emotion (Second Chances, SKIN), her thrillers will keep you guessing (By Death series), and her romantic comedies will keep you giggling (It's a Dog's Life and Charmin Marvin Romantic Comedy series).

She honors the stories that come to her – and some of them are crazy and break all the rules and cross multiple genres!

To go with her fiction, she also writes nonfiction in many different fields with books available on resume writing, companion gardening and the US mortgage system. She has recently published her Career Essentials Series. All her books are available in print and ebook format.

Connect with Dale Mayer Online

Dale's Website – www.dalemayer.com
Twitter – @DaleMayer
Facebook – facebook.com/DaleMayer.author
BookBub – bookbub.com/authors/dale-mayer

Also by Dale Mayer

Published Adult Books:

Psychic Vision Series
Tuesday's Child

Hide'n Go Seek

Maddy's Floor

Garden of Sorrow

Knock, Knock…

Rare Find

Eyes to the Soul

Now You See Her

Shattered

Into the Abyss

Seeds of Malice

Eye of the Falcon

Itsy-Bitsy Spider

Psychic Visions Books 1–3

Psychic Visions Books 4–6

Psychic Visions Books 7–9

By Death Series
Touched by Death – Part 1

Touched by Death – Part 2

Touched by Death – Parts 1&2

Haunted by Death

Chilled by Death

By Death Books 1–3

Second Chances…at Love Series

Second Chances – Part 1

Second Chances – Part 2

Second Chances – complete book (Parts 1 & 2)

Charmin Marvin Romantic Comedy Series

Broken Protocols

Broken Protocols 2

Broken Protocols 3

Broken Protocols 3.5

Broken Protocols 1-3

Broken and… Mending

Skin

Scars

Scales (of Justice)

Broken but… Mending 1-3

Glory

Genesis

Tori

Celeste

Glory Trilogy

Biker Blues

Biker Blues: Morgan, Part 1

Biker Blues: Morgan, Part 2

Biker Blues: Morgan, Part 3

Biker Baby Blues: Morgan, Part 4

Biker Blues: Morgan, Full Set

Biker Blues: Salvation, Part 1

Biker Blues: Salvation, Part 2

Biker Blues: Salvation, Part 3

Biker Blues: Salvation, Full Set

SEALs of Honor

Mason: SEALs of Honor, Book 1

Hawk: SEALs of Honor, Book 2

Dane: SEALs of Honor, Book 3

Swede: SEALs of Honor, Book 4

Shadow: SEALs of Honor, Book 5

Cooper: SEALs of Honor, Book 6

Markus: SEALs of Honor, Book 7

Evan: SEALs of Honor, Book 8

Mason's Wish: SEALs of Honor, Book 9

Chase: SEALs of Honor, Book 10

Brett: SEALs of Honor, Book 11

Devlin: SEALs of Honor, Book 12

Easton: SEALs of Honor, Book 13

Ryder: SEALs of Honor, Book 14

Macklin: SEALs of Honor, Book 15

SEALs of Honor, Books 1–3

SEALs of Honor, Books 4–6

Riana's Revenge

Published Young Adult Books:

Family Blood Ties Series

Vampire in Denial

Vampire in Distress

Vampire in Design

Vampire in Deceit

Vampire in Defiance

Vampire in Conflict

Vampire in Chaos

Vampire in Crisis

Vampire in Control

Vampire in Charge

Family Blood Ties Set 1–3

Family Blood Ties Set 1–5

Family Blood Ties Set 4–6

Family Blood Ties Set 7–9

Sian's Solution – A Family Blood Ties Short Story

Design series

Dangerous Designs

Deadly Designs

Darkest Designs

Design Series Trilogy

Standalone

In Cassie's Corner

Gem Stone (a Gemma Stone Mystery)

Published Non-Fiction Books:

Career Essentials

Career Essentials: The Résumé

Career Essentials: The Cover Letter

Career Essentials: The Interview

Career Essentials: 3 in 1